The King of Good Intentions II

by Los Angeles songwriter and novelist John Andrew Fredrick picks up where we left off cliffhangingly, unsure whether John and Jenny, the brilliant and charming on-again/off-again couple who play in the fictitious fledgling indie band The Weird Sisters, will break up or not—as a couple or as the principal members of a getting-great band.

Reconciled after an infidelity-that-can-be-explained or at least atoned for, *King II* opens as The Weird Sisters are on tour during the fateful day Kurt Cobain's suicide is announced. This undeniably hilarious sequel pits the little jangle-pop band we're rooting for against an evil record label CEO'd by a guy who believes in aliens, various nefarious bookers and sound guys, drunken "punters," and lunatics and maniacs galore that Jenny, John, bassist Rob, and new and uproariously ridiculous new drummer Raleigh encounter on the zany road.

A quintessential LA novel as well, *King II* finds John, the not-so-humble but endearing narrator, confronted by yet another dilemma of the femme fatale kind, as well as grappling with his deepening love for and attachment to Jenny, his beautiful girlfriend and bandmate and former piano prodigy.

As *II* ends (with John getting a job as a PA on perhaps the most ludicrous video shoot in rock history), it sets up *The Hollow Crown*, a third installment—for Fredrick, without meaning to, and almost accidentally, has written a goddam trilogy.

ALSO BY JOHN ANDREW FREDRICK

The Knucklehead Chronicles

The King of Good Intentions

The continui
hilarious mis
rock band ca

John Andr

& really rather quite

dventures of an indie

d The Weird Sisters

w Fredrick

THIS IS A GENUINE BARNACLE BOOK

A Barnacle Book | Rare Bird Books
453 South Spring Street, Suite 302
Los Angeles, CA 90013
rarebirdbooks.com

Set in Minion
Printed in the United States

10 9 8 7 6 5 4 3 2 1

Publisher's Cataloging-in-Publication data

Fredrick, John Andrew.
The King of Good Intentions II / by John Andrew Fredrick.
pages cm
ISBN 978-1-942600-00-8

1. Bands (Music)—Fiction. 2. Musicians—Fiction. 3. Rock music—Fiction. 4.
Los Angeles (Calif.)—Fiction. 5. Love stories. I. The King of Good Intentions
Two. II. Title.

PS3606.R4367 K56 2015
813.6—dc23

This novel is for my dear old dad, William C. Fredrick The Great

"Who has not squirmed and covered his face with his hands as the dazzling past leered at him?"

—Nabokov, *Ada or Ardor*

"Where there are many shooters, some will hit."

—Dr. Johnson in Boswell's *Life of Johnson*

"That Beauty of which we are sometimes tempted to ask ourselves whether it is, in this world, anything more than the complementary part that is added to a fragmentary and fugitive stranger by our imagination, overstimulated by regret."

—Proust, *Within a Budding Grove*

"This whole thing about a person meeting another person first— it's all so arbitrary and cruel."

—Whit Stillman, *Damsels in Distress*

"What do you think I'm angry about?" "What we're all angry about. You're unhappy."

—John Updike, *A Month of Sundays*

"No cord nor cable can so forcibly draw, or hold so fast, as love can do with a twined thread."

—Robert Burton, *The Anatomy of Melancholy*

"The first prerogative of an artist in any medium is to make a fool of himself."

—Pauline Kael

"He must needs go that the devil drives."

—Christopher Marlowe, *Doctor Faustus*

Prologue

All hail to those who'd flock to this
Music mecca, Los Angeles,
In search of fortune & of fame,
Great hopes & dreams to forge a name,
Climb the charts, no one-hit wonder;
Defy the odds, rend asunder
The parlous world of indie rock!

Ye bands who, lab'ring 'round the clock,
The fickle public's gaze implore—
The punter & the record store
Clerks who'll stock your works in bins
(Post our poster, won't you, then?),
Bookers, goons in A&R
Who'd 'gainst all odds make you a star—
Hark! to me and hear mine story,
Then *say if one's quests for glory*
Are worth the price of priceless soul:
To sell one's all for rock & roll.

Part One

One

he doughty, white, midsized minivan cants left, hard, and a touch scarily, as, changing lanes into "the fast lane," it vrooms down the long declivity that is the southbound Grapevine on Interstate 5. And as the outer outskirts of Los Angeles hove into spectacular view the endless springtime sky, too, stuns: white hot white and streaked pink and blasted raspberry, it swirls and quavers with freakish springtime heat and odd red clouds, only daubed here and there with mitigating, pacific blue. The sky's every bit as overwhelming as the weirdly euphoric feeling you sometimes get when you first glimpse "home" after being away even for, say, just over a week and a half, as the four passengers in the van certifiably have been.

The air-conditioning, never very icy or reassuringly powerful to begin with, has of course been flicked off owing to the intense, long climb the van's just climbed that is "The Vine": there's the very real risk of the radiator overheating (that's the obvious), and furthermore it's a drain on gas (that's the not-as-apparent). And money's something this expense-conscious lot has to be meticulously mindful of, especially as prices at the pump have gone up *again,* and now hover 'round 1.20 dollars, which is crazy. They're saying it's only a matter of time before gas tops off at two bucks a gallon! Fuck! What next? A latte or a loaf of bread for three *fifty* or more? Ridiculous. Word is, over yonder in Old Europe many roadtripping Europeans these days don't even bat an eye at the prospect of forking over more than three dollars for a litre of "petrol." What's the deal with *that?* A litre's not even as much as a gallon is, last I checked. I mean, why don't they just send their Euro-wallets or firstborn children straight to His Majesty The King or Queen via The Royal Mail? Just put a fancy escutcheon-or-fire-breathing-dragon-emblazoned-type stamp on them and mail them right in to the palace or castle. Jeez. Ridiculous. What in the world is the world coming to, anyway? Absurd. If that's what it's coming to—no thanks. With those kinda prices, you'll never hardly be able to go anywhere, not even for spring break or Christmas, for Christ's sake.

The four riders in the van are virtually bathed in bright white light and the van itself, inside, is overwarm and kinda clammy. Having the front windows intermittently down hasn't helped much— it's that toasty. And the back side windows, though tinted a queasy aquamarine, only open via hasps, five ungenerous inches at best. It's almost hotter with them like that, winged forth and too whooshy-sounding anyway, so they're often closed less than a minute or even seconds after they're unlatched, open for but a couple of jarring gasps max. It's Tuesday, early-afternoon, and now that the mondo hill's been nervously, sedulously crested and "the air's" just been put back on, all's a bit more bearable, temperature-wise, in the so-called cabin.

On the outside, the doughty white minivan really does look like it's been through a thing or two, as they say. And it has: the plashed mud and pine sap of rain-dominated Washington, the soaked, whirling hay and surprise mists of horribly boring Oregon, the dust and viscous grime of Central and Northern California are all grafted or plastered onto the wheel wells, on the sides of the singing tires with their humming monotony, on the trembling footboards, all over the bus's puggy snout—everywhere. They, the foursome inside, always try to reserve a white one from the Enterprises on Hillhurst Avenue or Glendale Boulevard that they faithfully rent from. Despite the fact that right now it's dirty as fuck they, the four, that is, figure it's easier for other drivers to clock a white van at night (night-driving's on the itinerary for sure—there are some long distances between destinations), and collectively they seem to prefer it, that color. The color that seems to suit them, the something-innocent-about-them that gets quasi-sardonically remarked upon from time to time by jaded club bookers and callow university journalists who try to act all Lester Bangs, all wise beyond their years. What a contrast to the kids, the true indie pop fans, who, as the band "loads out" after each show (for by now, oh reader, you surely must have twigged that I'm describing an indie rock band on tour, in a van), come shuffling up to smile shy smiles full of tortured-early-twenties or late-teens pain and say hello, great show, and ask about the 7-inches, bashfully inquiring something like *How many songs from the new album did you guys end up playing tonight?* Or: *Do you guys have, um, like, any of your first cassette left or, like, anything on transparent purple, green, or violet-colored vinyl, numbered, hand-colored, limited pressing?* Or: *You don't have any XS babydoll T-shirts left, by any chance? My roommate's got a gnarly midterm tomorrow and she begged me to bring her back one. I really, really hope you have one 'cause she's been kinda down lately and is flunking every subject this semester. I think she's been wearing the same sweatshirt and jeans for two weeks straight now so it'd be nice to get her something, um, new to wear and stuff.*

Or (if they're not shy): *Know who you guys remind me of? You guys remind me of [insert cool hip band name here].*

And nine times out of ten the band the guy or girl compares you to is a band you either a) have never heard of, or b) sounds nothing at all like you and now you have to nod and pretend and smile all factitiously like you know what the hell the kid's goddam talking about till he or she gets bored or till you make up some transparent excuse and get the hell away yourself—like you gotta go get something from the van, or you forgot you were having your appendix out at the local emergency clinic.

Inside the kinda-careening vehicle, where the ultimate (as in farthest) bench's stays and bolts have been crescent-wrenched out and the bench itself left behind, orphaned, humped into the airless practice space in North Hollywood, the back's space's been expertly and systematically stuffed to the roof with music gear and bag and baggage: three amps, four guitars, one bass, a drum kit plus hardware (bunged into a pale yellow thrift store-scored golf club bag), the "merch box" (now, thankfully, nearly empty of T-shirts, CDs, signed posters, and 7-inches), guitar stands, etcetera, plus sleeping bags and duffle bags and one elegant suitcase for ballast.

The caramel and vanilla-colored interior is pleasant enough, but the van's seats aren't particularly comfortable, though neither are they unbearable (though the inside-the-cabin road hazard called "dead ass" does set in). The lone bench, the one right behind the driver's seat and the "shotgun" seat, isn't *quite* long enough for even the shortest of the four to stretch out and lie down on, so the preferred sleeping-space, and one all four members share fairly, in alarmingly hypersensitive and kind of comic awareness of duration and rotation, is a space made deliberately and *above* the planed amps that have been stacked against the lone bench: it's called "the perch." It's usually makeshift-upholstered with a nice, thick, unrolled sleeping bag or two and furnished with a couple pillows (or "drool pads," as the four charmingly refer to them); and it's kind of heaven, especially after one's been driving for five or six hours and has gotten little or no sleep after the hard day's gig-night before. One can catch major "Z's" there, for sure: oddly, it's even a bit hard to hear the blaring stereo, even at its most quote-unquote rockin' volume, when one's "be-perched," all right, on account of the space is womby somehow, an insular-ish, wondrous thing.

There are a number of plump, little, satiny, purple, star-shaped throw-pillows (a.k.a. "junior drool pads") strewn 'round the cabin and the band shares them indiscriminately like they themselves are occasional somnambulistic communists. There's a ten gallon blue, white, and mint-colored plastic Coleman cooler that resides between the driver's and the shotgun seat (and in which half-melted ice pieces slosh 'round in curious contiguity with the eight-ounce sparkling water bottles and plastic bags of breakfast fruit and assorted Yoplaits and wheat bread and honeybaked turkey and English cheddar and spiced mustard and mayo containers therein contained). On the floor, in the door wells, wedged in between the arm rests, are rogue road snacks and 50.7-ounce designer water bottles both empty and half-drunken from, and a flannel-lined black cassette case caddie that holds maybe thirty tapes. There's a nice black logbook with all the dates the band have done (nine gigs, well, eight, as one was last-minute cancelled, two in-stores, including one *stupendous* noon show at wonderful/venerable Stanford University, a godsend, which for the most part accounts for the mercifully light merch box); two fat road maps, folded importunately, one coffee-cup and rain-stained *Thomas Guide of the Western United States*, one quite expensive leather purse, three cheap polyester backpacks, several black-backed, spine-bent Penguin English and Russian novels plus a well-thumbed paperback copy of *The Canterbury Tales*, many music magazines, fanzines, weeklies, and assorted transparent red, screaming yellow, pink, or turquoise plastic bags filled with thrift store or curiosity shop *bric-a-brac* and vintage plaid button-down or "cowboy" or ironic heavy metal T-shirts, glamorous mohair and Gallic-cool cotton blend Lacoste cardies, rare vinyl records and an assortment of import CDs that really aren't that hard to find in a store at home, in LA—it's just that, for this band, like any band, "thrifting" and frequenting used book and new and used record stores are the preferred on-the-road daytime activities. There's only so much time you can theoretically spend with your band mates, talking or lunching or yawning or day-drinking or plotting rendezvous and set-lists before soundcheck.

For it is a truth universally acknowledged that rock and roll touring, at no-matter-what-level, is a *lot* of waiting around.

A lot of it.

And you need activities, however meretricious and meaningless and banal, to fill the void, kill the time that's killing you, killing us all. You have to kill it before you have to go and *live* onstage for your forty-five minute set plus a two-song encore if you're collectively "feeling" it and the crowd "deserves" it. (It's no profound thing that even a dum dum like Peter Frampton perceptively called his most famous and obviously best selling double album *Frampton Comes Alive*—because that is what live gigs, even if they aren't that good, kind of make you, "the artist," *and* the audience *do:* i.e. *come alive.*) And for the most part—apropos of this "thrifting" motif—if you don't purchase something from a store you've lolled about in for the better part of half an hour, you feel like you haven't *accomplished* anything, really.

So out on tour you end up with heaps of things in the aforementioned colored plastic bags that you don't need or even really want, like the import CDs you could get back home at Arons or Finyl Vinyl or even the cooler corporate branches of The Wherehouse or Licorice Pizza or Music Plus or Rhino in Westwood on the goddam Westside. Or you end up buying stuff of super-iffy authenticity like a guitar that Donny Osmond supposedly owned and gave away, or an official Peter Tork lunch box or playdoll that looks suspiciously like a G.I. Joe with a wig and a bass stuck on it, or a chintzily framed picture of Pete Townshend windmilling blood all over a bitchin' "Fireglo" Rickenbacker 330 or beautiful walnut Gibson SG.

There's this nebulous, metaphysical sense of accomplishment that you get merely by being on tour in that you have succeeded, for however much time, in *not having to work an odious quote-unquote straight job.* Even if it's just for three days in a row, half a week. Thus, and for that magnificent amount of time, you are a bona fide "working" musician—not one who's just daydreaming about touring as he or she rings up another purchase and hands change or answers a rachety office telephone or rakes leaves into heaps from a veritable suburbia of long lawns or scoops them from yucky gutters. But that feeling of accomplishment is not the same thing, same feeling, more's the pity, unless you have something tangible to show for it when you come home from being "on tour." Something like a stack of mint condition Beatles bubble gum cards (i.e. you are a Beatles nerd), or a rare promotional poster for a Japanese date The Fab Four did in '66 (if e.g. you are an even bigger Beatles nerd), or a signed, framed lithograph of one of Yoko's "poems" (i.e. you were drunk or high or both). God knows that something tangible's not going to be (doesn't *have* to be) very much money—unless you are in Roger Waters' or Kenny Rogers' band. It doesn't have to cost much at all; it's just a sort of souvenir. You might drool over a vintage jasper-colored lava lamp you spotted in a head shop you ducked into for a lark; you might marvel at the golden-framed copy of that hexagonal, still-sealed, first pressing of the infamous 3-D Rolling Stones 1967 LP, *Their Satanic*

Majesties Request, that hangs above the register at the Rough Trade, say, on Haight Street; but at 400 dollars and 269 dollars, respectively, you're not *even* gonna think about how you might put either of those "finds" on layaway or anything.

And like layaway's even an option at a record or head shop anyway!

Anyway, keeping track of the stuff that—especially after a gig—just gets chucked any-old-where into any old band's van is another sort of game to play. How, sometimes, after a few dozen backstage celebratory beers grabbed from the slimy flotilla of them bobbing in the sloshy aluminum vat and half a pack of wolfed-down Marlboro Lights, one can even find one's own *head* sometimes is a major mystery. Things get lost easy. Evaporate or disappear. Turn right back up sometimes. Sometimes not. For instance, the cheap black vinyl logbook is a frequent fugitive: the four of them are always foraging for it, it seems, overturning junk like mad Black Friday shoppers, scrambling to find out the address of the club they were supposed to roll up to and unload at seven minutes ago. A magical mystery tour—every indie tour is. It's a mystery whether you'll make it to Athens, to Bloomington, to Cinci, to Dallas without killing yourself *or* your band mates—even if the tour's going grand; it's gonna take some kind of magic these three weeks, three months, three years just to get you through any given Tuesday tour day. With its blood red and stark white oblong The Weird Sisters sticker affixed to the back of it, the logbook's not that hard to spot; and it always and invariably turns up—but only after three of the band members panic a little.

One of them never or only very rarely frets, however—he's the bassist. He's tall and dark and dorkily handsome without being aware of it, the handsome bit: the dork element he's doubtlessly aware of; he plays it up in fact on account of he's not really a dweeb, just a guy who puts people at their ease by putting himself aw-shucksly second, and often down. He's got the even-keeled demeanor of a boat captain (*there's* a ludic pun), and it's a good thing too 'cause the other three are to different degrees and in different ways querulous and one might even say downright "uptight" on occasion. They're firstborns, all three, and it's just not acceptable to them for things not to go as they've planned. (And most things "rock" rarely, as anyone with any exposure to "The Music Business" knows, go as planned!)

Curiously, there are two anthracite-gray barbells banked against the bench/backseat (as if they don't get enough exercise, these four, schlepping their gear up narrow horror-stairs to second-floor venues or a handful of mop-and-beer-breathed basementy pubs), but only one band member ever touches these, the one who owns one black, old-timey-doctor-looking bag that he uses just for seemingly innumerable and astonishingly specialized and distinct hair products plus a scary, jet black, incredibly oversized, professional-appearing blow-dryer. You'd think that bag'd belong to the demurely pretty young woman who's riding shot, but it doesn't. It's the property of The Weird Sisters' drummer, our *new* drummer, who as we meet them is sitting directly behind her, the pretty and only girl. It's the sort of serious-looking bathroom apparatus, the drummer's blow-dryer is, that you could picture someone rigging up to a heavy-duty, dirty orange extension cord and marching out to his or her frosty front lawn with in order to scatter into the misty street some yellow-red oak or red-green maple leaves in late autumn.

One last material thing, as far as tallying up or inventorying all the stuff in the van goes: under the lone back bench, next to the barbells, unless there's what the four call a "cargo shift" like what's aforementionedly happened above as the van changed lanes, rides a not-ornate chess set that's encased in a red, imitation leather case. (Sometimes, in other words, being slick-surfaced, it slips out like a "So there!" tongue from under the seat and has to be heeled or patted back under it.)

But most notably inside this vehicle, right there right now, what there is is there's a feeling of keening, ineffable sadness—made even more palpable as it has been preceded by a sort of unanimous euphoria. For The Weird Sisters, this little—you might even say *purist*, modest, unspoiled, and genuine—indie rock band from Los Angeles, not forty minutes ago and com*plete*ly out-of-the-blue, heard the "single" from their debut CD on the lone alt-rock radio station in Bakersfield, California.

And hearing it on the airwaves, their song, has made them, collectively, respectively, and to varying degress, really, really happy.

The ensuing sadness, however, has, precipitously enough, come as a result of listening to the radio as well, its horrid, inexorable source. For as the driver, the frontman and leader of the group, toggles the crackling dial to try to get reception on 106.7 FM (the Bakersfield station having fizzed and faded statically away), the powerful "Legendary KROQ," the on-air DJ makes the following startling, terrible announcement: *This just in from The Associated Press: The body of Kurt Cobain, lead singer of the multiplatinum band Nirvana, has been found at his Seattle home—the result of an apparent suicide. Authorities have yet to reveal more details at this time, but a wave of infinite sadness washes over all of us here at the station as we mourn the passing of a great artist, husband, father, and human being: Kurt Cobain.*

Two

ell, now. There's where I might start—were I, assuming and subsequently maintaining an omniscient third person persona, to try to pick up my story from where we last left off at the end of *The King of Good Intentions*. Kinda dramatic, yeah? Thrilling, even—maybe?

"That's a helluva—dramaturgically-speaking—*protasis* you got there, son," a good old boy/Rhodes Scholar/playwright-maybe/kinda-neo-Faulknerian fuck might remark over a nice glass of top-shelf

Scotch or sherry or bourbon: "A mite *melo*dramatic, perhaps, but a pretty darn good way to start with a bang—if you'll pardon the less-than-fortuitious expression."

It's certainly somewhat jolting; you gotta give it that—ending the first chapter like that with the "tragic" (depending on your view of suicide) death of an icon, "the voice of a generation," the reluctant, pretty "poster boy for Generation X," milk carton kid equivalent for The Grunge Era in general; or maybe just another fucked up leader/songwriter of another fucked up band in a fucked up world.

Hi there. *Hello.* Hey. It's me—John, the fucked up leader/songwriter of The Weird Sisters, the fucked up ('cause all bands are fucked up) band in the fucked up van, just as all songwriter/bandleaders are, to varying degrees, of course, fucked up, too. There: that's better. Now the mask's dropped and the guard's down and the too-arduous artifice needn't be kept opprobriously up. Well, then: You might be wondering what the hell Jenny, my girlfriend and key band mate (she's the one riding shot, the other singer and guitarist, who used to play keyboards as well), and I are even *doing* going on tour and playing music together considering what disastrously happened maybe six months prior to this. Considering that she'd discovered, *without me being the one to confess to her,* that I kinda/sorta half-or-fully cheated on her with this awful, pretentious chick called Sarah. Sarah-Who-Hates-Me's what I called her on account of even though she seduced me, she averred that she despised me and didn't really even consider me a real live person.

No kidding.

After that sort of a denouement, you might have expected we'd be a double bundle of wrecked affections, Jenny and I, unanswerable accusations, woe and unhealable hurt and whatnot. Expect we'd never even speak again, let alone become a real "couple" again, a couple who not only *work* (at being in a band, of course), but also *live* together. Shocking, huh, or maybe not. Either way, I'll get around to telling you what happened in a little bit, okay? How biddable *she,* Jenny-dear, thawed (I won't say melted), then got back together with me, reconciled with me, forgave me, gave in, carried on being my wonderful girlfriend and talented band mate. But first I've gotta tell you about our new drummer, Raleigh—Walter our old drummer's replacement. 'Cause despite all the stuff you may have heard about what pains-in-the-ass drummers (*and* their seemingly omnipresent Yoko-ish girlfriends) can be, this new kid's (he's, at twenty-two, around eight or six significant years younger than the rest of us) *sui generis,* one of a kind. One of a not-good kind. In so many ways. No shit. I already kinda started telling you about him, Raleighboy, via the barbells and the hair products and hair-dryer and all of that, I shouldn't wonder. You know how there's this expression that goes: "By their friends ye shall know them." In a way you could *also* say "By their *possessions* ye shall know them as well." And maybe even know them better than how you know them by their chums and sidekicks and mates."

Okay: Guy brings some extra weights to lift on a one or two-week indie rock van tour? Guy's looking to show off or keep up an image of himself as Mr. WorksOutALot? Mr. *Weakie?* Mr. I-Don't-Know-About-You-Hard-Partying-Waste-Cadets-But-I-Like-To-Party-By-Keeping-In-*Shape? Hey*, guy! *Hey.* Wanna get some extra reps in? Wail on your pecs and get those biceps "jacked" and "pumped"? You do? Okay, then: *Fucking free-lift my nine-hundred-pound Fender Twin Reverb amp up these four-flights-a-stairs instead, why dontcha?* Do *that.* Jerk-and-clear my goddam *gear* instead, okay, mate? I'll tell every pretty girl I meet and can't approach 'cause my girlfriend's right there, in a band with me, standing hawk-watchfully right next to me at the merch table after the show and evil-eyeing every quasi-attractive lovely under forty-three in the club—I'll let her know what a stud you are, all right? Put in a word for ya. No *problem.* Happy to. Here: Take my guitar and my backup while you're at it, plus my suitcase full of effects and tweed guitar leads in scarlet/gold and purple/red and tuners and plectrums. Go on, then, stud. Work it. Work *out.*

I mean, Jenny and Rob and I just gawked sometimes—and of course laughed under our collective breaths, and somewhat (*some*what, mind you) bemusedly shook our incredulous, road-weary heads at him, Ral, that is, as he'd do some curls after a gig, or first thing in the morning, in some kind soul's living room, someone who'd given us floor space to sleep on—not, to our minds, turn into a weight room or goddam gymnasium.

Raleigh. You're not going to believe half the things I could tell you about him. One time, I think it was somewhere on the way to Portland, southern Oregon somewhere, some place with a thousand million towering pine trees, anyway, Raleigh was driving and I was navigating and Jenny and Rob were fast asleep, making the most of the "drool pads." We were sick of listening to music, Ral and I were, and when that happens it's sort of the shotgunner's road etiquette, sort of their obligation, to keep the conversation going and stuff so the driver doesn't' fall asleep bloody blinking madly and kill everyone on some winding highway at 7,000 feet above the hypnotizing tree line that evergreenly gesticulates beneath a somnambulant sky of bluest iris blue. I remember looking out the well-smudged windows and seeing scarlet flowers along the sun-spangled roadsides, and teeming plumes of psychedelic, glimmering Queen Anne's Lace, great leaves shimmering greenly in the affably waving trees.

"All right, Ral," I'd sighed. "Go on. What do you wanna talk about?"

"Okay, let's see," Raleigh said. "Hey, John?"

"Yes, Raleigh?"

"Do you know that band Imperial Butt Wizards?"

"Yeah?"

"Imperial Butt Wizards," Raleigh repeated, but like he was gearing up for another thought.

"Uh-huh," I quote-unquote said. I was starting off all mellow, like someone admiring a collection of antique gloves or someone's pet book of photographs of various barns or silos or breakfast tacos from Austin, Texas. I was chill. But I knew that *some* sort of shenanigans were in store for me. There had to be with Raleigh. "What a*bout* them, Ral?"

"Hey, John?"

"Yeah?"

"Do you know that band Anal Cunt?"

And here I shook my head "yes" and opened my hands up like a priest or pastor or Jesus Christ himself supplicating his flock—as if to say, "And *so?*"

Longish pause. Then Raleigh said: "Anal Cunt." Pronounced in the same fashion, like he was learning a sublanguage of the taking-the-piss family of languages, like he was doing some exercise from a *Teach Yourself* book.

"Uh-huh, Ral," I this-time-more-pronouncedly sighed.

Pause encore. Several long minutes passing. Jejune suspense. Queer feeling of queasy anticipation. Then, the inevitable:

"Hey, John?"

"*What*, Raleigh? What *is* it? Just *say* it! Jesus, Ral, you have a way of—"

"John?…"

"*What*, Raleigh, *what?!*"

"Nothing. Nevermind."

"*What*, Ral? What is it? You can't just—"

"Hey, John?"

"Oh, my God, Raleigh," I said and doubtless threw my eyes up toward the skies and trees.

Pursed-mouthed silence for sure now—that ensured there'd be a shorter-than-usual "beat."

"Jesus fuck, Raleigh… *What?* Am I supposed to beg you here to—"

"Do you know that band Lisa Suckdog?"

I was looking straight ahead now, not at him, but I could tell his— to say the least, mischievous—eyes were trained right on me.

"*Jesus*, Raleigh: yes, yes, I know Lisa Suckdog. Lisa *Suck*dog, Lisa *Suck*dog. Watch the road, Raleigh. What a*bout* her? What in the fuck is the—"

"Huh-huh," Raleigh said in a Beavis-or-the-other-guy way. "Lisa Suckdog."

"Oh my God, Raleigh," I said, turning his way now. "You are just the most amazingly—"

"Jeez, man. You don't have to get all bent out of…I'm just trying to have a friendly conversation here and keep awake so that I don't drive this van off a cliff or something. God, John. Sorry I harshed your mellow or whatever."

But by that time he'd, in a word, gotten my goat, gotten it, and was meekly-smugly parading it 'round the silty county fairgrounds, as it were. It happened all the time. Drummers, boy: I'm telling you. They get a clue re: something that can make you go straight out of your mind, bug the living fucking shit out of you. They hammer that shit to fucking death like a tom-tom or floor tom at the mercy of Keith "Allmighty" Moon or John "Boom-Boom" Bonham. Or Raleigh did, at least—that's for sure. Never faltered.

Then, around six or seven winding-twisty climbing miles later: "Hey, John?…"

And such-like otiose proceedings of similar circumlocutional fatuosity that pass for sparkling badinage in an Astro Van on tour: immeasurably insufferable.

And me the bait taking—every single time, unfailingly.

And why? Because I never ever learn, do I? Do I? I do not. No. Not me. Not this guy. Never. Not a chance. Nope. No, sir.

Rob and Jenny had *way* fewer issues with soigne Raleigh than unkempt I did: For one, it took all of two rehearsals for it to become apparent that Raleigh was utterly (and predictably) puppy-dog smitten with Jen, *loved* her, fawningly, droolingly, as an object lesson in perfervid, lovestruck obsequiousness—and three hang-outs after practice for us all to see that Rob was some kinda big-brother-buddy-slash-goombah for Raleigh to look up to. And Rob, who just like my good old best friend Sterling, loved *anyone* who loved *him*, lapped it up with a smoking kettle-spoon, thought Raleigh a kook in a *good* way and got an immense kick out of palling around with him, teaching him the ropes, the ropes I, of course, would love to use to string his ass up with. And Jenny, though she'd never in a million years admit it, was, you could tell, sort of minorly giddy to have a young and pretty handsome fellow fucking ga-ga-ing over her left and right. So I guess it was just me who was bugged to the max by our latest Sister. Good old, pernickety, curmudgeonly *me*. There I go again, having a little whinge and a moan about another drummer. How picayune, in the grand or the small scheme of things; how silly, to let someone who *hits things*, "the skins," get under *yours*. What a spastic waste of life and time. There must be more important things to think about, dwell on, mull over, contemplate. Like global warming or what to have for lunch; or why people learn French (other than for *reading* it); or why not *one* of my friends who grew up Catholic believes in God, especially the ones who confess they thought when they grew up that they were for sure gonna be nuns or priests or maybe Pope; or why, at the end of those exercises in abject beauty and untrammeled sentimentality we call The Movies, the director never shows (as the swooping camera panoramas, pulls away, to the string-heavy swell of molten music, as the quaint little town goes back to good old normal after the big old mushrooming drama/kerfuffle) say, a sweet, cute little girl getting punched in the face with an overblown-up tetherball; or a powerful, natty businessman tripping on a slab of raised and root-shifted pavement and totally *eating* it; a roofer just fucking *nailing* his already empurpled thumb with an industrial-issue claw hammer; or a doily-faced little old lady choking to death in a tearoom, her superannuated-apple mug going even more puckery as she strangleholds, then magic-tricks the pristine tablecloth; a shit-grinning "retarded" personage stuffing a butterfly into his already food-caked gob, or a rabid dog with a dog (a littler one, of course) in its mouth.

Or—for another instance of something better to think about than how, when you are on tour, someone in your band can fairly jumprope repeatedly on your very last nerve—how about this: the fact that, as everybody knows, in a serious committed relationship or a marriage, say, one party *always* loves the other more than the other party loves him or her. And how what nobody ever talks about is how said more-in-love person more often than we realize or acknowledge has a greater sense of emotional self-preservation, or maybe even ruthlessness, and who ends up getting less hurt, in the end, when all goes smash and the love runs out, than the party who seemed all along to have "the upper hand."

Huh.

Or this: How come everyone, even if they aren't particularly superstitious, talks about how things come in *threes*, but no one talks about how, sometimes, things come in *ones*? Haha! Rather than ruminating on Raleigh and his opaque ilk, wouldn't it be better for me to think up variations on Hofstadter's Strange Loops or try to write a comedy screenplay, a biopic period piece, buddy picture starring bumptious Boswell and laughing Johnson? Aren't there better ways to spend one's time than analyzing to death people who aren't even really all that deep or interesting? I mean, I didn't mean to go all Henry James or pretend-Proust on you. Just you look at all those goddam commas, those apodictic, boohoo appositives! Anyway, when someone—and here I'm back to addressing The Raleigh Question—not just gets but fairly trampo*lines* onto your last nerve, well...*and* you have to be stuck in a van/a band/on a stage with him plus backstage pre-the gig? Watch him masticate Cocoa Puffs or Cap'n Crunch or Count Chocula for *dinner*? Endure innumerable silly jokes and that worst sort of joke, The Practical? Yep, Raleigh was/is a practical joker—someone who, in my humble estimation, is for all intents and purposes a practicing sadist, the denizen of Lilliput who delights in humiliating bigger others; from the most "harmless" sort of "hey-I'm-just-having-fun" kinda gag—like, say, taking out a subscription to a gay porn 'zine in someone's name—to the über-prank of the bucketful of saltwater over the inviting door, the practical joker's object's to *mortify incontrovertibly*. Think about it: The practical joker, that sick fuck, isn't content merely to get the better of unsuspecting *you*; he's gotta show you he *knows* you know that he knows he "got" you: He comes right out like a fleering jack-in-the-box and takes horrid credit. And the more the merrier in terms of audience. Even better if his or your friends bear witness to the "fun." That's how you know he's cruel as hell: he wants points, too. He wants a gawking gallery. That's greedy, if you ask me. Fuck, I hate jesters like that, and Raleigh's a real card, a total jokesmith, a joke-jockey, one like you've never met, let me tell you.

You just can't win. Kick up a petulant fuss when you get goofed on—you're a spoilsport and party pooper. Laugh along at being made muchly merry of? You're still, at best, the chump. Not just *a* but *the*. Big distinction. However mean-spirited the burlesque (and, as you'll see, some of Raleigh's monkeyshines weren't just monkeying around), the gagman comes out on top and you come a cropper. Every single time. The fucker's fucked with you *and* fucking fucked you and there's fucking nothing you can do the fucking fuck about it without fucking looking even worse, for fuck's sake. Wasn't it Freud or Erich Fromm or Franken or one of those other heavy hitters who theorized about the inherent hostility of regular old verbal jokes? Let alone ones that are practical (what an ironic term, anyway). You practically, virtually crack a guy's shorn shin with a hockey stick or trusty 2 Wood—that's technically considered a form of "joshing." Just as one category, if you think about it, of irony is sheer invective: like it's all ironic and stuff to go insulting a guy directly to his face, the way, say, characters in Shakespeare's comedies (and tragedies, too) famously do: e.g., *Thou be-slubbering knotty-patted gorbellied rump-fed coxcomb whoreson of a poxy tatterdemalion slave's fortnight-old skidmark—you wet spec of offal lodged in M'lady's Thursday pantaloons!*

Anyway, ever notice how infinitely puerile practical jokers are normally the sorts who aren't very good with the old noggin, the brain? Words: not quite their forte, of course; not what they're best at. Your more-evolved, twisted "wit" who gets off on practical shenanigans might spin it theoretically to the point where he's arguing that he's actually giving you an ontological *opportunity* to show you can take a joke, not take yourself so seriously. To be "punked" is to be tested and then some, they aver—and either one passes or fails. But I ain't buying it. Like those sorts of japes, reader? Put this book down right now and get lost, why don't you? Don't wanna know you. Don't want your company. Piss off, okay?

Ah, leave it, why don't you, I tell myself; *Think happier thoughts, get positive, get over it, lighten up*, I tell myself.

Can't.

Fuck it: let's get this out: not to be done with it but to amuse me and maybe you—and vent, as well—sure, there's worth in that.

Okay: to wit: and going back to the black bag motif: see if you agree with this: guy has more than three hair bottles of hair products (the absolute limit being shampoo, conditioner, and either a spot of leave-in conditioner or, at *best*, a finger-full of gel or a rumor of mousse), guy's a probable *total hassle session*. Way vain. Way self-involved. Way too prissy and particular. *Way* a program. (guy's *gay*—that's another story: gay guy's entitled to as many unguents for the head as he wants to stuff into his "valise" or "portmanteau" or "rucksack," okay? That's certain. Gay guy's another category entirely. He needs "product" and stuff like that to counterbalance all the unsubtle, rampant homophobia in our unfair society, all right? He needs that shit.)

Not-gay guy, however (and Raleigh was/is *sans doute* not a "lord" or "faggot" or "popesmoker" or "bum chum")—he has four and *more* hair products, tubes and bottles and cans of them. He's *not* a go-with-the-flow sort like Rob the bassist is. The kind of guy, in other words, who's, well, like *me*. Who, after a gig, needs just a few couple hundred beers (in order to have a gambrinous shot, at least, at a good night's sleep), a little puff on a spliff, then an army or horse blanket or tacky plaid or patchwork summertime-style sleeping bag and a couch that's not too convex or evocative of some twelfth-century torture prototype photograph from the Louvre or the V & A; a shower in the morning (and not even a lake-drainer—just a rinse-off and *maybe* a fresh towel, or at least not a too-used one); a no-nonsense cup of black coffee and a refill plus a buttered bagel or day-old Danish or a shard of toast on a paper towel—and he's good to go. But Raleigh? Sheesh. Where do I even start? Especially when the phrase "Don't get me started!" even more aptly applies to *him*. I mean, he's a *great* drummer—*much* better than Walt, our old one was—but as a *person?* Wow.

A further example, then, of how Raleigh could irk you right out of your wig? There you are, let's imagine, trimming the hedge in with your trusty pea green gardening sheers: Raleigh saunters up: "So, hey—trimming the *hedge*, huh?" Or you're scouring the after-dinner dishes, up to your arse in sitcom-like suds and sweat and red-hot water: Raleigh ambles in: "So, hey—doing the *dishes*, eh?" Or, there's you changing guitar strings or reading a book or dipping a crispy shrimp roll into a vat of deliciously quivering sweet and sour sauce...or flying a kite...or camped outside an appalling mall, sitting on a beach chair, beer in hand, and spectating a preposterous sidewalk stampede on the so-called Black Friday after Thanksgiving...and there's Raleigh, sidling up and...you get it, now, surely. Certainly you do.

I'm a horrible exaggerator—that I know, it's a fact, I admit it—but that's *exactly* how Raleigh is and no mistake. 'Twould drive a saint crazy, 'twould, having to deal with him. Especially in close quarters, like what touring claustrophobically brings. The near-perpetual proximity. The commingled vile smells and relentless screaming-hangover breakfasts at countless "greasy spoons"; the bathetic aftermaths of cracked gigs, and crestfallen demeanors after crummy turnouts, bad sound, bad performances, bad vibes. Eventually it would drive a saint barking mad, touring with good old Ral who drums so well. Bet you any money, after three archetypal days in the van with Raleigh, the saint would "go 'round the twist." Get up from The Lotus, after infinite self-counselings *Du calme, du calme, monsieur,* or *Father, forgive them they know not what they do—and besides, he's a* drummer, *for heck's sake.* And said saint would just *not be able to take it anymore.* Then, at a Rest Area or Gas Hutch, in a blindingly-lit, eerily tranquil Denny's in the middle of Nowhere, Texas or in the sparkly-spangled lobby of the *one* nice hotel you've gotten to stay at this whole long tour, the holy guy'd go stick one of his wandering-the-desert boots or at least a supple sandal right into Ral's left rump, shielding his eyes with a sort of hand-salute as he does so, so's he doesn't risk missing, making sure to keep that light, that sun, that chandlier-lambency out of his face so he can get his "shot" at Ral sorted, landed.

Either that or he'd up and take Raleigh by the lapels of one of the groovy green-and-purple paisley shirts he wore onstage sometimes and go: "*Right*, you. I am a saint and all. Saint am I. A bona fide one, too. You can look me up in *The Big Book of The Beatific and Sanctified*, okay? I'm in there. Twice, at least, though I'm too humble and everything to go poring over it day and night, okay? Therefore. Established. My saintliness. But *you*, you have tried my holy indulgence to its sacrosanct, frayed ends, to the precipice of patience itself, the very edge of the cliff of tolerance—so much so that I'm mixing metaphors here like a politician.

"Hey," the saint would "aside" to the audience (if we could film him); "*Hey* there. Have you ever tried to lose weight by subsisting on rice cakes or carrot sticks? Most of us saintish types just fast and pray and all that rot and kinda just take the hunger pangs and have done with it, you know? But that gets old after a while—even for us. Plus, all that fasting can lead to (and this is what your sanctified, your super pious, your spiritual leaders and gurus don't tell you) splashing out in a not good way, i.e. binge eating, gluttony, scarfing largely then purging and what-all. Anyway, rice cakes, after you've munched two or three hundred of them in an arid row—rice cakes, I daresay, only succeed in making you positively *ravenous*. There you are, chomping contentedly on your third or forth one and suddenly, next thing you know, you're running to the Frigidaire to go gargle non-nonfat egg nog and chug a turkey, whole, spitting out the bones and the marrow as you go. And carrot sticks? Don't even get me started on carrot sticks!

"Raleigh," the saint might conclude, "you are the *rice cake* of rock and roll. Your band's own personal carrot stick. I'm heartily sorry to have to tell you that, but you *are*. I mean, God forgive me for not softening this with a palliating metaphor or something, but you're also just, well, you're just…you're a fucking *idiot*."

Talking to him, Raleigh the drummer boy, almost every time you did so, was like having one of those conversations that start off with someone uttering one of these two diabolical phrases: "*I have to tell you something*" or "*We have to talk*." Know what I mean? The kind of idioms that never, or at best hardly ever, presage anything good, anything *you* really want to talk about or have someone tell you. Have you ever noticed that, reader? Those locutions *never* ever adumbrate anything *positive*. *Oh* no. It's never "I have to tell you something: I'm giving you ten thousand dollars just for fun"; or, "We have to talk: I am going to support you lavishly, in Honolulu, Hawaii, no less, for the next five years while you try to make it on the pro tennis tour at age thirty." It's never anything like that. It's always that they *have* to tell *you* something and that something's simply *awful*, like they're pregnant (with another man's child; and the man's your favorite uncle or erstwhile best friend, one you've known and loved since third grade), or that quote-unquote we (it's really *they, them, them themselves*) have to talk because, somehow, the new car you ransomed your life for went into a deep, wet ditch while the friend who borrowed it was drunk and insuranceless. He's really sorry—he didn't know how to tell you; the good news, however, is that quite a few of your favorite tapes flew out of the car's window before it burst into tall flames! That's a positive, right? Isn't it? At least there's that. Look! Creedence *and* Echo and the Bunnymen! Fancy that. Good as new. Almost, at least. One is. I'll replace it tomorrow. I was going to the record store anyway! If I can find a ride, that is. Cool? Okay? Sorry. Really.

Know what? What I think I'll do is just pick up the tale from the Cobain announcement/eulogy and fill in the proverbial blanks from there. That all right with you? Ah, I'm just messing with you like always, reader-dear. Having fun at both our expenses. Take me with a grain, why don't you? A grain of pure grain alcohol, that is. Ha! Or, better yet, take me with a *gram*. There's a party. That'd be a blast. That'd be kicks. And like I said: hey there: glad to see you again. Glad you could make it, come to the show. Ready? Buckle in, then, and come along for the second part of The Weird Sisters' wild and wicky-wacky ride. It's gonna be bumpy; it's gonna be *rocky* (ha!). It's gonna be rollicking-good and twisty-turny and fun. You're gonna meet some new people (a tall, bright, slender, laughing-happy-insouciant, super pretty, sparsely-be-freckled, black-haired girl with blue blue eyes like the twinkling sea; an even crazier record producer/exec than our good old out-of-his-gourd former producer McLeary was; more artists and writers and actors and posers and geeks and freaks). Mind you, maybe we'll catch up with some familiar former acquaintance. For these characters are, almost all of them, in their tumultuous late twenties—where allegiances shift and drift and friendships fade and bloom, flowerlike, and then maybe burst and there they are, in rumpled petals, in a glorious mess on the ground. And there you go wondering "what ever happened to...Krash or Jolia from your local Britpub, Kaz and K.C. from those dank, dark clubs you play too much like Spaceland, The Lingerie, or Molly Malone's, Three of Clubs and Madame Wong's West; Fais-Do-Do or Largo. Where are Jim, Jem, Joe, and Jo Jo; Mike C., Mike B., or Mikael with a "k"? Anyone know where *they* went? Seen them around? Stacy, Kayci, Lacey, Mackenzie? Fuck if I know. And what about Mike Fuck? Mike Fuck! Oh, my God! Remember *that* guy? Hahaha: what a winner, what a card. Haven't seen Mike Fuck for *ages*. Nobody has. No idea where he...and we never see Johnny T. anymore, do we? He just faded away. His band had a big thing in *BAM*—just last year, it was. They opened up for Jane's Addiction, Lions and Ghosts, X, and then they just sort of... faded away. No shit. I heard about that. Maybe he's in the studio or joined an ashram, got lost in Central Mexico or upped as a grunt marine; moved to Joshua Tree (*everybody's* flocking there it seems since the Gram Parsons *Best Of* came out on CD). Jesus: and what about Tracey? Lost touch with him, too. No one's heard from him in yonks. Did he fuck right off/right back to Cleveland, Princeton, Pittsburgh, Cinci? Dallas, Detroit, Daly City? Beantown, Chi-town, downtown Vegas?

Los Angeles, boy. Where they disappear as mysteriously as they predictably appear—and don't you forget it.

Anyway: if it happens, if we get around to it, if all things logistic fall into place, we're maybe gonna go on the road with an ambitious and industrious and three-sevenths-of-them college-educated indie band and read about some pretty thrilling stuff, yeah, and maybe some sorta sultry sexy sordid stuff, too. A few little melancholy-making (it can't be *all* fun and games all the time) things perhaps are going to come in to the authorial equation, but it's not going to be *boring*, Sydney. Not ever will it boring be, is what I'm skewed-syntactically saying here, echoing that immortal line in *Syd and Nancy*. I promise you. Not even the boring bits are gonna be. Boring, that is.

You'll see. So, let's get going. Let's see what's going forward in The Weird Sisters' world, why don't we? Yes, let's. Let's jam.

Through the glass darkly, then, and lightly, too—you've gotta have a balanced view. Let's have a little look-see, shall we? Peer into the impenetrable prism of the past. The reverse crystal ball of the what-went-on. Catch up. Fill you in. Apprise you of perimeters, particulars. Let you know what has gone down and come up and worked out and…not.

Time. It's been said to be a bandit, a thief, the ineluctable monster that masticates us all in his Marvellian "slow-chapped maw"; but I like to think of him as more of a *maniac*, a lilac-eyed *lunatic* who's clambering up the fortified gates outside of which we, all of us, tremblingly wait. There he is, Mr. Time (hiya!), smiling, half-laughing through the sharp knife in his sharper teeth, with, for good measure, a sharpened, ready machete or, traditionally, archetypally, a long-handled *scythe* in his big-buckled belt and a well-worn cudgel in his free hand (God knows apelike, strongman *he* only needs the one wing to scale the barrier, somersault over, get going, get to work, have at us, hack away; he's been around for*ever*, he's old as the hoary hills, but he's still in hella great shape).

Good Ole Father Time.

Old Reaper. Old friend. Old fiend. Old *faux-ami*.

He's coming.

He's a *killer*.

It's comic.

Well, *al*most.

Comedy—and life itself is nothing if not tragically *that*—isn't pretty. But at least it can be pretty funny. Here's hoping so. Here goes. Here we go.

Here.

Three

f the four of us, only Raleigh, really, had more than a passing interest in Nirvana as a band from a fanboy standpoint. Jenny and I were way too into dark, underproduced, jangly pop like what *we* played to get too into what grungey "Kurdt" and Co. were all about. But we were collectively affected, for sure. How could one not be? Almost everybody who cared about so-called alternative music at that time was. You couldn't get away from him, Cobain, in the media, that is, any more than sorry-tragic he could get away, it seemed, from *them*, the media pundits and parasitic paparazzi and fawning fans, the frat boys and homophobes and über-jocks he begged not to come to his gigs. There he was, Cobain, looking dolefully goofy or posing playfully ironically at you from every music magazine and record store display, with a cooler, big-striped, varsity-striped, or fuzzy tan or teal cardie than you'll ever own—and you can't buy one just like it 'cause first of all it's from the seventies *Sears* or something, and sold exclusively in the Pacific Northwest; and if you did get your hands on one and go asporting it you'd just be some total clone, some wannabe. There Kurt's songs are as well, there his pains are, his variegated hair and lost-boy stare; his cries and whispers, screams, on the radio, in the shopping mall, the Pep Boys and Auto Zone, the coffee house, at someone's backyard party, in their basement studio,

on their Walkman as they walk or jog by you as all you're trying to do is buy a goddam sixer and…there they are again: Nirvana. Pumped in and amped through to the liquor store's gimcrack Radio Shacks before the cooler door shuts tight behind you. There's some kid riffing arrhythmically any one of the songs from *Nevermind* as you walk past his suburban bedroom. The choppy strains of "Smells Like Teen Spirt" or "Come As You Are" are wafting up from twenty million adolescent American's basements, out from many thousand British sheds, from tiny amps in Europe and Australia and all over Asia, too. Guy lives in an igloo or shanty, guy can't afford a Happy Meal or Ramen feast, guy lives in his car down by the reservoir—he's still got his Squier Strat plugged straight into his truck's lighter socket so he can fumble through "In Bloom" or "Lithium."

After a few obligatory "How sad's" and "I can't believe it's true's," and "What a drag's" and "Unbelievable's" we drove on, dipping down now into the somewhat flat part of that part of the thrumming freeway, past Castaic, past Newhall (where all the LA cops live so that they don't reside, presumably, right next door to the people they have to bust), silently and pretty darn stunned. Till, that is, Raleigh, with tears in his quavering voice, asked if we could please pull over for a second: a request I had to nix, seeing as we were already late for a meeting at our record company's offices in central Orange County before the last gig of the run, also down in the dreaded OC. I nix, yes, but not before appealing telepathically to Jenny and Rob for "seconding" and "thirding" so's I wouldn't (for the nth time this tour) have to be the bad guy.

In other words, the guy I've kinda more than gotten used to having to be.

Now the bad guy's a role, if you're gonna front an indie rock band, you'd *best* get used to, have down, and fire yourself up for playing— and playing again and again and again. On a budget and aren't "big" enough for a tour manager? Put on your flak jacket, fearful/fearless leader of indie rock band: when *anything* goes wrong, anything at all, you're gonna get it, boy—especially if, as I mentioned earlier, it was the case with three of four Weird Sisters, anyone's even slightly "uptight," i.e. more often than you'd think or like. 'Cause the road just amplifies any aberrant characteristics one might have. The *admirable* qualities one has, the ones that get you through the day when you're at home and doing your thing—those just kinda stay status quo and stuff. But the pesky peccadilloes? The quirks and the anomalies? They get, out there in gigland, out there on the freeways and highways and byways and frontage roads and city streets and alleyways to the "load-in" for the next night's show? They get the neon highlighter, as it were. As our dear, sweet, volatile Irish/English former producer McLeary used to say, just as there's a laggard or dullard or rear-bringer-upper in every group, be it rock or a package tour group touring Ancient Pyramids-and-Tea Shops-on-a-Budget, so is there a fall guy, blame cushion, impugned-and-accused-burgher. And just as someone, sucking his thumb and disoriented in the indefatigable native sun, hearing the strains of the voices of the guided group get more and more faint—just as that sap gets snuffed up by a crocodile, say, so is there a*nother* someone who's in a fashion going to have to take the fall for having lead him, the dum dum, in maybe some sort of official capacity, toward the fatal swamp. That's *you*, team/band leader: the guy with the crunchy, outdated, inaccurate-to-begin-with city map in one hand and his headachy head in the palm of the other, going "But they *said* the goddam club's on Fifth *Street* not *Aven*ue, for Jesus's sake! What's the matter with this town?!" While your band mates, no matter how amiable or symp-or-empathetic do their level or not-so-level or even catawampus best *not* to wear a look like, "Oh, not *another* fuckup (this is the twelfth one today—but who's counting?)!" on their tired, contorted faces. Which only somehow makes things worse. *You*, sir or madam—you're the guy who's fully at fault when the crooked booker cheats you out of twenty-plus percent of your "guarantee" or there's only one queen-sized bed for the four of you at the Last Ditch No-Tell; or you have a shite show 'cause you didn't get a confounded goddam sound check. Not even a line check. (A "line check," for the blessed uninitiated among you, is when you just get the levels on the drums and the bass—the "back line"—and then get the fuck off stage.)

"The road" itself's in part to blame, you know. I mean, band gets along like bacon and eggs as long as they simply practice, get a demo tape together, do some local shows at the local clubs. They invite one another over for barbecues and "movie nights." Walk arm-in-arm down garden paths and riversides with train tracks that you can just spot in their photo shoot. Come over, have a beer or two, mate! Drink my last one—go 'head: I'm not thirsty! I'll pop down to the corner shop. And while I'm gone, fuck my girlfriend sideways, if you want; she's in the master bedroom and waiting for you in the bright white lingerie I bought her. Sure! That's fine. The shower's cool, too. Let me get you a clean towel, okay? What am I saying—"girlfriend"? We got engaged last week. No, no, no. It's no big deal. You go ahead and have her, bro. I think she really likes your bass-playing/your vocals on that one song/the way you move onstage/the way you always try to throw me off at the end of our new hit single, the one we haven't even "laid down" yet. Fine and dandy.

But if band in question eventually makes enough of a name for itself so that it gets to sally forth to some one-off a couple of Podunk or Tumbleweed or even Steel-and-Glass burgs over? Look *out*.

And get them a *tour*, a proper one, booked by a salivating, avaricious, actual booking agent, get them stuck for days on end in a godforsaken van as they travel 'cross the land of purple mountains' majesties and waving fields of grain? Look even more out, mate. Yikes. Look out for flying Lorna Doones and one guy or girl throwing a hissy fit, reaching the snapping point, crying or fuming in a black or red booth by him-or-herself at an all-night diner at four in the fucking morning while her or his band mates, stressed to the max and bereft of patience, wait in the idling Econoline or Astro after having taken turns pleading with the melt-downy one to *please* get in so they can carry on to Austin or Boston, Williamsburg or Raleigh-Durham, old El Paso, grand Seattle, Battle Creek or Kalamazoo.

Good-paying gigs get cancelled last minute (how in the hell did *that* fucking happen?—the goddam "guarantee" was *five bills* and a case of *bottled* imported beer!). The cool, new, effervescent posters and glossy, glance-engrossing stickers never make it from the record label to the club's viscous and superlatively yucky walls. The god-awful marquee reads *The Word Sitters* or *The Ward System* or *The Wyrd Sifters*. The hospitality backstage is sliced turkey that's so additived and processed and insidiously fat-injected that it's now become *pork* or something. There, in the mingy little room where you wait and tune up and munch something before the big gig, there's bread that's more cardboard than carbohydrate, and some fruit from the winter of 1983.

All your fault, fearless leader guy or girl.

The drummer's girlfriend and her supercilious "plus-one" plus her "plus-one's" equally haughty friend were forgetfully left off the guest list and the first "plus-one" is making a capernoited scene and a half, holding up the already totally parched and jigging-with-impatience-and-frustration queue at the kiosk?—that's all your lookout, managerless frontperson. *Your* doing. How come you didn't fix it? How come you didn't *plan* for this? How could you have neglected the VIP needs of the drummer's girlfriend and her fifteen dozen friends? Are you gainsaying them—is that what you're saying? Did you leave them off the guest list on purpose? How could you have done that, you dick? You fucker. You *didn't*? Yeah, sure. So you say. So says you. Like I/we believe you. To crown all, of course one of the plus-one's friends has another gig to go to later that night so now you're the dunce who's gonna make her late, you callous asshole. But there you go—only thinking of you, huh. Looking out for yourself 'cause you're the big *star*, the feature attraction, the lead ego, the guy who got us into this fine rock and roll mess in the first place—so get us out of it, okay? Fix it. I was/we were happy at our jobs at Big Five, the Shell on Grand, as a parcel post delivery operative, in the warehouse of The Magnificent Cat Food Manufacturing Company, Inc. No matter what you think, no matter what I told you, *I didn't* mind *having a job where I had to wear a paper hat, okay?* It wasn't all that bad. Certainly not as bad as what I'm having to go through now? *Hey!* Where's my *sand*wich? I said *gyro* not *Hero*, goddammit! How do you expect me to have a good gig when I haven't had a decent meal all day?! This won't do! I'm not *having it!* Don't you *get* it? This is a *sub* and I expressly requested something on a *pita*. How many times I gotta tell you?—*no tomatoes*. This thing has sesame seeds on it and yes they *could* be brushed off and stuff but what if I'm allergic to them and I don't even know it? What then? What if I have a seizure from them right before we go onstage? Or during the second encore. I already *had* two subs this week, don't you see, *and I'm sick of them, okay?* Sick! There's screaming yellow mustard on this and I thought I said Dijon, all right? Like, what the *fuck!* It's not like I'm in Spiñal Tap! It's not like I asked for cocaine and caviar! Though, actually…that's what I'm going to insist on for my next "project"—the one I'm in when I quit this fronted-by-you-only-think-of-you band. Just kidding. Kind of. Hey, man! Where's the stupid bathroom (and you've never in your life ever set foot inside this venue so how the fuck would *you* know) at? (*Oh God,* you think to yourself, *I not only associate but actually* hang out with *people who add "at" to questions of whereabouts! Kill me; kill me now.*)

How come there aren't any records of ours in this big chain record store we're wandering 'round in here, huh? In this paltry Mom and Pop. They got Wet Wet Wet and Winger. They got Warrant and the Wedding Present, Wire and W.A.S.P. and throwback Wishbone Ash, those blokes with the torn jeans and outrageous muttonchops, Cher hair, and bunhugging mondo bellbottoms. Where are *we?* Hmm? *They don't have our CD!* What's the good of me taking time off from my job at Kinko's or Big Beefo's Bigbeefburger to do this tour if our album's, like, nowhere record store-wise to be found? We have an industrial dolly's worth of them still in their boxes in the back of the van; so why can't those compact discs be in record stores where they belong in*stead of* in the back of the van? Who's going to go browsing through the back of our van? Only people who are breaking into it!

Breaking into it in order to sell our very CD to the very record shops that don't have the record in the first place! People at gas stations and truck stops and rest stops and pig-in-a-blanket dispensaries and 7-Elevens and Flying J's and Circle K's aren't gonna just come up to us and go: "Hey, are you nice-lookin' fellers selling that new album by that new alternative band we've heard so little about? How much is that CD, any old way? Lemme take two if y'all would be so gracious as to sign a couple of them durned things. Hell, give me three—the wife just got a CD player for the twins' two-seater baby buggy!"

What are you gonna do *now*, John? What are you gonna do about it, huh? How come—[if there *are* records there]—we don't have a white section card of our own but are just filed under the goddam W's? How come there's no dis*play*? Product placement? They didn't get the stickers? They didn't get the *flyers*! What *did* they get? The memo? Ha! The Post-it? They didn't even get that. They got some Post-its, but they're not our promotional Post-its; they're just regular old Post-its; they're just, like, *blank*. All queasy-crapulous yellow and shit. Great. Just great. I can just tell this gig's gonna go great. Really well. Really. What a way to start the day. We coulda slept till three instead of having to get up at, like, 2:47, man! I'm so tired anyway! Exhausted! I've never been this fucking tired! And we gotta play four *hours* from now! We gotta do a*nother gig*? Oh my God. I thought we were supposed to have a *lunch* buffet, a weenie roast, a Roman orgy organized for this event? And by the *way*—I lost my favorite pencil: have you seen it? Do you have it? Where'd you put it, John? I know you borrowed it last! It's silver—yeah, that's right, a silver pencil. Of course they make those! I got started using them in Art School. I do the daily crossword puzzle with them! Don't you remember? It's got a Mickey Mouse e*raser* on it and it's my lucky pencil, 'kay? My grandma gave me a box of them as a going-on-tour present and lost all but one by the second gig and I can't flipping *find* it and I'm fucking freaking the fuck *out* about it! I can't find my Walkman, my wallet, my glasses, my gloves! You need to take me back to the strip club from last night so I can look for my wristwatch [kidding: The Weird Sisters never did strip clubs—but most bands do, that's for certain. Told a lie: we went to one: Jenny insisted, as a dare. It was awful. Portland, I hate you. Portland, USA capital of strip clubs USA, you *suck*.]. I must've given it to Amber. Or Cindy. Or Barbarella. No: Trixie. The one with the… I'm losing my *mind* here, okay? Haven't you seen it lying 'round here somewhere, John? You were supposed to re*mind* me about something I asked you to remind me about—I distinctly remember telling you to re*mind* me of something, so how come you didn't? How should *I* know what it was—that's what I asked *you* to remember! Jesus… What?! We're going on *now?!* I thought you said "In fifteen minutes?" My friend who lives here, goes to school here, isn't here yet! He's bringing a couple of super-important friends of his, er, ours from *high* school, man. We can't go on yet! Tell the sound guy you can't find your tuner, the set list, your capo, guitar strap! Say our manager's not even here yet with the revised and updated guest list! They know we don't have one? You *told* them we don't have a manager?! How *could* you? *Do* something, John! Stall! I thought the sound man said fifteen as well. Plus he's an eejit. What a fucking ogre. Did you hear that guy? What an oaf. What a goddam amateur. This is *total* Amateur Hour. He hates us, anyway, that guy does. Did you see the face he made when I extra-politely asked for a touch more reverb on my kick drum? I just *know* he's gonna sabotage our set—I can sense it. I always know a hostile soundman when I see one. Where's the set list? Let me see it! We can't do *that* song right before *this* one! How *could* you! What were you thinking? They're the same tempo and key and the bridges are practically identical! Didn't you twig that?! Didn't you notice? *You* wrote the songs, Mr. I-wrote-the-songs-guy; Mr. I'm-gonna-get-all-the-songwriting-royalties—how come you didn't *notice?* Hoity-toity! God! Jesus! *Really!* Marry-come-up! I mean, come *on*…

Remember when in *The King of Good Intentions* I told you my one, terrifically novel, money-minting T-shirt idea (e.g. *Bands are Stupid*)? Well, the aforementioned thwarted jeremiad's why I came up with it, where it comes from.

The people in your band—they're all like that. A little bit at least, they are. But of course I am embellishing just a mite here for comic effect and because that's what I *do*: go over-the-top, go overboard, rachet things up a notch or two, blow it all out of proportion so that we both can have a little laugh. I can only imagine what out-of-control egos going at higher levels than the low level/first album just out level we were at were like. Very *Spiñal Tap*, I'm sure. That movie's not just whistling Dixie: there are *zillions* of Nigel Tufnels out there, in Technicolor verisimilitude, readying their teapot tempests, viewing their at once shrunken and little self-important lives through metaphorical shrink wrap. There's one "Nigel" at least who lives not two blocks from you. Hell: these days, when everyone and his second cousin plays guitar, he's probably only two doors down. You hear him "practicing" from time to time. You've heard him at the outdoor bar at your favorite local restaurant chain as he talks and talks and talks about what his imaginary phantom "band" is gonna do when they cut their first album and then become "huge" and start furnishing the walls of their respective dens with gold, then platinum, records. Ha! At least Jenny and Rob would more often than not *catch themselves* behaving like the above. The sordid "road" gets on everyone's nerves—*no one's* immune to the nettlesome/jarring/deleterious/disconsolate effect it has on you. Jenny and Rob were more than capable of having at least a half-laugh at themselves. And often a full. Rob especially. But *someone*, I'm not sayin' who, would *never* deviate from the inordinate crabbing, carping, quizzing "norm" I've labored to illustrate for ya in the previous pages.

You thought it was me for a sec there, huh. No, sorry. Raleigh all the way.

Isn't it funny how often we *trompe* ourselves, our most sanguine selves, when we meet people and immediately start gilding their personality-lilies as soon as we find out that they like a lotta the same junk we do? Especially when it comes to taste in things like bands and things—music stuff.

Imaginary case-in-point: there you are at a balmy-leafy springtime backyard brunchy get together, knowing nobody, practically, two or three people tops, none of them very engaging, and most of them crashing bores or thundering dunderheads and/or assorted party-dullards. You spend a lot of time watching the beautiful clouds jockeying above you and mooning about outside, then inside, from room to richy-rich room, from enormous kitchen to plantation porch and back again, till you give up and go back out to the vast grass lawn and finally vow to just get drunk as quickly as possible and leave it at that. You "meet cute" (like in the movies, maybe: at the champagne fountain or simultaneously reaching for a drink from the pineapple drinks tray) a nice-and-friendly-looking girl, say, who *must* know she looks quite good in her cute new saucy "do" and sheer flower-print Easter dress, vintage, fetching as anything. Perhaps even someone with actual manners has introduced the two of you. Thinking you'll "hit it off," get on fine, like a house afire, have *so* so much in common.

So the two of you are standing talking on the nice grass plot with the pristine, rhomboid badminton net right next to the scintillating purple pool, over near the exploded gladiolas and the frothing carnations, and you get to bantering or minorly flirting or whatnot and something comes up that unveils *her intense interest in and love for Jane Austen.* Miss Jane Austen! Well, I'll be dashed or damned: I *love* Jane Austen, you tell her. Fancy that. What a terrific coincidence! Turns out she digs Dorothy Parker, Sylvia Plath, Iris Murdoch, Anne Sexton, George Eliot, Simone de Beauvoir, Margaret Drabble, A. S. Byatt *and* that chick who wrote *Jane Eyre* whose name escapes both you and now-laughing her. She, *too*, has been *meaning* to get around to Susan Sontag's *much*-neglected unreadable fiction! *And* has *heard* of Nadine Gordimer and been meaning to read *her* as *well.* Get out of here—you know Jean *Rhys?!* You've *read* her? Probably my all-time favorite—next to Joan...Didion! Of course! Me, too! (Jinx-on-a-Coke!) You and I are the only people at this *party*—and maybe the West Coast of The United States of *America*—who've even *heard* of Jean Rhys, by the by! Let me freshen your mimosa, get us both a glass of "fizz." Want another canapé? Yes, the blueberry crepes are simply heaven, quite divine. Though not so melt-in-your-mouth as the the melt-in-your-mouth-ish blintzes are! You think so, too? How odd. How very. Do you happy—oops, Freudian slip!—do you *happen* to know what time it is? No? Well I do. It's time we were better acquainted! Hahaha! I just made that up. I had better scatter lest I let myself run away with myself here. I'm Darcy, by the way. You must be "Lizzy" Barrett. Bennet, rather. That's what I meant. I was thinking of Syd Barrett. Completely different fictional character, isn't he?! Hah-hah-hah! You're kind of amazing. You know who I'm talking about? If you tell me you know the early Floyd as well I'm going to scream. You do. *The Piper at the Gates of Dawn*? Wow. And the jingly singles? Really? Wow. "Candy *and* a Current Bun"? Hahaha. "Arnold Layne," of course. Of course! Marvelous. Do you know who you look like, by the way? No? (I hate when people say that, mind you, I think it's so cliché.) Ready? *No one I have ever met be*fore! Hahaha! I've always wanted to say that to someone—and I picked you. Thank you. It's not bad, isn't it? I've had that line for two years now and never found anyone, um, worth trying it on...I'm serious! I wouldn't kid you about such a thing! Come on, now. You should try flirting with me a little. I think you'd like it! Oh, you thought that that's what we're doing here? Ha! I haven't even got a *shirt* on yet, my dear. Anyway. *Any*way. You've got to be kidding me—Jean *Rhys*? Jean *Rhys*? Really?! *The Wide Sargasso Sea*? Oh, you're correct—no "The." That's right. And that's not even her best stuff, is it? I like the early one that's set in Paris. That one's brilliant. Uh-huh. The one where the narrator's kinda crazy. Real sad and everything. Kind of a downer. In a sort-of-sexy way, though? Kinda just hanging out and all down and out and stuff in all the seediest bars in The Left Bank? *Defi*nitely depressing...but in a good way! You're so right. I'm *really* glad I met you! Uh-huh. This is too funny! Whoda thunk?! Just amazing. Just unreal. I'm sorry? Did I overhear you tell someone that someone made you have a tape of The Beach Boys' *Smile* sessions? Not just *Smiley Smile* but the actual...? You have *got* to be kidding. You're having me on now. No? Hey, listen:

marry me, okay?! Wanna get *married?* You think I'm kidding, eh? Do
you think the hosts would let me used their phone to call my mom?
She said to call when or if I ever found someone who… Listen: What
are you doing later? A rush-job blood test is well in order, I think—do
you still have to get one of those here in nineteen eighty something?
If you'll marry me, that is. They say you should never turn the idea
of marriage into a joke, though—when talking to a woman, that is.
You're very attractive. Did I tell you that enough hundred times? Well,
just as long as you're a *Beatles* girl and not a Stones. Hahaha! *Both?* Me,
too. Though obviously not a…obviously. Though if you had to, you'd
go with…*whew*! Exactly. The Beatles are just…the *nonpareil*, right?
Right. You think so? You think the Stones made better records? As
opposed to singles? Well we are just gonna have to agree to disagree
on that one, miss! It is "miss," right? You don't already have a husband
or anything like that? One who's six-ten and about to come over and
get me in a headlock or punch me in the face? Actually, you're right!
The Stones did make better albums! Kind of. I don't know, though—
hard to beat *Revolver, Rubber Soul,* and *The White Album,* though.
Hmmm. Maybe get this question settled over dinner sometime, if you
wanted to or something. Do you like steak, by any chance? Lobster?
Sushi? Italian? Romanian cuisine? Specialties from the Continental
peasantry? Sound good? Basque food? Sauerkraut? Sauerkraut's
disgusting, huh. Dinner next week, then? Okay? Sure. Great. I mean,
if you…yeah. Exactly. You know: maybe. Whenever. Precisely. Tell me
something: Are those little spots of *topaz* in your pretty emerald eyes?
I thought so. I knew it. You'd call those "almond," right? They really are
really pretty, you know. Oh, don't mention it. Everyone should notice.
Don't *men*tion it. How terribly pretty you are—really. Yes, really. I don't
really say that. To people. And what a lovely name you have. Quite.
Really. You don't think so? It's common-ish, you think? Oh, I don't
think Anne [Kathy, Cindy, Elizabeth, Jane, Mary] a "common" name at
all, at all. You're welcome. This whole time we've been here I daresay so
wonderfully, amicably chatting I've neglected to notice that you are, I
daresay, a *beautiful* girl. It's all been so interesting and diverting I haven't

had time to see and now say that you're quite gorgeous, actually. No, I mean it. Really. Of all the pretty ladies at this perfect party—and there are a quantity, aren't there, you just can't help but notice?—you have got to be just the most, by far...I mean: you're beautiful. How remiss of me. Oh, stop it yourself. Just stop. Thank you, you are oh-so-kind. I hope you'll forgive me 'cause *I* sure won't. Hahaha! Four Hail Mary's, three Our Father's, huh. You're *Cath*olic, too! Jesus *Christ!* Oops, I'm sorry. I always meet the *greatest* Catholic girls. I mean, not *too* many, you know. Just sometimes. Recovering? That's funny. This is too much. Ridiculous, I *know.* I can't believe I met you. At least you gotta make me a tape of that tape. *Then* maybe marry me.

Her head tilts back, she laughs a little too stentoriously and puts on a show of her just slightly/cutely fucked up teeth—the muckle-mouthed smile that makes her even *prettier*, especially as you now know you've met, and conversed animatedly with, for more than twenty minutes now, no less, *your soulmate*, the *one*, the girl you've waited all your lonesome life for.

I can't believe this, you think to yourself; *what are the odds?* Whodathunkit? Did you check your horoscope today? *I* did, and it didn't say that *this* native'd be meeting wonderful you! It must be fate, kismet at *least*. Celestial interference sighted, sir! Set the controls for the heart of the sun. Set the controls for the heart of the sun sign! Haha! Brilliant. Couldn't help it, but... Plan the wedding, shall we?—complete with Maldives honeymoon. I'll ring my Bulgarian pastry chef first thing in the morning. Get him designing straight away a five-tiered *gateau du marriage* that'll be the eighth wonder of the world. He's simply remarkable, Klinic is... How many kids you want? Two? Me, *too!* Well, I don't want any actually but now that you mention it, two'll do, be just fine. Let's make one this afternoon, in fact. Ha! Kidding. Don't go thinking I'd sleep with you on the first date or anything. Two, then. A curtseying sugarplum of a pretty little so-smart girl and a nice quiet so-cute boy who'd not be too terribly unkind to small and cuddly animals—just the occasional magnifying glass to the anthill or cat put up in a homemade balloon-and-sand-bucket aero-thing for him to shoot down with his pellet gun as it floats over the sparkling lake our summer home looks over? The girl— Jane? *Jean?*—in a fuchsia pinafore and plinking Chopin on a muted pianoforte as the lovely little lad sports with his bright red toy train set or reads his *Hardy Boys* or learns High German in a lacy, hypnagogic reading nook, then bounds outside to cut the heads off the golden gladiolas and birds-of-paradise with his practice epee or foil or sabre. Hahaha! *Naughty* boy. But not too naughty. Just naughty enough. Oh my God, I just remembered: *Charlotte* Brontë! She's the one who wrote *Jane Eyre!* Look at the crystallized geraniums in the flowerbox outside our house! And there you are, at the kitchen window, directing "the help" at our first Thanksgiving, smiling as I bring in firewood by the helpful armful, crunching by in my good old Wellingtons across our shimmering lawn, a lawn of fine, new virgin snow and all our newly-realized dreams-beyond-our-wildest-dreams. And no, that's not our primary domicile, my love—just a ski cottage we keep. (Away from all your wonderful friends at the club and the mellow-humming sun of Central California I would never keep you long, my pet.) Oh, look! There's Nanny with the kiddies. Twigging what you and I want to do in the kitchen in order to "christen" it, Nanny calls Jane (or Jean) and John Jr. outside to build a eudaemonic snowman waving *Hey.* Waving *Just you fuckin' try and be as happy as we are, neighbors we don't know and never see!* With the bairns bundled and gloved and shoved outside and weebling around in the patchy slush and mud as the day heats up, we make love at the sink, you hoisted up by the thighs, then sitting splayed and moaning as I get myself in you hotly, quickly like you like (oh the eyes-at-half-mast look of love-lust in your so-fine eyes!); there's me standing thrusting and you come so hard and good it makes the peppermint hot chocolate we make for Nanny and the family when they come excitedly panting-smiling-chirruping in taste just so delicious.

So you get her number, this ultra-pretty, literary party girl you're planning on bedding and wedding, and call her the next day (unlike most guys, who wait a conventional unimaginative three). You make a dinner date. Great. And there, at the nice seaside restaurant you splash out for, with its canting candles and obsequious sommelier, she goes needling all your hope-balloons as she either a) talks too much; b) talks hardly at all; c) talks about herself incessantly; d) talks about her incredible ex, a guy called Grady, Yale, (and he went to *Harvard*—how ironic!) or Remington, and how she'll never get over him as he was a dreamboat finance guy, six-five, plus a Shaolin master of Tantric fucking. Or else she: e) stands you up; f) makes some crude allusion to the fact that it's apparent already that you are—ouch!—gonna be *such* good *friends*; g) whispers that Grady, Yale, or Remington was *Jewish, you know, a Jew*, as though that's the only type or race or religion of guy she's, like, ever been or, like, you know, ever will be, like, attracted to; h) brings one of her friends, blithely figuring aloud that of *course*—you're such a nice *guy*—*you* won't mind if she/he joins before they have to rush off to that hot young author's launch party downtown; i) farms her perfect nose clandestinely when she thinks you're not looking; j) orders the most expensive entrée on offer, and two starters, then plays fork-hockey with it, her food, and says she doesn't want dessert as she has to turn in early on account of she's going shopping *mañana* with this new guy she just met and was certain she already told you about; k) spends the whole time talking French to the waiter, a Spaniard; l) turns up forty-four minutes late—but who's counting?—in sweatpants and a T-shirt and looks like someone's just fucked her arseways, fucked her silly, pulled out half her hair; m) observes that, physically, you remind her of her brother/her father/her snotty, corpulent second cousin she thought she always hated—until she made out with him one night her "blackout year" in college ("But not that I'd hate *you* or anything," she helpfully adds); n) intimates that she's friends with a coven of B-list actors and actresses who are all "incredible" and "amazing" and "just, like, incredible, you know?"; o) quasi-creative combinations of all of the above.

An *almost*-alphabet of expectation-dashing *faux pas* and girl-gaffs. I don't even wanna hint at what I was gonna write for "p"! Let's just end by saying she's a high-heeled walking datemare in low-cut, tight teal sweater and even-tighter, black and boner-bringing pencil skirt; or maybe she wore a tantalizing romper, unbuttoned *just* enough to make you mental, and tastefully diaphanous nylons that make her great "gams" a sort of waking, walking hallucination. The girl you were supposed to spend the rest of your life with, right?! Your dream-thing ideal.

Right.

And all because she liked some of the same heavy-duty classic nineteenth century (she also said she was crazy 'bout good old George's *Middlemarch*, *Mill on the Floss*, and even goddamn *Scenes From Clerical Life*) chick lit you did and frosted *that* metaphorical offer of emotional cream cake with a fifteenth-generation tape of Brian Goddam Wilson's "Teenage Symphony to God" or whatnot.

Yow. That bitch! Who's even *heard* of *Scenes From Clerical Life*! What a horrid, duplicitous girl. How dare she so definitively dash your prospects for walking hand-in-hand off into the sunset or the university library together! Whatta downer.

Now, meeting Raleigh and playing with him drumming the first few times was *just like that*—only the platonic, bandly version of it. Just that sort of motif where you think you're gonna love this person, be their greatest friend till the end of the world and beyond.

He got us all jazzed, Raleigh did—at first. Rob and Jenny and I. He'd answered an advert in *The Pennysaver* we took out that read:

Drummer wanted for four-piece guitar band. Smart and punctual. Much more post-punk than punk. Occasionally showers. Influences: The Cure, The Church, Sonic Youth, The Jesus and Mary Chain, New Order, and esp. The Beatles. N. Hollywood lockout studio. First LP already recorded and out soon on up-and-coming indie label. Must be able to tour. No druggies, no Walters. Call John or Jenny— (213) 448-6263

(We put the "No Walters" bit in there as a funny inside joke and also because Walter, our as-I-already-mentioned last drummer, and his "wife" Nastasha, Jenny's former landlords and roommates, had really fucked Jenny over on her security deposit—but I'll tell you about that later, maybe.)

Over the telephone, Jenny interviewed, then vetted Ral for at least a meet-and-give-tape session. Their conversation, she recounted, went something like this:

"Hi. I'm answering the ad for the drummer?"

"Oh, hello. How are you?"

"Fine, thank you."

"Let's see. John isn't here right now but you can talk to me, I guess. What's your name?"

"Raleigh."

"Hi, Raleigh. So, um, I've never really 'interviewed' a musician over the phone before but let's see. Um, what made you call on the ad, then? I suppose I could ask you that."

"Well, I really like all of the influences you listed. And I just moved here from Utah and I've been looking for a band but it seems they are all Guns N' Roses clones or they don't, you know, like, have a bass player or a singer. I want to play in something cool that has something going and it says here you guys have a record deal...?"

"Yeah: we got signed to a small label. Medium label, actually. I don't know. I don't get that involved in all that label stuff. I don't really pay attention to all that industry stuff, actually. 'Signed or dropped? Signed or dropped?' You know? I hate that stuff."

"I know what you mean."

"Better Records—that's what it's called; they're down in Orange County."

"Really? Orange County?"

"I know. Do you know it?"

"My dad lives there now. Originally I'm from Utah. My family is, that is. I just moved here not too long ago."

"Where do you live?"

"Hollywood."

"Oh. Okay. We're near Hancock Park. So, um, *Raleigh*, right? What do you listen to? I've overheard John ask a few people that over the phone, I guess, plus how long they've been playing and what they're looking for and all that stuff—if they have a tape or something? Do you have a tape? But I should really just take down your number and let you talk to *him*. 'Cause, like I said, I…anyway, is there a number where you can be reached so John can call you back, please?"

And on it went for a little while longer, she said, and I'm not going to burn you out with the full-secondhand recount of the initial conversation or anything but it went well enough, Jen said (and Raleigh seemed "normal" enough), for her to give him our address of so that we could meet him so that we could play him some of our stuff and see if he was cool in person. And of course he liked all the bands we did and knew them too—he wasn't shamming. Some guys do, you know. Ring you up and make like they're president of the fan club of some band they've really hardly heard of—just to get you to audition them. And especially when you tell people you have a recording contract—even a little one on a tiny imprint.

Anyway, it seemed like old Ral wanted to be in a band for "the right reasons"—and of course that was cool. Why *do* people wanna be in bands, anyway? Especially if you believe, as I do and as I have irrefragably shown you via my aforementioned brilliant band-related T-shirt idea, that "Bands are Stupid"? Riddle me *that*.

Let's consider: Most guys wanna be in bands to get laid, get paid, be made famous, make millions, not work, make their friends envious, impress their peers, get back at their exes, and get their exes back. Get back at their fathers, their mothers, their teachers, their pastors. They wanna tour (and sleep till three in the afternoon in glamorous rundown rock and roll hotels) in exotic, sexy cities like Berlin and London; Madrid; El Paso. (Dude! El Paso's *awesome*— if you know where to go. And where *not to*…like [comic pause] El Paso…hahaha! Keep going on to Marfa then Austin, man—believe me: don't stop; don't even fill up the *tank* there; drive!). Increasingly, they, these muso types, these guys in all *kinds* of rock bands, wanna throw away their paltry or puffy *per diems* at tawdry cheap-o strip clubs and in Tahoe and Vegas, Reno and Laughlin; and at sundry rip-off Indian casinos strewn up and down California. They want free drinks and free strings and free advance CDs and backstage passes to Lollapalooza and complimentary drumsticks by the dozen and dumb (or really smart, really wily) girls with big hair in tight leather pants to sit on their taut denim (or leather—if they are metal, if they are glam) laps at The Rainbow on Sunset who lispingly ask them "*What* band did you say you were in again? You're, like, *hic*, the twelfth guy tonight I've, *hic*, like, met who's, like, a, like, *hic*, musician."

Some of them wanna be artists, play music, get better, learn to *really* write, create an immortal medley worthy of early McCartney, or Mercury, and May, get *off* on *Rock with a capital R*. Some want to "just put out a 7-inch on colored or swirly or white vinyl or make a cassette-only EP" and "make a statement" and get the fuck off stage, as it were, retire, quit the building, make like fat Elvis, become a glamorous emeritus. Some want to make records but never play live, cultivate an image that never applies, curry favor with a fandom that never materializes, or snub the world and be mysterious, be affected, wax reclusive, court mystique. Some, scared shitless about the real commitment that is big time studio audio recording, want to rehearse and rehearse their stuff to death; and then make neurotic excuses not to lay down tracks "just yet." They don't care (or at least they say they don't) that the enormous roar that screams from their practice space will not be heard much farther beyond those four walls, will dissipate and float out over the air of an oblivious-to-them city, county, or rural route, no less. Some want a "music career"—like what Sting, what Clapton, what Flea, what Lemmy and other guys who have one-name handles get to have. Bono, Edge, Stipe, Neil, Malkmus.

Malkmus?

On they plod, the careerists, in quest of a "house" with "just one once-in-a-lifetime girl" who possibly looks like the "back in the day" version of Heather Locklear, or Heather Graham *any*time, or one of the Heathers in *Heathers*. They're aiming for "a coupla kids" and a "nice backyard" and a "piece of the publishing" in bands they didn't write one word or melody for.

Those are called "mercenaries." See also: most drummers. See also: most singers.

Some want *three instant best friends* to share their dreams with, share their sorrows, share out the two-topping backstage pizza they got instead of a paltry "guarantee" or fee. Three best friends, musical musketeers, one-for-all-and-all-for-one against the big, bad music world. Three *confreres* forever, whom they'll eventually, murderously resent—resent because, well, if "familiarity breeds contempt" in normal human circumstance, it breeds mega-loathing in most band-oriented sitches, which, after a time, come down to commerce, sadly, not communal community. The old joke, the old saw goes that being in a band's like having "three girlfriends at the same time." Sound good? Sound grand? I've done that in *real life*, okay?—the-three-chicks-in-rotation thing. And it's a full-time waking, sodding *nightmare*. My best childhood friend and college abroad and at-home roomie, BJ, had this mathematics prof that he TA'd for senior year? *He,* the prof guy, he didn't think so, think the three chicks thing was a hassle session of grand proportions. Oh no. The guy was Bollywood-heart-throb handsome with an IQ they couldn't measure, not even at NASA—plus a laugh riot. And he always, unfailingly—with his very Oxford don/pukka wallah/plummy voice—admonished old BJ: "Ting is, you must needs alvays have a rotation of *tree* women going *at all times*: at all times, mind you. Unfailingly. Dat vay, someting goes incontrowertibly disastrously wrong with *wun*, der are two *udders* in the running. Two to choose from till you find de wariable, necessary turd, you see. At *all* times, mind you. Not two, not four—four izz incontrowertibly too many to be a-juggling. One drops out, one is summarily sub*tracted*, the next romantic integer *must* be added to the pleasure-equation rotation, don't you know; and quick as you can snap your fingers *thus*, you must find one replacement, one. *Two* women equals a—how-do-you-say—powder keg on tenterhooks? One or the udder? Haha! Okay. Right. Bloody vell right, my dear young friend. Quite. Anyway, wid two on your hans you have a potential squabble or troublesome, serious *show*down, as it were, that vill *not* be enjoywable to you in the *slightest* degree, old boy. *Tree* is onliest number to guarantee satisfaction in the disunified field of sexual endeavorings. Believe me, dear boy. *Tree* is onliest the way to go. Latterly, I have been supplementing my teory by tinking: dey don't need to be wery extra-ordinarily *bootiful* or anyting—but it iz, as everyone knows, much easier to obtain a *bootiful* girl dan 'tis to 'see' or especially 'bed' one who is only fractionally attractive. Easier than the calculus, certainly! But that is for another lecture, another time, perhaps, old bean!"

"But what if all three women find out about each other somehow?" I remember BJ reportedly asking Dr. Kamadeva-Rati with baited breath, twinkling eyes. "Won't that be worse, Dr. K?" "*Au contraire*, dear boy," the good doc apparently retorted (and BJ's hilarious imitation of his favorite prof was made all the more savory by virtue of the fact that we'd just seen Peter Sellers in Blake Edwards' *The Party;* it was playing at our college's ancient classic movie house). "Negative," the professor continued: "Da tree find out about each udder, dey won't know *where* to turn, accusing *in* turn one den de udder one till de parallel paradigm that materializes is tree monkeys fighting in a bag—'all against all,' like the Hobbesian *Weltanschauung*, don't you know. Do you know dis vunderful philosopher of de sixteenth century? Yes? Good. Hobbes? You've heard of him? Most excellent philosophy, mind you. For *Vestern* philosophy, dat is. The universe contained in a burlap sack. Hahaha! Anyway, as da tree have it out, as it were, one can slip quietly away and begin recruiting tree *new* ones for one's new carnal rotation. But *two*—and the putative two find out about each udder? You will be 'monkey-in-the-middle,' as dey say. A particularly op*prob*rious position, my dear young fellow. Most unfortunate. Hard as Hilbert spaces or, for the untutored, my friend [i.e. not *you!*], differential equations. Mark my words, old chap. Take my tip: *tree!* Tree is *thee* prime number indeed as far as de womens go!"

Ha!

Okay, then: musicians. Where were we? Some want to "meet their heroes" while "killing their idols." Some want to do interviews (the only time, it seems, anyone actually *listens to*, takes seriously, what they have to say) so that they can say outrageously hubristic things or brag about how humble they are, how "just glad to be here," how "grateful to each and every one of you who bought our *new limited edition specially priced for a limited time only double live album on marble-colored, numbered vinyl.*" Some want a new Fender Jazzmaster from 1966 in Sea Foam Green or Olympic White; or they go coveting the Cherry Red Gibson ES 335 that Donny Osmond gave to one of the guys in his backup band. Most know that electric buzz you get when you work a new song through to the very end for the first time and you're fairly lifted off the ground, metaphorically speaking, flying 'round, levitating, in orbital, ecstatic, incomparable, unmitigated joy. Sir Keith Richards, Esquire can tell you all about it, indeed he can. Recently he opined that that's what he does it for—it's not for the money, the chicks, or for you: it's meself I do it for, he said, I rock for me, mate. I'm Croesus-rich and I don't care what you say! Money doesn't matter a whit! I rock for me, for the feeling I get when the jam gels or parts of a riff come together and, out of nowhere—bang!— you've got a *song!*

Or something like that.

Some guys are just looking to play in a cover band and night after night mechanically churn out "Jumpin' Jack Flash" and "Century City." There they are, up on some dump's or cave's malodorous stage, striving, straining to get the harmonies right as they sing "all I really wanna do is, baby, be friends with you." And goddammit, they do, they do wanna be friends with you—especially if you can get them an audition for the big time, 'cause Sting needs a new percussionist/music director, Mandy Moore is touring Europe this summer festival season and looking for a decent drummer who can double on percussion and matching backing vocals, and Stevie Nicks's longtime keyboard player just took a job producing, can't go to South America, Japan, New Zealand, can only do the North American "leg" of the worldwide tour.

Some—ye *gads!*—live to rock in *"tribute" bands*; they used to be a *George* but now they are a *John*. Took them ten years and three Beatle-bands to realize it but there it is. Those guys frighten the hell out of me. Those *gals* do, too! Seen Cheap *Chick? Lez* Zeppelin? Judas *Priestess?* The Beat*elles?* These I have not made up. Who could?

Guys and gals in tribute bands, they've often got the *exact same rig* as the heroes they impersonate—they've got the exact same *wig*, too. And the most curious egos, like something atavistically megalomaniacal that's rubbed off on them from pretending to be prancing Prince or jumping Jim Morrison or that Janis-someone. Elvis started rock and roll (if you don't count the countless black guys who *actually* started it); and he started *rock and roll impersonators* as well. They'll be around as long as the poor who are always with us will; The Clash, God bless their demotic lyrics, bone-white socks, and sleeveless Levi's jackets, went and gloated way too early: phony Beatlemania will *never* bite the dust. The proverbial poor, maladroit tribute groups like More Than A Feeling, Stairway to Heaven, Born on the Bayou, Are You Experienced? will *never bite the dust: no dust of any kind.* (Disclaimer: if there are any cover or "tribute" bands out there who are *actually* called any of the aforementioned names, I don't mean *you*; I don't have you and your sad little "fan base" in mind here, okay?; so don't go calling your second cousin twice removed who's in law school.) And speaking of cover or "tribute" bands, the creepiest of the creepy creeps that play in dodgy-creepy "tribute" bands are *guys who were in the actual band the tribute band is paying tribute to! Ils existant!* (See also, e.g.: Creedence, The Beach Boys, Love, et alia). Check the Sunday Entertainment/What's On section of your hometown award-winning daily rag and see for yourself: one's got to be playing your town this week sometime; one's got to be.

Here comes one. Here one comes, or better yet struts in his ostentatiously neo-maccaroni way, down Sunset, say, right outside the landmark, shack-like, world-famous Sunset Grill right next to the flagship Guitar Center in Hollywood 90028—a recognizable guy in a notorious "tribute" band. Let's have a look at him. Nay—

go to, go to: let's do more than *that*. Let's give him a regular virtual imaginary audition, the old once-over, shall we? It's what he's up for, looking at, keening for anyway. See his ginger-red rug, the startled-porcupine motif coif, his lank frame, that big-collared seventies long sleeve shirtsleeves rolled up "just so," the shirt itself unbuttoned to his growling navel, showcasing the maculate, depilated chest? Look at those eldritch and quite frighteningly too-blue eyes, that mutant schnozz like he's balancing a log or a cucumber or an armless Ken or Barbie on the end of his unmistakably remarkable face, the not-good skin on his not-clean, super-sallow mug and a sly, wry nanosecond smile as he passes by in super-skinny, wide bell-bottom blue jeans and platform shoes in pale blue suede blue. Who *is* he? Whom does he *remind* you of, dash it all? Can't you guess? Who does this guy think he is? Well, *that's* an ambiguous question! Hint: Do you think he's sexy? Come on, sugar, do let him know. Well, there's a clue. Dead cert: it's Ron "Stew" Stewart, Rod's arguably most brill, best, and most renowned *doppelganger*, man. You do an eidetic double take watching his eidetic walk. Was that just…? No? My word: 'e looks just like 'im! 'ave you not seen 'is act, mate? He's King of the Clones, bro. And furthermore *Ron Stewart's his real name*. No joke. Beat *that* with a silver-tipped walking stick and riding crop from the official Ascot shop. He's got Rod down to a "t," Ron has all right; his vocal range tops six full octaves; he does a "You Wear it Well" that's even better than the note-perfect "Maggie May" he trots out at the end of the first set, which of course starts with the big bang of "Hot Legs" and Ron skip-shuffling through the woo-hooing audience to thread his way up the thinly-painted black wood stage steps in time for him to ask, as the band does the first go-'round and preps for the dramatic vocal: "*Who's that knocking on my etcetera.*"

The fanciful imaginary boulevardier in "Every Picture Tells a Story" must've swaggered just like that down the Champs Elysees in his imaginary salad days! Look! Rod "Ron" Stewart musta spenta modest fortune at the Rock & Roll Ralphs (Sunset and Poinsettia) deli counter or the produce section, stuffing his Y-fronts with costly salami, rutabagas, cobs of summer corn. I mean, guy's practically got an entire cornucopia down his skintight trousers.

Fuckin' 'ell!

If you'd seen the geezer strutting past while you were munching a melty double-chompburger on the patio at The Sunset Grill you might just spit a pickle, as it were, snorkel your paper-coned Coke out your own goddam weezer. Just you *try* not to gawk in awe or to laugh grandly at the easy target of ridiculous ridicule that he may be. Ah, but Ron's having the last one (laugh, that is) 'cause he makes more in a month than you and your scrappy/scruffy "original" indie pop outfit will pull in in "mechanicals" after your second, notoriously difficult, "follow-up to the debut LP," LP, even. Ha! Word is that Ron exclusively drinks Wells Bombardier English Premium Ale or Makers Mark or cheap plonk—Rod's own poisons of choice. Don't try and buy him anything but, mate: you'll be wearing it well yourself. Word is Ron irefully spit-sprayed a former Bunny's screaming décolletage with Jack Daniels when she, in fetching a mercenary drink for him, well, *she* thought it wouldn't matter that the barman at The Mansion poured the wrong thing. And paid for it and dearly. He couldn't "quote ya no Dickens, Shelley or et alia" but he sure can work a mic stand like it's one of them there tap dancer's sticks. He's probably bobbing off to Guitar Center to sort out a new one—he goes through mic stands like pusillanimous WWI "Giovannis" or "Giorgios" from Firenze or Bologna reputedly did with factory-new carbines. Oh how he crushes the fuckers, contorting them (and himself) in miming Rod's on-stage fits and plethoric poses and faltering fare-thee-wells.

You see, the whole "tribute" band experience is just one big laugh parade, one honking *charade* of a mirthless joke. If you've ever seen some copycat band try and *be* Pink Floyd or Led Zeppelin—down to using the same vintage amps and guitars onstage—you'll know exactly what I'm saying here. The whole thing's just this kind of sham of pretense and sorry parasitic false nostalgia: there's the band up there, faking being *a band that doesn't exist anymore, or if they exist still, they probably shouldn't*; and there's the audience out there pretending to enjoy themselves like they're really seeing one of their favorite acts, live and in-the-flesh.

And maybe the guys in the homage thing have the songs and the riffs pretty much down (to varying degrees). Sure. All right. Okay. But there's unfailingly something so *off* about them. Like the the drummer doesn't look anything even re*motely* like "Bonzo," not even close, or the guitarist is four feet too short to be a believable simulacrum of David Gilmour. And the crowd's just so forcing it, make-believing down the lane. And the hypberbolic whoops and the obsequious whistles and the obligatory wows and woo-hoos are all so hollow and sad and painfully quixotic—like two going-bald men pumping each other up to get hair transplants or the latest miracle follicle-renewal unguent treatment.

Your French intellectuals and meta-theorists like Derrida and Foucault and Baudrillard and Houellebecq and Louis Lebeau have absolute *field days* with characteristically American junk like imbecile tribute bands. Tribute acts are like *Disneyland*: this ultra-phoney thing that's like a monument to *some place that never really ever existed.* You can just overhear them, those grousing Gallic critics, what they'd say if you saw them at a gig by, *par example*, some outfit called The Brown Sugar or The Strawberry Fields or Down on the Corner. There they are at The Roxy or The Whisky as, let's imagine, Wish You Were Here or Misty Mountain Hop are up there and posturing, boogieing away, waving their silk scarves or whipping their shaggy locks or wooly dicks around at the mob crowding the packed club's dance floor: "Regards zis unmeetigated *ee*diot wiz zee microfone, Jean-Michel! And zat ree*deek*ulous human homunculus hologram of Jimmy Page! *Quelle blague, non?!* Zees Americains fools—how you say?—sinking zay are real rock starz zemselves! What a travesti! *Sacré bleu!* Zis is not juste a metaphore for zeez Americains, non? Zis is how zay really are! Zis is very twue."

Some rockers, even dumber than the dumbest ones, dumbly get into the stupidest of all things: *hard drugs.* Because the guy they idolized as they mimed to his stuff in their bedroom mirrors did, perhaps. Because it was a sullen, rainy Tuesday in Boise or Baton

Rouge or Visalia where they come from and someone dared them or warned them not to, said don't do it, you'll regret it, one hit and you're hooked, dumbfuck—a goner, forever. Because they thought that once they became a fucking junkie Edie Sedgewick and Nico-alikes would come running at them with mattresses on their backs, handing them their sopping panties before the first round of flirting's even half done with. Many's the horror story of rock *qua* heroin chic and tales of how the wasted protagonist wakes up with the needle's damage done still in his golden arm, or with a Hollywood harlot next to him who's turned all shades of purple-blue. Not one drug story ever ended well, not even with a factitious lesson learned (horrid phrase), not even the aforementioned Keith's notorious endless saga, if you ask me. Hurrah—Keef's unkillable! A verifiable survivor! Big *wow*. He looks like he should've been dead *thirty years ago*. At least by the time the egregious *Black and Blue* plopped out. Hard drugs and rock and roll drug-martyrdom are the most monumentally gormless clichés *ever*.

If you ask me.

Which—you didn't. I know that.

But still—who wants to hear another cliché, rock or otherwise?

Me neither.

Want more? Some band guys work a "day job" at Guitar Center (where the "Rock Look"—vest, piercings, long shagged hair à la anyone in mid-period Pink Floyd, facial hair, jeans and boots and tight black tee—actually quote-unquote helps, inspires confidence in the rube who's thinking of buying a beginner Strat or budget axe that knocks off Slash's trademark, low-strung, goddam Gibson Les Paul); some install fine art or work as extras in the movies or as production assistants, getting barked at by second assistant associate directors, ragged on by the grips and best boys. Some tie their hair back and "man" the register at your local Rite Aid or SaveOn. One songwriter-guy Rob was friends with was a Corporate Hortocultural Hydrationist (he trimmed and watered indoor ferns for downtown firms). Though we had a good long laugh about that, the guy had the last one in that he made sixteen-an-hour doing it, under the table: there's nothing funny about wages like *that*, for work like that.

Like Jenny does, some work straight jobs. Really straight straight jobs. They're accountants or stockbrokers, mechanics, telemarketers, assistants to tooth-pullers, gumshoes, or ambulance-chasers. They work in banks or at anonymous offices; they work as "Temps" (*I* did, *I* do); they're fry cooks or waiters or book clerks or messengers; caterers. They deliver shit: flowers, memos, packages, medical supplies; bags of groceries, bags of weed, bagged bags, bags full stop.

One keyboard-guy we met on tour told us he was working as a UPS scab during a strike and he delivered a "test pressing" of his band's first 7-inch to his own address! One drummer I know (and love) serves writs to startled scofflaws and assorted scammers. He's been doing it so long, ringing ominous doorbells, being the bearer of bad news in lengthy legal document form, that he has even "served" a guy he was once in a band with, a guy from his high school. "Billy!" he goes. "What's *up*? How are you, anyway? How've you *been*, man? Oh no thanks—I can't come in for a beer, or come in at all, actually, but thank you anyway. I'm working, to tell you the truth. What am I doing here? Well, actually, I have something for you…no, it's not our old promo picture. Ha! Good one. Nor lost royalties neither, I'm afraid. No, I'm afraid she wants a divorce, Bill. Here you go. I have some papers for you and something for you to sign. You've been served. Sorry about that. My apologies. Best of luck to you, man. Hey—you playing any music these days? No? Oh, well. Take care. May be time to break out the old bass rig again…good to see you, though. Though not under these circumstances, obviously. How did I know it was divorce papers? Hmm, that's a good question. But I think it's 'cause the manila envelopes the 'papers' come in always look a little mangled. Like someone kinda rammed the sheets in there real forceful-like. See you around, Billyboy. Look after yourself, now, all right, okay? I'm really sorry, Billy. I really am," he said.

That go-getting young urban professional in the sun-bright cubical next to you at your humdrum "yob" at Croppers United

State Mutual Insurance and Trust, Ltd.—he with the unique ties and meticulously pommaded "do"? He might just have a clandestine thing going you've got no idea about: as the five-string bass player for a heavy metal mariachi band called Atomic Taco or Aztec Zacrifice. She with the prim outfits and ideally cut-and-platinum-tinted bob? She just might front a Blondie "tribute" band, own a walk-in closetful of platinum platform shoes and whore-red heart-shaped "shades," dabble over weekends in oxycontin and threesomes in Laurel Canyon hillside hot tubs.

Some have secret trust funds or get monthly checks from Mum and Dad ("One more year, dear, we'll support him, his pipe dream of fame and endless shots of cucumber-infused vodka, backstage groupies and a Japanese Fan Club." "But he's just not, um, very *talented*, Harold-honey! He's hardly what *anyone* would call a *star*. Even though he started with guitar lessons in fourth grade, *he still plays like a fourth grader*. And when he sings, dogs and cats go running!" "There's *lots* of young people out there in Hollywood like that, Helen-darling—and some of them, why, some of them, I say, well, they get lucky! Get their big break. Why not our Goffrey/our Rodney/our Greggory James?").

Some move *ensemble*, as a band, from Tampa, Ann Arbor, from 'Frisco or Boston. Many come from Ireland. They come because of one man. No, not Margaret Thatcher. Not *him*. That man is Jim Morrison. Here in LA, you've never met so many ex-pat paddies in positive, swooning love with The Doors's notorious frontman, the first rock fraud, the *faux*-est of the *faux*, The Lizard King. Are all those wonderfully amiable Irishes so soused, you sometimes wonder, that they can't see that the Doors are the most overrated band *ever*? The absolute *worst*?

I mean, HI, HOW ARE YOU? HOW HIGH *ARE* YOU?

Some are that charlatanish, puerile thing, The *Collector*. Otherwise known as the nerd, the geek, the dork, the boffin. The dweeb, the kook, the freak, the music gear accumulator. The connoisseurs of whatnot, lisping their unquenchable lust to acquire and display and talk, talk, talk about what they've got, got, got. They've got Fender Telecasters or Fender Jazzmasters in every color, custom colors, or a *seriously* enviable record collection, sedulously alphabetized of course. They don't just have a couple hundred records and CDs like you and I do— plus the cassettes you can't bring yourself to part with. You're gonna have to do something drastic like *get married* if you wanna lose those.

Anyhow: collector types. Just look at the unopened copies of *The Beatles* ("The White Album," on white vinyl!) or a first-run pressing of that one hexagonal blue record the Rolling Stones did (unopened as well) or Sparks' first LP (as Halfnelson, worth easily five or six hundred thousand million dollars). They've got rock dolls and puzzles and Russian doll puzzles of The Ramones. A veritable kindergarten of box sets and buttons and bobbleheads. Japanese/Italian/Australian promo posters and vintage blacklights to light them up. They've got your obligatory Blondie lunchbox and would *kill* for a Beatles "Baby Butchers." Personalized picks and picture discs. I know a terrific engineer (a non-nerd, great guy) who tortures dorks at his parties by abracadabra-ing from its thick, round plastic sleeve a picture disc of Neil Diamond that, when you play it, plays Black Sabbath's *Sabbath Bloody Sabbath*. It's a *boner* rarity, to coin a phrase; it's apparently unappraisable (not that he'd ever sell: the drooling looks on the dopey rock-oafs who prize such things—*priceless*). See them madly spinning backward with geeky, covetous awe. "You guys wanna see something utterly bizarre?" he asks in the middle of one of his frequent get togethers. Why yes of course what *is* it? Tell us, show us, what have you *got* there?

Thing is, the thing about getting into music (and getting into playing it, playing in bands and things), the thing, I say, about getting into getting into music is, is, it's just so…it's just so *easy* to get into.

And the collectors, little acquisitive accumulators, as artists/ musicians themselves? Never any good. As Dr. Johnson tells us in one of his better *Ramblers* or *Idlers*: "No man ever excelled in painting, who was eminently curious about pencils and colours." To be sure, there are artists and great ones who must need become collectors (every famous person I have ever known gets more and more free goods sent his or her way than you would ever believe, madam)—but that's only after they've "made it" and have to fill the void that opened when they filled the void in themselves with the thing called "success." Whatever that means.

Many modern LA troubadours live in the van they drove "out west" in, clubbed the eastern seaboard in, the great Midwest, the Bible Belt, the heart of Texas. Let's meet five glam guys and their beat-to-shit Econoline. The tacky bumper stickers and disconsolately discarded vodka bottles tossed away outside give it away as a band van. It's sitting inland; it'd be great to have it out by the coast, but the fuckin' cops, man, The Fuzz are stricter nearer water. Plus the piss-yellow Jersey or drab blue Delaware plates make you an obvious target for The Man, man. Eventually, van life gets old and the band secures living room space from friends "back home" (so many of them go back home, after not making it here in the time span—two months, two years?— they "give" themselves "or else"). Next, they get a cheap, unfurnished apartment or find a flophouse on Western, off Olympic, on a not-safe block on Washington, or Santa Monica Boulevard, adjacent. You can hear them rehearsing in squats, abandoned warehouses, purloining electricity, one step ahead of the irate slumlord or the aforementioned cops; you can watch them existing on unboiled Top Ramen or popcorn and hot dogs from your Arcos, your 7-Elevens, your Circle K's and Kwik-E-Marts. Witness them arguing over who gets the last scrape of peanut butter/plop of strawberry jelly. There they are, drunk on bad wine or budget gin, the bottles clinking obstreperously on the cement or parquet floor, talking, talking, talking about how what they just "jammed" out's "a total hit," sure to land them that record deal, that coveted opening gig, those chicks at The Rainbow, The Whisky, The Roxy, The Lingerie, an endorsement deal from Vox, Charvel, or Miller Lite.

They finally get a gig (a very lame pay-to-play-thing in some Hollywood alleyway hellhole or the Tuesday midnight slot at some dark, dank, dead joint deep in the Valley). They shill, they shill, shill, shill. The sound of it, their shilling, is like the whoosh of a whoosing hi-hat. You meet them (especially if you are a pretty young thing, 'cause that's, they've determined, their putative "target audience": pretty girls who will bring other, different-looking pretty girls to their gigs, which will in turn get them known as a band that has "a following" of mostly cute chicks—hey, it's why they got into this rock thing, ya—which will in turn get them *guys* flocking to their shows 'cause the *guys* heard there'd be *chicks* there, chicks galore, dude—the club they played last week was fucking crawling with them!) and they don't let up till you swear that you'll "come down" to their big gig at a tiny place on a Thursday night (the midnight slot) so that you can "check them out." They'll put you on "the discount list," just six or seven bucks at the most at the door, doors open at eight, and don't forget—there's a two-drink minimum after 7:00 p.m.

Grand total to you: $51.50. The minimum on the two-drink minimum, they forgot to mention, is twenty-five dollars and twenty-five cents for a watery domestic draft or slapdash well drink.

Sorry 'bout that, dude. Come on up to the VIP room, though; you can't miss it, look for the mystery stairs and the slack red velvet rope, unmanned; here you go, have a promotional condom or this-here drink ticket, take it, take it, thanks for "coming out," take it, take it, take it before our drummer or our stupid fill-in bass player asks me for another one to give to his mom's best friend/the guy who's his "ride"/his cousin from Canada, Grenada, Barbados, Taiwan.

Some are pretty boys, pretty as the prettiest boy in Rock who ever lived (that would be the aforementioned young David Gilmour of the aforesaid The Pink Floyd—I mean, seen the footage? Seen the goddam guy in *Live at Pompeii?* Dude looks not just like a *lady* but a *foxy* lady, to twist/borrow an already very bad phrase). While others (many, most) are sin-ugly in a way that's just kind of *cool* (fresh outta the Bill Wyman/Ron Wood/Sir Charles Watts school of stunning unsightliness).

Some of these music guys are, well, *girls.* Women. "Ladies who rock." And some are pretty girls and some are girls who are not so very. Chicks with picks!—and sticks! Every day there are more of them, getting lessons *and* learning the lesson mommy must've taught

them: not to even think about getting involved with rock stars—
or *any* dopey yokel in a two-bit rock band, for that matter—but to
become rock stars themselves. Though they still, at this late date in
feminist hegemony, have to fight for their rights to rock out. That's
a fact. They're still looked at as sex and fetish objects and decorative
anomalies. And being asked beyond-ludicrous interview questions
like (via venerable Lady Kim Gordon of The Sonic Youth): *"What's
it like to be a girl in a band?"* It's getting better for them. People are
rooting for them. Hell, I've seen it with respect to our Jenny up and
down the rockist spectrum! People talk about the way she rocks more
and more these days (instead of how she "rocks" some tight jeans or
an open blouse motif that showcases one of her stunning red or lacey,
blazing black bras). It's showbiz still, sure, but women are bringing it
all back home, they are, all right.

Why, here one comes with a nice guitar in a nice case—a singing
female songwriter off to a rehearsal: a rehearsal with herself. Her
name's Ravenna or Sienna, Rhapsody or Sage; and she's thinks she's
the shit. (She also thinks, deep down, that she sucks, what's the point,
but nobody needs to know that, now—it's a fake-it-till-you-make-it
kind of thing.) Her original drummer quit to go to enter the seminary;
her bass player left because, well, they were dating and aren't now.
She broke up with him after she walked in on him snogging her ex-
best-friend from middle school in Cambridge, Renton, Rochester,
Columbia. Since then she's done some "Open Mic" nights and
is looking to do a proper gig, to find "the right producer," to open
for someone who's a somebody (not just anybody, some Charlene
Nobody, some nobody just like *she* is). She's hoping beyond hope to
get her "demo" plugged into a show on The WB or some Showtime
show that—unfailingly, five minutes from the ending—features
pained, victim-ish lyrics, vocals plaintive and aquiver, gentle strums
and dramatic pauses and maybe some "safe" strings or something,
as pads or patches. She's got a tasteful vintage flower-print summer
dress on and some real swell Mary Janes or granoblastic combat
boots and her well-cut hair's dressed in an impressive, careful mess.

She's wearing a black motorcycle jacket over the dress (a pale yellow, little old thing with cream-colored spaghetti straps) that's the envy of nearly everyone she meets at swank clubs and spendy bars and opening galas (how soft it looks, what epaulets, what straps and flaps): she also thinks she's *such* a hyacinth girl: just you gawk at how lovingly she paints herself, how she arranges her striking hair like so many baby's breaths or beautiful thistles.

She never knew her father/her identical twin brother drowned in a summer lake/her mother drank her sorrows away and goddam wasn't "there for her," and maybe made her have Borderline Personality Disorder (she doesn't want her therapist to confirm that iffy fact, though; when the term comes up she squirms or goes ballistic!). She had a real rough girlhood. Or, she has it rough 'cause she *didn't* have a tough upbringing. She had it so great as a kid that she'll *never recover from it*, her ideal childhood. She moved here, to Los Angeles, this music and movie mecca, from Cleveland, New Zealand, Rhode Island, or Thailand (where she was teaching English/studying Buddhism/fucking a French guy/finding herself/partying too much— but she realizes it now and that's all the past, it's gone, it's over). Or all of the above. How she just loved *The Waste Land*! She read that one in high school. She handwrites poetry herself, she does, favoring purple paper. Poems pour out of her: about her fugacious relationships, about every boy who's ever taken her virginity or her perspirate-delicate hand on a starless, midnight, full-or-gibbous moonlit walk. Between *billets doux* to her many *beaux* (some say she's really very pretty, though, gosh, she herself doesn't know if she'd describe herself like that: she's o*kay*, she guesses; lots of girls are gorgeous here, in Los Angeles, the town she likes and hates so much; if guys think that, well, who's she to go and stop them?), she sends longish monthly letters to her Congresswoman or Senator about how the bees are dying and the corporations are lying and so many whale meat steaks are frying in Russo-Sino-Japanese frying pans.

The ornate inlay on her aubergine-and-sausage Guild guitar's the color of untinctured marzipan.

Her favorite artist's Johnny Cash.
Her preferred whiskey: sour mash.
She lives in Brentwood with a cat.
She's gigged in New York laundromats.
She really wants a record deal.
A major would be just unreal.
But she'd take an indie thing.
Keep control of everything.
An actor boyfriend would be nice.
But a nice guy would suffice.
As long as he knows her career
Will always come first—won't it, dear?
She's sick of dating total jerks.
Alas, a new jerk's in the works.
Damn his epicenish eyes—
She believes his every lie—
Until at last she sees the wrong
He's done: and puts it in a song!
Wonderful and oh-so clever—
All her friends say "Her best ever!"
Well, two of them at least: they said
They "really liked it—not half bad!"
She might have booked a cool show:
The World Famous Troubabour!
(She really hopes they call her back.
Till then, she'll have another Jack
And Coke, okay, you got this round?
You're just too sweet—you new in town?
You have a label? Hey, that's great!
I have a demo—we should date!)
She hopes you'll sign her mailing list.

One thing that makes her really pissed:
When people chitchat at her gigs—
"They sometimes act like total pigs.
Tonight the room had such a din
As farmers put their livestock in."
(She knows that didn't make much sense;
You got the gist nevertheless.)
It's really hard to keep the faith
(the odds in favor aren't that great),
Playing to a crowd of seven
On a Tuesday at eleven.
She knows she isn't just some waif
Whose goal is just to play it safe.
She's an artist—yes, she is—
And going to make it in The Biz.
Give it everything she's got
Work it, give it her best shot—
For perhaps another year—
But after that she's outta here:
Back to Texas, South Dakota—
Till then, another Jack and soda.

Now. Next up…*them*. Let's talk about *them*, shall we? There they are. Who? Who are they, this them? Some brand new band, looks like. New kids on the chopping block. Got some songs and need some gigs. Went vintage outlet shopping and "thrifting" for suitable duds, threads, outfits, stage clothes. Shirts, pants, boots, jackets. Now they're ready. Ready to go rockin' in the free world! But first things first: first they have to *get ready for their photo shoot*. Their very first *photo shoot*. On Fountain, on Melrose, on Willoughby, on Grand downtown—they're having their picture taken by some grasping amateur, some Scripps Institute or New York Photography Academy (there's one on Hollywood Blvd.) novitiate. Some shutterbugging *idiot* who thinks he's Ingmar Bergman, Annie Leibovitz, or Jacques-Henri Lartigue. My heavens, my *stars*, don't they (the new band) rather look like little eighteenth-century emperor-sized douchebags or little marquises of self-involvement as they line up and pose themselves against that obligatory brick wall, over by those banal train tracks, in that cemetery (for Goth bands only, *s'il vous plaît*). Okay, now let's get one with you guys looking really serious/really happy/really pensive/really silly/really douchey. Really, really.

Look how tall that one pale guy...well, his *hair* is tall, at least. He's a walking human shortcake himself, but his follicles fan out to the nearer stratosphere. It's the height of a Marshall Stack, his "do"! (Eww!) *Actors* in "this town" are notorious dwarfs but rock has its midget-ish ones as well, lugging their Napoleon complexes onstage along with their keyboard setups.

I'll bet you any money the Fauntleroy in the aqua tank top's the *drummer!* Classic! Where d'you think the singer got that prodigious necklace crucifix? Melrose, Sunset, east Ventura Boulevard? Thing must weigh near thirteen pounds. His new shoes are worth more than your car. Does he know that? Does he care? Look at the chick who's doing the styling and art direction for this photo-picnic; she's obviously his latest conquest, new main squeeze. How did he get her? *How* did *he* get *her?* She's incredibly beautiful. She makes you want to kill yourself. Nietzcshe really must've been right about the whole no-God thing. Her smile makes you want to scream "What am I doing wrong?!" Her lips protrude till two weeks from Tuesday. Tits do too: they stick out all the way to your craven, envy-driven libido. Her face just breaks you. She towers two heads above the guy. He hasn't got a job, a bank account, a clue, or even a gig at lowly Madame Wong's West on a Monday at midnight yet—but he's got *that*, God bless him, he's got *her*, goddamn him. Goddamn him straight to lower *Hell*.

Go to, go to. *Du calme, du calme.*

Incredible. And she's not even an utter shrew like The Weird Sisters' old drummer Walter's girlfriend "Nasty" Nastasha was. She's cool, in fact. Not cold: cool. Cool enough. Very cool enough, in fact. Went to Spence, someone said. Did all four years at NYU. I thought I overheard her talking about quantum physics and the differences between translations of *Madame Bovary*.

Oh the humanity!

Is she *a drug addict?* Did "new band" get her hooked on smack, this fucking lucky rocker's inamorata? Or, instead of spending her pre-grad school year abroad did she sign up for some sociology prof's research study wherein she was to go to LA, let her life go to the devil, and start dating a poncey glam rock frontman and report back after nine months? What the Sam *Hill's* the *matter* with her? There's no explaining a) the Bermuda Triangle and b) the Lost Colony of Roanoke or c) why she's glam-guy's arm candy.

There is no God. There can't be. God's gone and done an Elvis. That's got to be the only explanation. Friedrich, you're so right. Sorry, God. I have loved You and got down on my knees for You, *to* You, all these goddam years, those hungover Sundays, and day-after humpdays, in vain, in vain, in vain. If You were *really* there You would hurl down a thunderous lightning bolt and break the fuck up this totally *de trop* singer and his impossibly, outrageously gorgeous girleen. Do it now, Our Lord and Holy Saviour. In Jesus' possibly apocryphal name we pray, Amen.

Singers are as bad as drummers, man. You've got "pipes," yeah? You can sing? Got a bit of range and all? So the fuck what. So can my dear old dad. So could my grumpy, gimpy granddad. Without fail, he baritones it to the tippity top of the varnish-burnished old church rafters every single sodding Sunday, dear old dad does, roaring his favorite hymns. Big deal. My dad, my granddad, your half-deaf great uncle—any guy off the street, practically. Any old vulgar gondolier or splendiferously be-pimpled kid desultorily scooping your Rocky Road or Peppermint Delight at Ye Olde Serenading Ice Cream Parlour, USA. Sorry, guy. You'll have to do better than that. You're not exactly irreplaceable. Hey, Frankie/Joey/Mikey/*Aaron*—put down that can of eco-friendly supermousse and help me hump my goddam amp into the van, *okay?* Jesus *Christ*, you fucking nimrod, you got hair gel all over my brand new tweed reissue Fender Vibrolux Deluxe! Thanks a lot. You're just as bad as our Ral. You ever met a *single* guy called *Aaron* who wasn't a *total* program, by the way? A complete dandy and drama king? I have not. Never. Every one a prima donna. Every one a momma's boy. Almost as bad as every Ryan, Sean, or Mychael-with-a-Y.

Even the way he *smokes* spells *diva, sissy, total headache.*

Check out the poor guitar player—he looks so very bored. He can't for five minutes keep his mouth from bobbing on a cigarette. He smokes in his sleep, this guy. They ain't done a single gig yet and he's already thinking of "going solo," or forming a supergroup with some guys he knows from some of the astonishingly beautiful and museum-like vintage guitar shops on The Sunset Strip. He's "so over it"—and it hasn't even started yet. He checks his hair six times a sec. The whole of the world's his hand-held mirror. Or at least, every other shopfront window he might pass is. His cornflower blue and weirdly piercing eyes seek them out. *His* girlfriend goes almost everywhere with him. She'd go with him to the loo if he'd let her. There she goes Yokoing off to the diner they, the band I'm yammering on about, go to *après* the shoot. She will have the fat-free iced tea and a couple of her boyfriend's fries—the ones that skidded off the greasy plate, away from the pile, redolent of ketchup and lunchtime dreams of future fame.

"So what are you guys doing tonight?" goes the drummer.

"I don't know…getting fucking loaded and fucking drunk, I guess," replies the singer, a tyro sybarite and singular purveyor of autolatry.

"Sounds good," says the bass man.

"Cool," the guitar-guy says.

"Are *we* invited?" the girlfriends coyly duet.

And the boys just laugh; and in quadrophonic chorus-unison go: "Nooooo!"

It's almost poetic, the way they talk (but not the way they rock—they're gonna have to "work on that").

"So: how many songs do we have now, man?" the drummer asks of anyone, no one, after more than a bit of a lull in the conversational action.

"I dunno, man," shrugs the singer. "Seven, maybe?"

"I thought it was more, man," bass-boy says.

"No, man," the singer mumbles. "There are some more ideas, but I'm, like, having…I still need to get some, like, lyrics for those, man."

"Depends on what you call a song," the guitar player philosophically breathes, the weird pierce, as it were, of his eyes given full effect.

"Just what do you mean by *that*, Bobby?" the singer counters.

"What I mean is, we need *better* songs, man," guitar-guy goes.

"What's wrong with our songs, man?" singer, outraged, says.

"They kind of suck, man," guitarist counters. "They're just not very…I dunno, man. They're just not very good."

"What are you *talking* about?" the singer says. "You kind of suck, man. Every one of those songs is a legitimate *hit*, man. Every last one of them. I mean, you fucking *wrote* them, man, so how can you *say* that? I don't get you, man. I don't get you at *all*."

Just look at all the bands in this town, wouldn't you just! *Look* at them! Just try not to! Make like Lot's wife and just you try and look away. They're *everywhere*. At the 7-Eleven on the corner. At the gas station, the beach, the barber shop (well, maybe not the barber shop), the Griffith Observatory (photo shoot!), Hollywood Boulevard (photo shoot!), Forest Lawn (ibd.!), Grand Central Market, Runyon Canyon (well, that's where people go for exercise—so maybe not there, either). The movies, the Fatburger, the shitty pizzeria on the zooming-busy corner, the gig by that hot new band from Stockholm or San Antonio or Sacrafuckingmento. They're coming in through the goddam windows! They're scratching along your eaves with their unclipped fingernails and their disgustingly tight paisley Brian-Jones-goes-to-Morocco trousers at full half mast. *They're on your roof*, having a "smoke break" right beside your bloody chimney, or they're busy parachuting down it, in order to get their promo picture put up in your precious daughter's pretty pink-and-yellow/animal motif-ed room while the moon floats big in the bright night sky and the stars sail on, away, away.

Lock your doors and windows *right now* if you, too, live in Los Angeles, reader; there's a pop group that wants in, wants a crack at playing you their just-completed, prototypical three-song demo, wants to put their flyer up on your refrigerator (the one for the pay-to-play gig they're paying to play next week—once they get paid themselves from their part-time jobs or if the check from their uncle comes, the one who was in Mountain, in The Blues Magoos, Paul Revere and the Raiders, or who once almost got to open for Country Joe and The Fish). These goddam xenobombulating bands, they want a chance to, as the old blues guy puts it, put a spell on you—put a spell on…while they cleptobiotically ransack your cupboard for anything even remotely snackable, tip over your refrigerator like an acoustic guitar's soundhole with a pick flicked down it, make off with a few of your favorite terry cloth towels and a bulk pack of toilet paper, act like those Yosemite bears you see with the yellow stripes painted down their snouts to let you know, *hey*, these here bruins know how to work your corkscrew and they *will* get to your picnic basket, toss aside the rotgut chianti and make straight for the Chateau Neuf du Pape.

"That's *cat food!*" you may well yell to one you might catch ransacking your pantry. "Don't *eat* that, mate! Let me make you some spaghetti. What?! It's all gone? The bass player ate it raw/right out the package when no one was bleeding looking?! What the *fuck!* You guys are *a*nimals! Or minerals. I'm not sure which!"

"Hey," you wanna shout at them from out your car window as you breeze down Sunset or Franklin or north Ventura Boulevard, "could you guys think of a *more* cliché way to pose?! *Get a tie*, you fucking fuckers! Get a *band.*"

They're called *Dick and the Fucks*, or *The Uselessnesses. Johnny and the Posers* or *Strip Tent. Elephant, The Dorks, Loon, The Mikes.* They're called *The Chairs*—and next week they've got a cool gig with a band called *The Lamps*, and *The Tables* are opening, taking a break from recording with this guy who produced *The Sofas.* If they could get *The Mirrors* to headline, that'd be just wicked-awesome, even better than the show they had with *The Spoons* and *The Forks*—after *The Knives* cancelled, those pricks, those posers. They're *Huge, The Old In-Out, The Tits, The Clits, The Oven Mitts*. They used to be called *Flick* but some band who got signed to a major bought the rights to the name from them for ten grand and now they're gigging as *Dinah Shore Jr.* They play hard, fast, punk rock so they gotta have a name like *Monet's Arsehole* or *Carnivorous Flowers* or *Riotous Delirium* or *One-Armed Skate Whore* or [*insert famous young hard-partying starlet's Christian name here with or without apostrophe*] *Herpes Outbreak*. If their "sound" is folky-pretty acoustic-based, like aural eider downs and cream puffs and fields of swaying wheat or barley, they maybe use their last names in a row or go by something softly pacific or oddly bucolic or sort of sylvan and punning and throwback—like *Mantle Goes Yard* or *Frobisher's Gardening & Bicycle Company 1883* or *Rolling Hills & Waving Planes*. If metal's their thing, and they're out to scrape people's faces off with trebly, crunchy distortion, it's *Strafer* or *Plutonium* or *Total Hell* or *Pandemonium*. I mean, they can't be called *Marshmallow Kisses* or *The Cat's Best Japanese Silk Pajamas* if their goal's to play Ozzfest before they die or split up; or split up, then split up the mega-royalties. And should they rock the Christian rock it's gotta be something like *In Excelcis Deo* or *Where Three are Gathered* or *Leviticus Says* or *No Onanism*.

And what about Prog?! They're...for heaven's sake, for the life of me I haven't a *clue* what a mulletheaded contemporary prog rock band'd call themselves. Thank the Lord for that. And on and on and on.

Hey, The Spoons, Chairs, Lamps, et alia: as my old chum Psycho once said: "If you aren't clever enough to come up with a cool, viable name for your band, you shouldn't *have* a band, man."

Some want to write the aleatoric, perfect pop song, an album as good as *Revolver, Let it Bleed* or *Beggars Banquet, Kimono My House, Bringing It All Back Home* or *Odessey and Oracle* or *Forever Changes* or *Physical Graffiti* or *Ram* or *White Light/White Heat*, or the astonishing version of The Glove's *Blue Sunshine* where Robert Smith resang all the songs. Those guys and gals often end up totally trammeled, victims deluxe of the rock and roll version of dear old Harold Bloom's *Anxiety of Influence*, petrified at the thought of "putting out" anything till it's *perfect*. (Hint: there's no such thing as perfect. I mean, John Winston Ono Lennon wanted to rerecord *every song the Beatles ever did!* What a *nutter!* What a *kook!* What *was* he—*on dope?!*)

Get this: I know a guy—all the right influences like your Robyn Hitchcocks and your Guided by Voices and your Stereolabs and your Beatles and Kinks and Stones. He's got a superb *look*, down to the fact that he's got a Sideshow Bob cut that drives the rock chicks crazy; plus *eerie-colored eyes like David Jones Bowie has.* Plus he's got loads of dedication, oodles of it—word is, he's been belaboring a debut lo-fi solo album on his Fostex four-track *for thirteen years now*. But he won't let you hear it! He won't let you near it! Though he's always "really close," he says. "Sometime this year," he's been saying for twelve. He ducks into his cleared-out clothes-closet four or five nights a week for nigh-on five/six hours at a stretch and tinkers away on his way-too-precious past master masterpiece. And all day long on langorous Saturday—pock-a, pock-a, la, la, la; vamp, vamp, vamp, vamp; boom, boom, boom. You gotta be a little crazy, a little hubristic-narcissistic, to want to make a record anyway, but, hey, come on, this is *ridic*ulous. I'll betcha he's *erased* more things, more riffs and licks and sonic "ideas," more entire songs and catchy choruses, than most bands will ever dream of or dream up or put down on tape. They say he's worn out two or three pairs of Senheiser *head*phones, yeah—and those things last forever.

The guy's no poser. He's the real deal/genuine article. A real *artiste*. Yet nobody will ever know it. He'll never finish it, his *tour de* no *force*. He can't. What would he do if he did? His identity as some mad burrowing wacky four-track machine-genius is entirely wrapped up in it. It's who he *is*. (Just like my dear friend Sterling who, on the verge of getting a "major label deal" disbanded his band—Milk Amplifier—and spent the next ten years gadding about and basking in the attention he got from friends and fans telling him what a shame it was he hanged it up, what a bummer; and how, now, no one will ever know what he could've done had he not freaked the "F" out and "broken up the band.") The, ironically speaking, "act" of completion, at this point, is unsubduable for the Four Track King with the crazy eyes. Forget it. Game, set, match. He can't finish it. Finish it off and send it out into the world? Hie himself down to the stationery shop and scoop up a deck of manila envelopes and neat white labels and do a mass mailing to record labels big and small? He can't do that! He can't *release* it—in both senses of the term. People would judge it. What if they don't *like* it?! Horrors! Curtains! It wouldn't be *his* anymore. Under his control. He'd have to let go of it. Curtains! Horrors! He's automatically reckoning they'd say (in a quasi-Prufrockian way): "He worked thirteen years on *this?!* Plus he wouldn't have a shot at a "do-over" if he actually released it. Never going to happen. Sad. But, to him, it's gotta be as good as *Pet Sounds* or it isn't worth a *shit*. Hey, tinkerer! Hey, *tinker*bell! Hey, you twitty, tinkering, musical Twinkie! *Pet Sounds* it*self* isn't as goddam good as *Pet Sounds* is cracked up to be, okay? Hahaha! Listened to it lately? I mean, it's *good* and everything, a lovely little album from some suburban music nerds in candy stripe/barbershop shirts who grew up five miles (it might as well have been five hundred) from the *actual* beach, but come on: *nothing* is as good as it's been built up to be!

As my chum Steve-o says: "*Everything* is overrated!" Name me *one* thing that isn't. Go on, then: tell me.

And it's true! So true. Everything *is* overrated. Think of some film, some book, some record you unwaveringly revere, that you've swooned over and told all your friends about till you're as blue-in-the-face as a Pictish warrior. It isn't really all *that* great now, is it? Come *on*. It's not gonna save the world or even fix you breakfast or fix your flat tire or wake you up with a tasty, mind-blowing blow job. It's really good, it's fucking great, it's fannyfuckingfanfantastic—sure. But it ain't all *that*, now, is it? Admit it. It ain't *that* great. Not when you really think about it. *Sgt. Peppers* (the mono version, of *course*—right, record geeks?), *The Rules of the Game*, *The Velvet Underground and Nico*, *Barry*

Lyndon, Isn't Anything and *Loveless, Swann's Way, Dr. Strangelove, Pornography, Clarissa, The Bell Jar, Eine Kleine Nachtmusik, Anna Karenina, The Notorious Byrd Brothers, Invisible Man, Psychocandy, Imperial Bedroom,* Franicis Bacon's *Popes* and *Triptychs, A House for Mr Biswas,* Bach's *Fugues, The David, The White Album, Dubliners, The Pretenders, The Discreet Charm of the Bourgeoisie, The Sistine Chapel, White Light/White Heat, The Interpretation of Dreams, The Marriage of Maria Braun,* Richard Ellman's *James Joyce, Wild Strawberries, The Idiot,* Chopin's *Etudes, Lawrence of Arabia, The Dream Songs, The Who Sell Out, Blue, Middlemarch, Zen Arcade, Some Like It Hot, Roxy Music, Who's Afraid of Virginia Woolf?, To the Lighthouse, Safe as Milk, On the Waterfront,* Hugh Kenner's *The Pound Era, Ram, Midnight Cowboy* or *Darling, Master of Reality, Pink Moon, Chinatown* or *Knife in the Water, Fear of a Black Planet, The Waste Land and Other Poems, The Village Green Preservation Society,* Walter Jackson Bate's *Samuel Johnson* or the more familiar and renowned *John Keats, The Garden of Earthly Delights, Smile,* Monet's *Waterlillies, Blow Up* or *L'Aventura, Axis: Bold as Love, Revolver, Rear Window, Labyrinths, Bringing it All Back Home* or *Blonde on Blonde* (if only one could turn down the goddam harmonica), *Seinfeld, Bleak House, Double Nickels on the Dime, The Great Gatsby, Odyssey and Oracle, Goodbye, Columbus, Beethoven's Ninth,* Boswell's *Life of Johnson, Heaven Up Here, Unknown Pleasures, Wuthering Heights, Hunky Dory* or maybe *Low, Rebel Without a Cause, The Portrait of a Lady, The Psychedelic Furs, 8 ½, La Gioconda, Blue Velvet, Power, Corruption, and Lies, The Good Soldier, Tonight's The Night* or maybe *Zuma, Dead Souls, Let's Get It On, A Handful of Dust, Two Wheels Good* (or, in the UK, *Steve McQueen), English Settlement* or the more beautiful *Skylarking, Murphy, The Importance of Being Earnest, Let it Bleed,* John Donne's *Songs and Sonnets, A Hard Day's Night* (the film), *Jane Eyre, The Best of Sly and the Family Stone, Pale Fire, Annie Hall, Three Novels* by Samuel Beckett, *Never Mind The Bollocks, Waiting for Godot, The Birthday Party* (the play, silly, not the *band*), *Raging Bull, Around the World in a Day* (this Prince only on account of it has "Pop Life" on it), *Lucky*

Jim, Forever Changes, Whipped Cream & Other Delights, Apocalypse Now, Rocket to Russia, Breathless, After Bathing at Baxter's, Chekhov's *Short Stories, Pink Flag* or probably *154, Troilus and Criseyde* as well as *The Canterbury Tales, The Naked Gun 2 ½, Tess of the d'Urbervilles, Physical Graffiti, Madame Bovary* or better yet *Sentimental Education, The Piper at the Gates of Dawn, Casablanca, Taking Tiger Mountain by Strategy, Straight Outta Compton, Metal Box, Neu!, Fast Times at Ridgemont High, King Lear, The Essays of Montaigne, Catcher in the Rye, The Simpsons, Pink Floyd Live at Pompeii* and blah, blah, blah— you could live without them. You could. You know you could. You'd survive. You wouldn't die. You wouldn't crumble. You'd be fine.

Even *Lolita's* just a novel. Just a little book that someone dreamed up, wrote, and revised.

Everything's overrated. It's just that we *want* amazing things to materialize so that we can get them on cassette, Japanese imprint 180 gram vinyl, deluxe bonus picture disc "gold" CD and DVD and limited or first editions signed by the overlauded author; so that we can set them on our bookcase shelves for our equally geeky friends and guests ostensibly to admire. So that we have something to cherish beyond our own illusions.

The author's just a guy, after all. Or just a girl. Not a god. Not a super creature. Flesh and blood. No more. No less. Yes.

Consider as well the musician whose excessive modesty really only masks his suppressed but massive ego.

Ah, psychology.

There he sits on your superannuated couch or severely wounded lounge chair at one of your hip soirees, your creaky weekend house parties, wryly smiling when someone asks him what he's up to these days—artistically, that is. "You know, it's astonishing to me," he says as he curls a long hank of ropey, straight, errant hair behind his left ear, "that anyone would even slightly care what sort of stuff I'm writing and producing. I'm amazed, in fact," he modestly asserts, "that anyone could care." He says this emphatically, insisting on his irreversible diffidence and insignificance, especially if his interlocutor's a "someone"—a someone who's perhaps more bored than he lets on to the "no ones," but at least he's making an effort to be nice, making a desultory show of how a sense of *noblesse oblige* (more rare than you can imagine in Los Angeles, let me tell you) can be an act of beneficence and bonhomie. The ostentatiously modest guy will—count on it—walk away from this chance opportunity to put on mild display his minimal significance. He'll walk away *more chuffed than you can imagine.* You *can't* be a musician and be sincerely humble. We're all of us vainglorious. Especially the modest ones. Especially those.

I have these two friends from the quaint little California seaside town where I grew up. One (I'll call him "Curtis" on account of *that's his actual name*) had been in "the record biz" as a big time A&R guy and then as an international salesperson for amps and things and then as a recording studio owner; the other ("Charlie") had a "skinny tie" band for a short time in the early eighties who made a good three-song demo and played a few local gigs, stirred up a bit of a fuss if only for a month or two. Maybe opened for INXS at The Arlington or The Church at the I-Beam in San Francisco. Had the demo tape played quite a bit on the Sunday night commercial specialty show, and on the 620-Watt Locals Only monthly college radio "hour" that's on from four in the morning till six or something and the DJ's falling asleep and the needle's stuck in the end groove for minutes at a "dead air" time; made a seven inch that got played on "Rodney on the Roq" and caught the capricious attention of a big indie label that eventually stopped calling. And now, more than a decade after the band gave up, split up, Charlie, the "artist" guy, has made himself small-town notorious for going 'round going: "Well, when *my* band puts out our first album…" And the "exec" guy, wiping his mouth with the back of his hand as he finishes off a Pilsner Urquell, pauses pregnantly, then goes: "Charlie, you don't *have* a band." Hahaha! Right to his face. Right in front of everyone at this splendiferously recherché barbeque in a town known for righteous traditional tri-tip. Priceless, I tell ya. Just immense. Good old Curt meant it as a way of getting Charlie off his ass and "out there" again—they really are true blue chums—but I suppose it's easier to talk about what you're gonna do than actually do it, in just about everything in life, not just music.

Some want to pay homage to the blues, "tell Tchaikovski the news," "get their kicks on Route 66," or "rock and roll all night, and party ev-er-y day"; have a shot at falling out of favor with the Flavor of the Month Club, or "just reach that *one* guy who, like, *gets* what we *do*, man." Some want to "take down the system" or "stick it to the man"; make the world a better place or shake the body politic—or slap its face. Some just want a house with a pool and a ping-pong table—or just to be able to "pay the bills on time," "book another session, man," and "make a decent living doing what I really love to do." Some can't stop, keep going past their prime, 'cause stopping would be stopping to *think* and thinking and rocking just don't go together all that terribly well, it seems. Plus they'd have to think of something else to do with their lives, their time, themselves. God bless and damn them, every one, the entire cavalcade of lesser stars and stars manqué, a mélange of wannabe jukebox heroes, local hopefuls and poser zeros, the about-to-be-has-beens and the coulda-been-a-contenders, the talent squandered and the mediocrity elevated by luck and connections; the sidemen and session men; and that queer, rare thing: someone actually really good—getting somewhere, for a record or three, perhaps, then becoming a sad-making or horripilating story on the egregious VH1's *Where Are They Now?* or whatever it's called *Behind the Music*; or going on, in even more rare instances, to be happy hanging it up, calling it quits, finding something else to do like becoming a cobbler or robber baron or avocado-farming part-time Piper Cub pilot.

Some sure do talk a damnable lot about themselves—what songs they've written that should have been hits, what cushy or big gigs they've done or fine girls they pulled "back in the day." The more they talk about themselves and how great their tour was or their music is or their playing is, the more they *suck*, believe me. The self-panegyricking blowhard holding forth, holding court in the lobby of the hourly rehearsal complex with two or three greenhorns dancing attendance on him? Even if he's a virtuoso (especially if he's that), he's *terrible*, a hack. But the guy quietly nursing his drink in the dark red booth in the even darker corner, going deep within himself before he has to go onstage, attracting no attention, brooking no obsequies, and ducking out just as the set's last chord clangs—*he's* quite possibly brilliant, the real deal. You launch the real deal guy into the orgulous orbit of the loudmouth, and the actually-talented guy will grow even quieter as the blabbermouth tickles up the volume on his already-deafening *monster* ego.

Happens every time.

Some *seem* cool—just because they're orchestrating an imbecile, banal "conversation" with a smiling circle of backstage groupies competitively wobbling on too-high, screaming red or shiny jet black heels or standing in front of a Marshall Stack the size of a single-family shanty-dwelling or bashing on a drum kit in a cage that puts you in mind of a torture chamber or of go-go dancers—but are actually utter *squares, total* Sarsaparilla-sucking über-nerds. Nerds who live, breathe, talk, eat, and practically evacuate music and only music all day and into the night. Have a chat with them for *le mauvais quart d'une heure* and watch your own eyes glaze ten times over: "Oh, the Techitronics 482VB's a *much* improved version, from a sonic sine wave point of view, over the 481 Mach 5.2. And so much different from the point *one*, man. A whole 'nother *world!* Whew! Make no mistake about *that*. Abso*lutely*. Let me give you a little demonstration on these iconic oversized Megatron royal blue Celestion Blue British speakers I just had packed into my old tweed Fender here with the British racing green piping (they only made a thousand of these, you know: real rare, very)…state of the art, you know…I mean, the sustain on the thing is just…miraculous…indescribable…I mean, listen to *this*…"

Some…well, that pretty much covers it. If you can think of another type, then you know more about musicians than I do, dear sir or madam.

One's put in mind here, summing up, after this superfluous and long harangue that I must need beg your collective pardons for (I'm so sorry; obviously I got carried away), of Dr. Johnson's observation on how all artistically ambitious types prefer themselves to anyone else, to all-comers. Johnson may as well have been talking about twentieth-century indie rock and other rock bands as he was excoriating ladies and gents from *The Age of Reason*. Here he is: "Every one wishes for the distinctions for which thousands are wishing at the same time, in their own opinion, with better claims." (*Rambler* No. 185, Tuesday, 24 December, 1751). In other words, everyone thinks he or she's got a shot at being "the next big thing" or at least, and more cynically, "the flavor of the month." In an earlier *Rambler* (No. 21) Johnson imputes this attitude to vanity and self-love: "Every man is prompted by the love of himself to imagine that he possesses some qualities, superior, either in kind or degree, to those which he sees allotted to the rest of the world; and, whatever apparent disadvantages he may suffer in comparison with others, he has some invisible distinctions, some latent reserve of excellence, which he throws into the balance, and by which he generally fancies that it is turned in his favor."

The thing with Raleigh was, he turned up to our new rehearsal space in The Valley, and he knew (and had ostensibly practiced) the songs from the "advance" cassette Jenny and I had given him when we finally met him at our apartment. He was polite and somewhat demure, and his style was a fit: he played really well, or at least well enough for us to ask him that very night to join the band. There didn't seem to be any point in deliberating, and we needed a drummer and badly; and most of the people who'd auditioned didn't have the right feel or the right fills (i.e. way too many of them, busy, busy, busy), or they just didn't seem to mesh with us. Ral seemed to get along okay with Rob in particular (everyone gets along with Rob) and he didn't seem like a total *poseur*—the three of us genuinely believed he was genuinely into our music. And he was. Is. But you know: you start playing intramural music with someone, then a few gigs, "play out," as the infelicitous, parvenu phrase goes, rehearse some more and a little run to Arizona ("The Zone") or up to The Bay Area ("The Bay Area," aka "Land of Snobs and Hippies") and back—and suddenly you're kinda stuck with him. *Kinda*: you *could* axe him, tell him "it's not really working out" or say "you're great but I think we're gonna keep on looking"—but it's such a hassle session auditioning people and most drummers in LA, like the ones we auditioned, either can't really play or are cymbals-happy tinnitus-merchants or unmitigated mercenaries. They want *pay*, especially when they find out you have that coveted thing, a recording contract, even a small one, one whose goddam agreement is written on a Post-it or an Official Barbie's Memo Pad or something.

And so: there "they" *are*, your new band mate —in your band, right there, right there with you. In your apartment for a party, or one of your "party of four" at some mercilessly-bright Denny's or Carrows, squatting at the meeting with your new record label (actually *chiming in* when they oughta *pipe down*), asking you to bring them back "a soda, some cinnamon-flavored Jumbo Beef Stix and a packet of onion-or-cupcake-flavored Sun Chips" as you pop down to the liquor store.

Four

 orry, Raleigh, I really am, I *would* pull over, you know, I'd like to, but you know we have a meeting with the Mikes before the gig tonight and we're gonna be late as it is," I said, trying my best to inject more than a modicum of heartfelt lament and empathy into my slow tone, slowing down the van in order to deal with a patch of phlegmatic traffic, farther down the 5 where we now were, outside Calabassas or somewhere. I felt bad for him, I really did. I mean, what if one of *my* favorite artists had topped himself? I'd be

gutted for weeks. I recall thinking it'd be good to be as compassionate as possible here; I'd never liked Raleigh, liked him even less than I never liked Walter (which was, admittedly, a lot of not-liking), but he wasn't a bad guy, really, and real good drummers aren't, even in a supermegatropolis (and as I've told you only fourteen hundred times now), all that easy to find. He was just a guy who thought Bob Saget or that watermelon-sledgehammer guy in the plaid golf cap was the hilt of comic comedy, and who laughed at "bloopers" and people getting hit in the crotch by broomsticks or hockey pucks or midget remote-controlled aeroplanes, and potty humor, and his own jokes, practical and otherwise. He was/is a guy who watches a *lot* of TV (Rob does too, but somehow the fact that Rob's an inveterate television addict kid doesn't chafe so much somehow—I don't know why); and, for a fellow who spends his free time hugging barbells and searching for mirrors to gaze into and worrying about his "body image," he seems to eat a lot of junk food, suck down his share of burbling, foaming sodas.

There he is with a mega-straw out the side of his pale-lipped gob, slurping a gargantuan Slurpee—like the kid who's successfully snuck away from Fat Camp and serendipitously alighted (after having got lost en route) on a woodsy-friendly, mega-sweets-and-cupcakes-stocked General Store. There he is: coming back from a jaunt (with Rob in tow) to a Hostess Bakery *outlet*—where day-old Ho Hos, Twinkies, Snowballs, Ding Dongs in *bulk* go on irresistible sale. In he walks (late, of course) to practice with a ponging *shopping bag* of Chicken Deelite or mondo bucket of Sir-Clucks-A-Lot, with the grease seeping through and making imperial map-like patterns on it, Burger King carry cartons or sacks of sock-it-to-me Jack in the Box, malodorous McDonalds, Beefy's, ChunkBurger, TacoLot, Okinawa Beef Bowl, Winka-Winka's, Senor Fishwich, Pig-on-a-Stick, Amy's Pies 'n' Burgers 'n' While-You-Wait Oil Change, Steinmanbergmanstein's Deliwiches, Bob-O's BobOburgers, Pickwick's Fish 'n' Chips, Smokey's Smokin' HotLinks-4-U, Dr. Fishwich, DumboBurger, The Earl of Sandwich, ChilliKing, Pete's Pizza Pitas, a box of Quickby's BiscuitBurger, Fatso's Downtown Falafel Hut, BurritoWorld, Hogie Hoganmeyer's,

Beefenberry's Authentic Philly Cheesesteak & Tahiti Teriyaki Palace, Hot-Dog-a-Roo-Roo, Chumpy Whippersnacky's, and/or...*ta-da!*... Corny CornDoggyDog's All-Beef FritterFranks.

You'd best look out! Ral's gotta steaming sauerkraut-and-cauliflower sausagewich from fucking *Sub*way or somewhere that lights and heats up a room, if you know what I mean; a drooping, dripping humungo-sized chiliburger from Fatburger with extra onions and a "fat" or "skinny" French fry medley; a mondo slurp shake with fudge Krakatoa-ing over its sippycup brim; *an assortment of* barbecued napalm-and-Agent-Orange beefwiches that he'd spread on his floor tom that'd take him half an hour to chew through and another twenty torturing minutes to wash up from. And on and on and on. No wonder Rob and Jenny and I had so much time to work out our bass and respective guitar parts! No wonder Jenny got so "very good enough" and more on rockin' lead guitar.

"Jesus, Raleigh," I'd woebegonely go, talking over our bombilating amps, "do you *have*ta eat that shit in here? I mean...can't you...?" and Jenny and Rob'd just turn up their palms from their readied instruments as I appealed to them with repeated longing and potentially conspiratorial looks: like, what can you do? Their collective eyes'd intimate: the guy didn't get his dinner yet; he just came from work and he has to work late sometimes; give him a fucking break, John; drummers get *hungry*; work harder than we do; he's just a kid and prolly still *grow*ing. And Ral himself would look up all squirrel-eyed from a double-decker crunchburger encased in a viscous paper flower of American-cheese-yellow tissue paper and an efflorescence of industrial-strength napkins and go: "Hunh? What? You [munch] guys [chomp] *say* something [crunch]...? And I'd avert my tired eyes for all of twenty seconds (adjusting Jen's amp, tuning a truant guitar string, double-checking the old pale blue Boss Chorus or off-orange Distortion pedal), and there Rob and Jenny would be, macking guiltily away on some fresh hell of pizzafied egg roll or FrenchToastFurter that Ral had gratuitously offered them and that they couldn't resist.

"You guys are the snackiest people I have ever *known*," I'd say, all incredulity; and the three of them would laugh and then usually Raleigh of course'd counter my obviously remonstrative observation by proffering from behind his kit a "Family Size" bag of white cheddar and butterscotch-flavored potato chips or a handful of "zesty-style" über-pretzels frosted with garlic and onion powder and pixie dust and—I don't know—buffalo-essence or oyster-enhanced imitation flavorings.

And the coyly "innocent" look on his kind-of-babyface would just make Jenny and Rob laugh like mad. And, sometimes, me too. Not that often, however.

"Can we just get back to work here?! Please?" I'd plead and they, the three of them, would, of course mouths full, go: "Umm-humm" or "Mummnkay." Then they'd do this sort of pantomime where they'd pretend to stop snacking away, but then start right back up again, almost like it was Fellini-choreographed, proffering one another Cheese-Bees and Munch-Its, Waffle Gobbles or Choco-Scarf-'Ems, Lemon-Flavored What-Have-Yous and GumbyTreats.

And there we'd be, *after* practice, so tired, so hungry ('cause junk food just makes you hungry for other, for *real* food), the four of us boothed at Mel's or Swingers or Johnny Rocket's or the boisterous Café 50's that was closest to our lockout; and Raleigh, wouldn't you know it, has got half his ham 'n' eggs and two outta three blueberry pancakes or strawberry crepes down his gullet before you've even looked up from putting the napkin on your lap.

On the way down to the record company, we had to stop for gas, as you might expect; we got off The Golden State Freeway and turned right on Rinaldi and pulled up to the pumps. *We hadn't had a "bathroom break" since Bakersfield anyhow so what the hell*, I thought. Of course Raleigh heaved the back side door handle back before we'd hardly stopped and popped out to find the loo; Rob followed quickly, too.

"That's terrible, isn't it," Jenny said for the third or fourth time, shaking her now-longer, well-past-her-shoulders brownish/cherry-hued locks and tucking the long front strands behind one ear. She was so the sort of girl who looks great with her hair long or short. She looked tired as hell then, though—but so cute. Sometimes the sun would hit her big root beer-colored eyes just right and make them go all palely opal-ish and she'd just be stunning, so adorable and pretty-pretty. You'd probably want her if you met her. Trust me.

"The way he…" I hung fire.

"Who?" Jenny said; she knew me so well; people you're sleeping with can't help but sometimes intuit your very every thought, almost: "You don't mean *Raleigh?!* You aren't still pissed at him for…"

"You're talking about Kurt Cobain…right. Sorry. I know."

"John…Raleigh's *clueless*—we know that. You didn't, like Rob said, have to rip him to shreds over it, though. Just because he's…"

"I know, I know, okay? I *know,* Jenny. I'm *sorry.* I am. I think he knows I felt bad about it; I shouldn't have lost my temper like that. But, I mean, the just-ridiculous chintziness of the guy sometimes just really ticks me off. I mean, those kids had *nothing*: they put us up and fed us last night. I mean…jeez! The one kid only owned *one* crummy guitar and…I mean…"

"No kidding," Jenny said, meaning she agreed with me saying Ral was a cheapskate gaucheburgher. "I *know*. It's over now, okay? I'm going to the restroom. Do you want me to bring you something?"

"Gatorade, okay? Let me have the credit card, okay?"

"Okay," she said and kissed me lightly and somewhat formally, like she did it only on account of she quote-unquote had to, and stepped down from the door she had opened and was holding onto. "The thing is—and I don't want to make too big a deal of this, okay…?" Jenny added and closed the door.

"I know, I know," I sighed. "'When will I learn not to go 'round teaching people lessons' is what you're going to say."

"Exactly," Jenny said—or I thought I heard her say as she walked away.

"Learn your own lesson, John," Rob, just climbing back in the van and overhearing us, said.

"Learn my own lesson."

"Right," Rob said and smiled.

"Right," I said.

I felt so awful—like when someone calls you *clumsy* in a social or athletic situation. Say that word right now: *clumsy*. It's terrifying. Or the term "fool." "You *fool*," someone says as you drop the bong and grotty, week-old bongwater waters the new, Persian-cat-white carpet, or they just go "Hey, fool" for no reason, as a way of saying hello, or "You stupid fool" or "You fucking stupid *idiot*"—and you instantly, even if your self-esteem is riding high or you pretty much most of the time think pretty well of yourself, go: "God, maybe I *am* a idiot, maybe I *is* a chuckleheaded dunderbrain."

See, we'd played Berkeley the night before—this little club that was totally inappropriate (a reconstituted pizza joint or Sizzler or God-knows-what, maybe a preschool or bike shoppe). And these two *kids*, a really young married couple, an acoustic duo called The Sleeping Beauties that had "opened" for us, had been the nicest people you could meet if you went on tour for five years straight. I mean, really beyond the pale in terms of being hospitable and sweet and complimentary, almost fawning—*al*most: otherwise we'd have hated them; well, the royal We would have; Jenny had a lot more tolerance for people who liked us, liked her, and Rob and Ral, dontchuknow, simply ate up plaudits from punters like you go for your gran's apple cobbler. So after the gig they, the couple from The Sleeping Beauties, took us home to their tiny two-bedroom craftsman flop box and bought a twelver of Bud (they had to have had someone buy it for them, some kind soul they'd deferentially accosted outside a humming Kwik-E-Mart or twinkling am/pm) and ordered and *paid for* a veggie 'za with half pepperoni for Rob and Ral and gave us their living room and one doll-sized spare bedroom to crash in and a modest hippie breakfast (toasted pita bread and *sprouts* or whatnot—some sunflower seeds and an exhausted avocado—and the last of their cornflakes and soy milk for Raleigh) in the morning. And as we're going, bidding them a fond fare-thee-well and thanking them profusely, hugging it out with them, helping tidy up, loading the sleeping bags and personal packs into the van like touring automatons, yawning immensely and anticipating an immediate stop for coffee and rubbing gobs of "sleep" from overtired eyes, Raleigh spots a stack of The Sleeping Beauties' homemade tapes on top of a dresser in the kitchen and goes: "Oh, *cool!* You guys actually have a tape, actually?! Mind if I take one?"

And the guy of the couple, this preposterously nice guy, Malcolm, starts *umming* and *erming* and shuffling his feet in his tatty pyjamas and then he mumbles that they "Usually ask, like, five bucks for a donation for their, like, homemade album-on-cassette."

And we're standing there just mortified, with a courteous mouthful of rabbit food from an organic paper plate that we're choking back out of politeness, as Raleigh goes "Oh! Okay, then!" and puts the tape he's plucked up *right back on top of the stack of obviously not-easy-to-sell-tapes that these sweet and talent-free kids had painstakingly hand-colored, right down to the cassette labels and spines, the whole shebang.*

They're not even shrink-wrapped, for fuck's sake. These indie kids couldn't afford it. Or maybe some of them were, shrink-wrapped, that is. Like they took some Saran Wrap from a drawer and drew it tight around the tapes and then had at it with a blow-dryer or or arc welder or Easy Bake Oven something, that toy from the sixties.

And that was it, for me. I'd had it. That was the last straw. Too many tacky, gasp-and-blush-inducing things had happened in just a week and a half for me to countenance it, *him,* any more. (You know how sometimes you get so hot under the proverbial hat you can't even say someone's name?) So I dug into my pocket and pulled out a ten-spot and gave Janet (that was the girl, the sort of child bride) the dosh and, biting a smile, said I'd take two, actually. Just to make a point, you know. Just to make a point with a mallet or a wrecking ball. You might say I was pissed. Beyond cheesed off. They put us up and feed us and break our fasts, however humbly, and you're too cheap to give them five measly bucks for all their efforts—plus insult them as "artists," like their albums not worth five Jack in the Box tacos or two Taco Bell Bell Beefers? Unforfuckinggiveable, Ral. I was trying not to look so livid but I know I wasn't pulling it off. As usual Rob and Jenny stepped in and ran interference (they are both so good with people, truly nice

people themselves, they are) and made even more jolly nicey-nice and
Raleigh thanks them (but not me who bought the fucking second,
and vestigial—and total charity—tape for him) at least, and into the
van we pell mell pile at last. And, naturally, Ral the Royally Oblivious
doesn't comprehend *anything* with respect to what he's just put us all
through and me personally and monetarily (ten bucks extra on the
road for a band that's barely breaking even is nothing to sneeze at);
and he's just goofing around with Rob and raffishly teasing Jenny and
chattering about the pretty-goodness of the gig last night and how at
least we played well despite the lameness of the venue and we navigate
the streets past the university and make our bouncy way onto the
jumping freeway. And it doesn't take more than ten costive minutes
on the old blue highway for me to turn it into the *ka*bluey highway;
for me not to be able to contain my ire anymore and explode and
absolutely excoriate Raleigh for his *appalling* behavior of maximum
tackiness. I mean, I didn't want to. I wasn't enjoying it. It's just no fun
at all "losing it" on someone in your band; in your van; with the rest of
your band in the van with you and the band mate you're losing it on;
it just isn't. But goddam if I didn't just "lose it" and hugely, despite the
fact that I'd sternly counseled myself *not* to, intended to be gentle for
once in my seemingly endless remonstrance of our dear drummer:

"Raleigh!"

"Yes, John," he sighed loudly, mockingbirding my tone, probably
guessing what was coming. "What is it? *What?*"

See, I thought: *He knows, somewhere in the back of his unconscious,
that* something's *amiss, though of course he couldn't tell ya what.*

"How the *fuck* did you think that was cool for you to pick up
those guys' tape and then put it *back* like that when they'd not only
put us *up* but treated us like *royal*ty?" I almost-shouted. "You have to
be the *most*…goddam *clueless,* discour*te*ous person I've ever fucking
known!" I said, yelling at him, practically, kinda. (Okay: I was yelling;
I admit it; but it was a sort of hushed yelling, not full-blown or
anything.)

"What do you *mean?*" Raleigh pleaded, real pain admixed with unknowingness in his small voice. "I didn't…"

"John…" Jenny said.

"I can't be*lieve* you sometimes, Ral," I said. "You're such a fucking…"

"John!" Jenny said.

"*Hey*, you guys…" Rob said.

"Band fight!" Raleigh said.

"Not funny, Raleigh," I said. "I'm being serious here. That had to be about the most tact…"

"John!" Jenny said. "*Drop* it!"

"There's an am/pm," Rob intoned and we wheeled in there and coffee'd up without a word.

And I swear to God after that we, none of us, said boo for nearly two hours till at last we stopped at a gas station somewhere in blazing Bumfuck Central California. The sky, I recall, was pale desert evening and the brown mounds of hillside in the distant distance looked ever so murderously mournful. No one looked up at me—not one of my fellow Sisters did. All the cheaply oxymoronic clichés in the world came swarming in: deafening silence, suspended animation, cool hotness, intense nothingness, screaming quietness.

And of course Raleigh, after what I'd said, after what I'd managed not to stop myself from saying, bolted immediately-dramatically from the cooling van and slammed the sliding door and headed toward the heads and Rob went: "Jeez, John, don't hold *back* or anything next time!"

And I started to feel even worse; and then even worse than the worse I felt 'cause Jenny went and gave me an eye roll that'd do for an actor from the RSC at The Globe that confirmed she, too, thought I was a total asshole for ripping on Ral like that, cheap shotly—in front of everyone and shrieking unsparingly.

What atrocious colloquies one has to have in bands! Or ought I not say "has to have" as I could just as well have kept my big mouth shut, let it go and all of that. *Fuck*, I remember thinking! *I'll never learn, will I?* What boots it, going a-teaching people lessons, one might rhetorically ask? What good does it do and for whom? It just doesn't do one bit of...well, whatever/never mind.

Thing is, though: you go out on tour for two days, you go out for two *years*—either scenario, you're the same kinda emotionally and physically exhausted at the end of it; and ready to snap. At your wit's end. On tenterhooks and on permanent alert. Knackered. Unhappily trigger happy. Ready to stick the boot or knife in at the drop of a hat (and other clichés). You've had bad food, bad days, bad dreams and no or little sleep on torture-couches and mogully futons and sofa beds with razor-sharp *Slinkys* or something similar coming boinging out from them. You've had bad gigs and *some* good ones that in *some* ways are just as *bad* as the *bad* ones were (I'll explain later). You're burnt from driving impossible distances (looking out the window as innumerable trees and telephone poles pass and their shades blur the van's bright glass with swirling, indiscernible, psychedelic color, like what the rim of a glass of single malt Scotch looks like when you "sniff" it around). You're tired of trying to read and catching a headache, or catching up on said lost sleep, drooling onto a "drool pad," waking up with a start as the van downshifts on the oh-my-God-we-didn't-slow-down-enough off-ramp, the jolt glides to a stop at the Union 76 or preferably an Arco on the other side of the meridian (it's cheaper, and they stock more/better "road snacks"). You're weary-ain't-the-word-for-it of getting off at the wrong exit and *never having more than fifteen minutes to be alone* and defecating in public and restaurant restrooms and malevolent toilets in tenebrous clubs where three toilet seat cover tissues aren't *even* enough to assuage you *or* your quavering bumcheeks, plus sometimes there *is* no toilet seat for a toilet seat cover to cover. Yeck! You don't really want to, but you're starting to *hate* the people you're closest to (uh, that would be *your band*; the ones you are closest to are now the ones you most want to get away from every opportunity that you can), gone through all this with, "bonded" with under extraordinarily adverse circumstances, through road-trials and tribulations *galore*. No matter how many tepid or too-hot showers you get in claustrophobic bathrooms meant for dwarfs or midgets in fully "sketchy" budget motels and at kindly people's houses and apartments and anonymous condos, you never really feel clean and they always feel cursory, those trickly wash-offs. Plus, you woke up *again* in the sweat-soaked-stiff clothes you wore onstage the night before.

You're verging on being sick of being someone's eternally gracious gladsome guest—quiet, polite, unnecessarily and inexplicably contrite—tiptoeing 'round their kids' knifelike attack-toys; apologizing 'cause you need to destroy, as it were, the loo again (per Rob, we Sisters would ironically call it "fumigating," e.g. "God, I don't think those wings or fajitas we got back there at The Truck Shack quite *agreed* with me, you know? I, um,...could you guys wait while I go *fumigate* every stall at the Rest Area, John? Thanks."). You're terribly tired of troubling them, your dear, sweet, excited-to-help-a-cool-rock-band-out hosts, for a tablespoonful more of wince-inducing instant coffee. Woefully, you know the menu at Waffle House like the back of your proverbial hand; you're "so over" being slightly or majorly hungover and you're even kinda tired of *beer!* How can that *be?!* The one great, count-on-able thing in life—barley-based beverages—and you'll burst into bitter, torrid tears if you ever meet up with a pint again. (Oh what twaddle: like you'd really turn down a pint of Guinness or Budvar if someone handed you a jar of that right then, mere *seconds* after you just said you're sick of beer.) You've been up-down/up-down for *days* now: you made a hundred and then some bucks extra at one gig 'cause Jenny sold an unexpectedly inordinate mess of T-shirts and CDs (we're smart like that: we almost always have her do the merch table; oh how the indie guy-kids and putative little lipstick lesbians like to meet such a *pretty* rock chick, get an up-close look at her nice plump lips, get up-close-and-quasi-personal with a girl with nice tits and an even nicer face who's *actually* nice as well: the nice girl whom they just finished drooling over and fantasizing luridly about for the full forty-five minute set), but the night before you had to sweat the sinking owner or the swindling doorman, haggle like a hag, 'cause she or he started hemming and hawing about how *the numbers were low* and *nobody drank* and *the independent subsidiary booker-guy guaranteed you way too much for a band your* size, *man*. And you lost the little tussle 'cause you gave up in a pet and took a hundred fifty less than you were promised 'cause you, too, are a "nice" guy and a not-good businessperson and, well, kind of a *patsy* when it comes to monetary-oriented confrontations. A patsy even though you're *fully* aware of John Lennon's dictum that in order to "make it" you gotta be "the biggest bastard on the block." Especially a bastard when it comes to getting what you played for: money you need to keep you going on the road toward getting more money to keep you on the road in order to keep you going as a band...that's going on the road—after their next record comes out—after you finish this tour from Outer Hades.

Mise en abyme: the hermeneutic thrust into the abyss.

Now, backing down, "uncle-ing" that easily, letting yourself be intimidated by a man or woman who fills in a schedule at a bloody *club* and just talks on the phone all day and gets to be consequence-free *rude* to scads of people half the time, you're just a big, lily-livered bastard and worry furrows your sweat-dirty brow: how are you gonna get to Portland/Olympia/Seattle/Vancouver now you've been *stiffed* a fuckin' hundyspot-and-a-half, huh? How you gonna make it up, what you lost, what you were counting on to keep on touring: how in hell will you keep cheap gas in the blasted van, get a dreary hotel at this late hour, dole out the sad per diems, buy a round of conciliatory drinks for your three "best" friends, the only people in the whole wide world who, actually and at this point, under*stand* what the *fuck* you've had to endure, what you've gone through, dealt with, suffered?

Hey there, hey *you* with your langorous fingers stitched behind your longhaired, daydreaming head, listening to the woofy four-song demo you just made on a warbling Tascam four-track cassette machine and envisioning how *great* it'd be to "go out on tour" with your tiny, fledgling, practically cryptonymous band! *Here*, have a nice big cuppa joe from the lobby of the uptown Travel Lodge: it's mud black or it's got gobs of that pointillist powdered creamer and a packet of raw sugar swizzled into it and it *still* tastes like Automatic

Transmission Fluid, only worse. *There*, have a nice fat chat with a girl with an angel face and a demon-red mouth and scary-pretty eyes of periwinkle blue: she runs the door at the bar you're playing in a town you've never been to (and, odds are, will probably never see again). No matter whether she's heard of you or not, she's *not impressed in the slightest*: to her, you're just another band-guy, an employee of the club of sorts too—and not even that: you're lower than a *temp*. Take your eight "drink tickets" and your piss-yellow "backstage" wristband and much luck to ya, band-guy; she won't remember you or your group past ten o'clock tomorrow morning! You thought she kinda liked you till you saw her kiss the bouncer, an Ozzy-alike with a butt the size of Boise. He's got a double-sleeve of tats and a spiffy cowboy hat and cowboy boots that probably cost more than your guitars and amp. Where's his *horse*, you wonder? And *she* (Siobhan, Missy, Mindy, or Scarlet; Yvonne, Chantel, Cherise, Yelena): has she ever even *seen* the sun? It don't look like it. A smile sincere's the strangest thing you'd ever see where *this* girl's concerned. It's like her pretty face with its professional scowl won't even let her grin.

Everywhere, all *over* Clubland and Barville, the socially immiscible soundman's sour or sleepy—just try to kiss his ass *or* sass him: neither matters, neither helps. Tell him hello from me and kick him in the shins, okay? Sure you *got your rocks off* playing original music (I told you and you know yourself there's nothing like it, not a chance), but you're *way* cash-strapped and well, sick of it, sick of being fucking broke. Each time you go to the register anywhere in the USA you're a trembling trunk of prodigious trepidation. The big, beardy (or bantam, John Lennon-bespectacled) clerk at the tiny music store sneers and/or rolls his own music-addled eyes as you flick the nickels toward the counter, play three-card monty with the quarters and the dimes, smooth a vestigial dollar bill and slap it down noiselessly—and have to start all over, counting. Then take your pack of Slinky Ernie Ball guitar strings without a bag, thanks, and slink away. Sure: you went home with someone after the show last night. Someone (now the shots she bought you have had time to wear off) who's turned into a crystalized, incapacitating, walking human *monster*, someone *you never want to see again for as long as ye both shall live.* Ah, but you will, you *will* see her again—just a different, yet no less lonely or trite version of her; you might meet her tomorrow night, in fact. Go home with her again—after the Chicago show, the Minneapolis fiasco, the pickup gig you got in Cedar Falls or Cedar Rapids 'cause a friend of a friend told the booker and the booker *actually had heard of you* and he had a that-day cancellation anyway.

And you go home with her not just to fuck the day, the gig, the drive away but more so to get away from (there's that familiar motif again), if but for five or six or seven hours, the three other people that mean more to you than anyone else in the world. The people that you could go two months *easy* without talking to right now.

You might go home with her that is—not me. Jenny, my girlfriend and band mate, probably wouldn't like that too very much.

And while you're at it, be sure to say hey to the bug-eyed bibulous bar bore who won't let you get on with packing up and loading out the last of your gear (even though the booker or bouncer's barking at you both). He bought your CD and he bought you a shot of Jagermeister-flavored tequila or bathtub gin; and now he thinks he owns you. I sure do miss getting hit in the face with his ravening horse-breath, his spluttering spittle, his ghastly stammerings on rewind-repetition, the monotonously fatuous "information" he's imparting, the lame and halt jokes you can't just half-laugh at or he looks at you like you're going to get it in the neck.

Say hey to the waitresses in East Texas, in Tulsa and Tampa and Tucson. Who look at you like death on account of your unintentionally patriotic hair's red from henna, white from fright (a trucker didn't check a single one of his seventeen mirrors, and your van got damn-near sideswiped), and blue from cheap conditioner from the Motel 6 or gel because what-the-hell—you're on tour!

You can be anyone you want now!

Anyone except yourself, that is—'cause that person's someone you don't even recognize anymore.

Boy do I miss being on tour. Boy do I miss all of that and then some. And yet…

Got a young, gung ho booking agent with an opening slot for us all set up for fall or spring or summer? An agent whose perfidious perfidies aren't *too* too pronounced? Got formidable "guarantees" guaranteed and—this time—*a tour manager* to tackle the pricks and bastards and bitches you meet who run clubs and bars and pubs and quads at sundry colleges and universities? Got a kindly, pretty little merch girl who finished in French or English at Columbia or Dartmouth—one who's cool and doesn't bellyache when you ask her to do extra stuff like find Raleigh 'cause we gotta go, or ask Jenny what's the matter, honey, when she's crying in the Ladies? Got a sixteen-passenger van instead of a bread box, with a trailer, too, one that won't fishtail on the Sony Bono Memorial or fly apart going over the breathtaking Rockies?

Sign me up.

Let's see: I wonder if I can get off work, wonder if the boss'll miss me at my job delivering fancy flowers or messages and rewrites of sitcoms or telescripts, my gig at the night shift call center, or the part-time thing hanging rich people's pictures or watering their plants or deep blue swimming pools? I'm really gonna miss, respectively: driving 'round in an iced flower-delivery van in darkest February; the receptionist/secretarial scowls when I tell him/her the temp agency sent me; the games of cribbage with wannabe actors as I take a break from the screaming switchboard or the proofreading broom closet on the vertiginous ninety-second floor; the looks I get from would-be aristocrats when the newly mounted painting's off an inch or two or their favorite orchid looks like it needs "talk therapy." The kids at the Downtown Inner City Rec Center are sure gonna miss me—the poor sods whose wrecks of parents barely slow down to drop them off, speed away like it's spring break, 1970. Maybe I'll be forced to quit my "yob" as a runner or waiter at an upscale Brentwood or Hollywood eatery: well, at least the bus boys and barbacks and hostesses'll only take two secs to say goodbye to: shorter time than the time it took

to tell the unctuous, second assistant "on probation" sommelier off
and fling my apron over his sebaceous, pretentious, French or Greek-
speaking head.

See ya!

Give us a week's worth of rehearsals and an hour and a half *tops*
to pack a bag and load the van and *we're outta here.*

Just to have a few kids come up after the show who wanna tell
you how much they enjoyed your first single, how they called in to
their college radio show to hear it, how they lobbied to have you play
the university plaza, the campus pub, the recreation center/alumni
hut. To hear that someone, smiling uncontrollably to get at last to
meet you, who seems like they mean it, who tells you that they drove
across three not-small states to make your gig; that they wanna keep
the beer-sheened set list and buy you breakfast tomorrow before you
both get back on the road. How incomparably gratifying it is to have
a jaded record store clerk-jerk go: "You guys are pretty *good*, actually.
Not bad at all." He's seen The Jam on their first American tour, he had
two tickets to Joy Division's ill-fated first American gig at The Whisky,
he's drunk beers with Bob Pollard, "like, a thousand times back in
Dayton, Ohio," and *he thinks you're worth stocking, your stuff is, that
is.* He'll "set up an in-store next time you guys come through," and "get
your poster up" as soon as he finishes "pricing the imports that just
came in on Tuesday morning." How immeasurably great it is to hear
your song on the radio, even if it's the frequency that only reaches
the dorms and downtown. And to hear it on commercial radio—as
The Weird Sisters have done a few times now, like the time on the
Grapevine? Unparalleled euphoria. How scrumptious to read the
preview review in *The Daily Paper* by the journalist who laughed at
your every joke, your each cute quip. He said you guys "live" were
better than the Pumpkins, The Pixies, The Posies, The Pastels. What
a fucking totally great *writer* that guy is. What a seer, tastemaker,
hidalgo, savant. Guy's a total genius. He knows The Pastels! Him,
you, and fourteen other people. He should write for *Rolling Stone.* He
should be the president. When you are king he shall be deemed poet

laureate and be allowed a harem of women in bikinis who went to the Sorbonne and who not only have great, sprawling collections of obscure and classic post-punk 7-inches, but also, unlike you, actually understand and can talk about Wittgenstein, Derrida, and why people like that awful band Galaxie 500. You felt a fool and ingrate 'cause you forgot to give him a free "T" and one of the special, short-run swirly indigo-and-white vinyl copies of your new single; you remind yourself not to forget to send him one when you get home, put a thank you note inside it with a sticker and some candy for swag.

And the people you meet that you've never met before! How they smile ever so sweetly and bid you welcome as they greet you at their door! How nice they are, what hosts, what sweethearts. They sure are "good people," those people. They give you their floor space, their basement, their attic; their blankets, their pillows, their futons, their sofa beds. The full run of their fully-stocked Westinghouse or Ice King. The Maytag, no less. You can wash and even dry your road-grubbed clothes! They'd even let you date their daughter if she wasn't still a virgin/just a freshman/in a coma/on the track team/ off at a Fire Camp for Repeat-Offending Juvenile Delinquents. They bring out the jollified best in you as you laugh off last night's "very off" gig. A really rotten show, it was; and you get to show that you don't take yourself so seriously while mowing the last of everything in their rumbling refrigerator.

When you leave there's not a leaf left, not a slice of American or crumbly loaf-heel.

They pack you a tasty lunch, and waggishly-adorably put with a purple pencil each of your names all cute on the fresh brown bags. You might as well take it: if you don't, you'll have to stay for lunch as well and you'll miss your next sound check or your meet-up with the Midwest Distribution Rep. Here: take this: just *take* it: it's only deli-quality prosciutto and mozzarella on fresh-baked ciabatta or organic peanut butter and farm-fresh strawberry preserves but it's way better than Winky's, than Arby's, than Wendy's for *sure*.

And yet, you know, it's always a risk, going out on tour. Never fails. You come back and the life you've left behind, metaphorically speaking, is transfigured, and not always or even often for the better. It's like you're Johnny Appleseed—but a Johnny who looks back over at his shoulder at his pillowcase rucksack with all his worldly possessions in it, the whole motif, and just goes "*Fuck* it! The Appleseedster don't need no fuckin' rucksack!" and keeps on walking down the shady lane without it, commando, divested of everything except his essential Johnnyness and the stick the sack was fucking stuck on. Maybe he über-dramatically hoists it into a verdant *arroyo* or from a lofty crag; maybe he just drops it the fuck on the leaf-strewn, stone-cold ground. Whatever. It's gone. And marry-come-up come what may; and a heigh-ho the wind and the rain and the devil take you if you get in my (touring) way.

Rob, for one, had actually lost his little apartment last time we "went out" for a couple weeks: He'd gotten home and his place, a "single" in a particularly malevolent part of North Hollywood, close to our rehearsal studio, was "out the window." Two months late on three months' worth of back rent and the *dueno* had changed the goddam locks on him, brassy Kwikset deadbolt, knob, and all. The old joke about "What do you call a drummer without a girlfriend? *Homeless*" applied to indigent bass players as well. And as he was "currently unencumbered," fresh out of a domicile he most certainly was to boot. Poor Rob. He'd had to move in with some of the young bucks and bright sparks on his softball team—a buncha guys, maybe four in all, who lived in a two-bedroom in Woodland Hills and who worked as little as possible (and in the movies, usually, as grips, sound guys, production assistants, and art department gofers) and who bet on sports to make extra money. This group of insouciant dufuses was nearly as down-and-out as Rob was: they'd flaked one too many times on the electric bill, rubberized too many checks, Rob said, so Water & Power had shut the juice off for good. Cleverly, the enterprising fellas had run a monster orange extension cable from their opaque kitchen window to the laundry room of their complex in order to keep Cable TV going so that they could watch the games they capriciously bet (and mostly lost) on. They were, some of them, electricians on movie sets, after all, so rigging up the illegal power source was cinchy as could be. At night they just sat in the dark, by the light of the gargantuan telly, curtains closed like blacked-out London windows circa World War II, pounding countless beers and sending up spectacular parachute-clouds of potent pot—sat in the dark so that the live-on-premises manager wouldn't bust them for nicking the complex's precious electricity. Hoping he, the manager, wouldn't spot the silver gaffer tape dully gleaming on the hot eaves and the bright line snaking out the dusty-cloudy, maculate laundry room window. You should've heard how they'd have to scream quietly when a team they bet on scored a touchdown or a three-pointer at the buzzer to beat the spread. You should have seen the blue-hued, ballooning clouds of dope smoke that diffused beautifully as they eddied 'round the swirling ceiling fan with its terribly tacky ornate lightbulb holders (now retired) and scraggly-looking chain. The thick black theatre curtains, more spoils ostensibly purloined from some "set," helped as well to squelch the yelps and cheers and sporty groans. I went over there just once, just to witness it, them, these glorious couch-jockeys watching "the game." And the place itself, which Rob himself (no great friend to hygiene—they were more like acquaintances) called "The Pubic Palace" on account of…well, you figure it out, reader, and try not to cringe or wince, okay?

Poor Rob. And yet somehow not so: for whenever he talked about his salad days with the softball team (it only took him a couple of dark and desperate months to eventually get a normal place with normal roommates and legitimate electricity), he'd wax almost wistful, affecting the devil-may-care attitude that when you're that down, with nothing left, really, to lose, it's freeing somehow, and there you are, unfettered, no lower to go. Without more than the littlest hint of irony he called it one of the most amazing and downright interesting periods of his life—even though he slept, I swear to God, *in the hall closet* of the damn place, and had no more than one, and usually from a fast-food joint, "square" a-day. One of the sports dorks was a handy carpenter on various PBS sets so he tricked it out, the front *closet where Rob slept* (I emphasize this in order to emphasize it), with one sleeping bag down, one sleeping bag up, his Echo and the Bunnymen-issue greatcoat draped over it. The closet itself, you see, the carpenter-chum had customized by reversing the brassy hinges on the flimsy door, then taking a florescent orange claw hammer to the shelves so that six-foot-plus Robert could stretch out in style. With touching solicitude, they, his almost equally-destitute roommtes, would tuck him in by shutting the closet's door for him each night. In retrospect, Rob almost rhapsodized about the whole thing: "There was never a time without a beer in the fridge—or rather the giant icebox we kept in the kitchen. It wasn't really a fridge 'cause we didn't have one on account of the power being off and everything. And you always had someone to watch the game with. Everyone got along so well. It's not just misery but poverty that loves company, I'd say. Nobody bothered to pool the funds to get the LADWP to put the juice back on, but raising money for a twenty-four-pack of Bud from the close-by Ralph's was totally cake," he said with an aw-shucks smile. Jenny and Raleigh and I would just shake our incredulous heads, but a part of me, and not a little one, could see where he was coming from. Urban camping. Suffering for your art. Waking up so down, with no lower to go, as down as down could be, every day an arduous adventure in getting by, getting through the difficult day, living well to make it through another rather challenging one and chug a frosty-cold "cold one" at the end of it and maybe take a wake-and-bake bong rip to begin. I had lived it myself, a similar suchlike nightmare/dream, before I'd moved in with Jen, that is. Had that beachside Santa Monica one bedroom I shared with my old bud Jaz: I knew well what squalor was. It was an old pal, that's for sure; an old acquaintance unforgot. It was too utterly absurd for *anyone* in their mid-to-late twenties in the early mid-nineties in Los Angeles with an almost-college education and no major head wounds or acid flashback problems to live that way, but all over the city there were people trying to "make it" as directors and rock stars and actors and stuff who lived downtown in dusty squats or stuffed into ramshackle Silver Lake houses in the hills where people kipped on tatty wood floors with just tatami mats or sleeping bags between them and a million slivers springing forth from them, in cold water flats in industrial North Hollywood.

Some of Rob's catch-as-catch-can softball slacker-buds actually had impressive degrees and things from Dartmouth and Penn and places like that. Well maybe not *Dart*mouth and Penn but Swarthmore and NYU and SMU and whatnot. RISD certainly. UMASS or somethin'. Reed. It was like they were squatting, but legally; hanging with the lads; laughing off imponderable improvidence and white collar squalor; competing to see who could take the longest no-hot-water shower with a bar of soap the size of a sucked-on after-dinner mint. Rob, oddly, was a sort of natural philosopher about it. He was right there with Hamlet, living out "The readiness is all" motif. The slings and arrows of outrageous musician-related misfortune: the fact of him living in a closet he accepted with hubris-free resignation and bemused stoicism. Maybe it was just a front but I don't know; some people truly *do* shrug off what The Fates and Furies bring, with an honest-to-goodness don't-care-i-tude that's real, sincere. If Plato's right that all men aspire to harmony and order, then there thrived indeed—the way *I* saw it—a sort of unique order and harmony at The Pubic Palace that had to do with how many greasy pizza boxes were allowed to pile up before the stacked trash seriously *had* to be taken out, out to the crazy Valley alleys where the black-and-blue community rubbish bins lived, tucked away from the mad swish of traffic on Ventura, Roscoe, Riverside, Van Owen; an order and harmony that had to do with whose turn it was each night to man the couldn't-be-more-black curtains and notorious orange cable like a participant in an on-land regatta so that the ethics and traditions of serious, couch-bound sports-spectating could merrily carry on apace.

This last time after touring all of us (except Jenny of course and probably Raleigh—which I guess just means half of us) came back broke as fuck—even though, as I've illustrated earlier, the band did pretty well, really, financially-speaking.

And tragically, that time, to make ends meet, to not sink, to not have to break down and lugubriously ring up his mom and dad in posh La Jolla, Rob had even "had" to sell a beautiful maple bass guitar with a *sweet* rosewood neck and ornate inlay 'round the soundhole. A super nice acoustic one, it was—Martin & Co., vintage of course, expertly crafted for maximum, buttery playability, and more deeply sonorous and sexy than the voice of Zeus or Theresa Russell after several cocktails. Unfortunately, it wasn't *his* bass that he'd had to pawn. Oh no. The thing had belonged to the old landlord who'd kicked Rob out. Rob had borrowed it from the guy, just to check it out, jam around on it for a bit in his living room, fool about with it and play some Doors songs with his friends, these "cats" he used to be in a stupid cover band with. He'd checked it out; now he was checking it *in*—in to a tawdry pawn shop run by a one-eyed Tasmanian or something, some drooling usurer with a smell about him and abundant hairs screaming from not-well-placed face-moles and flaring nostrils. Rob always hoped (against hope, of course) to get enough "scratch" together so that he could get the instrument out of hock and give it back to the guy 'cause they'd been pretty good friends, actually. Well, friends before the guy had swapped out the locks and left Rob roofless, all of his possessions flung out on the strip of palely sunburnt lawn in front of his "unit."

He wasn't a bad or particularly amoral guy at *all*, Rob wasn't—not in the slightest. He meant so well, never wanted to screw anybody over ever. Or almost never. Mostly. Who knows, really. And do intentions count toward morality? (Discuss with examples from ethics, philosophy, religious studies, fiction, poetry, moral essays, maxims, your gran, Miss Manners, Emily Post, et alia.) It was just that Rob was, well, a goddam *musician*. Didn't Mommy warn you? Haven't you learned *your* lesson by now? It was one of the ineluctable hazards of the so-called trade. You're friends with a bass player in an up-and-coming indie band—uh, *don't lend him ruddy* squat *if he's about to go out on tour.* Not even if he's the pastor of your parish or whatnot, some kind of certified moral authority or guru or saint or part-time kindergarten teacher. Not everyone, but some people who come back from being on the road have a sort of *sauve qui peut* attitude. What Rob did, ripping the guy off like that?—drag but, like, what can you do? Hang it up and go slave nine-to-five for "The Man"? Buy a tie rack and work out your 401K (whatever *that* is)? Get a haircut, a night job, a time card, a straight job? Sooner the rack and *screw* than the revolving bedroom-closet tie rack. Sooner a bout of water torture (seawater version), being hanged by the thumbs, beaten on the feet, head plumped into a stone-cold vise, the tessellated type.

Rob wasn't the worst, though, of the scamming musician scammers who scammed scammy scams. This *one* guy, Paul Small, a frontman/friend in Rob's old band, the cover band? He *actually bought life insurance policies from Stage Six AIDS patients.* Imagine the audacity. Just think of the unconscionability. Another guy we casually knew from "the indie scene" in LA at that time intercepted and cashed his neighbor's unemployment checks. His name was David D. Davis and happenstance or the gods above had placed a guy named Davis D. David right next door in The Fairfax District, on Orange Grove. Unreal. Unreal that the guy who was getting ripped off left and right but mostly right never found him out. Unreal.

One chick, another freelance bass player/actress friend of Rihannon's—Veronika-with-a-"k" or something, this really tall girl of Russian extraction with an orchid-beautiful face and freakishly crazy and scary-beautiful swimming pool-blue eyes and only a trace of a fucked-up accent (so sexy), got this dubious thing called "Stress Disability" where she just claimed her job was too much for her; so they sent her to a quack shrink and the quack shrink vouched that the big, bad work world *was* too much for her, much too much; he checked a box or something on a questionnaire. End result: they paid her *not to work* on account of the stress the work caused her when she had to work, or even if she *thought about* the idea of *thinking* about going back to work, was too much for Veronika-with-a-"k". She'd worked for six months straight with a labor lawyer on how to work out working the system so she'd not have to work. And it worked, her scam. Nice work, Veronika. Nice job. Nice going.

We ribbed Rob ambivalently about it every once in a while, the pawned bass, the complete Hackabout story, joshed him about how we'd have to keep an eye on *our* stuff when he hadn't had a job in a while or had just got off tour. He always got this infinitely sorry/ fucked/guilty look on his face as if to say "I know! I'm so so sorry I had to do that, but...but...I mean...like...I had to. I'll get it back to him one day. One day, man, I'll make it up to him. If the pawn shop hasn't sold it yet, you know. I mean, it's only been six months on a...oh *shit!*" NB how Rob said "I had to do that" instead of "I'm sorry I did that," and note how we invariably let ourselves off the hook, how language comes to our "aid" somehow so that we can live with ourselves, save face. And it's funny, isn't it, how for someone who's close to you, when they do something that's kinda/sorta minorly morally reprehensible, your affection for them isn't diminished in the slightest. Maybe it chips away a bit at your respect for them, but respect's trumped by affection every time. At least with me it is. Perhaps on account of the multiplicity of sins I hope to be forgiven for. Raleigh, who'd call you out on the most ticky-tack things—a cereal box not properly sealed or if you moved his floor tom a centimeter back—just looked at Rob like he was even more endearing on account of his follies and transgressions. But if it had been anybody else but Rob who'd perpetrated such a thing, Ral'd probably call them "the lowest of the low" or "a total sleezeball" or a "scumbag-and-then-some." And Jenny (who had a very *laissez faire* attitude toward what others did that bordered on nihilism, or at least was profoundly pessimistic or maybe just apathetic) just went into denial mode, like she'd just rather forget she ever heard about it, the bass-selling incident. For Jenny's was a very live-and-let-live sort of sensibility, I think—*she* wasn't judging—maybe because as a piano prodigy child and all, she was always herself being judged like hell—by panels and peers and scholarship committees, eccentric/exclusive piano-teaching despots of draconian notoriety; by audiences at scary-hushed recital auditoria; and by Daddy: her first teacher and personal ogre.

In one of the first radio interviews we ever did, Rob talked about his "powerless" days. We were in the broadcasting studio at some kinda big radio station in the middle of Middle America—Bakersfield, actually—and the DJ, when our time was up and the mics were off, asked us about life in LA as an LA band and Rob told the guy (and the three of us) this: "Those times when I lived in a closet were totally 'gnarly,' actually! I was of course totally bummed and weirdly not. What can you do? I have these friends—they're amazing. You realize LA, for a city as completely deeply shallow as it is, has people who are *the* greatest, do-anything-for-you friends—who are amazing. I kind of got into it: I mean, I was living in a *closet! I know*—right? Ridiculous. Like, you look around and go—*me? Really?* This is what my life is right now? No. Can't be. This is not what my high school guidance counselor and I talked about. [Ha-ha-ha's from everyone. Then Jenny going: 'She *should* have!' Then more ha-ha-ha's] This is definitely not what I went to junior college for almost six years for. Not at all. But it was somehow just so funny. There wasn't anything I could do about it, really. I wasn't going to quit music and move back *home*, that's for sure. I mean, I had a roof over my head. A, like, six foot by three foot roof. I kind of had to just go with it. I can laugh about it now 'cause I don't (currently) *live* in a closet. [Ha-ha-ha's redux] I *could*, though. It could happen again. I hope it *doesn't* but, you never know. It's kind of like a *surf* mentality and as you know I grew up surfing, living in Huntington before my family moved to San Diego, La Jolla, actually? I definitely saved money living there 'cause, like, what female's gonna wanna go out with a guy who has come that low? None. Zero. So I didn't have any problem with dates 'cause I wasn't getting any [insert 'Aw's' from the band and interviewer here]. Maybe if *we were a bigger band* [and here Rob looked at me as if to jocularly say: "Hey, John, get on that, wouldja? The making us *huge?*] I wouldn't be facing the prospect of coming back from a tour again and having to reside in a closet the size of, um, *a closet!* These guys [us, he indicated] know that I lived on a boat when I played in a cover band—that was almost smaller. Though I must admit it was a *bit* more enticing asking a girl to come back to my boat as opposed to 'Hey, wanna come back to my place—it's kinda small, though. Surprise! It's a *closet!*' Pretty funny. Not many girls are gonna go for that. No matter how drunk at a beach party. I told the others when I joined The Weird Sisters that that was exactly the kind of guy I am—the kind who plays music in order to meet chicks. (Though not really. I just like saying that 'cause those guys [and here Rob looked at Jen and me] are so *arty*. This was when it was just me and John and a drummer called Walter. These guys tease me about it but, hey!—*whatever!* I don't see anything wrong with meeting girls if you can meet them.) Anyway, the *cover* band I was in in the eighties, unlike my *current* band, made money. I made a living at it, playing music. A sort of one, I guess. Yeah, actually: I got by for sure. It was a drag for sure but still kind of fun. For sure a *super* down time in my life—but this tour is cool, you know. The West Coast. Seattle and back. And Bakersfield—when would I ever get to see Bakersfield?! That's pretty nifty for a guy who grew up playing the same Beatles and Doors and "My Sharona" at fern bars in the OC! All I want to do is rock and hang with my friends, anyway. Drink beer. Have a good book to read. That's basically it. Meet a nice girl with a trust fund. Haha! She doesn't have to be nice—just beautiful! And with a trust fund. Hahaha! Pretty basic. I had my bass and my surfboard and my books and my friends. Pretty cool. Sure: from sleeping in a closet I sometimes woke up looking like one of the figures in the early chapters of an anthro text, but still. It was like being on tour, I guess. Except I never went anywhere except to look for work or to the 7-Eleven on the corner to get a coffee or a six-pack. It was like being on tour without going anywhere or having to play any shows. One thing I will always remember is when three or four of us guys who weren't working that day (there were a lot of days like that then) would go get lunch at Shakey's for the "Buncha Lunch Special" where it's all-you-can-eat of this greasy pizza and over-fried chicken and I *think* it was spaghetti for somewhere around five or six bucks?

Oh my God. We were like these *food-Vikings* or something! The look of the people on the faces who were working there when we'd come in! Total terror. At the end of it, one guy would have an entire pizza or a chicken bucket down his pants to take home and another guy a tableclothful of those potato wedges they have? There were times when they just let us have the whole place. Like, cleared it out, almost. Hilarious. And at the end…and they would get so confused by the time we were outta there that they'd only charge us—seven guys or so—for one or maybe two Buncha Lunches. Hey! You guys here at the station don't have a lunch buffet set up for us or anything, do you?"

There's a Rob monologue, for ya. There you have him. That's Rob.

He was quite a smart guy who, thus far in life, had done the least possible that he could do. You know people who say routinely: "Well, it was the least I could do"? Trying to play down the fact that they'd done something heroic like throw some sand on top of a little's girl's hair that'd caught fire at a beachy barbeque birthday party? Well, Rob did that. Seemed to live that phrase, I mean. He frequently said: "It was the least I could do. And I *always* do the least I can do."

He was quite a smart guy who had been a dumb kid who did dumb, dumb-kid things. He'd joined a rich-kid church group by the shimmery South Orange County sea and corrupted them and sold them pot for a while, just his junior year of high school, that was all. He'd had a threesome with "two twins," [*sic*; though he knew he was making a funny malaprop/pleonasm when he sometimes, you could tell, deliberately "redundanted" like that]. They were these Barbie-blonde friends of his fabulous actress sister Rihannon, *and he'd gotten both of them pregnant!* (Not many did he tell about this by the way, and Jenny and me in confidence, so please be discreet.) He'd started a fire in junior high drafting class, put out a "slow" kid's right eye with a slingshot (he was nine, and hadn't meant to, of course, it was an accident; they were just fooling around). He'd gotten kicked out of junior college (long story—but who succeeds in *doing* that?) *twice*, thrown a TV out a fifth-storey hotel window (not his window, not his TV), nearly died bodysurfing a fifteen foot swell at the world famous

"The Wedge" in Newport Beach, been arrested by mistake, twice in the same night, *in Mexico*; had two separate girls at a dance club pour two separate drinks over his one head *in the course of one night*: and both girls had mistakenly taken umbrage at some less–than-gallant thing that Rob hadn't done! (There was this grabby Rob-alike, apparently, at the club the same night). He had gotten a DUI from The Harbor Patrol *while sailing* (so I guess that'd make that an *S*UI), been fired or laid off from four and a half jobs in five years (though, to his credit, he almost always got another lousy crummy one right away), and had had—though he would never in a million years let you know it—his giant heart crushed by sundry sad-sack strippers, slumming preppies, law students and legal assistants, actresses, more strippers (which was weird 'cause he never seemed to *go* to strip clubs. He would just *meet* them randomly and all: at the supermarket, or in line at the DMV or neighborhood Koffee Klatch or whatever).

He'd had sex with a *midget*. (He would never ad*mit* that she was a midget, this midget he'd had sex with, but I saw her—she *was*. Totally dwarf. Pretty darn close-to six-foot-three-when-he-stood-up-straight, Rob had fallen madly in love with a chick who in high heels was four-seven at *best*, I swear. This Asian chick who was, admittedly, uncommonly elfin and beautiful in a way only Asian girls can be, but *way* too portable, if you know what I'm saying. He called her, not maliciously, "The Spinner." She had a voice higher than Bob Marley times Cheech and Chong. He'd brought her to to one of our gigs. She stood on a kelly green plastic chair near the soundman's sound board and watched him, Rob, him and him alone, it seemed, intensely, with humongous eyes, like she thought he might put down his bass at any minute and run away and she'd have to go sprint-toddling after him and bring him back. When they broke up a few months later, she'd tried to kick him, missed, and ended face down in a muddy puddle, Rob'd reported. "She nearly drowned," Rob said with a straight face as all of us busted up, doubled-over.

He considered that he'd saved her from drowning. But of course he didn't crow about it: it was the least he could do to pull her up by her tiny-little spinner-torso and dinky spinner-armlings.

"What do you mean, exactly?" Raleigh had naively, unimaginatively asked, when "The Spinner" came up one afternoon in one of those bandly conversations you're always seeming to have—when you're in one, that is, sitting around before a gig or taking a break from flogging some new song in your dimly-lit rehearsal space. "She was like a gymnast or something?..."

"A *spinner*," Rob'd replied, like, *You've really never heard that term before?* "*You* know, Raleigh: a petite little girl you can just sort of...spin a*round* when you're...*you* know..." Rob had explained, making great fun of himself as he pantomimed "having" a pretty little girl by her Ripley's-tiny hips; he told stories about himself as though he wasn't he, Rob did, as though he were talking about some *other* sap; he made a motion like turning around a girl from the "girl-on-top" position to the "reverse-girl-on-top" sex position by way of mimely illustration.

"Sor*ry* I *asked*," Raleigh laughed dryly, uncomfortably. I don't think he liked to think of Rob having sex with someone—it was, for Raleigh, like picturing your parents or something. "Gosh, Rob. Wow."

"Don't be!" said Rob.

"Is she actually...?" Jenny had softly ventured.

"She's not a midget," Rob said quickly, patly. His head went slightly back like someone was about to foxy box him right smack in the face, then his chin sort of jutted, his lower lip distended defensively, as he tilted his head just discernibly. "*Or* a dwarf—if that's what you're thinking...*John!*"

"*Totally* a midge," I kiddingly contradicted him. "*Full* midgetby. Bang on. All the way. At Disneyland, you wouldn't be able to take her on..."

"I'm *not* going out with a midget," Rob'd protested, incredulously and unconvincingly as well, laughing at himself as per usual, and at me and my silliness, as well. "I mean, I wasn't. I think we might have broken up, unfortunately."

"Of course you're not," I had backed off, biting my lip, tongue, too, but only metaphorically. "Of course she's not, I mean. She's really actually quite pret…that's too bad, Rob."

"Of course not," Jenny had added, giving me a scalding, scolding look. "She's just really…"

"She was just a spinner," Rob sighed. "Like I said."

"Exactly," Jenny'd said, her big, soft eyes getting smaller, softer. "Uh-huh. You're not going *out* with her; you're just *spinning* her."

And at that, Jenny's funny joke, the four of us busted up like you *would* believe if you've ever, and you have, I'm sure you have, found yourself not being able—no matter how hard you try—to stop laughing.

"You guys are unbelievable," Raleigh had added after we'd finished. "Just…unbelievable."

"Thanks, Ral," I said.

"You don't even want us to start in on *you*, Raleigh. I mean…" Rob said chummily, ostensibly relieved that the conversation had swerved away from his curious love life.

"No, I *don't*," Raleigh retorted. "Sometimes the way you guys talk about women is…"

"You don't mean *me?!*" Jenny said.

"You es*pec*ially, Jen," Raleigh kidded and offered Rob a bag of chocolate-covered pretzels. "Mmm?"

"Yeah, right," Jenny countered.

"Yeah, Jenny," Rob joined in. "You're kind of misogynistic, sometimes, I noticed," Rob jested, peering into the Ral-proferred bag as Ral dispatched a three-hundreth-or-so mondo-pretzel. Then Rob got a look on his face like he was having to make a very important decision, like where to go back to finish college or what to have for lunch; and his hand danced above the bag like some move a Hindu dancer might make in silhouette for an audience of Brahmins or foreign dignitaries.

"You guys are completely ridiculous," Jenny laughed lightly, then shook her head "mmn-mm" as Raleigh held the colorful navy blue and old gold bag forward, toward her, and shook it about a touch.

"*You're* the one who famously said that the one thing that women have in common with men is that they both like the company of men!" I chimed in.

"I did?" Jenny said.

"Yep," I said.

"I don't think she meant *us*, though," Rob laughed.

"Definitely not," Raleigh said through his food. "Def-in-it-ely not us in the *slight*est."

"Oh, *give* me one of those," Jenny said and everyone sort of tittered.

One

aleigh was the first one back to the van the Tuesday afternoon I'm telling you about, the day of the report of Cobain's demise. He was ready to go when I'd finished pumping and paying; Rob had, as I mentioned, come back a bit earlier (with an armful of glittering aluminum junk-filled mini-bags stuffed with crackling crunchy salty/sugary snacks) but then he went back into the store to buy more, or get water, or to use the loo again, or go 'round the corner of the store in order to light a furtive cigarette on account of he had quit smoking, but not really, not on the road, at least. When McLeary, our old producer, had hectored us all about being incorrigible carnivores, Rob, in the nicest, most fond-of-irascible-McLeary way, had said: "Okay, I'll quit. But not eating meat. I'm not going to do *that!* I'll quit smoking instead. That will be my personal protest against all those reasons you gave for why the planet is fucked because of McDonalds and Burger King."

Rob had "quit" smoking at home in LA, basically, there exclusively, is what I am trying to say here. After the gigs on this jaunt up to Seattle and back, he'd bummed so many smokes from me that I had to tell him, "Um, these things don't grow on trees, Rob!" in a mock-petty-but-I-really-mean-it sort of way. Rob had given me a whole fresh pack of Marlboro Lights—tamped it down and the whole motif—the night before in Berkeley; he'd taken one out and comically held it up for my approval of his purloining it; I didn't really care. Rob was so funny about smoking; he knew he didn't look like one, a smoker—too All-American and happy-seeming; people who didn't know him were always mildly surprised to see him bob off to the far corner of a backyard at a house party and light up a Camel with that one-hand-cupping motion. Seeing him with a smoke was like catching your Jack LaLanne-ish dad or Fred MacMurray having a fag on the sly. "I don't look at all like a guy who would smoke," Rob opined every once in a while. "People are always surprised when I ask them for a light."

Any old way, I'd slid in and "removed quickly" the Vegas Gold-colored record company credit card (there's an actual color called "Vegas Gold," by the way; how odd is that?) and punched the right buttons and waited for the receipt. Jenny loved and frequently remarked upon the wonderfulness of the fact that filling stations had pumps nowadays that required *no human interaction*. I loved it when she said snarky stuff like that. Stuff like what you'd expect a quasi-misathrope's very own favorite über-babe *to* say.

I was sitting waiting in the front seat when Ral shoulder-shoveled open the sliding side door. I made a somewhat-anxious steeple of my fingers and looked back at him as he packed his carcass back into the back seat. There were just the two of us; now was the time; I had to say something, despite the sitch being both ghastly and appalling.

"Raleigh," I said, all serious-remorseful, turning toward him, but not all the way. "*Listen*, okay? I'm really sorry about the way I bit your head off back there—I really am. About the tape. I shouldn't have. It was just I…I shouldn't have reacted like that and…look: I'm sorry I was so harsh."

He made some faint noise like breathing puffily out the side of his mouth or spitting out a little fleck of oregano that had stuck in his teeth after a battle with some spaghetti.

"I mean it," I said, quick as a mad bull charging (as another really big, fat big rig farted fatly by). "I shouldn't have chastised you so badly. I shouldn't have said that. Made those, um, recriminations. That was wrong. And I'm sorry about Kurt Cobain, too. I know he was one of your…"

"It's okay," Ral said, leaning forward like someone pushing an overloaded shopping cart, the ice in his Big Gulp sloshing discernably. "Forget it. It's all right, John. All right?"

He picked up from under the bench seat one of his appalling, imponderable barbells and started doing some easy, gentle reps while simultaneously sucking on his soda straw; and as Jenny and Rob came back with an opaquely milky and diaphanous plastic bag loaded with winking Cokes and Arrowhead waters, I got out and decided I'd use the loo "just in case" before we got back on the awful 5 and braved the preposterous "five o'clock" LA and OC traffic for our meeting with our record label before the last gig of the run that night in Orange County at this place called The Doll Hut—a sink of iniquity if there ever was one.

I had been there once to see some gig and it'd been kinda… grubby, with longhaired castoff be-tatted, be-pierced veteran punk-rock-mostly types and grubbers kinda just stumbling and bumbling around and bouncing off each other: the kinda bar that's the antithesis, in a way, of the bar where everyone knows everyone else (and where it's so dark that your toes are accosted by a black-painted step up to the stage that you don't see and thus go flying with your arms out like a banshee).

This would be the sort of roistering soak-magnet of a rathskeller where, by the end of the night, *no one knows his own name,* instead of "everybody knows your name," as the wildly-popular contemporaneous TV jingle-thing goes. This was a bar where clusters of people clustered knowing none of the other clusters—and having no intention of clustering together at all.

So Raleigh sat seething, kidding himself that he was okay with me, 'cause if he didn't tell himself that he'd have to face the fact that he's a petty, petulant, unforgiving, grudge-bearing fuck who can't accept someone's apology for hurting him—or can't deal with the fact that he *can* be hurt. Some people really are like that, you know. Raleigh's physiognomy says it all: he's kind of a baby-faced guy, or fox-faced guy, or baby fox-faced guy, unthreateningly handsome and, curiously, fascinating to a certain kind of woman who is, somehow, programmed to be vulnerable to his pointy-faced, smiley-faced, fox-baby-faced or whatever charms.

I don't know why, but just then I drifted away in my mind to this husky-voiced, super preppy, sort of wonderfully beautiful tomgirl I briefly dated in college. You know her, you two've met: she's the super-cute *brunette* who could drink you under the table, match you beer-for-beer, and who starred on the field hockey or lacrosse team at her outrageously expensive boarding school. The one whom you couldn't believe everyone at your college or university wasn't rushing, didn't think she had just *the most heartbreakingly pretty face.* How could she not be Alumni Week Queen or Laurel Princess! How come no one's flung her the keys to the city or let her cut the ribbon to the new Harbor Pump? How come no one seems to *notice* this girl?! She looks so tall—even though she's really not. How does she do that? Her vocabulary's just amazing. A self-described, "full-on word-weenie." (You don't want to *know* her verbal SATs.) Her conversation is so very excitingly all-over-the-place: moreover, would you get a load of her in those white jeans/that prim bun she's pulled her great, straight hair back into. Molly, Muffy, Maddy or Mallory—the whipsmart one who triple-majored in French, art history, and "Quarters." The one who makes you laugh like hell, who looks so prim and adorable in her Fair Isle sweater and nice tight corduroys, or sweatpants and Weejuns, especially when she burps like an eighth grader when you chug "glugs" with her after afternoon classes on Wednesdays and Fridays. She's the collegian who gets sort of honorarily adopted by some fraternity without her ever having rushed a sorority, or even stepping foot inside a one. Or if she did rush one, she's the one who's just done it because she's a legacy (Delta Gamma or Pi Phi only, please) and she never goes to any of the functions hardly except her "Monday Night Meetings."

As far as your romance with her goes, she was scrupulously truthful when it came time for her to end it with you at the end of fall semester. Your last semester in college! Hers, too—on the five-and-a-half-year-plan, on account of she had to take time off for skiing the Alps or trekking in Pakistan. She told you all along she was just looking for friend-sex, wasn't into something serious, wasn't looking for an attachment of any kind or for a boyfriend because, hello, like *duh, she already has one.* He goes to Williams, to Penn, or to Princeton; to Georgetown or Wheaton or Amherst or Emerson. He's waiting for her to join him so that they can live out their super-privileged lives in an L.L. Bean or J. Crew catalogue/at a beach house in Maine/or in "good old" The Hamptons or Pawtucket. Why do you look so sad, so lachrymose—having to say goodbye to her at graduation? You knew she was going on to grad school back East next fall, maybe joining Chip, Skip, or Tripp in Oxford for his Rhodes Scholar *annus mirabilis.* She was just having fun—and so were you! And it was! It *was* fun. So fun.

Of course you're sad; you've never met anyone like her and you're young enough to think that she's the last girl you're going to meet who's quote-unquote unlike anyone you've ever met.

Dammit!

Here she is: I can't forget her and I don't want to. You were so great, Molly, Muffy, Maddy, Mallory. So cute and such a "one-of-the-guys"—but one of the guys you'd really like to, um, fuck. Really like to fuck.

That didn't come out right. Oh well. Here's she, *her*, M, as she remains in my head, in my memory, the über-girl you wished was your collegiate sweetheart but whose heart was elsewhere—though her willing, supple, nubile, surprisingly plump-busted body was oh-so near.

When she felt like it, that is.

Here she is; she playfully touches your sleeve or your thigh (if you're sitting with her, just you two, away from the once-a-preppy-always-a-preppy throng) as you two talk at a party or at her place; she uses your Christian name so much it hurts. You know how you never tire of a pretty charmer/super stunner using your name? Well, Muffy/Molly/Mary, et alia *over*used it.

Here you go:

"John, the sex was nice—great—amazing. So wild and lovely while it lasted. [Voice way lowered here, so as not to be overheard by the older people at her very small, very elegant and casual-for-preps soiree/graduation party] I mean, the time we did it in my mom's sauna, on the rooftop of the art department, *and* on the polo grounds that *one* night, and then on the sink in your roommate's bathroom when you lifted me and couldn't get my Lantz off! Oh my *God!* John! Amazing! And what about the time in my convertible Karmann Ghia when we went beach/overnight/car-camping—I know that *that* is something I will never quite forget! Thank you truly so much for that. You made me laugh at how many layers I had on as you put yourself inside me through my shunted pink panties, the ones with pale green piping? You did! [whispers even softer here]: That was *terribly* sexy, John. How frolicsome we were. There's no harm done—Tripp, Chip, or Skip sees other people, too; we're both too young to settle down—at least until we're twenty-eight-or-seven and done getting our educations. And *listen*—you're *sure* to meet someone better, less crazy, less *je-ne-sais-quoi*, someone who will love you like I never could or can. I'm sure of it, hon. Less off her trolley. Remember Fassbinder? That film of his we saw called *Liebe ist als Kalter der Tod?* So good, that film. And how true that phrase is. "Love is as something-or-other as death." I wish I'd keep up my German. Oh well. And besides, you yourself are off to England again anyway, aren't you, John! For how long? Nine months? John, John!—that's gonna be *so* amazing, John-John! Do you have any idear how a*maz*ing that's going to be? You don't want me, anyway. Not *really*. My butt's so fat this year from all those cheddary *nachos* you force-fed me. Just look at it! (Don't look at it!) I know you always liked it [even more heartbreakingly pseudo-intimate whisper here]. You'd be bored with me if we were actually... *you* know...oh yes you would. Please don't ever forget "our Wednesdays." Fridays, too, sometimes, huh. Ah! Those were just so very great. I can't believe you—the way you let me put on Bowie's *Low* each and every time. I don't know why I love that record so. Why I love to you-know-what to it! Ha! And why it was the only album I ever wanted seriously to drink beer to as well. I'm strange, I know. It was either that or *Here Come the Warm Jets*, right? You always said I was the only girl you knew—or ever *would* know, probably—who even knew who Brian Eno *was*. How funny. How can anyone go through life without him, I'll never know. All the Roxy Music stuff too! Wow! So good. I mean, *any*way...well. And...where was I, anyway? Have I had that much to drink?! John, don't let me drink so much! Oh! Listen: the future girlfriend you're gonna have? Just make sure she's *not* N.O.K.D., okay? Just kidding. I'm sure she'll be an angel. Involved with all things eleemosynary. President of her chapter and a model and actress and Rhodes Scholar or something. Ballerina. Beautiful *and* a *tiger,* too, if you know what I mean, this new girl who'll take my place in your...let's talk *books*, okay? Did you ever make it through *Ulysses? I* sure didn't. I was so exhausted by *The Magic Mountain* that all I read these days is Cheever. And Sylvia Plath, I guess. She's such a college-girl cliché, though, huh. I'm starting to *hate* her, actually. Seriously! Can't stand that blonde bitch! Hahaha! Time to put away those childish things, I guess—and *authors* too. I can't believe I took a German *Lit* class just for fun my last semester—even though it was "in translation".... The professor kept asking me out to dinner; and I told her, in my awful German, that I was seeing someone! But she just wouldn't listen, dontchuknow! And besides, that whole 'experimental phase' I had was just *so* freshman year and all...oh, John. Oh I so [burp! excuse me!]...I so wish Daddy were here. Not just to see me graduate and all, but so that he could meet you, tell you all about "the old country." Thank you. I miss him every day. Do you want another G and T? I'm waiting a bit before I have around twelve more, I'm telling you. How come I'm so nervous this evening? These *parties* Mummy has! Anyway: Daddy: What's the good of having castles in Killarney if you drink yourself to an early...we Irish, you know. Irish-French-Norwegian, really. Don't worry: I'm not going to cry. Just give me a sec and I'll be okay. I'm not going to cry at my own goddam party. Goddammit, I *promised* myself. Wasn't...thank you. You're too kind, you know...maybe time to retire that good old varsity Lacoste sweater, though, by the by, my dear. You *always* look so good in it, if you know what I mean. Hahaha! Only kidding. Kind of. I had to laugh when I saw that line in *The Official Preppy Handbook*. Ha! That was one of the 'burns' the girls at my old boarding school would use. Hideous, we were to each other. Just the worst. Still, Brooks has such good things after Christmas, you know. Hint! Ask for Merton; he'll take care of you. Get his name right ("Meryton," not "Mer-tin") and he'll treat you like a king. My horrible little brother practically worships him. Did someone introduce you two? He's not really "horrible," actually—just to me. Aren't all little brothers? Does it strike you like it does me? Small parties are so "very," aren't they? Just the right motif. You *have* to meet my grammy. She's French and just a riot. This is all her furniture, you know—the envy of most of Old World Montecito; most of it from the days of the First Republic. It's bad form to point it out, but you *must* inspect the chairs in the library. Even though I can't imagine you would care about such things. Such plush things, so ornate and elegant they are—though I imagine literal *table* talk bores you positively stiff...my God, she's such a scream, my grammy. We all call her "Ma Mère." She's, of course, *very* uppish and strange, but *tres gentile*. So different from the Irish side, my Dad's side, of the family. I wonder what she'll make of you. I told her *all* about you; she insisted I invite you. Writing to her's how I got my French so almost-good. She came all the way from Monte Carlo. Monte Carlo to Montecito. Hahaha! 'Right, *Monty*?' Hahaha! Remember that guy we met at the back bar at the El Encanto?! *Do* you? 'Monty!' Montgomery St. Cloud. That can't have been that guy's real name! What a fake James Bond he was. And who on God's green earth wears an *ascot*

these days? I mean, come on. In California, no less? Wow. Telling us
the diff between Choate and Exeter—as if we care, huh? The guy
thought he was Cary Grant, no less! Hahaha. You were *so* funny and
got *so* plowed you called him "Minty." You don't remember? Then it
was Montly, then *Monsy*. Hahaha! I'll never forget it. You got so drunk
I had to drive…drunk. I think I was. I must have been, I'm sure. My
tolerance for alcohol these days is *frightening*, don't you think? Good
thing I drove, too, huh, John. If *you'd* driven and been pulled over?
Yow. At least I could talk my way out of it to a cop. God knows I've had
the practice. What a wally he was, really! 'Abso*lute*ly, Monty,' you kept
saying. 'Abso*lutely*.' 'You should be in a commercial simply advertising
what a blast it is to be upper class.' That's precisely what you told him.
You did! Honest! I can't believe you don't remember that! I just loved
that. *Quel* motif, for sure, for sure. I thought I'd bust my cocktail dress.
You *know* I'll always keep in touch with you, John—treasure what we
had. I thought that I should tell you that. Uh-huh. I'm off to Sri Lanka
week-after-next. 'For my present'—I didn't mention it? Auntie gave it
to us, me, I mean. Darn. I thought I told you. [Her perfect little nose
goes scrunchy here and makes the archipelago of charming Irish-ish
freckles—there are only a few on her high cheekbones and across the
bridge of that too-cute proboscis—coagulate, unite.] *Heck*, of course
he's going with me. I hope you understand. We've planned this trip for
so long, now. I hope I never ever led you on. I'm rather sure I never
did. Kiss me goodbye now. Take *care* of yourself, anyway. Look after
yourself over there. I'm really going to really miss you: I will. Write to
me from London, won't you? I'm *horrible* at writing back. But you
could've guessed that, huh. And thank you for the book on Yeats! You
remembered that the "Innisfree" is just my favorite poem ever. "Nine
bean-rows will I have there, hive for the honey-bee, and something-
something-something in the bee-loud glade." Beautiful, so beautiful.
How sweet you are, John. Now I wish I'd got you something. I'm really
sorry—completely forgot to. Look: just borrow anything you like
from the library and bring it back never. Ha! There isn't much there
that you haven't read but I do know there's a Lord Tennyson that you

might like. Sorry I didn't get you a present. I'm awful, aren't I? Wait! There's a signed copy of that book *The Pound Era* that Mummy, for godsakes, isn't ever gonna read...Hugh Kenner taught here. Have another canapé! Carl's crabcakes are just divine. They're indescribably delectable. Carl? Oh, Carl? Come over here a second please. Are there more crabcakes? Won't you just pop into the kitchen and see, then have Chalmers bring my friend a few, if there are any? Pretty, pretty, pretty please? Thank you, Carl. (He's getting up there now of course but Mother doesn't have the heart to—you know—let him go.) For four and a half years everyone asked me: 'Why live right next to campus when your family home has so much room?' Well, I'll tell you: it's Carl. Carl's why. If I lived at home I'd be "twenty stone," as the English say. Just enormous.) I'm so glad for you to be going back to England, you know. Another year there—how nice for you! You know what? I think I've lived on chips and salsa, plus beer, of course, for my entire college career! Besides my little sister's living here again. They kicked her out of Ojai Valley School. That girl—she's such a naughty thing. Do you have any idea how hard it is to get kicked out of *Ojai Valley?!* You practically have to burn the place down while blowing the headmaster! How I wish it would rain! Didn't you just love all the rain we got this spring? It's snowing *gobs* back East, you know. I envy all my friends back there...just one more glass of "champers," or should I have just one more beer with you? So many have we had and all. So many Millers, Buds, Coors, Miller Lites, during my 'Miller Lite Phase,' Heniekens, Becks, *Staro*pramen, Czech*var*, Samuel Smith's, Tsing*tao, Guin*ness. Practically 'round the world, we went, beers-wise! You know I love to *day*-drink, don't you? And what *is* it with me and cheap beer, anyway? And good beer too. Maybe I will write to you from Aix, Toulouse or Paris on my—*our*—way back from Sri Lanka. We're not sure where we're going, where we'll inevitably end up. Goodbye, then...yes, I'm sure, I'm sure I love him. Or, at least...please don't *ask* me that right now, okay? He's got way, way, *way* too much money and his horror-family consider me an angel and him a ne'er-do-well of the first water. Hey! Let's try and play some tennis soon.

Before I go, I mean. I don't have much time, but a set or two before I go? I'd love that. Now that the weather's getting better after the weird rains in spring, Mummy's had our clay court seen to. You know how I love to play on clay. And the ones at the club, they don't keep up very well—if you ask *me*. My boyfriend doesn't play, the silly! He's a *golf* guy. Why, I'll never know. Never understand the attraction. "A good walk spoiled" is what I always say. It's not even a *sport*, is it? I mean, someone, by my definition, has to try and *stop* you from doing something for it to be a sport. That's what *I* think, at least. Otherwise, *bowling's* a sport—and you can't be smoking and drinking like a fish and playing a sport at the same time, can you? Oh, that's *your* theory, isn't it? I got that from you. That was your motif. Hahaha! I'm telling you a theory of *yours!* Hahaha! How funny of me to forget and go spouting it at you, Johnny! Mummy would be nothing less than absolutely ec*static* if he and I got married, like, the day after tomorrow or something and I spent the next five years of my life barefoot and preggers with, like, fifty-seven babies running around. She's very tight with his 'people,' as we say. They're cute as buttons, too, even though, as I said, they're horrors, but I don't think I'm even close to being ready for the whole marriage motif. Would *you* be? Hardly, huh. I *know*. I mean, eventually I'm sure I'll want gaggles of little babies and all of that but not before…oh! There's my History of American Painting prof! *Must* say hello to her, okay? I can't believe she came. Listen: Contrary to what you may think, I haven't slept with all that many people. I can count them still on…well, I can't do *that*, but it hasn't been that many. I hope you don't think ill of me, I really don't. Don't give me that look! *Please*, John. Kiss me one last time, okay? Thank you. So sweet. Okay, sure: There *were* a few during sophomore year when Skip, Tripp, or Chip left for school in Nice for the second time, but… And no one after you. God, that'd have been horrid. And I would never tell you, anyway—even though there wasn't anybody, really. God! Why do I keep *telling* you things? I tell you *everything*, don't I? Everything I shouldn't, huh? Haha. Take care, my love. Say goodbye before you leave, okay? Don't take 'French leave' like you and

I always do, okay? I want to kiss you properly goodbye, I do… What's *that*, Mummy? Sorry? What did you say? *Who* is?! He's pulling up the *drive*way?! He's *here?!* I thought you said his flight was cancelled! Ma Mere said…oh, now I get it. You *guys!* Priceless. I can't believe you keep a secret like that…and at my graduation party too! Incorrigible! Oh my gosh! You know how I hate surprises! Even good ones! Right, John? Must rush off to meet him, then. Does my hair look at all okay, my dear? My hair looks kind of flat right now. Flattish, at least. *Oh* my God. Just my luck. Ugh. *Good*bye, my darling. Kiss-kiss, kiss-kiss. Be seeing you!"

Back to Raleigh then. As I was saying. Ral's the girls' man (but not a ladies' man—there's a big big diff), the boy you wish the lumberjack/asshole/commitment-phobe you're currently dating would magically turn into. He remembers not just your birthday but the exact time it was he met you. I mean, two-forty-seven or something. He pets your cat (it lets him, it trusts him instantly)—it's on his lap, they're both of them Cheshire-smiling; he's down on the floor with your dropkick lapdog, your purblind sheepdog, your pooch that looks like someone knitted it for Christmas. He brought lunch to your workplace (of course he made it; it's tuna fish, your favorite), he gave you *the best* backrub you've ever had (and he didn't even *try anything* after), he sent you flowers after you took his blankity blank into your mouth. (You've never done that for anyone before!)

He's so considerate, you could *scream!* He never doesn't wanna go for ice cream or take a walk in a park and "just be together"; or go see a movie where beautiful Julia Robertson, say, plays a beautiful dork or beautiful, dark-haired, charming Hollywood harlot who trips on a sidewalk in Terre-Haute (where her dying family members are) just so that some rich, just-happens-to-be-vacationing-in-Terre Haute hunk of a dreamboat dream-cake can pick her up from the pavement just in time to whisk her off to to the Champes Elysees or the Via Dei Condotti where, as she ugly-ducklings down the lane, wondering if she's actually in love with this studly-goofy Patrick Gere or Richard Swazye, she's accosted by an oracle sort of Tiresias-ish guy with wire rims that give him an owlish aspect and perfect English and an encyclopedic knowledge of the history of all Euro-royal families (played by Gerard Mastrioni or Marcello Depardieu). He pegs her as a secret princess twice-removed or something, the owlman does, and she goes off (reluctantly, mind) to meet her new "people" but they're so not all that marvelous or wonderful—Julia Robertson kind of doesn't like that they shoot the heads off fawns and baby bunnies with powerful, heraldic, gold-flaked rifles and gas-powered crossbows and sip tea and say cutting things in the sixteen languages they fluently speak. So of course, La Julia has a real crisis on her hands here, and comes to realize, like, a whole buncha stuff, and she rushes back (not tripping, not once, signifying she's symbolically "on her feet now") across cobblestone streets as mogully as Mt. Chamonix, only to find Mr. Rightly has left the luxury hotel building—only he's hasn't! He didn't check out! He's right there with a lorry-load of flowers and a twinkle in his already impossibly bright eyes and a nice, big, throbbing, palpable bulge in his immaculate yachting trousers!

"The End."

That's the kind of stuff Ral not only put up with, but checked the times for in the goddam bloody *LA Weekly*.

If you were the girl dating him, not once did you feel like you were imposing or smothering or oppressing someone with your love when you told him "you just kinda wanted to talk"; there's no game on TV he has to watch (he hates sports, in fact: actually makes fun of them, their silly, elastic allegiances and their fans' irrational loathing for players on the visiting team—who used to play, of course, for the home team). Of *course* the sports-prejudice thing has *nothing* to do with the fact that he's not athletic at all, has a sort of doughy quality, and a long, girlish, super-straight, dirty (but not dirty) blonde ponytail perfectly pulled back at all times. He himself looks a bit like a chick—that's what it is! Therefore he gets the chicks (and they're usually pretty pretty—gotta hand that one to him) who deep down would rather themselves *be with a chick*, but they can't on account of they're Catholic or their homophobic Basque gran would just croak if she ever found out that Steph or Bets or Stace or Trace is a "lezzie."

Raleigh looks a bit like a boyishly handsome Danish or Finnish or Latvian zoologist—one who wouldn't hurt a tsetse fly. With his glinting, circular, silver-wire rims and slow, wry, shy smile, he looks like he just got back from a day spa, had a pedicure *and* manicure. He looks way out of shape—but looks can be deceiving. He's incredibly strong. Hits the shit out of the drums. Which, in turn, makes him a big hit when it comes to hitting chicks. He's the drummer, so he's gonna get all the chicks anyway (drummers get *all* the chicks—no one knows why; that's why all the one-liner musician-jokes take drummers as their subject: pure envy), but I have seen him *tête-à-tête*-ing in so many club corners with just *the* prettiest girl in the building, in the entire town, probably. She looks like she just came from being crowned for something (Bean Queen, Harvest Princess, Pumpkin Bunny). She looks like she's just walked in from cutting some fluttering purple ribbon or giving a sesquipedalian pep-speech to the octogenarians at the Rotary Club or the plum-faced Girl Scout troop. She looks just like a younger, taller, prettier version of big-time, A-list movie star Julia Robertson! The people of her little town fête her just because she deigns to breathe the same air they do. Though she's not in the slightest aware she's a knockout. And do you know what he's usually doing, Raleigh? Doing with her? He's drawing with a silver pencil her meticulous portrait in his stippled sketchbook, the one that, like his "hair" bag and barbells, he ports everywhere. He's not going to take her home that night; he wouldn't even dream of it; he's going to listen to her carping about her stupid, immature boyfriend, in fact, tilt his head sympathetically to all she has to say. He's going to get her number, though—*and* her address. He's going to keep in touch with her, all right, call her (from work so he doesn't have to pay for the long distance call) and write to her—long, long letters. What a rarity! No one writes postcards, even, these dark and unromantic days! He's going to invite her to Los Angeles, the big city, Hollyweird, where, coincidentally enough, she's always just *dreamed* of going, offer to squire and show her around, never be more *anything* than fascinating, unless it's more into her than even she is…into herself, that is. Which is a lot. Of course it is! (She's "hot.")

And then he's gonna sleep with her (but not on the first night she's there—oh no, that'd be moving too fast; he'll take the perfectly fine foldout sofa bed, thanks; just cry out if there's anything you need—except carnal relations—and I'll come running). He's gonna make her fall in love with him and leave her hometown honey in the tear-besprinkled small town dust and tarmac. She moves here, gets her own apartment, and he dates her for a "long" time (six months is a long time these days, in relationships)—till "it's not working out any more," till "they both mutually [sic] felt it was time to move on." It's a bit brilliant, how Raleigh operates. You had to admire his strategies and patience, his mono-minded follow-through. There he'd be, three months from the night he'd sketched her, with this total little alterna-Snow White by his side at the Teenage Fanclub gig at the Roxy or the Sonic Youth-curated ArtFag Festival downtown. You go up to his apartment to pick him up for practice (his boat-like, baby blue vintage sixties Merc broke down a*gain*) and there she is, watching jentacular cartoons or coloring comic books and drinking Pepsi and having cereal with him on a latish Saturday morning. Didn't I meet you in Omaha, Orlando, Oakland, or Oregon? Oh! Hi! Now I remember you! You're heartbreakingly beautiful, you know? Do you know that? Uh-huh. Honestly. Easily as pretty as any of the girls here in Southern California. No kidding. You really are. And no, I'm not just saying that. You should be a model, an actress, a hostess, someone's mistress. A hostess at The Playboy Mansion's what I really think I meant. You didn't think that I meant *Carrows?* Oh and just kidding 'bout the actress bit. Ha! We *all* hate actors and actresses 'round here. Oh, sorry. What I meant was we all hate actresses unless you are one. In which case, we love them. And you *are!* How great! How'd they turn out, your most recent head shots/classes in movement/auditions for those Cancer Society infomericials—good? I'm sure you'll be a great one, get an Oscar, go do Shakespeare in the Park, Strindberg at Stratford-on-

Avon, Pirandello-in-the-Projects, Chekhov summer stock, and Pinter in the dead of winter. Next stop—Stoppard! Oh, stop it! Just *stop* it. Talking to myself here, trying to rein me in. Sorry. Got carried away there, positively giddy at the prospect of seeing you again. And with our Raleigh too. You just turned twenty-three, then!? Congratulations. Congratufuckinglations. Sincerely. Completely. Wow. So you kept in touch with Raleigh, eh? How sweet. He drew you, huh? He did? Wow. How interesting. And wouldn't deign to tear the page out and hand it to you, finishing with a flourish, as it were, 'cause he wanted to keep it for himself, yeah? Have something keepsake-like to remind him of you. He *is* so sincere, such a sweetheart, a fairy prince. And *so* funny too—the way he pranks his also-a-drummer-from-Utah roommate on an almost daily basis. Oh, don't I know it! Nice to see you again. Take care. Be seeing you. Ready to get going, Ral? I'll have him straight back soon as rehearsal's over, okay? No after-practice-drinking-bouts for *this* guy. Promise.

Brilliant.

And how do I know all this? Well, Rob of course. Rob told me. They're tight that way, Raleigh and Rob. And Rob and I are, too.

Hey, fellas, hey you young geezers: Want to get chicks? First, get some chicks...no: haha. There I go riffing on the old Steve Martin bit about how to become a millionaire. Okay: listening? Want to get chicks? First: become a drummer. And if you can't do *that*, treat them, chicks, that is, like you are perpetually disinterestedly drawing their portraits. Like nothing matters but what they are saying. Like someone could drop a grenade at your feet but instead of taking the time to go kicking it nonchalantly away you just have to capture gallantly the way their beauteous eyelashes turn up just so, just so *ravishingly* so.

It's such a pother, isn't it, all this pother about getting women? But it's the only pother worth bothering about, sometimes, isn't it?

Right, guys? Right.

Two

LOGBOOK: WITH FIELD NOTES

Friday: Bakersfield: Jerry's Pizza—Seventy-five dollars vs. fifty percent of door after Soundman's one-hundred-fifty-dollar fee; two CDs sold; horrible sound. Thanks, Soundman. Worst sound imaginable. Inconceivably bad. Soundman irascible as all hell. Worst ever. Big surprise. Pretty okay turnout: fifty people, maybe, but no one really seemed to get very into it except two or three guys who stared at Jen, as far as I could tell, from the overlit stage. Until Jen did what I dared her to, which was unbutton her already pretty sheer blouse down to her belly button practically & give the crowd a nice bra-show. Then, all those frat fucks & "country" bumpkins from the pumpkins perked up, all right—not just those initial three "bros"! The Blanched Bats, the openers, were pretty cool & surpisingly melodic for a ragtag, Buzzcock-ish, local-yokel, Bakersfield garage band. And any opener who gives you their CD but insists on buying yours? Golden. Though I'm sure it's not just 'cause they want us to try to get them a gig in LA.

Saturday: Santa Barbara/Goleta: Zelo Bar: Eight-dollar cover: one-hundred-dollar guarantee; one CD sold; great article in The Daily Nexus. Great article in The Santa Barbara Independent. Unfortunately, it, the second article, was on Sloan, the fuzzy/jangly/ kind of catchy Canadian band on Geffen who were playing the other, bigger, better alt-club in town. Hence: crowd of thirty-five or so, including the something-like-fifteen people working there—seven cocktail waitresses, at least, who kept coming up every thirty seconds to see if we wanted a ten-dollar well drink or beer in a Euro-thimble. Very depressing. Nice to see some of our old friends, though—many of whom are still "doing music." Old friends of ours, or of mine, really, The Woodmen, opened: nice, jangly, inoffensive pop with cool Rickenbackers & not-cool Les Pauls. We didn't get the entire "guarantee"—something about some mix-up with the regular sound guy. Big surprise. Ergo, no guarantee. Sound guy got seventy-five of the hundy-spot. Great *gig*, sound guy. You really rocked the house tonight.

Sunday: San Luis Obispo: SLO Brewing Company; Twenty percent of door after Soundman's fifty-dollar fee, Doorman's seventy-five dollar fee; one Weird Sisters T-shirt given away to nice Soundman (nice oxymoron, huh); twelve people total in attendance, twelve paid; should not have worn Clark Kent glasses onstage. Worst gig ever. Worst openers ever, this married couple called The Squallabies whose every song sounded like not a "B" but a "C" side of a James Taylor or Christopher Cross song. Yikes. They took four hours between songs, tuning & talking & putting on & taking off their paisley "hippie capos," those cloth jobs that look like ankle bracelets for stuffed unicorns. One kid bought a 7-inch because he was drunk I think & thought he was at a Dead show or maybe thought he had a shot at Jen—I don't know. Touring's ridiculous, it just dawns on all of us. Me esp. Total haul: fifteen bucks. Horrible. And to think I didn't drink more than one or two pints before this gig 'cause I wanted to be "on." I should've had one or two hundred. Beer there pretty good. Publicist promised us a feature in the college paper, but they cut it, she said, on account of they had to run a story on the Lettuce Festival & a review of Hootie and the Blowfish's sold-out show at the local track or something. Like it woulda helped. San Luis a college town where, curiously enough, people don't seem to be art-inclined or literate at all, but instead concentrate on things like whether The Grateful Dead are gonna play the Lettuce Festival, or whose hog will take the purple at the monthly county fair.

Monday: San Francisco: The Paradise; (plus in-store at Tower Records: 4:00 p.m.); one-hundred-fifty-dollar guarantee; six CDs sold; two T-shirts; one 7-inch; & no "product" "moved," curiously, at in-store, even though our "single" is on Live 105, the big commercial station, <u>around two to four times a day sometimes, friends say</u>! Perhaps not so curious as Tower had stocked a grand total of <u>zero</u> of our albums. We had to consign some from our cache of them. And still no one "bit." This <u>bites</u>! For a lark, I "made" Jenny walk around the store with some of them & ask shoppers if they had heard this CD. No one even gave her the time of day. San Franciscan alt-rock fans just as jaded as ours are. Hard to sell to. Or just Gay with a capital "G." At least Rough Trade in the Haight had two (albeit one *used* one—I hate to see those in the bins so soon!) of our album, & the poster was up in the smoke-colored window. At least there were nearly seventy-five people at the club gig. Plus writers from <u>The Chronicle</u> & <u>Bay Guardian</u> were crossed off the guest list. (Doesn't mean they <u>stayed</u>, though: this SF band, The Flaming Brandy Apricots, has a buzz going even in LA. Total cunts. They didn't even say hey at sound check, they split right after their set, & their <u>appalling</u> drummer came up to Raleigh & in this big, fat, phony voice said "Hey, I really dig you guys—what you're doing, man. Do you got an extra pair of drumsticks?" & didn't even give them back to him, the twat. What a <u>cunt</u> that twat was. I hope a waiter here in North Beach/Chinatown where we're staying with friends serves him a cooked squirrel or cat or a live rat one day.

Tuesday: Palo Alto: Stanford University: Noon Show—free— fifteen-hundred dollar guarantee; <u>ninety-eight CDs sold</u>—nearly <u>two boxes</u>; fourteen T-shirts; Oh My Fucking <u>God</u>! The Weird Sisters totally <u>rock</u>! Rob & Raleigh had these two super-cute Asian Art majors come along to lunch with us post-gig. Rob bummed that we had to get on the road pretty lickety-split, as "his" Art major, Joyce, was pretty darn cute with a nice laugh. The two of them almost got in the van & came with us to Oregon. Rob super bummed when then decided to stay & study for midterms instead. Jenny oddly friendly with them— which she is decidedly not always with pretty girls of the Asian or <u>any</u> persuasion. She can be quite the competitive-with-other-good- looking-chicks chick. It's hard to predict, however, who she wants to bristle at, however. You can never tell who she thinks her rivals are. (Good thing she doesn't read this logbook; or at least I don't think she does! Oh well. If she does, Hi, Jen! How's the tour going?! Love you!)

Wednesday: Eugene: John Henry's Tavern—<u>CANCELLED</u>; (plus interview at KVWS); five CDs + five pairs of tickets given away to <u>a bloody show that didn't happen</u>. Total chicanery/amateur hour. The owner gave us a pitcher of <u>light</u> beer, if you can believe that, & said the booker fucked up & a frat boy band had rented out the joint so that they could play *covers*. Hate Oregon. Scene of so many hideous idiocies. There's no <u>light</u> beer in fucking Oregon. They were <u>totally</u> just fucking with us. Tried to negotiate with the frat band to see if we could play anyway, try to sell some CDs. No go. "This is our gig now," one of them said, puffing out his chest. "Besides," another wonder chimed in, "no one's heard of you guys." Splendid. Jenny, bless her, told me she unplugged the power sources on their effects boxes when they weren't looking. Guess that's why, as they started up the first song (a Dave Matthews cover, of course), you could only hear the drums & vocals. We got out of there, pissed & bummed, of course, <u>fast</u>, Rob & I finishing a pitcher of <u>real</u> beer in record glugging-time.

Thursday: Portland: Satyricon (plus in-store at Jackpot: 3:00 p.m.); two-hundred-fifty vs. one-fourth of door; four CDs sold at record store; zero sold at gig. Terrible gig. Oregon <u>sucks</u>. Continues its sucking streak at fucking sucking. Hate Oregon. Always have, always will. Rain, rain, rain followed by more rain, then drizzling clammy mist with intermittent showers, followed by intense downpour. <u>No one</u> has a sense of humor here. Absolutely zippo. Report was there'd been only eleven sunny days all summer up here. No wonder no one smiles. They sure didn't appreciate the fact that Rob walked around SW & amazingly wonderful Powell's Books with his mustard & true-purple Lakers T-shirt on. Forget the names of the opening bands. Horrible skronky grunge stuff with guys in olive drab military shorts & tank tops & drums that pummeled you in a not-good way—total

& complete mismatched bill. We had to stand outside the venue to wait till we went on, other bands were so bad. I mean, there was just no getting away from the squalling terribleness & girls with forehead-piercings & neck tattoos & guys with…forehead tattoos & neck-piercings. I sometimes wonder if Oregon has unwittingly entered itself in a Worst State in the Union Contest. We've had such bad shows here & everyone, even the preschoolers, has dreadlocks. White-people dreadlocks. I think many of our enemies here are fellow Californians—but of course it's not cool to be a marauding Californian taking up precious forest space & taking tofu out of the mouths of the real Oregonians, so…no one admits to having even heard of our state. I mean, I get that you have to slag off "Cali" (God, that term jangles every available nerve) in order to fit in here, but, jeez, tie-dye, do ya have to go out of your way on your tractor to do it? Esp. as the whole state is an Irony-Free Zone, it seems. Just look at these townies in Cat Hats & college kids in U of O green & yellow all over the shop! They look like they just came from rolling around in the mud right after a breakfast of LSD-laced organic sprouts & flaxflakes. Where can I buy me a "I Hate Oregon" bumper sticker? Washington, maybe. Oregon: where people who have given up on their dreams move to. Something like that.

Friday: Seattle: Crocodile Café; one-hundred-seventy-five dollar guarantee + dinner vouchers & drink tickets; two CDs sold; three 7-inches; nicest (albeit bewildered) grunge-centric/"flyin' the flannel" crowd we've ever played to; they were probably very, very high & very, very drunk; convinced they thought we were from Scotland, hence "exotic UK outfit"; in fact <u>The Stranger</u>, an alt-rock rag like <u>BAM</u>, said we were "veddy British-sounding"—wonder what they bloody well meant by that, the wankers?

Sunday: Day off; (travel day; long drive)

Monday: Berkeley: The Starry Plough (plus cool interview at super cool KALX: 2:00 p.m.); one-hundred-fifty vs. forty percent of door after Soundman's seventy-five dollar fee; three CDs sold; three 7-inches; two CDs & two 7-inches stolen by hippies or dirty, thieving streetpeople, probably. Everyone too cool to clap, too cool to yelp, even, eating tofu & organic mac & white cheddar cheese. So the few cheers there were sounded like someone talking with a wad of cheesecloth in his gob.

Tuesday: Anaheim: The Doll Hut; Tonight: last gig of tour; door split three ways among the bands. Six buck cover. No idea who the other bands are. Which mattereth not, on account of I, for one, never want to see or hear a band again. Maybe even our own included. TBA.

Three

hen I came back from using the gas station's loo Raleigh was in the driver's seat, taking over for me, and laughing at something—all three of them were kinda giggling when I jumped in and urged the side door forward. Now, normally, having him there, driving, freaks out the "control freak" in me 'cause he's got a seriously plumbous foot and is bat-blind. Other than that: great driver. (Raleigh wears his eyeglasses driving, sure, but I am convinced that he still can't see: countless times I've, onstage especially, tried to get his attention and he just seems to look right through me, missing my every "cue." Or is it because…? I wonder sometimes.) Ah, but I was

feeling particularly magnanimous (read: guilty) and easygoing—the way you do when you've just raked someone over the proverbial coals much harder than you meant to, and your worst, most shrill self's just come out uninvitedly to play. I'd have much preferred it if Jenny took over behind the wheel but what the hell; the rush hour traffic was gonna be a positive massacre anyway, so Ral wouldn't be able with the tap of a blue Puma tennis shoe to put my heart in my throat anyway. There's been times when, going up (or more particularly *down*) a winding, mountainous, gasp-inducing highway I've been near tears with fright. Okay—not just "near" tears but actually shedding them. And I *don't cry*. I don't. Ever. Or rarely. You could crush my foot with something made by John Deere and I wouldn't weep. I would think about it, that's for sure, but I probably wouldn't go for it. It might be because sometimes I think that there's so much that's weep-worthy in this wigged-out, wicky-wacky world that once I started (crying, that is), I'm sure I'd never ever stop.

Raleigh pulled out onto the frontage road and—*what-the-fuck?*—passed the onramp to the 5 South.

"I think you missed the turn, Ral," I said as gently as humanly possible. "The turn was right back there."

"Oh, we meant to tell you, John," Raleigh said, "we have to go back to Bakersfield—I left a drum key at the club last week, and a pair of brand new sticks."

"Get out of here!" I said, in the way that you mouth/tongue sort of pssts it out.

"We took a vote," Jenny said, unable to contain her laughter or keep a straight face.

"And you were outvoted," Rob said. "It'll only take a couple hours. *Fuck* the meeting with The Mikes, anyway. There weren't hardly any records in the shops, right? 'Better-than-*what*-Records?' That just isn't right. Not good by any stretch. Those guys are *total* amateurs."

"I think Jenny left her *bra* there, too—isn't that what you said, Jen?" Rob added.

"Very funny, you guys," I said. "Turn around, Ral," I expressionlessly said.

"But we already voted!" Jenny said in this plaintive voice, a voice incapable, of course, of keeping a straight face, as it were. She was really laughing now. The kind of "larf" laugh you get before the *big* horking laughs come and you totally lose it—usually in places sacred or over-serious, like church or a courtroom or at a funeral parlour or when someone you barely know is crying right in front of you, asking you for a major favor or a handout or a ride to visit their great aunt and you hardly even know them or like them or you instantaneously dislike them and wouldn't mind if they stubbed their toe real hard right then or if a bird bespattered them with a birdshit the bird took after it had had just the biggest lunch of its fucking life. Or when a child is fake-crying and you have totally busted him and the more you mockingly cackle at him the closer he gets to crying in earnest. Ha!

"Uh, I didn't get a vote," I said, tripping into their trap, as it were.

"Basically, we voted that you get no vote," Raleigh said, and then the three of them started cackling like eighteenth-century Bedlam-denizen/inmate madmen and one madwoman who'd been tickled by the Head Key-Keeper's fresh-from-the-fireplace poker or something. When they'd *almost* finished cachinnating, Raleigh reached into his daypack and pulled out a black homemade tape and put it in.

Even Raleigh's daypack bothered me. It's amazing how sometimes someone's *thing*, possession, purse or bike or hat—esp. if it was a real *dumb* fucking hat like a too-small coonskin cap or one of those fully be-feathered alpine jobs or natural khaki fisherman's thing with all those *loops* and brassy *holes* and stuff all floppy and outdoorsy all over the place—sitting there all innocent, hasn't done you a footling bit of harm, could just send you *fuming* somehow, make you want to *crush* things or scare small children half to tears or death. Driving over the San Francisco Bay Bridge on the way up north, I remember looking at that smug, all fat-with-Raleigh-stuff pack in all its screaming kelly green glory and thinking: right now, more than anything, more than I want a personalized license plate or a Shetland pony or world peace or a record review in *SPIN*, the thing I would *enjoy most would be to grab that pack and kick that pack in its smiling teeth and hurl that pack out the window and as far as I humanly-Olympianly* can *hurl it, over the San Francisco Bay Bridge's crenellated railings, into the drink below.*

Anwway, we have this in-the-van band rule that the driver holds sovereign sway over the stereo: whatever he or she wants to listen to, he or she can. It's a sort of safety precaution, you see, so that the guy or girl at the wheel has every chance of staying alert (esp. late at night if we have a long haul between gigs) and keeping the van out of hair-raising-just-to-peek-at-them ravines and away from freeway pillars and lost cows and telephone poles. The driver always has his or her pick, even if its nothing, silence, even if it's Andrew Dice Clay's notoriously unfunny *The Day the Laughter Died* (seek it out: it's so not funny it's hysterical: and it's a *double* album—unreal) or the *egregiously* barfy T. Rex or Galaxie 500 (I would beg, just plead with all my might, for Ral not to put on Luna, for instance, the even more appalling band the main Galaxie guy came up with after Galaxie broke up) or Big Star, bands whose teeth-jarring, über-trebly vocals to this very day *make me want to kill myself*; and of course that just made Raleigh leave the cassette or CD of those groups in as long as he possibly impishly could).

And wouldn't you know it but the tape Ral put in produced the too-familiar strains of Blue Öyster Cult's incomparably wonderful "(Don't Fear) the Reaper" and just then the song came pulsating over all four speakers, the infamous arpeggiated opening blasting forth like a rockist call to arms.

"Oh, no! Not again," the other three of us seemed to go at once—on account of, as another jokey joke, Ral had made a ninety minute Sony Deluxe Gold cassette of "(Don't Fear) the Reaper" over and over and over again: I think he was able to fit it on twelve times per side.

It's a classic classic rock song, one of the greatest, way ahead of its time, for sure, and one that gets you "pumped," especially when you're driving. Of course. And it was funny when Raleigh put it in when we were stuck in a ridiculous traffic jam outside Seattle on our way to our gig there, and we all of us kinda got obsessively-compulsively into it, seeing how many repeats we could collectively take.

Somewhere around three sides of the cassette, if I'm not mistaken. Absolutely mental behavior, that.

But the BOC *redux* was gonna send me over the edge. And besides, Raleigh wasn't turning around: he was going faster, in fact.

"Very funny," I reiterated. "Joke's over. Come on, now. Cut it out! Turn around now, please. We're gonna be..."

"Late!" all three of my gamesome band mates yelped at once in a trifecta of the old jinx-on-a-Coke motif, with Rob making his voice like a retarded personage's or a deaf one.

Horrible.

"The look on your face!" Jenny said, as Rob threw his laughing head back and tossed a "drool pad" at my head.

"So glad you are amused," I deadpanned.

"You get so intense!" Jenny laughed.

And I hucked it, the pillow, the "drool pad," back at Rob and smiled in order to show I was a good sport and that I knew it was all "in good fun" and stuff; but no one, not even I, bought it, as it were. They knew they'd "gotten my goat" and there they were, parading it around the county fairgrounds or whatnot, roping it like a steer and dragging it along behind them in the dust-devil-strewn afternoon, then *roasting* it unskinned above a crackling campfire.

"Go-in'-back-ter-Bak-arse-feeld!" Raleigh sing-songed, and Rob started making banjo-ish sounds and Jenny clapped her pretty little hands—all to my mounting annoyance, which Ral must've noticed, as just then he turned the van toward the onramp north. And "flipped a bitch" at just the *very* last moment. It was a good thing there were no cars for miles or anywhere on the overpass.

"You guys are a *riot*," I said expressionlessly. "Really quite hilarious."

"Quite hilarious," Raleigh echoed, in a kind of deaf-guy voice—very uncool.

"Ah, come on, John," Jenny said as a tad bit of the mirth that came in the wake of Ral's practical joke revived. "We totally had you going for a minute there."

"Yep, you sure had me," I said, all dryly and stuff.

"Like we were actually going back!" Rob said.

"Come to think of it, though…" Raleigh said and faked like he was going to make yet another U-ey, changing lanes and looking over his meaty shoulder.

"*Stop*, okay?" I shrilled, losing it a little; and that of course just killed them and their abcedarian uproar held sway once more and they started "busting a gut" again like anything.

"Hilarious," I said, desert-dryly. "Don't even fuck around like that."

"'Don't even fuck around like that,'" Raleigh echoed, even more mockingly this time.

"Yeah," Jenny said, making her voice all mock-mannish and husky, "don't *even*. 'Don't *even* fuck around with *him!*'"

"Very funny," I said again. "Thanks for humbugging me, you guys. Nice. Real nice of you. Nice band."

"Nice band," Jenny said in a really husky voice just then. A husky, stentorian voice that kinda reminded me of…

"Jen?" I said.

"What?" she said, kinda Exorcist-ish, or like in the tone of a cowboy with a head cold who hadn't had a campfire-barbecued buffalo or beefalo steak in many-a-moon, which of course cracked schadenfreuding Ral and Rob up into an encore.

"You're kind of being a bit of a 'B' here."

"No, I'm not. I'm just…"

"You kind of are," I said.

"Band *couple* fight!" Raleigh said.

"Shut up, Raleigh," Jenny said.

"Shut up, Raleigh," I said.

"Well, at least you didn't say she was being a 'C,'" Rob, ever so helpfully, added.

"Or an 'A,'" Raleigh chipped in.

"If anyone's being an 'A,' Ral…" I said.

"Ooooooh," the three of them chorused.

"I'm going to take away all of you guys' snack priviledges," I said in a mock-schoolmarmish voice and wagged my finger around.

"*Uh*-oh," Jenny said. "You guys are in for it now!"

"*Us* guys?" Rob said. "You love road snacks as much as we do, Jen!"

Which was pretty funny 'cause Jenny was just then in the process of reaching out to Rob for another handful of Chocodiles or Twixlers or Goldfishies or whatever.

"Busted!" Raleigh said. "So busted. You guys are too funny."

"Chocodile, John?" Rob fake-offered me.

"Hilarious," I said.

I was going to add, just for Raleigh's benefit: "And, hey, try not to get us killed in a fiery crash, *okay*, Andretti?" but I realized that'd only make Raleigh employ his lead foot to "step on it" and he'd only freak me out even more so I just shut the fuck up and picked up my paperback copy of *The Canterbury Tales* (its colorful cover strewn with crow's feet, its pages and textblock marbled with water stains) and pretended to be able to read it.

Four

hen it comes to love, there is the notion of someone "really" understanding you and that of the *illusion* of someone understanding you—and in some ways they're really the same thing. What does it matter whether the someone who is the boyfriend of the girl who's yammering on about how he really "gets" her really "gets"

her or not? If she thinks it's so, it's solipsistically so. Until, that is, she doesn't think he "gets" her anymore and, for whatever reason—she's bored, she finds the things he does that she used to find amusing are now starting to "get on her nerves," she starts to "thrill" inside a little bit when a "new" boy comes along who makes her laugh or even nervously *sweat* in a way that she realizes deep down is sexual. Now her boyfriend's theories, his notions and ideas, that once seemed solid and thought-provoking but not *too much* so, now they appear iffy, dubious, sketchy, etcetera. She starts to think that the two of them are "growing apart," and that they have "changed." "The tragic thing about life," the immortal Jean Renoir famously said at the beginning of the incomparable *Le Regle du Jeu*, "is that everyone has their reasons." The key motif here is that Renoir acknowledged the *tragic* element in my reasons not "seeing eye-to-eye" with yours. Thus, perhaps our need to be "understood" is far greater than the need to be loved. Perhaps they're the same thing. Perhaps love is *only* Understanding with a capital "U." But people are so complex, so psychologically convoluted that in a quick trice you can go from thinking you have them completely figured out to going "I don't 'know' this person *at all!*" Some several hundred zillion years ago I was working with a pretty good psychologist in order to get over a lost love (I'm not saying it was Jenny, and I'm not saying it wasn't). One time when I kept nattering on wondering aloud "Why would she [my ex, that is] *do* that, how come she thinks *this?*" Well, the shrink kept going, "Well, I don't know her." Point is, the psychologist was operating from the epistemological standpoint of assuming you *can* know someone. You see: I'm starting to think that that's a fallacy.

Anyway, if love is understanding and understanding is an illusion, then perhaps by the transitive property…um, best not to think about it.

Love: it's like this big, bright, somehow beautiful moth that's fluttered into your lamplit living room. It flitters hither and thither and you can't leave it alone 'cause eventually it's gonna go zigzagging into your closet and mow your wooly vintage cricket sweaters. You turn out the lights and open the door and hope it'll find its own way out, floating free in the big, bad world for a while, darning the air doing delirious arabesques just-for-fun, till it either gets munched by a sparrow or visits you again. But it won't bend to your will. You try to cup it in your lotion-soft hands and there it goes away again—in the crenellations of your curtains, atop lampshades awash in the starlight coming through the open windows. You're close enough, you almost have it, you gently clap your hands together, think you'll get it by its wings, and suddenly it's the softest dust, pulverized, in your guilty palms, like a trick some conjurer has played but not pulled off, quite. You sneeze. But it's nothing to sneeze at, love. It's not. And there you are, nauseated by what you've done—and you tried so hard not to harm the poor thing.

What are Jenny and I, lovers, band mates, doing in the same van, the same band, living together in a big apartment Hancock Park-adjacent/west of Koreatown, if you're wondering, those of you who know that, when we last left off, at the end of *The King of Good Intentions*, Jenny had been told by this chick Sarah who really despised me, actually, that she and I had slept together. There they were in conference as we had just gotten offstage at our first big gig (it was only our second gig): an outdoor/Saturday festival at USC. And the distraught, distorted look on Jenny's pretty face told all as Sarah walked spitefully away.

Do you wanna hear about this now? I can give you the scoop if you want it. Well, the song and dance of apology and remorse I did for the next three weeks at least could've, it seemed, gotten me into a veritable Julliard of regret and contrition. My one "saving grace" was that the incomplete sex Sarah and I had had, had been, verily, *coitus interruptus*; and *interruptus* by *me*, not the police or a porn director or one of Jenny's friends or—God forfend—Jenny herself. I'd stopped mid-fuck: fact. And that fact was the "in" for, interestingly, both Jenny and me. You see, you cheat, or in this case, half-cheat (call it that, go ahead) on a girl, she's crushed, betrayed beyond, wounded in her pride and in the heart of her being and affections, looks at you like you're coated with baby-vom, baby-vom from a really big, like, Guinness

Book-type baby. In order for her to forgive you—if there is even any chance of that—she has to have some "out," some way to "save face" and her dignity. That's in part why some guys, married guys mostly but bachelors, too, always aver that *even if she walks into the room while you're porking someone else*—deny, deny, deny. "That's what they *want*," my long-married chum Dumphries always says. "If there's even a shadow of a doubt in their minds," Dumphries says, "a *pale* shadow of a doubt at that, they can go on living with it, and with you, if and only if you get them to see that their eyes were deceiving them somehow, that what they thought they saw wasn't what they thought they saw. If ever my wife, God bless her, walked in on me and there was a twenty-year-old busty coed with her twinkling, pretty ankles waving at Cecelia from atop my shoulders and the girl's screaming my name as she's fucking multi-coming...it *never happened, okay?...* It's *not what it looks like, okay?...* Honey you were *dreaming, okay?...* We were doing some Ancient Babylonian *wrestling* or something for her *act*ing class. *It wasn't sex*, okay? We're just *friends*, we just *met*, she's *ob*viously gay, can't you see that? She was drunk and I was fighting her off of me! I mean, they *want* to believe you," Dumph opines when the topic crops up, "no matter if they work for NASA or the CIA or they work a pole on Tuesdays at your local at-the-edge-of-town strip club; you give them what they want—which is a way to believe you (sorta) and be able to live with themselves. Deny, deny, *deny*. That is the only way. I love my wife, I'd kill or maim someone for her. Walk in front of a truck. Hurt is the last thing I want her to be. It's also the last thing she wants to be, so I'll give her what she wants, see? I love my wife...I don't wanna *fuck* her...but I love her more than anything."

Some guys—believe me—actually believe shit like this. Say it, too. No kidding.

Take Cholmondely, more of a tennis acquaintance of mine (for those of you who don't spend your lazy-hazy rainy afternoons leafing through *Debrett's*, it's pronounced "Chumly"), whose similar attitude is this: "She quote-unquote catches you—of *course* it never happened. It never did. Even if she walks in on you with someone somewhere.

Check this. There I am, in our hotel room in Mexico—yes, *it is our fuckin' honeymoon*; no *shit! Bet your sweet bippy, it is!*—and Anastasia barges in as the maid's basically *flossing her teeth with my fucking cock.* Not good, right?! *Uh*, oh! She comes back early from parasailing or a foot massage from flirting with the pro there or some shit—*marlin* harvesting, or whatever she was doing; snorkeling or whatnot; *I* don't know—and sees me. I'm in the reading chair in the room and the girl's on her knees in front of me, going downtown, if you know what I'm sayin'. Fucking *beautiful* little Mexican gal. Fucking *beautiful!* Of course she's flabbergasted at what she *thinks* she's seen, the wife is—ready to jump on the next plane and all of that. Go straight to the American Consulate or whatnot. Hahaha! Call up Carlos Escobar to come bump me off from Columbia or wherever. Hahaha! And I convince my dear little honeymooning honeybunny that *we were looking for my wallet*, okay? It wasn't all that hard, believe me. She'd already had around fourteen margaritas (and three Bloody Marias for breakfast), so I just kind of got her to come with me to the bar in the hotel and have shots till she blacked out—she's just screaming at me like anything, and the whole time I'm telling her she's out of her mind, nothing like that ever could've happened, ever, and blah, blah, blah. It wasn't what it looked like, baby—blah, blah, blah. I couldn't find my wallet and I was going to get her some kinda Mexican artifact for a present or something and the maid was helping me look for it, my *wallet*, that's all. I would *never* do that to her. Never in a million years. I had just come back from the pool and my trunks were loose 'cause I was *changing* into some dry ones and then freaked 'cause I thought I'd lost it, my billfold. Just then the housekeeper came in without knocking to do the room, I'm gonna lodge a complaint, yadda, yadda, yadda, and all of that…and guess what? It worked. It *worked*, you know? Whew. Think she really wanted to believe she'd married a guy who could 'do that to her?' No way. Like she wants to find that out. About me, the guy she fuckin' *married*? Nuh-*uh. Last* thing that girl wants, believe me. Or have to tell people, her family and shit, that that's what happened on the five-star honeymoon they broke their precious little piggy banks to send her on?! Like, for *sure!* Never brought it up again. No, she did not. Not one word. We've been married now—what?—eleven years? Oh, my God. Have I…? *All* guys cheat, all right? And every wife thinks she's the holy one-and-only exception—that *her* husband doesn't participate in any extramurals. No, sir. Not him. None whatever. Never has. Never will. *Fact.* Hey, by the way, wanna see some pictures of my kids? There's some pictures of my kids—they're both in the USTA Juniors Program, out there killing kids *much* older than them—at least a grade or so. That's Preston, nine, and this is Penelope, eight. Aren't they something? Forehands bigger than yours or mine…they fucking *crush* the ball. And a lot of these tennis brats they play, I'm telling ya…you wouldn't believe the things they pull. I'm teaching my boy to make 'Tournament Calls.' You know the term? When in doubt, call it 'Out!' Haha! You ever heard that one before? I don't want him to learn to *cheat* on the court or anything. Especially when so *many* of these little bratty fucking fuckers are learning early how to 'hook' the shit out each other. There's only been two or three matches where Preston *didn't* have to call in an ump on one of the other little cocksucking tennis-brat fuckers. But you know: it works. And what I said about denying? That works too. Fuck if it doesn't."

So the "out" *I* had was that I loved Jen—and it was true on many levels, plus what does that nebulous term "love" *mean* anyway?— so much that I "put the brakes on" something I had gotten myself into and had gotten out of, however gracelessly: even though that something was some "skank's" (Jenny's word) horrible vagina.

And of course that I loved her with all my heart and would never, ever, ever, ever, not-in-a-million-years, ever, ever, *ever* do that to her ever, ever, ever a*gain.*

The other caveat I had in my favor was that I could "swear up and down till my face was blue" that I was trying to think of a way to "come clean," tell her, confess like some St. Augustine on Ecstasy or Benzedrine—and that I hadn't found the words, couldn't manage it, couldn't face myself for what I'd done. Me—*word* guy. Mister Dictionary. Mister Glib. Couldn't find the words as the tears pearled down Jen's soft, bright, pink-sweet cheeks. As she sobbed out her jealousy and betrayal-pain. A pain that, for all women of a certain age, becomes almost cumulative, as though they're crying not just for you, about you and how you, an evil devil of certifiable ruthless evilness, hurt the shit out of them, but *for all the guys they've ever known who've let them down*—from Daddy Himself to High School David, from Summer Camp Darin to Junior Year Abroad Professor Darlington, from Later on in Junior Year Abroad "Mr. Darcy" (not his real name but what her friends called him behind his back, on account of he was English and proud *and* prejudiced), to Senior Year Dan, from Post-Collegiate Bewilderment Derek to Working World David *II* (he was so different from David I, so so different, especially in terms of, well, *his penis*), from Late-Twenties Married Darryl to Rebound Dumpkin, and, at last, from How You Mistakenly Thought for So Long He was Dependable Donny to *you*, bad you. Horrid, awful, shithead, *fuck*head, bastard, cheating, stupid dickhead *you*, you dickhead.

There are several camps, so to speak, in relation to this topic, the shopworn subject of, as they say in Chaucer's English, "bewrayal"—I can see their proud pennants and snappy standards flapping in the blustery distance; watch them wiggle and flutter like spermatozoa swimming in air, not womb-water. These camps—they traverse Time, the Past, the Present, and the Future. Their dazzling ambassadors and/or stewards may now ride forward and begin haranguing re: the curious topic of relationshiply infidelity. One herald, riding hard, in a pet, sweating mightily through full armor, beaver down, cries "Rubbish! What you've supposedly gotten away with is utter nonsense." Go ahead and trot out your best cliché, fair and valiant warrior; I know what it is: "Once a cheater, always a cheater!" "What you did," says gentlemanly he, "was cheat on her, you lying, cheating, fucking, troth-bewraying *bastard*! A girl that sweet (and loyal too) and you go and do that?! You were looking for it. You *bloody* well knew what you were doing and the fact that you pulled out, so to speak, doesn't speak in your defense. Not at all. It's a *mute* point.

Haha! You fucker! You might be right.

This camp's either had someone "step out" on them in the most mega way or they're walking exemplars of the phenomenon in psychology called the reaction formation: they're so aware of their own yearnings to treat the world and everyone in it of the opposite (or same—let's not forget ye olde homosexuality) sex like one big fuckhole that they "cry foul" in the shrillest, most strident voices imaginable.

Another camp, cantering up casually in blood-stained hauberk and smeary tunic, but with no broadsword "to hand," using an urbane tone, like someone talking to you as he opens not a can but a *box* of tennis balls used exclusively for posh grass courts, goes: "You didn't really fuck anyone but yourself here, brother-squire. You're sorry for what you've done and it only happened—or partly, even—once. The affronted maid hath, thus, an opportunity to exercise her powers of forgiveness and be-shrive you. Move forward! Now you know deeply the Tolstoyan take on love: 'To know love,' he said, 'one must make a big mistake—and then mend it.' Here's to the metaphorical needle and thread!" [Pardon the anachronism.] This camp's major fear, it seems, is they're afraid they'll, they-themselve'll, fuck up and won't receive absolution at the hands of the other person and more importantly from themselves. How sad to be someone who's not forgiven him or herself for what they've done. No one's perfect. Everyone screws up sometimes."

Yet another camp rep—such a smart equestrian!—comes on up, side-passing in on his trusty gingerbread thoroughbred. He's in courtly garb, fit only for repose, taking one's ease, and not "the field." He comes counseling all and sundry to "hold their judgment in abeyance, along with their tart tongues." Hark! He waxes philosophical, quotes texts from many traditions, diverse epochs, eras, schools of thought, and rightly proffers his opinion that nothing means anything till later—when its full purport comes clear one day. If it ever does. Maybe it doesn't. He offers water, cool, in a silver goblet, fine, plain, and ancient. Drink! His unrolled scroll buckles percussively in the whipping wind. He's maybe had *therapy*, learned to look at life dispassionately, disinterestedly, parsing the situation like some Joycean artist/demigod pairing his mottled fingernails as the hurly-burly kaleidoscopes and whirl-swirls around him. His musings show how detached he is from taking life too seriously, too tragically, from being Hamlet's "passion's slave"—a good and bad thing both. His punctilio is admirable, but maybe he's not taking into to consideration the fact that people can't help their feelings, and that it's human nature to cry *"The Jew must burn!"* Someone's gotta pay for this! There's gotta be a verdict. Conclusions must be reached and entered into registers—if only in the mind. (Finger-pointers and liberal burghers, PC watchdogs and that?! Don't get your bunhuggers and granny panties in a twist over the aforesaid expression! Look it up! It's from a play called *Nathan the Wise*. Seminal psychologist Karen Horney makes reference to it in one of her many wondrous-brilliant and super depressing volumes. It only alludes to the fact that the rabble *have* to have their man, as it were; they gotta string someone up once their dander's up. That's all. It's not personal.)

I cry your worship's humble mercies.

One

ircumstances conspire to keep people together or to repulse them from each other; it isn't *all* our fault. *Tempura mutantur et nos mutamur in illis.* And everything *doesn't* "happen for a reason"—I will maintain that till my dying day—but effects do have causes and Jenny and I ended up patching it up, "getting through this," then getting a massive three-bedroom place with an engineer/producer friend of ours called Keating. You'll recall that, near the end of *The King of Good Intentions*, Jenny'd been unceremoniously evicted from the room she rented from our old

drummer, Walter and his "wifey," Nastasha—an eighty-six-ing that I'd played no small part in, presumably, in that Walter and Nasty's major "objection" was that I was basically *living* there, or coming over there too much, at least, taking advantage, not being deferential or diffident enough, and, even more gallingly-to-them, happy with Jenny, happy as a Chumash before the Spaniards and their priests came sailing by the beaches of the land that would eventually be called after Saint Barbara. A happiness which, perhaps, rankled Nastasha in particular because a) she always seemed to think and actually mentioned that Jenny could do better, do better than me, at least, that I wasn't "a catch," hardly a good-enough boyfriend for her sweet, piano-and-guitar-playing "friend," and confidant, and roommate; and b) she was a miserable *little*—in both senses of the term—person.

I called a band meeting amidst all of the sitting on my futon, talking in soothing, apologetic tones to Jenny's chuntering back as she cried and sniffed and sniffled and occasionally turned 'round to accept a wad of toilet paper (but not one of my attempts—the first few days, at least—to embrace her) or to look at me with a hurt look or a touched one or, with, thankfully, incrementally diminishing frequency, a vexed and angrily impassioned one, with Jen, Rob and me solely in attendance and I for one voted that we kick Walter, as it had been a long time coming anyway, out of the band. Jenny gave the vote an apathetic "bye" (perhaps because she was too hurt to care too much about a stupid band when her goddam idiotic boyfriend had gone and "been with" someone else), and Rob reluctantly said "aye," and so the Walt "out" motion was carried and I told him on the day I went to help Jen move her stuff into storage. (Excepting, of course, her piano which some burly-friendly Latino piano movers had to move.) She was back staying at my roommate Jaz and my place after stopping for a tense, sad-making, not-hardly-taking-my-calls week with Sandy, her friend, an avid bicyclist who worked in the downtown law office Jenny worked at. Jenny didn't want to burn her out, her friend, and besides they were getting on each other's nerves, she said, what with the working together and sharing Sandy's cramped one-bedroom. So, after much coaxing and many promises, with me first caressing her with my voice 'cause she wouldn't let me touch her literally at first, with me then, after a real while, wrapping my assuring/imploring arms around the waist of her heliotrope sundress or (initiating makeup sex) lifting off the loose blue tank top she wore over it, with me at last kissing her and etching her back and fondling her front and joining my hands from behind and in front down below and getting her wet and then hoisting her gladly onto me and we made love standing up, through her pale cream panties, I recall now—after all of this, and so many in-betweens and soft words and little flashes of "looks" (so hard to define, interpret, even though you have, at the time, a pretty good idea what they mean) and sniffles and bitter little bursts of grateful laughter and stolen kisses on salty, parted lips stained with tears that it would take *eons* to tell you about, we found a spacious place and affordable, a little closer to busy, dirty Western than to languid, trendy, rich-people Larchmont than we'd hoped. Off Wilshire. A street called Lorraine. Signed a two-year lease and moved right in, giving our love a place to pupate again. Jenny's and mine, mine and Jen's.

Again.

Two

aleigh got us to the Better Records offices after an hour and a half of fighting a quintessence of Southern California traffic, bumper-to-bumper, the four of us marionetting in our seatbelts as Ral'd speed up too fast when a break in the congestion appeared, then have to brake like mad to avoid rear-ending a touristy family of four going off to "The Happiest Place on Earth"

in their rented van or something; or some "OC Boneheads," as we facetiously, snobbishly called them, in lowered Hondas and backward California Angels or Stussy caps, listening to Incubus or Primus or Dave Matthews or Social Distortion or Guns N' Roses or something equally appalling on car stereos louder than a police loudspeaker, a jet engine, or a drunken Roseanne Barr.

Gotta say here, it's weird *passing* the exit that you'd normally use in order to de-freeway—the one you'd take to get home—when you're on a trip. We woulda got off on Los Feliz Boulevard (where you get your first glimpse of the towering First Interstate Building as its tall, lone turret bullets majestically into the, dare I say, often quite impressive LA sunset sky) and gone west past the front part of gargantuan Griffith Park. But we kept going down the 5, past downtown, past the 10, and on and on, and at last crossed the "border," went behind "The Orange Curtain."

Passing Los Feliz thusly, though, I sort of wished we could just blow off The Doll Hut gig and the meeting with The Mikes, the two guys whom I alluded to earlier who ran the little indie label we were signed to, and just go home. With Cobain gone, Nirvana fans and sympathetic indie rockers all over the map were just gonna wanna get magnificently baked and stay home wallowing in *Nevermind* or *In Utero* while vigorously pounding über-beers or Jägermeister shots in remembrance of Kurdt. Maybe they *might* want to go out and have a few hundred glugs in order to distract themselves, have some slummy Baudelairean night out, but they weren't gonna wanna go see some semi-twee jangly psychedelic pop band they'd hardly or never heard of—no matter how much the very cute chick on lead guitar "rocked" or how catchy the songs were. They'd probably be more interested in losing themselves in heavy metal or something, headbanging to the punk and "rawk" songs Nirvana'd been influenced by as much as Kurt and Company'd certifiably liked folky Neil Young and the acoustic Beatles.

Well you know for a fact that we, being a super conscientious, good, little, ambitious, and capitalistic band and all, couldn't, didn't go blowing off the last gig. Like obedient good little slaves to capitalism and the record business, we continued on our very way to the record label headquarters in Anaheim. In case you're curious, the Better Records offices are almost in the darkling shadow of the Matterhorn, practically—a few long blocks from "The Happiest Place on Earth." I'm not saying that our dear, old, utterly incompetent, and/ or amateurish label was a somewhat Mickey Mouse operation but… hey, if the Mouseketeer hat fits, stick one…somewhere. We often, and bitterly, joked about how if the people who worked at Better spent half as much time promoting our record as they did hanging out at the "roach coach" that seemed perpetually to be parked in the back lot of the label's offices, well, we'd be full-on rock stars by now or something for sure, hanging with Sting or Bono—Sonny Bono, that is.

"They aren't a record label so much as a music-oriented mari*juana* club," Jenny coyly said one time, which cracked up Rob, Ral and me to no end.

But it was a bit bitter, our laughter, for sure.

Indeed, *apropos* the weed thing and the people at the label: the three or so times we'd gone down there—one to meet everyone and pick up the contract they'd offered us, two to sign the contract, and three to "take a meeting" re: what they were and were not willing to do in terms of promotion—*everyone*, all twelve employees plus The Mikes, had seemed high as Rastas on spring break, high as hell, as Snoop Dogg or any dog who's lapped up one of the "honey slides" you forgot you dropped behind the couch. As I've told you, we had a single on a major station, the one in San Francisco, and Bay Area people couldn't buy our disc unless they special ordered it from Amoeba or the great mom-and-pop (now gone, of course and sadly) Mod Lang in Berkeley.

Three

aleigh swung the van with a desperate vengeance and more than a modicum of tire-shrieking into a parking space back of the Better Records building; the engine cut with a baritone gasp and a grindy shudder, then settled somewhat borborygmusly, like it felt something, like it knew something, like it was thinking "Haven't I taken you guys far enough? Do you really need to *do* this gig—for your glorious careers and everything? Can't I just go back home to the parking lot at Enterprise? *Please?*" Poor thing: as if getting up-over the Grapevine with all kinds of band equipment isn't work enough it then has to stammer and zigzag through mad urban traffic for upward of an hour and a half.

The Better Records building's this industrial behemoth in a faceless complex. The Better façade and back entrance they painted school bus yellow—God knows why. I don't wanna even think "color theory" right now and how yellows often symbolizes caution. Or danger. Think about how in nature when yellow and black, for instance, are juxtaposed—look out, nature lover! Bad badness instantaneously ahead. Snakes, bees, wasps, monitor lizards, yellow fever (malaria, yeah), the screaming yellow meemies, warning signs (Dangerous Curves, Falling Rocks, Drunken Lithuanians), cowardice, jaundice, underhydrated urine—yellow is *not* something we aim for.

So we all piled out of the hardy Astro like people with minor or major back injuries pulling up to Emergency Ward arteries. Stretched out. Did imitation Canadian Air Force exercises. Yawned, laughed with relief to be off the road and almost done with this tour, etcetera. Bay Area-to-LA is just *this* much too long of a drive for anyone who's not a trucker or a speed freak—or a speed demon. Or all three. Of course, Raleigh and Jen headed straight for the Better Recs loos.

Predictably, there was a Better team member, our favorite, in fact, Franklin was his name, walking back from a "roach coach" down the alleyway. I always thought of food trucks as lunchtime things but there perpetually seemed to be one hovering 'round this particular part of the world. Franklin was "our radio guy," and in his paws he had perhaps the most mondo burrito I'd ever seen. You could've mistaken it for a rolled-up beach towel or a flour tortilla-colored lunch pail if you didn't know that Franklin was the last guy to go sunbathing or swimming or carrying a lunch pail, though he lived in beautiful Newport, about ten blocks from the beach—as far as him not being the beach type and stuff went. He had us all over for dinner right after we signed to Better and it was as though his beachy apartment was anything but: like he still lived in Lawrence, Kansas, was still going to KU, where he went to school. All of his curtains were these thick black jobs and there weren't even any seashells strewn around on the end tables or coffee table or in the loo like beach people always seem to have.

Smiling away, Franklin caught (of course) Jenny before she could get to the entrance and gave her a big, fat hug and greeting. In order to hug her he had to hold out the burrito way away from himself and with one hand like it was already rubbish and rancid or something, or like it was some furry animal wrapped in a tortilla-blanket of sorts and that was dangerous and that would bite her if he didn't keep Jen out of harm's way—the animal's way, that is.

"Hello, The Weird Sisters!" he said to all of us. "Glad you made it back safe! Welcome back! Good to see you guys. Really good. How were the gigs?!"

Now Franklin is about the nicest person you could ever want to meet: the kind of guy whose demeanor and delivery is so sincere that you think in your even semi-cynical way that it's *got* to be an act. But it isn't. It's real. He really is that nice. His temperament must demand it somehow, though I don't know how he does it, keeps it up. It's as though he can't stop beaming and nodding at you; it's crazy. He's gotta be on some kinda happy pills in the literal sense. No one

could be that clam-happy all the time and not be. He has a particular
jones for Jenny (who doesn't?) and Raleigh (go figure!): the former, I
guess, 'cause Jenny, as you know, is inveterately, terribly nice herself
and Franklin comes off as tickled to death that he gets to work for, in
a way, and know personally such a babe (he probably doesn't count
among his close acquaintances too many girls like her as he's sort of "a
total nerd," albeit a totally adorable one—though you never know, do
you?); and the latter 'cause he and Raleigh love to geek out on all the
hip new bands and their releases, i.e. those whose record is hot and
who's touring with whom and who got "signed or dropped, signed or
dropped," as Jenny parodically, periodically puts it.

All the hip new bands I'm starting to feel I couldn't care less about.

"Hey, Franklin!" Raleigh said and teasingly added: "At the 'roach
coach' again I see! Just like the last time we were here!"

Way to state the obvious right a-fucking way, Ral, I thought. *At
least you're consistent. Nice one.*

"Well, it *is* my break right now," Franklin demurred, smiling
shyly, finishing chewing a Bogarty mouthful. "Hey, you guys! Hey!
How's everyone? Actually, though, Raleigh, you know, we're basically
done for the day, except for the meeting with you guys, and besides,
um…did you hear about Kurt Cobain? You did? Okay. I wondered if
you guys had heard. Isn't that terrible? So sad. We're all so bummed.
Really sad. No one at stations, obviously, is taking calls right now
unless they're from Courtney—which they're not, of course, the calls,
I mean. They can't reach her for a statement. They've been trying to
reach her for a statement but they haven't been able to get a hold of
her. Of course. Leave her alone, is what I say! Terrible. The media.
None of us can believe it. In fact, almost everyone except for me and
Stacey and Mike Mays has left for the day, in fact. Tuesdays are slow
days, anyway, in that most stations have made their reports by now
and are having a breather before the next week has to be tallied and
stuff. The warehouse guy is here still, I think—I have to help him fill
some orders for tomorrow. You guys' record's getting steady onesies/
twosies each day. Not great. Not yet, at least, I should say. But, like I

said, onesies/twosies. Here and there. Not bad. We'll get more pretty soon here—never fear! Each week a few more, in fact. Not bad. The chains all stocked it. Most of them, at least. Many. I'll have to check on, uh, that. Not sure. I wish Sylvia was still here—she got some new reviews for you in *CMJ* and *Magnet*, I think. Pretty cool."

Sylvia Doum was the Better publicist. *Very* pretty, in a weird kinda way, sorta—giant green eyes, screaming red-black hair with streaks of red in it, great little figure (if you, like Rob, didn't mind "spinners"), lots of instant turn-off (if you were me) tattoos. She wore perpetual flowerprint dresses or dresses with things like skulls or bats or drawings of smoking grilled cheese sandwiches on them, in*tense* vegetarian, sported very-high, scuffed-leather combat boots (on her really weirdly too-big-for-her-petite-frame feet), a mirthless laugh, strange sense of humor, *talked* a *lot* (what else do you expect? But I mean, like an auctioneer on biker crank—that much), very extra phoney in a "*Hi*, how *are* you?" sort of way. To look at her you couldn't possibly imagine for an instant she could stand to hear more than a bar or two of our music; she looked like she'd eat you for a punk rock pancake breakfast, then go put on Black Sabbath followed by Motorhead and then chill out/digest you with a bit of the more intense passages from Swans, Skinny Puppy, or Ministry.

It was very un-rock of her that she bragged that she got up every morning at five-thirty on the dot, no matter how late she'd been out the night before. Everyone else in "the biz" acted all amazed if you ever even hinted that you got up before nine or ten. I sometimes wondered why Sylvia remarked so often on how she rose "betimes" if it wasn't just her way of being "different" from everyone else.

We're all of us looking for recognition of some sort, aren't we just? Howsoever we may.

The only in-common thing we had with her was the Beatles in that just as we were intensely in love with them, so was Sylvia Doum hell-bent on *also* publicizing the fact that, in her considered and quite well-informed musical opinion, "the Beatles ruined pop music forever." She never said her own name—in answering the phone or ringing some editor up or in some bellowy conversation at a stupid gig—without saying her whole name. The *one* time she went to one of our shows (the record release party at Club Lingerie), one of our friends/fans asked me: "Hey, John—who was that screaming black-and-red-haired girl *talking during your entire performance?* She's *really* good-looking but—my God—she just wouldn't shut the fuck *up!*" And then, as if on cue, Sylvia swanked right up just as our band friend's question was evaporating in the blue-smoke air of the packed club and, thrusting forth her hand like she was trying to give it away as a consolation prize or just get rid of it, said: "Sylvia *Doum*, Sylvia *Doum*—and who are…who are…*you?*" (The friend, to his credit, just pfff'd and walked away, toward the bar to get, presumably, another free well drink or domestic beer with the free drink tickets we'd shuffled out to a few stalwart Sisterheads and close friends. And I realized at once: Sylvia Doum's truculently drunk!)

What a character: sort of smart in that dumb way that air-minded, over-eager publicity people *only* can be—as in sometimes she just talked really, really fast without seeming to think at *all*. E.g. when our CD first came in from manufacturing and Rob, Jen, and I had zipped in Jen's car all merrily and excitedly as an ungrounded electrical socket down to the OC to pick up our allotted box of "advance copies" to try and sell or give out to our friends and families and McLeary and stuff (our very first record! Oh, my God—it really exists!), we'd done a pretty big-time phone interview with a pretty well-respected 'zine from back East and the whole time Sylvia'd chimed in at the most inappropriate times, making us sound like total novices; and moreover throughout the conversation she'd refered to Jenny as *Jenna* and to me as *Sean*.

Jenny *hated* her, naturally. I was glad she, Sylvia Doum, wasn't at work that afternoon. She reminded me a lot, but without being fully Goth, of our old drummer Walter's girlfriend, Nastasha—the epitome of the total bitch who *seemed* all the time like she was ever so sweet and smiley-friendly. She'd told Rob: "You know, getting a haircut at a place other than Supercuts wouldn't be a *bad* idea for your image, you know. There *are* other options."

And she, like everyone, liked Rob; that, it appeared, was her way of fucking flirting with him.

Though Rob, poor as anything, poor as me at times, even more poor, too, *did* tend to get some pretty iffy haircuts—like he'd gotten drunk with one of his "Pubic Palace" friends and had the brilliant idea to go scrabbling in the kitchen drawer for a dull pair of scissors that had been long-ago retired from a shed for having been used too much on various wild hedges and huckleberry bushes—but you didn't have to go and point it out to him, Sylvia Doum, Sylvia Doum, now did you?

Raleigh she'd only met twice, but each time she'd gone, "Who are *you*, exactly? So you're *in* this band?"

So Raleigh, who never hated anyone ever (except of course *me*, probably), would, when the topic of Sylvia Doum came up, go: "I don't really *care* for her all that much." Like he was for an instant the Caterpiller in *Alice*. You should have seen what Raleigh did the first time he met Sylvia Doum. He was of course munching on something—a candy bar, I think—and when Sylvia Doum said, "Who are you, etcetera." Raleigh just shrugged and took the Mars Bar or whatever out of his mouth and held it out to her like a lollipop he was urging her to take a bit from. He could be really pretty funny sometimes. And I mean, it was the perfect thing to do 'cause Sylvia Doum was one of those people who—you just know—can never laugh at themselves and who pull these *awful* faces with no attempt whatsoever to hide what they think of you, or your snack-related antics.

Hilarious. Plus hideous.

And speaking of enmity and stuff, for sure Sylvia Doum hated Jenny 'cause even though she was a idiot, she wasn't stupid; I mean, the two of them smiled so intensely-tightly at each other even a toddler could've seen that *some*thing in the animosity-between-really-good-looking-women category was up. Like Sylvia Doum, in trying to conceal how jealous she was of Jen, only succeeded in pointing it up all the more.

Of course I can't prove it, but I think she may have been the first person in history to use the utterly useless and obnoxious phrase *Just sayin'*. She was a real pioneer, that good old Sylvia Doum the publicist.

She really was so pretty, though, that, from some angles, she reminded me a lot of an older, littler, Mandy Moore, but with punk rock hair. But from *other* angles she reminded me of *Roger* Moore, a younger Roger Moore, but with—again—punk rock hair.

It was very confusing. At first. Then you just realized that you thought she was probably the most obnoxious person in the known universe.

Except for this guy Bob Chalet we knew.

About whom more later.

"Really?" I said in response to Franklin's little sales report as Jen and Ral ducked into the back hallway. "We're selling a few 'units'? That's great, Franklin. That makes us very happy. Way to go, team."

Then I told Franklin he ought to go eat that mondo-burrito before it turned to cold, coagulated Mex-truck muck.

That made him laugh.

"Definitely. Thanks, John, I will. Hi, Rob," Franklin said and high-fived him as Rob walked up just then. "Yeah as I said, hardly anyone's around but I am definitely coming to you guys' gig tonight. Stacey's going too. Sylvia has her parents in town so she can't go. It's not like she would…anyway…I think she was really upset about Cobain. A lot of people are, I think. Amazing, huh. We're all so sad, you know. I still just can't believe it."

I just nodded sympathetically.

"You probably weren't all that into Nirvana, though, huh," Franklin added.

"I heard them too much on the radio. And Raleigh played *Nevermind* way too much in the van, so I can't really be objective here to begin with, but, no, they weren't my thing."

"Sure," Franklin said.

"But that doesn't mean—you know—that I don't feel sad about it. People are so weird about suicides—especially when it's someone famous. And an icon like Kurt Cobain? They get all pissed-off and indignant and 'How could he have done that to his kid?' No one but that guy knows what he was going through, you know? Maybe he just had a very bad day and…didn't make it through it, is how I see it."

"Interesting," Franklin said. "I never thought about it like that."

"I could go on and say how it totally triggers a latent fear in some people but…let's talk about something else! How've *you* been?"

"Oh, fine. You know me: living for good music! Really happy with your record, how it's going—that's for sure. Now: How was San Francisco, anyway, you guys? I think I might take a trip up there this summer—and I will make a point of stopping by the station to thank them personally for playing the hell out of your single. That is so great about the single. That is not an easy station to get something played on, let alone—what?—three times a day! Incredible! Yeah! San Francisco's such a tough market, no matter what. I heard about the Stanford gig, too. My guy Wally B. at KZSU (you know that's the Stanford station, right? I knew you knew—just checking!) filled me in. Awesome! Apparently you guys did great! They *loved* you guys. Seriously. Don't look at me like that! They did. Swear to God. And the rest of the tour was, um, okay? *Pretty* good?"

As Franklin stood there biting his lower, the plumper, lip, rooting for us to've had a tour on a par with, oh, The Stones in '71 or something or Led Zeppelin basically every year, I remembered our roommate Keating, who as a record producer had had lots of experience with "label people," had told me: "Look, John—always remember. They sit at a desk all day long and run out to the warehouse and talk on the phone and drive the van to get the 'product' from the manufacturer and forklift it around all day—*and every single one of them would trade places with you in a heartbeat, no matter what you're going through on the road.* They probably got into the record business because they dreamed at one time of being up onstage and having people worship them; so if you tell them when they ask you how your tour went, for instance, go complain about how hard it was and how broke you are and how you never want to see or smell a club a*gain*, it's only gonna crush their buzz twice! Their buzz has already been crushed by the fact that they work *in* music—not *do* or *play* music."

"I get it," I'd replied.

Keating went on: "That's exactly why so *many* of the chicks at major labels are very cute. Not all of them, of course, but lots. It's, as everyone knows, a glamorous industry, so the super attractive but musically talentless girls who try and get jobs get their resumes shuffled right to the top of the pile, not "put on file." How many times have the *un*cute in LA been told "We'll keep it on file." Fact. Some of those total babes at labels, now—they get VP positions or 'Senior' Head of Marketing or whatever. Some. Not all. I would love to meet just *one* who knows Sabbath's entire catalogue or even the first four Eno solo records! If I ever met an industry chick like that, who knew her stuff instead of who got dropped from Hollywood Records or MCA that week and who slept with half of Duran Duran I would ask her to marry me right then and there. Misogyny? Nope. I don't think so. The same thing could be said for most of the *guys* in music. You know? No one knows music like the people who actually make it, not sell it. There are a few A&R guys who play and produce—two or three here and four or five in New York and quite a few in London, but that's what you'd expect, right? It's really sad. They're just 'suits,' most of them, people who work at labels. Do you know Sindi H. Blithering (you've heard of her, right? She's like a 'ten' and a half, total fox) or Mary Anne Parkby (blonde, great boobs, *great* smile, mad as a box of frogs, signed Smashing Pumpkins and Christina Aguilera or someone on the exact same day). You do? Okay. Those are the glam girls. And they kinda know their stuff—but not really. They may or may not and to varying degrees realize that the record business is all about image—from the bands to the chicks and guys who get their picture in *Hits* and fucking *Billboard*. At least, that's what I think. What do I know? (A lot! Haha!) But many of the women who keep on top of things, who make forty thousand calls a day on your behalf, who make someone-like-you's record maybe sell and get posters up instead of lying around in the corner of a store collecting dust? Some of those girls are *not* the glam girls. They might even have faces like a horse crossed with a mouse…or like a horse crossed with a mouse crossed with a *camel*. The highlight of their week is getting standing-room-only/industry-only tickets to some 'buzz' band from England or Japan that they go see but can't see 'cause the place is packed and they can barely see the frontman. So, the rule is, when a horse/mouse/camel face asks you how your tour went (unless they know that your van slid off the road in Colorado and, like, all thirteen of your crazy band mates and road crew died in a fiery, snowy crash), you wink and flirt and smile and say 'Oh, my God—it was just a*mazing!* Just incredible. Oh my gosh: I wish you could've come along. The wonderful, glorious Midwest…I *so* wish you coulda been there with us!' And you sit back and let them vicariously participate and pat you on the back and fantasize about it and be a part—even if it's only a tiny little bit of it—of your rock and roll dream. Remember that, then, John. I'm telling you. It really helps. Save your moaning and groaning for your friends and fellow musicians like me. Especially as I *love* road horror stories 'cause I can't stand even the *thought* of touring. The idea of touring comes into my head, I immediately get rid of it. Plus, as you know, I think live music is just *stupid* unless it's really bad tribute bands! Hahaha. Except The Weird Sisters, of course. You know I'm into *you* guys. You know I love going to those tribute shows! Anyway, save your complaining for guys like me who spend all their time in studios, thankful every single day of their working life that they aren't in some poor band that has to get out there and *tour*. Hahaha."

That Keating—he said some pretty philosophical stuff sometimes. And I just loved his prejudice against live music. Of course live music is dumb. Give me a record to listen to any day. Give Keating and me (and maybe quite a few of you who've got this novel on your lap or propped up on the kitchen table as you eat your super-sugared cereal) a piece of goddam vinyl. Your record's going to be around for eternity, mate. Your big live gig at The Roxy or The Whisky or the auxiliary Baskin-Robbins on Santa Monica or some pizza "arena" or pinball joint is over in thirty-or-so minutes and the punters who were there and afterward jabbering-nattering on about how *rock* you were and how a*mazing* you were are going to start talking about an even better show they saw last week/month/year within, like, fifteen minutes after your amp's cooled down and the strains of your last chord have evaporated in the club's hazy air, believe me.

Keating, boy—I can't wait for you to meet him; he's a total "character." He was so different from our "old" producer—the equally charming and kooky McLeary—in that McLeary knew "fuck-all" about the biz; and the people in it. We used to just laugh at his naïveté when he'd say stuff like this: "Give them [any record company off the street] a bell, see if they're signin' anyone. Ace! Ring 'em up, see what they say. See if they want an ace record from a number one band. Easy-peasy." As if it was easy-peasy as snapping your fingers, getting a record deal, finding a label! The funny thing was, whenever we called McLeary out on professing to know the ins and outs of the industry, he'd look all hurt, like he'd been pinked with a white-hot lance fresh from the blacksmith's tongs or something. These artistic types, I tell you—thin-skinned as hell, every last one of them. Tetchy fuckers to a man. Even the stuff they know fuck-all about they want you to think they fucking know all about.

I thusly remembered well what Keating had told me when I told Frankin: "It *was* great," and watched a thin, "knowing" smile spread across his soft-kind face; "That gig. And the other gigs…uh, some good, some bad. You know. Mostly good, though. Pretty okay! All in all, a really good tour, Franklin. Lots of great gigs, in fact. Quite a few. Some. *One*, actually. Hahaha. No. I'm joking. Half of one—haha! I'll tell you about them later. Manson's gone for the day, huh?"

Mike Manson, I think I mentioned, was the Mike who'd signed us.

"Actually, um, I have to tell you something," Franklin said, lowering his voice conspiratorially and all. "He's—I guess I can just tell you—not going to be working here anymore. He's gone. Not just for the day and stuff. He…resigned. He told Mike Mays Friday and all of us yesterday morning. This is hard, John. I'm really sorry."

"You're kidding, right?!" I said.

Franklin looked down at his untied, discount high-top basketball shoes. "I wish I was. I…I'm hoping nothing's going to change for you…I mean, well…you know you guys are one of my favorite, if not my favorite and…I just…"

"It's all right, Franklin," I said.

But of course that's not what I meant.

"We'll just see what happens, is all," Franklin said. "Just—you know—talk to Mike Mays and see what he has to say. It's all so new. And with Cobain, um, passing away like that…"

"Sure," I lied. "Thanks for telling me, Franklin."

"Oh," he said. "No problem, John."

Mike Manson was the Better partner whom Stacey, the label manager, had made listen to the album we'd made with our old producer McLeary; he was the one who'd signed us, convincing the other Mike, Mike Mays, who was more of an old punk and pure rockabilly and straight-ahead *rock* guy, to have us on the label. Mike Manson had "gotten" what we did. A Kinks and Zombies and all-'round sixties music freak, he liked bands with *songs*, with *melodies*— and poetasting lyrics that went with them, beyond the "Hubba-hubba, baby-baby/Let me be your yes not maybe" kinda stuff that was everywhere, music-wise.

Stuff like:

If I can't have you, baby, tonight
I'm gonna start a total fight
With any body in this bar
And then I'm gonna gun my car
Through the front door of the bar
Then you will know who me and my friends totally are
All right, all right, all right!
Let's fight tonight, tonight, tonight!
Rock, rock, rock, rock and roll!!!
Rock, rock, rock, rock and roll!!!

'Cause we got some rad tattoos
Pimped out rides all red and blue
See that Chevy in the parking lot?
See that girl who is so hot?
By "Last Call" she's gonna be with me
We're gonna get down, can't you see?
Get out of here and get it on
Then drive my hot rod 'round till dawn
Breaks in this sad town's sky
Every day I wonder—why
But till then I'm gonna get so wasted
This drink's the best that I have ever tasted
Don't even think of talking to her
That chick right there, though you bought her a beer
That chick you want—too bad, she's mine
I'm rockin' rollin' all the time—yeah
I'm pounding drinks, it's totally ace
Look out—I'm gonna pound your face!
Rock, rock, rock, rock—and roll!!!
Rock, rock, rock, rock—and roll!!!

Mike Manson was "our" guy, all right. Mike Mays on the other hand had only "gotten" the notion that *one* of our songs was a sort of "hit"—and that's, we suspected, why he'd agreed to have us on Better. And he'd been right, for, as you've already heard a hundred times now, it was getting a lot of airplay in San Francisco and a couple of other, smaller "markets." Mike Mays's idea of a band was a bunch of tough-looking fucks in slick suits or "wifebeaters," with tats and hats (*hats*, I tell you!) and biker vests (*leather* vests) with no shirt (no *shirt!*) smoking two Camel Lights apiece onstage and pounding three chords to death to the beat of a locomoting paradiddle at deafening volume. Rat-a-ta-TAT, Rat-a-ta-TAT—over and over and *over*, thumping a drooling-dumb and imbecile crowd into dumb, stunned submission. Three or four Johnny-strum-latelys plus a drummer mouth-breathing on a giant stage as they pogoed around and got their goddam legs as wide apart as possible, out-posturing each other, more like a Cirque du Soleil dress rehearsal than a music performance. The more a band did cartwheels and breathed fire and tossed midgets and the like, the more Mays thought they were the second coming of Elvis or The Beatles or David Cassidy or the Red Hot Chili Peppers. The more they "sang" about having sex with hookers sideways-arseways in the back of a fully "cherry," candy apple-red or screaming yellow muscle car (amidst maybe some spent crack pipes and a gallimaufry of fast-food wrappers), the more Lennon/McCartney he thought them. He was a music and musical dumbshit who, like most other music/musical dumbshits, liked the dumbshit sort of music that other total dumbshits were dumb enough to like dumbshittingly. A dreaded group called Social Distortion—the *most* egregious band of be-tattooed, talent-free, stupendously stupid, knuckle-draggging, posing *posers* in the history of rock (next to the aforementioned egregious Red Hot Chili P's)—was far and away his favorite band, his Holy Grail, Sacred Cow, and über-band in one. Know them? Mother Mary, I hope not. I hope you don't. Poor you if you've heard even *one bar* of their utterly unlistenableness. They don't have an *ounce* of it, dear reader. Not an ounce. They're really a piece of shit. They. Really. Are. A. Piece. Of. *Fucking*. Shit.

Know how people throw around that term? How they say to their priest or pastor, for instance: "Hel-*lo*, Father, how ya been, ya piece of shit, ya? How's the wife and illegitimate kids?" (Try it with an Irish accent—it's marvelous.) You know how that expression is just a phrase and all, just an expression and stuff? Well, just this once, just this one time, I want you to picture, in your most vivid, lucid mind's eye, *an actual shit piece*. There it is. See it? Look at it. It looks like *shit*, doesn't it? *Look* at that shit, wouldja? Just *look* at it! Disgusting. Got it there, in your mind, then? Good. Well, that's Social Distortion. Social "D." That's those music-oafs for ya. A piece of *shit* really-truly *is* them. Someone puts on one of their fucking records and you look around and go: "Oh my *God*—what *is* that? What's that *smell?* Something smells like *shit* in here, all of a sudden. What *is* that? Oh, oh—someone put on Social Dis*tor*tion. That's what that is. It's them again. Jesus, open a window or…take that shit *off*, please! *Please!*"

A few years ago (or yesterday—I don't know, who *cares?*), *eminence grise* rock royalty-member Tom Petty drawled in some national or regional rock rag or other that "rock and roll doesn't have to be *good* to be great." And though of course old TP—opining away to some salivating reporter, presumably—was being glib and cagey-like, he's kinda got a point. Music—it *is* fucking stupid, after all, isn't it? Whether it's Wolfgang Amadeus or a quondam tipsy shepherd with a home-fashioned bucolic flute trudging home from the misty or golden evening fields: whichever geezer you're talking about, his job's basically to come up with a little melody that even a drunken cretin might recognize as "Uh, kinda catchy, very nice." He likes it, drunken cretin does, it touches him somewhere. Or it doesn't, so he switches the channel on the radio or in his mind or walks out of the chamber room or concert hall. When's it coming out on 180 gram vinyl with a double-gatefold jacket and a swanky cover designed by old Storm Thorgerson of Hipgnosis, this song? If it's any good at all, halfway through it, "Crety" is singing along in his very dumb way.

It's a hit!

Perhaps.

But when he said that, good old Tom Petty didn't mean that stupid is guaranteed golden, I don't think. He didn't mean that your rock, you groovy kids out there, is good just because it isn't great. What do I know, though? I'm only one expert/genius/oracle/guru. It's only one wonderful, tasteful, experienced, brilliant, singular, extraordinary, polymath, didactic, arrogant, incredible, insightful guy's amazing, unparalleled, considered opinion. That's all. And Social D. has only sold four zillion million more records than The Weird Sisters has, have, or ever will.

Je vous en prie!

"I'm gonna go eat this, then," Franklin told us then, giving me an unbearably compassionate look, something tremendously horrendous. My face must've waxed completely canescent at the news re: Manson quitting or something 'cause Franklin kept looking at me with this super pathetic look like he'd just found out I had penile cancer or advanced leukemia or a case of double shingles or something. "I wasn't sure if you guys had heard or not," he continued with a kind of ostentatious kindness that was truly terrifying. "Then again, how would you have known? Don't worry, though. It'll all be fine. Everything's gonna be okay, believe me. Really. I'll let Mays fill you in. He's in his office—go on in."

He smiled his most apologetic, shrieve-me smile (it couldn't be more "I'm sorry") and held the enormous heavy door for me. It was psychologically comprehensible that Franklin *would* have said such positive, sanguine things when, in actuality, his outlook as far as we, The Weird Sisters, were concerned was most nigrescent. In meaning to reassure me, us, he'd accomplished the opposite. Everything's going to be okay. Sure. Okay. Okay maybe, maybe—after you get over the heartache of losing a label deal you've found (it's really, really hard to get a record deal, people—harder than you can ever imagine) and have to find another one in a hard-to-find/super-competitive market. *Kinda like the love/romance business, this record business business,* I thought just then, freaking out a little bit in my incontrovertibly worrisome way.

By the way, don't you fucking hate it when people, even if they sincerely seem to have the very best good intentions, tell you not to worry? Especially when worrying is exactly what you should be doing. Especially when worrying's something you're really good at.

I really, really, really, hate that.

Four

"ou guys are a 'chick band'—definitely," Mike Mays was ponderously intoning as Jenny and I sat there, across from him, in some chairs on the other side of his vast, very shiny, ebony desk. The seats we were sitting in seemed like they might've been purloined from a school cafeteria or an Elks Lodge or encounter group for coprophiliacs. Mays had his freakishly large hands locked behind his gargantuan Charles II head and his long, be-jeaned legs up on the desk and crossed like he'd just finished a hard day's night's work or a five-star meal and was thinking of ordering some Russian brandy in a properly-warmed snifter. He had the same long-ass curly Restoration hair that Franklin did, only Franklin slicked his back in a sort of a rogue ponytail that bobbed away like a startled animal heading for the safety of a bush or a hole in the ground under an unbudgeable boulder, whereas Mike Mays let *his* wig fully cascade all over the shop, i.e. down his massive shoulders, out the window, into another zip code. It was like someone'd precariously placed a rare, black, box jellyfish atop his head. He had that "tick" that super-long-haired guys sometimes have of flipping their locks back, one side then the other, like they're shaking off the devil on one shoulder, an angel on the other, or balancing out their dandruff. It was useless, Mays's flipping of the hair, of course, on account of they just jounced right back, his hair hanks. They looked like considerably formidable theatre curtains, all sable—something off Broadway, or from Aldwych, the West End. The London *Fringe!* Hahaha! You half expected some Liliputian characters from Molière or Congreve to come forth from beneath Mays's mop, disseminating super wit or foppish repartee or something in voices

like they had sixteen little plums lolling in their mouths while they talked, pulling back ornately embroidered greatcoats to shew a pretty turn of leg or unveil a silver-hilted rapier dripping with glistening poison. The funny or not so funny thing was, Mays didn't look at Jenny *once* the whole time he was telling us that we were a band that appealed to women way more than men, that women were going to make up The Sisters' "record-buying audience" and putative "fan club." Not even once, I noticed, as he was saying hello and welcoming us back did he look Jen's way. It was as though she didn't exist or he was gonna get in trouble with his mom or his wife if he so much as *glanced* at her with these deep, dark, deep-set dark blue eyes flecked with brilliant marmalade spots and drops beneath big, black, beetling brows. Once or twice only did it seem like he pointed this unbelievable *horseshoe* of hairy hair around his mouth in the general direction of Jen (he had a positively *florid* Fu Manchu going in the most "fuck-you" way), but it could've just been he had a crook in his neck from looking at himself in the mirror half the day or something. I'm not saying Mike Mays was a full-blown misogynist or anything, but you'd as like find in his office a barking mad drunk leprechaun with a pot of gold and riding around on a Shetland unicorn as you would a book by Simone de Beauvoir or Naomi Wolf or *The Intimate Unauthorized Unexpurgated Biography of Helen Reddy* (if such a thing exists) or any Joni Mitchell or Linda Ronstadt record. It struck me then as it strikes me now that The Weird Sisters were the only band on the label with a *female* member. And there were at least twenty bands on Better, if you included the ones that'd put out one record (there were lots of those) and then just split or gave up.

As we sat there, Jenny and I, I wondered idly if Rob and Ral might wander in later: Rob hated all things label-wise nearly as much as Jenny did (he thought of labels as pirates, shysters, scammers in a takes-one-to-know-one way, I guess). As opposed to sitting in an interminable and (to-him) pointless meeting, he was much more interested in foraging for free snacks, paling around with Franklin (who got the biggest kick out of him, who thought he was *the* funniest guy in the world), or going off to one of the label's many vestigial rooms to watch the humongous TV they had for screening videos and things, playing videos games or something. Franklin had probably found some lark's tongue soup and turtle *tartare* for Rob to eat—plus some caviar and pâté and *filet mignon*, with a lobster shooter chaser. (Yeah, right.) What I mean was, Franklin had probably gone with Rob back out to the pig-pink food truck so that Rob could order a couple of megatacos that, in terms of eating them, might be like swallowing a blistering tube of molten fire. In terms of hurling them at someone, they'd be like flaming discuses, certified weapons you could *hurt* some fucker with. They gave you mitigating limes (which, actually, do nothing but fuel the firey flames of unjoy in your scalded, smoking mouth), and then laughed at you, the Chicano/psycho-smiling guys in the roach coach taco truck did. They had these looks on their faces that said, yes, *güero*, we *are* sweating bullets in here, just dousing our *chingaso* blue or red bandanas, working our *culos* off, dreaming the *norteamericano* Dream; but, shortly, you will put a little red or harmless-looking yellow pepper in your mouth and you, *gringo*, you will taste the taste of a man's throat burning like the white hot fires of hellish *infierno*. Indeed, yearn you indubitably will for gallons and gallons of cold *leche* to pour down your poor, purplish mouth, your mouth like a dragon's breath, like a furnace, like Central Mexico at noon in summer. *Salud, güero.* Enjoy your beautiful meal, *pendejo* white boy. And don't even *think* of asking us for sour cream! We've made these bad boys sour cream-proof all the way."

I had eaten from that truck—once and never again. It was so good, a possible addiction. But you paid for the spicy, savory flavor for hours and hours after. The second time we'd gone down to schmooze with the label people Rob'd ended up outside in the alleyway, sitting on a couple of orphaned cement blocks, Rob-head in hand.

I knew immediately from the look of him what he'd gone and done: "You ate one of those tacos again, didn't you?" I said. "Oh no, Rob."

"My head!" Rob said, making a visor of his left hand, studying the asphalt, moaning, groaning.

"Oh, *no*, Rob. Are you gonna be okay?"

"I don't *think* so. I don't *know*, man. I don't know what's worse—my head or my tongue. My tongue's like a flaming pepper on *fire*. I think if I ate another one—and I *might*; I'm that stupid, all right?—that I might go *blind*, I swear. Keep me away from that truck, okay? I mean it. Is it still there?"

I'd looked over and sighed and umm'ed and Rob had gone: "Oh, nooo! Make it go a*way*."

Raleigh must have wandered away to use the phone; he said he had to ring his dad, check in. Ral was probably bummed it was only a local call because, as I mentioned, his pops lived in Tustin or Fullerton or somewhere, having moved long ago from Utah. And besides, I couldn't blame Raleigh for shying off somewhere, anywhere other than where Mays was. For Mays was, at six-five, intimidating, to say the least. People in LA (and especially the OC) don't ever *really* look at you, make eye contact—not even when they want something from you. (They almost all of them want something from you; it's something you adjust to—or you move back to Dallas or Provo or wherever. Almost all of them, I said—not *every*one.) But Mays, he was different—he made *too much* eye contact. It was discomfiting to the max. Unless you were, as I mentioned, a chick: then he never looked your way. Strange. The world is replete with ineffable nutters. But the record industry has a plethora of them, all right. More than enough to go around.

"That's how I see you," Mays continued. "As a 'chick band.' And you've gotta find that 'chick' audience that's going to appreciate you best. That's gonna make up the bulk of your 'chick' audience. The only thing is, *chicks* [and here he drawled the term out to around fifty-two sententious syllables]—*chicks don't really buy records*. Ask anyone. Ask *them*. 'Do you buy records?' you could ask them. 'Do you ever go to record stores and just...do you ever purchase *anything* from a record store?' And: 'Um,' they'd go, 'what are *those*?' Or you could ask them: 'What do you listen to, sweetheart? What kind of *music* do you like?' And they'd be all: 'Oh, *you* know—whatever comes on KROQ!'

Stuff like that. 'I listen to *everything! Like, whatever, like, comes on the radio!*' Pah! Chicks don't buy records. So: there you go."

"That whole 'I listen to everything' thing is such a cop-out," I said placatingly, hating myself all the way, even though I couldn't have known it just then, that I was being a total label-lackey. "You're right, Mike."

"*I* buy records," Jenny said neutrally, disinterestedly, an aural shrug. "*I* buy them."

Good going, Jen.

And then of course the world's record longest pregnant pause.

"Well, of course *you* do," Mike Mays said, smoothening his enormous Fu Manchu, the facial hair-affectation that made him seem, weirdly, younger than he was, younger than we who in our late- and middle-twenties were, even. "Of *course* you do, uh, um, Jenny. Sure, sure, sure. You're an artist. I *get* that, I do. And, and, and…but I'm talking about *reg*ular people. The average…oh, speaking of which: Can I have the record company credit card back? You used it just for gas and stuff, right? That was the deal we had, wasn't? Right?"

"Uh-huh," I said.

"I buy a couple of cassettes, in fact, a week, maybe," Jenny continued, "I may not buy as many as John does, but…"

"Good. That's great," Mays cut her off. "I'm sure you…hey. You guys add a lotta people to your mailing list? Get a bunch of people to sign up? Give Stacey the information, will you? We need that data asap-pronto."

Then he held out the back of his hand and fluttered it, his long long fingers, that is: "The credit card?"

Jenny charmingly tucked her pretty, just-discernably-in-need-of-a-wash cherry red/brown hair behind one ear and reached into her purse and plucked it, the golden credit card, from her wallet and handed it to him in what I thought, idealizing her of course, was a pretty queenly fashion. She had to stand up and lean forward in order to do so, over the prodigious desk, as, mannerlessly, Mays didn't rise up to meet her or even get up and come take it from her, as would've been polite, the right thing to do; and I noticed Mays kind of quickly look away as Jen's unmistakable décolletage spilled forth sort of unmistakably voluptuously toward him from her sheer white V-neck T-shirt, her uniform, so to speak, something she knew she looked casually/effortlessly great in, as she gave him the golden "plastic," blouse opening, bra showing. *He did it pointedly,* I thought. It would've been more decorous/considerate, I think, to at least *glance* at them, just them, her swelling breasts, her cleavage. I mean, she had great tits, Jenny did. Ask anybody. Not just kind of—*great.* Even guys like me who aren't at all or even especially "boob guys" had to hand it to her— nice *breasts,* Jen; nice *rack.* Sometimes the term *Cover of Supermarket Bodice-Ripper* sort of leaped to your libido-consciousness when you caught her décolleté out of the corner of even your not-leering eyes. And in some weird way I thought right then that it was kind of rude, if you will, rude of Mays *not to* sneak a peek. I mean, he was kinda, as head of the label, like a boss of hers or something—pretty wrong of him not to let her know she, the employee/artist-slave, was pretty sexy. Guy runs a record label and doesn't check out for more than a quick nanosecond some wonderful breastals that are right in his fucking CEO-ish *face?* —guy's kind of a dick, if you ask *me.* I mean, what a fuckface. What a *weirdo.* That's just plain *wrong,* don't you reckon? I mean, give them a break, okay? Pay homage. Obeisance. Be a goddam *gentleman* once in a while, for a change, for chrissakes, and at least glance, you bastard. Pay tribute to those, as Dr. Johnson—backstage at some play and frolicking among thespians—called them, "bubbies that excite [my] amorous propensities."

The big, black, bright desk Mays sat at was cluttered, of course, with legal papers and memos and brightly colored papers and important-looking manila folders and press photos and demos on cassette and fountain pens and pencils—the latter two fanning out from an oversized "Official Sex Pistols Fan Club Coffee Mug" and "swag": trinkets of all types, many used as promotional items, spread out higgledy-piggledy. Trinkets from other record companies, mostly, it seemed, as far as *I* could tell. Some of them pretty vintage-looking: like a Sopwith Camel model airplane that said "The Jefferson

Airplane" on it, and a khaki-colored ceramic bowl of frothing, pyramidical "cream" that had "Cream" emblazoned on it. There were also a few knick knacks of a space alien nature: bobblehead faire and rubber erasers with lightbulby heads all eyes and ghost-white pates and spindly arms and legs in grotesque orange and green. Plus one of those unimaginably unimaginative steel ball thingies that click-clacked distractingly back and forth: the sort of seventies thing that could've only been construed as spoof of the prototypical "American Business Guy."

"Thanks," Mays said. At least he said that.

"You do know, Mike," I said, "that we have a national tour planned, booked, I mean, for fall—to Boston and back. And, uh…" I sallied, then trailed away, already so oh-so utterly already defeated in that I knew just then that I was practically just talking to myself, making a woebegone soliloquy.

I was of course hinting at but of course not coming right out and asking if we were maybe going to get the bleeding credit card back come September when we were meant to be touring again—the biggest tour of our lives, one that had taken me arduous weeks and weeks to set up and that still was sort of more penciled than penned in, if you know what I'm saying, with great gaps still between, say, Athens, GA and Boston, MA; Minneapolis, MN and Seattle, WA. And what with Manson resigning, who knew what the future held. For aught I or anybody know, Mays would drop us from the label—quasi-hit song on a couple of commercial radio stations or no. It was best, I remember thinking at the time, for me just to play it cool—something, as you may have rather divined, I'm not very good at playing. Mays's allegiances, loyalties were, to anyone with an ounce of perception, as substantial as trifle—and as good for you. And I could go you one further and say he was as fun as warm beer on a hot Friday.

Warm beer and melted trifle.

"Well. Hmm. We'll talk about that, uh, um, John," Mays said, "when the time is right. When it's closer to, uh, well…when the stars and planets line up. When they are 'aligned,' as they say. How's that?"

"Oh. Um. Okay," I said, startled as someone walking along in a dark twilight wood—only to come upon a row of yellow trees bright as the sun.

I didn't want to look Jen's way right then; my guess was she was trying not to make a face.

"Do you know about The Pleiades People?" Mays asked, leaning forward, making a sort of disingenuously professorial tent of his humongous hands.

"Is that a band?" Jenny said mock-innocently, brightly, turning back up the treble in her tone.

Nice one, Jen.

"Hahaha!" Mays laughed, throwing his big black mop back, exhibiting his great teeth, then looking straight ahead, in between us, straightfacedly, very, very serious. "No."

Blank looks at Mays. Blank looks traded between Jenny and me.

"It's not 'a band,'" Mays said with a strange sort of dreamlike insolence, like he was remonstrating with a couple of very good children who'd done something uncharacteristically very bad.

More looks of blanky blankness.

"You've never heard of them?"

Blanker looks, if possible. I could've sworn that normally unflappable Jen had thrown her shoulders back—like when someone tells you they're radioactive or pregnant by your favorite priest or great uncle.

And then, just then, Raleigh, slurping a thickly-frosted coconut cupcake, wandered in to Mays's office. The cupcake was so big I thought for a second he was about to take a fatal bite of a claymore bomb from WWI. He took a seat in a chair that was just to the right of Mays's desk, closer to him, and in front of us, sitting like an eager benchwarmer might sit at the feet of a psychotic coach who would never put him, the benchwarmer, in the game, not ever.

"May I help you?" Mays said like some kind of super urbane, futuristic ticket agent and flipped his long-ass hair back *again*.

"That's our drummer, Mike—Raleigh. You've met him," I said; I was really tilting at windmills here, urging a sort of familiarity as a kind of over-earnest, desperate statement, like: "You *know* him, and you *like* The Weird Sisters, Mike, and you're not going to drop us from the label, just because the one partner who liked us, backed us and stuff, is gone: You wouldn't *do* that. You *couldn't*. You couldn't *pos*sibly! You're going to give us money to make another record and you're going to give us tour support for our national tour. Please, please, please—you are. Thank you in advance, in fact."

"Oh, sorry, sorry, sorry," Mays said. "Hi."

"Hello," Raleigh said. "Hi. How's it going?"

"Fine," Mays said, like he was talking to an agile toddler who was badly in need of a change of diaper. "And how are you?"

"Fine."

"That's nice. Nice to see you."

"Nice to see you, too."

Jesus wept. Then Jesus picked up a bench from behind the backstop and hurled it with all his almighty Jesus-powers at the umpire's tiny head.

"You're the drummer, huh," Mays inanely said; then, by way of an answer of sorts I guess, Raleigh took a pretty theatrical bite of the cupcake. We had to wait to sort of let him finish smacking his lips and swallowing, licking his lips and wiping them with a greasy party napkin, then gulping a little, running his tongue 'round his teeth, making a kind of monkey-face to shift the chocolate crumbs 'round in his mouth, then down.

Words just can't do justice to the…

And there was, just then, as you might imagine, a prodigiously imbecile moment of great stupid suspense: as in, when is this Mexican standoff of stupendous platitudes and nice niceness going to end? Silly grin on Raleigh, his eyes darkly sparkling; weird gurning look from Mays. More pauses. Beat. Beat redux. Frozen inanimation. Awkward pause continuing. Blank looks on both sides. Stalemate of whopping oafishness. Jenny and I now exercising our necks like people with really good seats at a professional tennis tournament. More dopey, bumbling smiling. Jenny's pretty face looking now like someone'd shoved the world's most difficult algebra problem in front of it. Me hemming, with assorted attempts at hawing as well. A musical scale of quizzical vowelly inquiries—ah, erm, I-ah, oh, um—going through my muddled head. *This is just doesn't half get weirder and weirder*, I think, as Raleigh, at last, goes: "So: what are you guys talking about?"

"The Pleiades People," I said chinlessly, instantaneously. It would have been impossible for me to convey—even were I momentarily transmogrified into a sort of neo-Charlie Chaplin or Buster Keaton or Marcel Marceau—with a look or two what I was hoping to convey to Raleigh as he turned around. The idea I was trying to put across was this: "Hey—don't ask *me!* I have as little a clue as you do as to what the fuck The Pleiades People is, okay?!" plus "Don't react with a big, fat laugh right now, please, if you don't mind. The person we are talking to is likely completely off his rocker and moreover he holds, in part at least, the fate of our first—and maybe our last—album in his daft, mad hands."

"Who?!" Raleigh said. "What's that—a band or something?"

Then Ral gave out a sort of horrid snort-laugh like he'd made an inadvertent zinger of a ridiculously topping good joke. Like, scored somehow or something.

"No!" Mays, Jenny, and I said at the same time—but of course with different intonations. Mays's: "You fool!" Jenny's: "Look out!" Mine: "Just you wait!"

"They're from space," crazy Mays said evenly. "The stars. Star people—or, not *people* but creatures, aliens, though I don't like that word because it implies…whatever. There's all sorts of new evidence. Old, too. We're learning things we've never learned before. They're really starting to become—how to say this?—more *known* to us, more…"

Snort! Raleigh snorted. "*Oh-*kay…you mean, like, *outer* space? You guys are putting me on, right? This is a joke, right? I mean, come on. Really. You're pulling my…"

Thanks, Raleigh, I thought at maximum thought-volume. *How very politic of ye*. But you couldn't blame him, really. You yourself might've gone right up to Mays just then and admonished him to have his head examined and pronto, greeted his extraterrestrial incomprehensibilities and crazy-strange enthusiasms with a *double* snort mixed with a theatrical throwing of one's incredulous head back, amidst sundry ho-ho-ho's of superior, fingerpointing knowingness and unwilling suspensions of dancing disbelief. But the unflappable, incredible Mike Mays, incredibly, continued unflappably, either ignoring or snubbing our drummer's snorty snub: "Listen: the Ancient Incas believed, as many ancient cultures from Australasia to Peru to The Hopi to the Norse legends that, er, were orally carried forth by the, uh, pre-Vikings, that Earth was in fact discovered by people who came from The Pleiades—a race of giants eight or more feet tall. Who come from the stars. A specific constellation. The Pleiades. One that's very bright and prominent to this day." And here he looked up at the ceiling like one, a Pleiadean (sic? a Pleiadoid? Pleiadedean?), had just come through the strip lights and was gonna have a cup of coffee with us and fill us in on what was going on not only in the celestial realms, but also for the last six billion years or so. Mays's demeanor and voice had seemed very professorial—like someone in a donnish monotone conducting one of those traffic school classes you have to go to if they catch you speeding in a construction zone or running over dozens of happy-laughing children carelessly crossing at a primary school crosswalk. Just then the florescent lights blinked, then surged some, with a little hissing sound, and flashed back and forth, unmistakably, like some Jungian synchronicity was going down, like a weird, buzzy sign of something weirder-to-come. Mays gave an odd, smug look like "See what I mean?" as though we were all of us meant to bow down right then and there or break out some hooded Druid costumes and fall into a human stone circle and begin the "chanting" process.

Jenny I caught rolling her eyes.

"Come on in, Stacey," Mike Mays beckoned to Stacey, the label manager, as she appeared like an apparition at the door. Stace was a cool gal who'd chanced to be at that big gig we'd done at USC, our second show ever and stuff; she'd been leaning against Mays's open door apparently and now she came forward and found a chair and said hello. She was one of a couple of record execs who'd got our information through the college radio station at SC, rung us up, and given Mike Manson a tape of the album we'd recorded on our own with McLeary. Without her, we would never—for better or for worse—have gotten our record deal. We might have gotten another record deal at another smaller label, but Stacey was mostly why, I'm trying to say, for better or worse, we'd landed on Better.

We'd taken the first thing we were offered—reckoning that the record biz was such a gamble anyway that we shouldn't look a gift horse in the snout. Great move on our part. Real swift. But, you know, in our defense, we were just kids, older kids, at twenty-seven, twenty-four, twenty-six (me, Jen, Rob), and we didn't have a manager, didn't know any better, either. What did we know? We knew we wanted to be a band, and "one that mattered" (cf. the opening of *The King of Good Intentions*), whatever *that* meant. We didn't want to be stars—or I didn't; I don't know about anybody else, really. I, me, I just wanted to do stuff, musically. That's all. That's what made all the "bullshit" you had to put up with worthwhile, worth it.

She gave us all a big, wide smile, Stacey did. It took up about the whole of her person 'cause Stacey's about the thinnest human you could ever imagine. I don't think she, for one, frequents the "roach coach" at all. All she seems to do is work work work and go see bands (which is more work, believe me) and drink around four thousand cups of coffee a day. She's amazing, Stacey; you'd like her, too. I know I keep saying that about people, but you would, you'd get a kick out of her if you had any sense at all.

You know how Patti Smith is/was scary skinny, as was Joni Mitchell and maybe Grace Slick too? Those chicks are *porkers* compared to Stace. She needs a double chili cheeseburger and a double order of double cheese fries and a double chocolate chocolate shake with chocolate sprinkles plus a straw made of hardened fat, all right, and that's just for *breakfast*, but she's "good people"—from Brooklyn, so we tease her sometimes about her accent. She makes fun of it too. She's very cool. A real kick. We love Stacey. But she should have a ham stack, crab melt, or triple Monte Cristo every night before she goes to bed for the next ten months. She doesn't look healthy, her. She's in dire need of a bunch of good old American, caloric, high-in-fat foods, if you ask me, me the nutritionist.

Yeah, right.

"Hey, you guys!" she hailed us. She had such a winning smile. "I heard from Franklin the tour was good, huh? Yeah? Awesome. Mike told you guys that Mike—Manson—is moving on, I take it."

"That's a drag, yeah?" I said.

"Hey, Raleigh," Stacey said.

"Hi there! Nice to see you!" Raleigh said.

"You, too. Yeah," Stacey continued with her not exactly charming and yet really quite endearing East Coast voice. "Manson wants to do something different, yeah. He doesn't know what, he said, but that's it for him, record biz-wise. Hiya, Jenny!"

"Sorry to hear that," I said with a look that, I hoped, conveyed to Mike Mays that, no matter what, no matter who was driving the boat or ship, we were still gung-ho indie rock diehards who were ready to do whatever it took to make our record go gold or silver or even tin; and that we weren't in the least nonplussed that a freaky believer in aliens and star-people had the controls, as it were, of the spaceship of our career. Spaceship? More like plummeting rocketship. Plummeting straight down. Or *Challenger*ing in mid-space.

"Hi, Stace," Jenny said warmly.

"Glad you guys are back safe and all. Anyway. Nah, it's cool, yeah. We're all still friends, right, Mike? Everything's cool. Everyone's just doing their thing, you know? Awesome," Stacey dissertated. "Hey, listen, I gotta talk to one of our more cool distributors for a bit (we're gonna fix that little hitch about your record not being in stores, okay?) but I will check back in a bit, okay? I wish I could say 'That won't happen again!' but, you know: The record business is sometimes just a crazy thing, yeah. Ya know? Unpredictable. Who *knows*, sometimes, right? Yeah. I mean, forgetaboutit! Haha! You guys love it when I say that, huh. I been here—what?—since college, since I was twenty-tree and I can't seemta shake it, dis accent. Ten years. Sylvia Doum can't make your show t'night, unfortunately, but I'll be there in spirit, yeah. My folks are in town too—Franklin told you, yeah? No? I'd bring dem down to the show and all—I would—but dere around fifty thousand yehrs old apiece and stuff. I'm gonna try and be dere. Do my best, ya know?"

Jenny and I just nodded and smiled at her and out she went, mincing steps. I don't know what Jenny's smile said, as it were; but mine must've screamed "Don't leave us alone with him, Stacey-the-label-manager! Please!"

"It's okay," I managed as she waved herself away. "Good seeing you, Stace!"

"So anyway," Mike Mays continued tonelessly, "we may move the label to New Mexico pretty soon. Wouldn't that be awesome?! Won't it? Totally. We may actually do that. Not sure. Somewhere closer to one of the Reservations down there, is what I'm thinking. Or maybe Roswell. But *everyone's* moving there these days. I want to be near the centripedal hub of things—once they come. Is it 'centripedal' or 'centripetal'? I fuckin' don't know. I swear."

"The Pleiades?" I said as neutrally as I could, like it was the faintest of questions, just to make sure I'd heard him right.

"Exactly."

"No kidding," I said as Raleigh got up just then, and walked out, pleading needing the loo. He gave me a quick look like "Cuckoo!" as he passed me. I was making what seemed to me an *at least* extraordinary effort not to guffaw. I, myself, was *this* close to pointing out the window in abrupt animation and going: "Oh, my God! I just saw one! A Pleiades! He was eating a bratwurst with roasted red and yellow peppers and sautéed onions while flying his supersaucer!"

And yet, at the same time I just nodded along like a perfect Yes Man, a company man, a record company suck-up, your obligatory would-be lapper at the teat of the most vulpine industry in the known universe, a "smellfeast" (as Dictionary Johnson might put it), a hanger-on. Wasn't an artist supposed to be a personage of epic recklessness, a Byron, a Richards, a Kerouac, a non-Pat Boone?" Fat chance.

Truth be told, I couldn't believe I'd just sat there while Mays suggested we consult some mythopoeic people who inhabited the stintless stars and whatnot, whose zip code was an astrological coordinate, presumably. Where were my most implacable principles, whither had flown my impregnable artistic dignity, my inexpungible independent pride, the old college try, the can-doism of callow youth and idealistic idealism? "Where is my mind?" as Black Francis pithily put it. Where was my mind? Nowhere, that's for sure. When someone is, in a completely gossamer way, utterly "out there" anyway, it's best to let them go floating in space, isn't it, ladies and gentlemen? Isn't it? Am I way off here? I mean, what can you do? What boots it anyway if we try and oar or reel them in? Nothing, nothing, nothing, nothing, nothing, nothing.

"Abso*lutely*," Mays continued, winnowing his brow and stuff and nodding earnestly, almost reverentially, like a vicar giving his flock a doctrinaire benediction and the go-ahead to exit out the foyer. "The signs The Pleiades have…oh! Hey! Have you guys heard the new album by The Hot Rod Harrys?" he continued.

"No," I said, as though obsequious me was implying that Mays should keep me there all night, making me miss the last show of the tour, if he really wanted to tell me all about them, the band he was gonna tell me all about.

"You know, they're our biggest seller. Let me play you a track from the new album, just finished, produced by D'Artagnan Andretti. Heard of him? You will. *Great* guy. Works as fast as his famous name suggests! No relation, unfortunately, but still. Met him on a driving range in Yorba Linda I go to from time to time to relax—'work out the kinks' kind of thing. Of course he races stock cars, too, and NASCAR, I think, but his spare time he spends in his studio in Fullerton—not too far from here. You guys should check him out for your next record."

"He's a race car driver *and* a record producer," Jenny said like a person whose disinterestedness could be palpably manifested, produced like a shoebox or something that one could pull from one's lap and set down gingerly on a desk.

"Affirmative," Mike Mays said, fixing his crazy blue-and-marmalade-sprinkled eyes solely on me, of course. Well, fixing isn't really the precise term 'cause they wavered so much, kinda cross-eyedly and stuff. But not really cross-eyed. It's hard to explain. Wonk-eyed, maybe. Creepy. I pictured Jenny breaking out twin checkerboard flags from beneath her chair and semaphoring them about and he *still* wouldn't blink her way. "Let me pop in this tape," he said. "You're gonna *love* this. We are *so* gassed about this record, I'm telling you. The entire label is. No expense spared. Full campaign. Also coming out later this spring is Danger Twins. Know them? I think it should be *The* Danger Twins, but no matter. Brother-sister thing. Or at least that's what the press kit says. Avant-folk thing. Great lyrics. Even better than yours, John. And yours are pretty good—if you care about that sort of thing. Man, these guys are totally out there. Here. Here's an advance cassette. You're gonna dig it. Great live show, too. Unreal… shame about Kurt Cobain, huh? Can't believe it. Anyway, these guys—they play everything on ukulele, accordion, banjo, and tape loops. The whole thing's tape loops. Not a live instrument in evidence! Isn't that incredible? Isn't that amazing?"

"No," Jenny said quietly, under her breath, though only I, I was sure, noticed it, Mays probably being nearly deaf as I was from all the loud music on headphones over the years. How would a guy like Mays ever get to the stage where he'd notice anybody but himself, anyway. To Mays, surely, Jenny was just being incredulous, impressed. I knew her. And I knew better. I half-expected her, a very talented, well-trained, and excellent musician, to get up and walk out right then and there.

But of course she didn't.

I stopped myself from agreeing with Mays. It's the little victories that…don't count at all. Who was I kidding?

"Uh-huh," Mays continued. "They start making out together onstage sometimes—freaks people *out*, man. No shit. Especially when people find out that Lucy, the 'sister,' has had a sex change and is now a *man!* Man! Hahaha! Wonderful. Incredible. Totally hilarious. 'She' goes by 'Larry' now! Can you beat that? We're putting out their four-track demos on hundred-eighty gram vinyl. Double-gatefold thing. Really cool packaging thing. Booklet, lyrics—the full nine. Some story. Totally indie. Indie rock thing. Wow. Rad, huh? Some of the demos weren't even done on a four-track. Some they did on a boom box at their so-called grandma's house right here in Orange County."

"Wow," I echoed.

"Right?!"

"Uh-huh," I said and loathed myself for it.

"*Right?*" he said again. "You have to *hear* this, though. This is a rough mix. Maybe the final mix. Don't know yet. I may have David Lord-Jaquerello remix it. Or maybe Ainsley Baron Lodge. The expense, though—when you are working with those 'big names'! Wow. The expense. Check this out."

He popped up and popped in the tape of The Hot Rod Harrys, about as "muscle car" a band as could be: you could just see their neck tattoos and bandanas in the over-the-top, crunchy, and vigorous guitars, hear their puny porkpie and fedora douchebag hats in the thumping bass, feel in the overproduced drums the "wifebeater" shirt of the drummer getting sweaty, and taste the pomade in the singer's hair in the wretched, dithyrambic, raspy, over-earnest vocals, his slick-backed, greased-out, fine-combed ducktail. After about a verse and a half, as the band went from full-on pedal-to-the-metal overdrive powerpunk to a ska-sorta breakdown complete with a *viva la raza* kind of *vato* or *esé* evoking or invoking some *cholo* on a street corner *macho*-ing for the *muchachas bonitas y calientes*, Mays turned the stereo down and leaned forward and looked left, looked right, looked left again like some paranoid meister expecting the cops to come busting in any minute: "Between you and me and you [Jenny, he meant] and these four walls, I think we have a fucking smash here. Unreal potential! Grammy, maybe. Many, many records sold. Total hit. Outta the park. Know what I'm saying? And these guys—my total *brochachos*, man. They went to my high school. No shit. Just listen to this."

"Amazing," I lied.

"The feeling I get is like the feeling I got when I heard you guys' single for the first time."

"Oh?!" I said.

"Only ten times that," Mays said.

"Oh," I said, but with a different tone now, of course.

"Amazing," Jenny echoed hollowly and made a face like she'd just sipped someone else's cup of tepid tea.

"I know—right?!" Mays tootled. "*Never* been more excited about a record—let me tell you!"

More zany looks and blank stares.

"Well, so we were just stopping by to..." Jen said desperately, at last, "you know, say hello and..."

"Hang on," Mays said. And here he fast-forwarded the tape and turned the stereo back up, occasioning an improvement on my hopes that I freakishly be suddenly stricken deaf. The fast-forwarding had landed him/us in the midst of a song that was, well, the same song as the one he'd played us—it was just in a different key. At least I thought it was the same song. I could've sworn the lyrics were identical.

Can you blame me if I envisioned Mays, just about then, dying as a result of choking on a shish kebab, being bitten repeatedly by a merriment of half-starved Gila monsters, torn apart, limb by limb, by the furious Eumenides?

"*Oh,* yeah," Jenny nodded as insincerely as could be—though Mays, of course, would never hear such a "note" in her tone, engrossed as he was in a band that he thought was the new Beatles or something. You could tell Jen couldn't take any more of this. And who could blame her? You could tell she would love to just wander off and find a nice couch to kip on for a bit before we had to go to The Doll Hut for the gig. She was always happiest either curling up to sleep somewhere (she really could sleep *any*where—one time Keating and I were blasting a Sam Kinison tape in our living room and Jenny was dead asleep in the middle of the day, her head barked right up against one of the speakers).

"Cool, huh?" Mays opined as he turned the stereo down a touch.

"You *do* know that our single is on Live-one-oh-five around three and sometimes four times a day, right, Mike? The single *you* picked," I ventured, quite graciously I thought, but with real vim; not at all in a desperate-artist-here sort of way.

"I know. That's awesome," Mays said.

"Posters in stores would be good, and giveaways, and actual CDs in the stores? I mean..." Jenny ventured.

"Awesome. We're on it. That's being taken care of."

"Is it?" Jenny said.

To call the pause that ensued merely awkward would be to diminish the legacies of sundry math dorks, foals, calves, junior high schoolers, and sweet, little, old, super-shy Laplanders the world 'round.

"Definitely. Affirmative. All the way. Franklin's trying to use that hype to get more commercial stations to add and spin your record. It's tough, though, you know. For independents these days. Very tough. Too many bands. You see this stack of demos here—see these? If only I had the power somehow to, instead of signing these bands that send us demos by the hundreds, make them disappear. Hahahaha! Wouldn't that be great? If I could just sort of make them stop. The music world would be a less sucky place."

I just wanly nodded and Jenny sort of telepathically shrugged her shoulders. But then Jenny started to say: "Maybe you could get the Ple—"

"*Please*," I interjected quickly, making a verbal palimpsest of what I was sure Jenny was going to sarcastically say, "let us know, Mike, what we can do to help out—you know, to help sales."

Mays looked up like he was anticipating some revelation of some sort or other: "Just...maybe...do a bunch more gigs? I don't know right now. I'm just so wrapped up in the new Hot Rod Harrys that I...let me get back to you on that. Try to get a tour with someone big. Someone bigger. You could try and do that."

"Sure," Jenny said blankly, and rolled her eyes—which of course Mays never saw on account of...as I told you—he never saw her period, really. Or maybe he did, 'cause, quickly, he said:

"Did you guys…try and get a manager to help you yet? It might be time," Mays tentatived. For a true *égoïste* he was pretty diffident every once in a while. Here was no full-time bumptious blusterer à la this inveterate "industry" guy Bob Chalet who was "interested" in signing us a while back but who, unfortunately, didn't, at the time, have an actual label to sign us to.

You kind of need one of those if you're going to try to put a record out by any band off the street. You sort of *do*.

Duh.

Just then Stacey came back with a geeky-looking geek with long-ass hair and a Pendleton shirt—goony smile, buckish teeth, very shy aspect about him, fully shoegazing.

"Sorry, Mike," Stacey said. "Excuse me. This is Trubert—he's here about the job opening as clerk at the store."

Better Records had a record shop a few miles away called Better Records. It was a very *blacklight and Indian incense* as it were sort of affair— looked more like a Head Shop than a record store. They had these cool lava lamps going everywhere and loads of imported vinyl. Most of the stock was domestic punk and rockabilly and ska and oi and hardcore and SST shit, with a bit of imported indie pop like what we did, but not very much at all, unless you're talking The Smiths, whose most obscure releases, plus the zillions of "Best of's" and comps they've released, always sell. It was way disorganized, it seemed, and like the lunatics were running the asylum and all; but at least you could find The Weird Sisters record there—and the poster was up, the four of us in individual lapis lazuli-hued portraits, with the layout redolent of The Beatles' immemorial "Let it Be."

"Hey, Trubert," Mike Mays said as Trubert shambled forward to shake hands, looking as he did so like a guy who had just tripped on a rock or a brick.

"Hi."

"Nice to meet you."

"You, too."

Strange smiles all 'round. Beat. Beat. Weird, pained, what-next looks exchanged. Beat. Another beat.

"Are you going to steal from me?" Mike Mays asked the Trubert kid at last and point blank and with a prodigious grin that was followed by a superfrown—like a seventeenth century galleon/warship captain might wear; one who, just as he's thinking he's won the day and can relax with a draught of sack, clocks with his telescope three-enemy-fire ships portside, the wind in the west; six guns ablaze, sea heaving, blood and smoke in the befouled air, cutlasses flashing in the hot bright sun off scintillant, choppy waters.

"Uh, no," Trubert said. "Like, why would I…"

"You're sure?"

"Uh, yeah," Trubert said.

"'Uh-yeah' what?" Mays said.

"Uh-yeah, *sir*," Trubert said.

"Don't call me 'sir'—makes me feel old. But you can call me 'Sir Mike, Your Supreme Lordship.'"

"Yes, Sir Mike, Your Lordship."

"Sir Mike, Your *Supreme* Lordship."

"Sir Mike, Your Supreme Lordship."

"Just kidding. Don't call me that. Who do you think I am—royalty? Hahaha! *Record* royalty? [swiftly dead serious now] Report to work tomorrow morning—at the shop. Six a.m. in the morning. Kidding. Shop no open till eleven a.m.…in the morning. Hahaha! That's wrong, huh. Redundant. Hahaha. Listen. Are you listening?"

"Yes."

"Kyle train you. Kyle cool. Find out if he stealing from me, okay? Report to me at oh-seven-hundred."

"At…?" Trubert said.

"Kidding. I don't even know when that is! I have not got up myself, not even on a Sunday, for—what?—the last ten years before, oh, noon, maybe, eleven-thirty. Mornings: basically a waste of time, right? Not rock and roll. Not rock at all. Listen: Just don't steal. Make tapes or something of the records you want. Just don't kype them, okay? Tape, don't kype. That's your motto. Like walk, don't run, only 'Tape, don't kype.' Got me? Plus push the records on Better Records—

try to sell those. I wish *we* did. Hahaha! Sell these guys's records: The Weird Sisters."

"Hey," I said and grinned.

"Yeah, sell our records," Jenny said, around five octaves lower than her normal voice.

"Hi, Trubert," I said so as not to burst out laughing.

"Hi," Trubert managed, and took, or so I thought, a furtive look at Jenny's breathing bust, I thought; then he colored majorly and looked back down.

"*Franklin!*" Mays maleficently yelled out the door. "Hey, Franklin, you geeky fuck! Hey, you long-haired, burr-haired, girlfriendless *id*iot! Try and sell some of our bands's *records* today, you lazy pussy! Try and sell The Weird Sisters, even though they're a little bit twee for the zeitgeist these days. [Here a horrid wink.] I know everyone thinks they can take the rest of the day off just 'cause some dumb northwestern spokesperson for a generation with a jazzmeister guitar went and killed himself but…"

He winked horribly right at me right then, Mike Mays did. And gave out a sort of laugh, mirthlessly, to boot. God, he was something, that Mike Mays.

"And *you*," he barked at Trubert buddy-buddily, giving the kid a start; "get to work…tomorrow, okay? Great to have you on board."

"Okay. Thank you, Mr. Mays."

"Don't call me that."

"…"

"Call me 'Bob.' Joking! It's Mike, okay. The only Mike we got now. Mike or 'Mr. Mike.' Got it? Okay. Now. Nice to have you working for us. Unless you are some kinda klepto—then you're fired in advance, okay? Now: Get the fuck out of my office and go get Stacey or someone to help you fill out a W-2 and help yourself to some of our goddam bands's shit from the warehouse, all right? The cut-outs only. Do you know what a cut-out is?"

"A cut-out is…" the kid ummm'd.

"No," Mays interrupted, superintending the conversation. "No matter what you think a cut-out is, it's not that."

Mad pause.

"A cut-out, Truman, is a record—on our label it is, that is—that was too good for the stupid fucking lame-ass *non*-record-buying public to realize was a good record, see? What am I saying?—a great record, I mean."

"Uh-huh," Trubert said.

"No, you don't see. See, a cut-out is a failure. Not on the part of Better, but on the part of idiots of the non-record-buying public's part. Do you understand now?

"I think so, sir."

"Thank you! Finally someone around here gets it."

"Thank you, Mr. Sir," Trubert said.

"Ha! Good one. Fuck you, kid. Fuck off now," Mays commanded, laughing affably.

"Thanks again, sir. You won't…"

"Regret it? Yes, I will. I already do. I regret it already. I can tell just by *looking* at you that you've got sticky fingers and I don't mean the fuckin' Rolling *Stones*. I know a thief when I see one, and you *are* one, aren't you, I'm sure of it—aren't you a lil' fuckin' shoplifter? *Aren't* you? Are you gonna be a thief the rest of your life—a thief and a fuckup?"

"No, sir," Trubert said.

"Yeah, yeah, you are. I pretty much think you *are* gonna be a thief and a fuckup, but…whatever. I have a seventh sense about these things. That's one more sense than a sixth sense, is what *that* is. What *I* call it, anyway. We'll catch you. You watch yourself—and what did I tell you your motto is?"

"Um, Tape…"

"Don't kype. Very good. Very well. Now: Get the hell out of my office! What do you think—you're already an employee and entitled to just stand around all day till the fucking lunch truck turns up? Get the fuck *out*. Go!"

"Thank you, Mr. Mike," the kid said.

"*Franklin!*" Mays yelped.

And Trubert, goggling at the way Mays had darned a grandiloquent and absurd arabesque of official dismissal in the air, like some pasha gesturing grotesquely, sending away a small army of deaf and dumb servants with trays piled with milk and honey and opium and manna, shied the hell out of there fast as a master chef or even you or I can make Quaker Instant Oatmeal.

"Hey, *you!*" Mike Mays shouted out the door again.

Trubert, turning 'round, having just barely made it to the door, gave an even greater start this time, like someone had shocked him with a family-sized cattle prod or put on, without warning, a Yoko Ono record with the sound all the way up. But Mays wasn't addressing Trubert. He was yelling at another young guy, real tall, all biceps and baggy blue jeans and earrings and brown, back-combed locks, who happened to be walking by just then. For a minute I imagined that it was one of The Pleiades People who'd ostensibly beamed down for a quick chat and a cuppa tea and Mays was just showing them who was boss around here—they might be eight feet tall and of superior intelligence and have spaceships the size of the Astrodome, but this was Mike Mays's turf, his label, a label he had sole control of now, no partner in now, what with Manson gone, and he wasn't taking any crap from determined or stray aliens. Not today. No, sir.

"What are you doing standing around out there?!" Mays said, as he got up to go stand in his doorway. He was having fun now, acting like Yul Brynner in *The King and I*, sorta. Only a Yul B. with extra hair.

"I wasn't…I was just…walking out to the warehouse to help Franklin with…"

"You're an intern, right?" Mays asked with a look of what I interpreted as ineffable disdain as Trubert muttered something and scuttled away, fully out the door by now and down the hall and safely away.

"Yeah, I'm an…," the intern guy said.

"What do we pay you for, anyway? *Huh?*"

"Pay? I don't get pay, Mr. Mays," the intern said. "Paid, I mean. That's why they call it an internship, Mr. Mays."

"Oh, is *that* whay—I mean why? Shut up, you fool," Mays said, all captious. "I know that. I was only joking you. Get back to doing whatever you weren't doing."

I got the sense that Mays was playing a sort of role, putting on the dog, as it were, acting like how he thought a big shot wack job vilipending record executive of the first water should act in front of a couple of "his" artists; but it was like his heart wasn't in it, ragging on the poor guy, like it was one big wink to him.

"Aye-aye, sir," the intern said.

"And don't call me 'sir'!"

"Yes…sir…"

"What did I just tell you? What are you—a sailor? A pirate? This isn't a ship—it's a record label you're interning at."

"Sorry?" the guy kind of laughed at Mays.

"At which you're interning, I meant. You hear about Cobain?"

"Excuse me? Kurt Cobain?"

"No, *Mike* Cobain. Kurt's brother. Of course I said Kurt Cobain. Who the fuck did you think I…I said, 'Did you hear about Kurt Cobain?' Did you?"

"Yes. That was, like,…"

"Terrible, wasn't it?"

"Um, for sure."

"Very sad. Okay: Good job, intern. Get back to work. Now listen," Mays said as he wheeled slowly back to his vast desk and sat back down. In his odd eyes the orange spots sparkled harder than ever, it seemed. "Who lets these dunderheads work here, anyway?" he twinkled, tittering. "These *blundering*, thundering dunderheads. These bumbling, blundering, thundering dunderheads! Ha! You should work that phrase into one of your songs, man. Jeez. I must've hired the kid myself. (Though 'hired' isn't quite right 'cause the interns of course don't get paid.) I probably did. Huh. I love my job. Don't you?"

"I was wondering, by the way, Mike…" I started. "Speaking of getting p—"

"Let me guess," Mays interrupted with a small, wan sigh. "And call me Mr. Mays from now on—now that the other Mike's gone. Joking! Why does everybody around her always look so serious?! You should have seen your face, John. Okay. So. You're wondering about quarterly royalties 'cause that's coming up and your record *has* been selling some and you've heard a rumor or two about us maybe merging with a major?"

I looked at Jenny. "We hadn't heard about any merger, I don't think."

"Oh no?" Mays said with a jutty lip-mouth.

"No?"

"No," I said. "Not at all. Should we have?"

"Really," Mays said in his inimitably seigneurial way.

I looked blankly at Jen by way of answering.

"Should we have?" I repeated. "So you guys are thinking of a merger—is that it?"

"Yes and no. No. I mean, we don't know. A definitely maybe. Probably. Who knows? Who cares? It's new. Some new campaign we have to hype the profile of the label. Who knows? *We* don't. No one knows anything about it. Even I don't. I probably just made that up, in fact. Mum's the word, okay? There's talk, there's a buzz, but it might be all made up by us. We're starting a buzz. A buzz on ourselves. You know: hype and all that shit [and here he waved his oversized hand, for aught I knew, as if to say it was nothing we would have to worry our pretty little, twee little "chick band" heads about.] I *knew* that single of yours was a hit, you know. The one I picked to be the single. *Knew* it. Knew it first time I heard it. Too bad chicks don't buy CDs, though. Really too bad. For you, for sure. That's 'ears,' okay? That's why the call me that. That's why I have this hair, see? I don't want anyone to see my secret weapon which is my ears which I use to hear whether something is a hit or a not-hit. I'm joking. You know that, right?"

And here I sort of cocked my head and kind of smiled away my understanding, assent.

"Okay. Or if some band is a band or a not-band. See?" Mays went on. "That's why I signed off on Manson and Stacey signing you guys. You do know that, don't you? I still think you're a 'chick band,' though. Definitely. There's where your audience is: in chicks."

"Uh-huh," I said.

"Uh-huh," Mays said. "Definitely. Believe me. I'm never wrong about stuff like that. I can't even think of the last time I was wrong about stuff like that. If Stacey were still here I would turn to her and say: 'Can *you* think of the last time I were wrong? *Can* you?' And she would go: 'No, Mike. I really can't think of when you ever *were* wrong about stuff like that.' See?"

"But you just said chicks don't buy…" I quixotically started to say.

"Well, that's the unfortunate catch-twenty-three, isn't it—catch-twenty-three being my little take on a catch-twenty-two that's got just a bit more of a catch to it, if you know what I'm saying."

Jenny stirred in her chair.

"Hear me out, okay? You guys," Mays continued piously, cracking his horrid knuckles, no less, "have been getting some great reviews, too: *CMJ, Magnet, Alternative Press*. Great reviews. Only—and you can probably anticipate what I'm gonna say here—*chicks don't read those 'zines!* Hardly anybody does. Press is great. Press does not sell records, though. Sylvia Doum…she…I don't know what the fuck she does, actually. But she's gotten you guys some real good press…which is great, but doesn't matter. Like I just said. So: What can we do? The mini-feature in *The Los Angeles Times* didn't hurt at all. Too bad it was during the week and not in the Calendar section on Sunday, but what the hell. Not as hip as *The LA Weekly* of course but fuck *hip*, man. Hip's for…who cares? Whatever. I hate the fucking *LA Weekly*. I hope they…you're doing great. The single's great. All great. Don't you think so? Franklin and…everyone are doing everything they possibly can. I think we're getting *Option, Contrast, Pop Culture Press* as well for you, too. Not that press means all that much—like I said. I don't really read those rags. Did I just say that? Thing is, reviews don't sell records. Good reviews, bad reviews, blahbitty, blah, blah, blah. Who *reads* *any*thing *any*way, these days? Who has time to? Not me. Not this guy. I would love to sit around reading Charles Dickens and the collected literary works of whaddayacallit Henry Rollins—hell if I wouldn't! I'd love to have my dick sucked by an eighteen-year-old *Playboy* bunny while sitting around reading Bukowski all day and drinking unlimited Bud. Smoking it, too! Haha! That I would. Who wouldn't? There's me, on a couch, being double-teamed by some centerfold twins as I read *Post Office* or what's that other one—*Women*. Fine by me. You read those? *Great* books. True tomes. Classic shit for sure. Quick reads. Funny shit. Best books on tape I ever read. Kidding. I read 'em. The real deal. Down and out. The *real* Los Angeles, man."

"Oh, so you lived in Los Angeles at one time?" Jenny said.

I did my best not to flinch, thusly perhaps triggering Mays's long shot realization that Jen was quite possibly taking the piss.

"No, not actually," Mays again said to *me*. Again. "But I've spent a lot of time th...bottom line? You guys, unfortunately, are a critics' band *and* a chick band. Tough sell. Wish it was different but what can you do? Press kits mean fuck-all. Everyone knows that. Never translate into sales. Never. Or rarely."

"But if we...when we go out on tour in..." I started to say.

"Listen," Mays began again before I had time to go on; his voice had that slight lilt people's get when they're done talking, and done with you if they are above you somehow, if you know what I mean: "if I paid my artists *royal*ties—uh, paid them on time, I mean, or even at all, in some cases—I wouldn't be in business very long, you see."

"Uh-huh," I nodded and the quavering needle of my personal self-loathing went into the farthest part of the reddest red. "Sure."

"I think we should take off pretty soon here," Jenny said diffidently, deferentially even. "Last show of the tour tonight, you know. Nice to see you, Mike."

The emergent note of obeisance in her voice wasn't gonna cost her anything on account of she had not one iota of respect or even a remote sense of *noblesse oblige*, I could tell, for Mays in the first place—especially now that he'd all but admitted that he ripped his artists off in order to keep himself a job. You must understand something about Jenny: she had a bullshit detector the size of Kubrick's Hal 9000. For most folks, that is. Not everyone. Not all the time, that is. But she had one. She just didn't have any use for trying different angles with difficult people. Her radar sussed out someone pretty quickly and then she made an assessment: there was no way she would ever in a million years try to convince someone of something or fight them or try to change them. It was like one of her fundamental beliefs. The best thing, she thought, you could do is take your pride and your dignity and get the heck out so as not to waste your time.

Without, I imagine, knowing it, she kinda/sorta put into practice Camus' maxim that there's no fate that can't be surmounted by *scorn*.

Which reminds me, reader dear—haven't you just about had enough of this scene? *I* have—I'll tell you that much.

"Right," Mays said. "Wish I could come. Have a good gig."

"Oh?" I said, fully pusillanimously. "You can't? Too bad. Are you sure that…"

"Sorry, man. Going into the studio to do some remixes for The Harrys. Well, *I'm* not doing them—D'Artagnan and our house engineer is. Well, I am and I'm not. I just…I don't touch the buttons, hahaha! Not me. The faders, I mean. No. That's for the experts. I just use my God-given ears, is all. That much I *can* do. Anyway. We'll talk. Good chat. You guys thought of a video for the single? You should do that. Make one. Get that organized. Lots of film school students up there in LA where you guys are. Make one for you cheap. Make it, we'll get it on MTV. Maybe. Or cable. Who knows? Who cares? We can't promise anything. Talk to you later, then."

He had an enormous coughing fit just then, did Mays—something fierce and frightening, like any minute one of his lungs would come out his mouth and flop down on the desk and join the party of super tchotchkes assembled there. And as Jenny asked him if he was okay, he sort of signed "I'm fine—don't fret" and then he bent down and rolled open the bottom drawer of his vast black desk and pulled out a long bong in the shape of and color of a banana, which of course had "The

Velvet Underground and Nico" stenciled or appliqued or something
on it; there was a hit of pungent pot packed into it already. "Hitski?"
he cough-spoke and proffered the thing my way but I waved him off,
going "Nah, no thanks, Mike. Gotta gig, you know." He shrugged and
took a grand chortle from the thing and billowed forth a billowing,
violet-tinged plume of roiling smoke and stopped hacking away. It
was like something mentholated or something, a purplish ghost that'd
visited and quelled Mays's, as it were, fit of internal combustion. It
should have been, Mays's act of breaking out a bong, a sort of crowning
wonder. But we'd seen and heard too much already for it to be all that
bizarre. I remember just thinking "Wow, you know—Mike Manson
was just this mellow, quiet guy in a blue button-down, well-groomed
and soft-spoken and well-mannered and very knowledgable about
pop music and really quite modest. Just so different from his now-
former partner at Better.

You mill around the record biz long enough and stuff, you think
sometimes to yourself, *Is there no end to the weirdness? Where will it
end?*

And the answer's always, always this: nowhere.

One

aving collected Raleigh and Rob (who had broken
out the chess set from the van and were playing at
a desk next to Franklin's), we piled into the van in
order to get over to The Doll Hut in time maybe to
get a sound check. But not before Franklin had us go
out to the warehouse to sign a few posters with some
fine-point royal blue and jet black Sharpies. Most LA bands don't have

money for a flyer to their Monday night Open Mic gig, let alone a royal blue and expensive silver-and-mushroom-colored promo poster with an independent record deal to match. So I reckoned we ought to have considered ourselves lucky by comparison. The thing is, most signed bands don't think about how lucky they are, period. They aren't thinking about the bands that are, in a manner of speaking, below them; they're thinking, and with no little envy, about the bands that have *so much more than they do*. And they're thinking "How'd they get *that*—especially 'cause they *suck*?" Or, "Sure they're *okay*, but we are so much better and why don't we have a new van/a tour with Dinosaur Jr./an ad in *SPIN*/a live guest spot on KCRW/a double-gatefold ten-inch EP or summer festival gigs in Germany and especially Sweden. How come *we* don't have that? As far back as nearly a couple of centuries before indie rock was "invented" our old friend the Doctor wrote about this phenomenon in *The Rambler No. 185*: "Every one wishes for the distinctions for which thousands are wishing at the same time, in their own opinion, with better claims."

In other words, there are too many bands, Sam. And Mays was too right.

'Tis well-known that a rock band's share of the bounty of money and fame is predicated on luck, right? Well, some. Some of it is. It's not all talent. It's not any of it talent-based with *some* bands—ones who have no songs, can't play, look like hell, and have terrible, collective *enfant terrible* attitudes. Most bands on Better Records, in other words. Ourselves excepted, naturally. Ha! See, Johnson's right and whatever you get—*it's never enough*. We didn't have anything personally against the other bands on our label. It's just galling—you might have gotten that impression from the preceding scene with Mays—to hear about how the label's excited and motivated about other acts and don't seem to "get" or care about us all that much. Especially when we have a song on the radio and have gotten, thus far, uniformly great reviews—even though there are only a handful of them, the reviews, and they're in little 'zines, mostly. And even though Mays was right about the whole press—good or bad—doesn't really matter thing. So: Nothing personal against any of the Better bands and the people in them. Not really. But still. I mean, the guys in The Hot Rod Harrys were super nice. They were from behind the Curtain so they'd *better* be! Ha! I remember meeting them the first time we went down to the Better offices; and one of them, Victor, was telling me how much he loved Kierkegaard. He was also all "Holmes, you know you guys ought to play some clubs down here other than The fucking Doll Hut, okay, *bro?* We'll hook you up. Our bands don't go together, you know, or we'd have you open for us and shit. I'll get you some refs, some contacts, okay? No worries. Mike Mays was telling me you were an English teacher or something, though, huh? You used to be? Just a sub? Righteous. That's rad, man…that's the only subject I liked in school, bro. *Old Man and the Sea* and shit. Motherfucking Steinbeck, too. Kurt Vonnegut—all that shit. That's when I first discovered Gabriel Garcia Marquez and Richard Rodriguez, man. I love fucking *Love in the Time of Cholera*, man, and especially *One Hundred Years of Solitude*, dude, but Rodriguez, man—that is one pissed-off Mexican. I could relate to him—you know I could, man…I want to go back to college one of these days and get my Master's in Chicano Studies. Yeah, I got my Bachelors' from Cal State Fullerton, man—I'm very proud of that, let me tell you, Holmes. Music major. Scholarship. *Hells*, yeah, man. Man, lemme *ask* you: have you ever read *Fear and Trembling* by Søren Kierkegaard? Danish *vato?* You know him? Shit. You me and around five other people in this world, eh? I tell you, man, the title alone spoke, like, right to me, growing up in the rough part of Santa Ana like I did. Eighteenth Street—no shit. You heard of the Eighteenth Street Gang, I suppose? The *real* rough part, if you know what I mean. Mother*fucking vatos* coming at you every sun-up, Holmes. Gangbangers, like, fucking u*b*iquitous and shit. People's drunk-ass dads outside at four in the morning waving a 'piece' around, thinking they're all big and *bad* and shit. Pinche Pancho Villas every flashy, fucking one of them. And me coming home late at night by, like, *minimal* lamplight as a little kid, carrying my Fender Precision Bass case through the *barrio?* Tweed, it was, the case. Cool *now*, right? 'Cause I lived to tell the tale. But at the time I was, like, 'Shit, I wish this *estupido* case was *negro*, man, so they maybe couldn't see it in the paling lamplight of our poorly-lit street!' I was barely big enough not to have to hold *that* fucking case with my spare hand—not just by the handle, you know? A scrawny-ass skinny little shit like *me*? Shit. Did I show you my bass? I take that thing wherever I go, bro. That bass is from the fuckin' *seventies*, Holmes. *Well* worn in. The best decade for Fender Basses *ever*, Holmes. No lie. *Mi tío* bought it for me when I was, like, little—like twelves or something. For reals. I think homeboy bought it for himself, then realized he couldn't fucking play it! Hahaha! He was one of these *vatos* that thinks the bass is easy 'cause it only gots four strings!… Yeah, man, I been playing with The Harrys since I was—what?—fifteen and a half. Do you believe that shit? We been a band a *long* time, bro. I been playing in clubs since I was six*teen* years old now. Do you believe that? Blows my mind. We been to Canada twice now. Little kid like me from Eighteenth Street. *Can*ada. Like, I never thought we'd even play L*A*, let alone a foreign country. I never thought we'd go beyond the old punk clubs in Huntington Beach or Long Beach and shit…you guys ought to tour Canada, though, man. Good bookstores, good *strip* clubs, *ed*ucated people up there, man. People *read* up there, man. People treat you *fine* up there, too—*real* good folks. Man, we did this jaunt to BC and back and all the people in the audience after the show? All they wanna *do* is get you high! They're like: 'BC, eh? *Best Cannabis* is what *that* stands for!' Hahaha! 'BC.' Fucking righteous, man. Canadians are just, like, the Mexicans of the North, all right? *Mexicanos del norte! Love* those fucking hosers. They read up there, too, like I said. No shit. You can talk *books* with people. Maybe on account of it rains or snows all the time exceteses in summers. I have had some *real* good conversations with Canadians, man. About Kerouac and all them Beats, bro. You probably don't like that shit, though, I bet…thought so. Anyway, you guys tour Canada as soon as you can rig it! You tell them Victor from The Hot Rod Harrys sentchu. Though hockey, bro, I will *never* understand that shit. *Never*. You ever watch it?… Me neither. My friends from my, like, 'hood took me to a LA Kings game once and I was all 'What *is* this shit, man?' Exactly. I thought the ice was real pretty until all these guys with ridiculous *cortes de pelo* come skating out and beating the shit out of one another. Hells, I can see that shit in my 'hood for *free, esé!* Hahaha! Anyway, talk about *fear.* Talk about *trembling?* Not that you could show none, right? Not in *my* 'hood, *esé.* But when I seen that book at the downtown library I was, like, 'Dang, I gonna read me that, like, *libro,* bro.' It's fantastic…you gots to check it out sometime, my brotha. He has this, like, *other* one where he talks about existentialism and God and shit. *Que huevos!* In a*nother* one (he must've spent, like, all his spare time writing books, you know?), he seduces this *fine* Copenhagen bitch and then *dumps* her, man. For no reason, *esé.* Just to see what it feels like. *Stone-*cold motherfucker. And he loves her, too. And regrets the whole thing. Crazy. Heavy stuff man. *Real* good shit, it is, Holmes. Makes you really think about things like love and shit. *Check* it sometime—I'm *telling* you! I *highly* recommend him. One thing, though: you can't read him high, though—I should tell you that. Too heavy. You wanna toke on this roach, bro? It's just *day weed* and shit but it'll mess you up a little bit, Holmes…say, bro, in your band, what do you call it when somebody rips one in the van?… You don't have a name for it? In The Harrys we call it a "maidstraightener"—like, in the hotel and shit, when the maid picks up your, like, *boxers* and shit, and they have that like fuckin' full-on *skid*mark from being in the van all day and shit? And the maid, like, *smells* them and like strands up *real* straight and like pinches her *pinche* nose, man? Hahaha. And holds them shits way away from her?! Hahaha. 'Maidstraightener!' Hahaha. Hilarious, huh, bro?… That's what we call it. The flatulence you get on the road, bro! From all that bad food? You know what I am talking about here, dontchu? Chuey? Our lead percussionist? Sometimes we think he's got a frog down the back of his pants, man. Hahaha. A frog! One time I was all: 'Hey, *Chuey*—what do you have down there, anyway—a *frog?!*' And Big Boy, our other percussionist, goes: 'No—I think he's got a horny toad.' Hahaha! 'A horny toad!' That shit cracked

me up. By the way: that fine *mamacita* in your band?—is she your
girlfriend, bro? She has got a *nice*...oh...really? She *is?* I thought that's
what they told me. Sorry about that man; I didn't mean no disrespect.
Dang, man, you are one *lucky* hombre, Holmes. She's *fine*, man. *Nice*
looking *Betty*. I just am kinda partial to the chicks with big...anyway.
Sorry, Holmes. Hey, though. I dunno about having a *novia* in your
band though, man. Know what I'm *saying?* Are you *sure* about that
shit? You're *sure* you're sure about that shit—having your girlfriend
right there?... Can't be easy, bro. Ah, I'm only pulling your leg, man.
Still...okay. I get it. *Can't* be motherfuckin' easy, though, huh. *Can't* be.
Hey and good luck with this label, man. These guys have taken real
good care of us—Mike Mays and them. *Real* good to us. They can be a
little weird, you know, a little out there, but for the most part they are
one of the better labels—pardon my pun. Hahaha! Take it easy, bro. See
you out there on the road. And don't forget: *Can*ada, man. That's where
it's *all at!*"

Franklin told us that there was probably going to be a kid called
"Flake" at The Doll Hut gig who had a little fanzine called *Pies*. And
who wanted to do an interview with us either before or after the show.
I reckon he called it *Pies* on account of records somewhat resembled
them? Or...? Who knew. It was a stretch but... *Platters* closer, more
apt perhaps, but probably taken by some kid xeroxing his 'zine out of
a basement in Omaha or Orlando? But mostly Jenny, Franklin added,
was who this Flake really wanted to talk to. Ah, but of course. The
record nebbishes go for the good-looking girl. Yeah, and you bet they
do. Never fails I have to deal with some geek gawking at her after the
gig. Before the gig. During. There can be four peeps tops at any given
show and two of them are up and at her afterward, trying to chat
her up, see if she has a boyfriend, telling her how great a singer and
guitarist she is. Mostly both of us play it very cool, but sometimes
Jenny goes: "A boyfriend? Right there, in fact—right next to you" as
I am tying up the guitar leads with a stupid smile on my sweaty face,
placing the effects pedals into the thrift shop suitcase we use to port
and store them in.

Part of this fanzine kid's deal, Franklin intimated, was that he loved to ask artists to reveal what their favorite pie was, like it would be utterly fascinating (and so much fun!) to hear that J. Mascis from Dinosaur Jr. dug him a chocolate cream with white chocolate sprinkles, or that Justine from Elastica favored Dutch apple à la mode. Franklin said he had a few more things to do before he got outta there and he'd see us at The Hut. Our quest for a sound check was quixotic at best as it was already eight o'clock and we were meant to play at nine. The booker'd left it up in the air, whether or not we could get up onstage before the show and test the sound onstage. But we knew what that meant: no check, most likely. In a way it doesn't matter whether you get one or no. You can have the most excruciatingly meticulous run-through, with a soundman like a golden god of musical sensitivity and willingness to please, twiddling knobs and faders endlessly, and still have the sound onstage suck. One thing we almost always found: that if the practice before the gig was good, the gig was bad. And if the practice before the gig was bad, the gig was good. The same thing, kind of, went for sound checks. So if we had them, we had them; if we didn't, we didn't. And besides, knowing this was the last gig for a fair while, the last gig of an already arduous tour, we could basically give a fuck. As I already intimated, with Cobain's death and all, a good gig couldn't possibly be something anyone expected. A good "turnout" was not to be presumed. High would run emotions, were any walking emotions in the form of punters, rock fans, fans of ours (a few, for sure), Doll Hut regulars and walk-bys, to come to the poxy gig. And with high emotions might not little concentration ride sidecar? No one would pay very careful attention to us is what I am trying to say. Only if we had the audacity to play a set of Nirvana covers (we did not; and besides, we did not know any Nirvana songs) would anyone pay us any—begging humbly your worships' gentle pardons for this pun—nevermind.

Okay so Raleigh was driving, Rob riding shot. We waved goodbye to Franklin and were vanning it past the roach coach when Rob, spotting two cute-looking girls with double paper plates of smoking tacos held up to their munching, pretty faces, told Raleigh to "Stop!"

"Hey, you guys!" Rob hailed them out the driver's side window, leaning forward. Raleigh, leaning back, had his left arm all bulky and casual and studly out the window. I could tell he was putting on his most fulsome, little-boy-devil smile.

The girls looked up but didn't say anything. Jenny and I were sort of on the edge of the back seat, watching, but pretending not to, of course.

"Hey! Do you guys like rock and roll?" Rob asked them, all bright and chummy, not like he was hitting on them (and like he was hitting on them).

"Not really," the less-cute but still-cute girl said. She had terribly sparkly, big, brown, mischievous eyes, the sultry half-lidded kind. The other one, I now saw, was just stunning in a way only stunning Latinas can be: perfect straight, golden, dark brown sugar hair, perfect teeth (she did smile a wee smile, but only for a flash of a half a second), perfect cheekbones and lips, cream-coffee radiant skin, big huge brown eyes too (but saucer-ish), wet, bright, translucent—to match her radiant, super-straight hair.

"We *used* to." The perfect one shrugged, tossed a one wall of hair over her shoulder, and curled her lower lip.

"Don't tell me—you like rap now," Raleigh said.

"So?" the sassier one said and made a horrible, obligatory, turn-down, dismissive *moue*.

"So you should come to our gig tonight—we're playing The Doll Hut here in Anaheim. Do you know where it is?"

"Yes," the sassy one drawled. "A *güero* bar."

"They're fourteen, Rob," Jenny said.

"What's *güero*?" Rob shouted.

"*Gringo!*" the pretty one said.

"*Puto!*" the not-as-cute-one said.

Uh-oh, I thought. "Come *on*, Raleigh," I said. "Let's hit it. Let's go. We've got a…"

"Just a minute," Rob said firmly but not in a too-admonishing way, turning to me; then he turned 'round to the girls again: "You guys are both really good-looking."

They were so acting all tough. And there was no way they were twenty-one. Eighteen or seventeen.

"Thank you kindly," the sassy one, who was a little bit more than chunky, actually, said sassily and did a curtsey. It was cute. The other one twirled like a little ballerina, spun 'round and flipped us off and laughed like she'd make the funniest joke in the history of Western civ.

"I mean it," Rob said. "That was cute! Don't be like that! You're twenty-one right?"

"*Twen*ty," the really pretty one said. She really did have an incredible smile—even her mock-smile, saucy as hell, was fetching as could be, staggeringly so.

"I'll get you in," Rob boasted. "I'll put you on the guest list. What's your name? You guys wanna come with us right now? I'd love to draw you both sometime," Rob said and winked Ral's way. "Come on, what are you guys' names. Please?!"

"I'm Betty and *she's* Veronica," the less-cute one said after the one flashed the other a look.

"Raleigh…" I admonished.

"Alicia," the perfect one said, nodded in a capitulating way, and smiled at Rob in a way that, really, was more like laughing at him. "And she's called Mayra. Thanks, anyway, though."

"Run away with me, Alicia," Rob yelped as Ral started to pull away slowly, his voice crackling with jocularity. "I'd marry you in a New York minute."

"You wish!" the less-pretty one said. "She has a nine-foot boyfriend who could kick your ass, fool!"

"Is he in The Hot Rod Harrys?" I yelped just then from the back of the van. Couldn't help myself. All the weirdness of the Mike-meeting and The Pleiades thing? God, were we all ready to get back to being a totally immature band on the run, on the road. I could try and rein Ral in, but me, myself? Um, no.

"Who the fuck are The Hot Rod Harry?" the Mayra chick yelled as Raleigh eased his foot off the brake pedal.

"Ex*act*ly!" I yodelled.

"He was talking to *her*," Raleigh said and threw his head by way of pointing. "But you're cute, too. Definitely. Come to our gig tonight. We're called The Weird Sisters."

"Laters!" the perfect one said.

"I'll make you a citizen!" Rob laugh-yelled as we pulled away slow.

"Rob!" Jenny barked. "You're horrible!"

"She already is one, you stupid *pendejo!*" the less-cute one jibed, lifting her taco plate by way of emphasis or mock-salute, dipping one leg and one big hip in a pseudo-genuflecting way.

"I'll make her a better one," Rob hollered as we picked up a little speed. *Thank God*, I thought, *we're outta here.*

"You'll make her a cheeseburger," the more-sassy one yelled back. Both girls were giggling madly now, I could see in the side mirror. "You musician guys all just end up working at fast-food places, anyway!"

"You better go get ready for your gig at *Fatburger*," the Alicia one shouted, riffing, then laughed so adorably it was comical, showing twin vampirish molars that hadn't been in evidence heretofore. We were all looking back at them through the side windows of the van and the rear view mirrors.

"Good one!" Rob laughed as Raleigh slowed back down to a halt.

"Ral—come *on*…" I said.

"You *live* at Fatburger, looks like," Rob said.

Uh-oh.

"Rob!" Jenny said—but she wasn't frowning.

And then, I could see by looking in either of the two big side mirrors on the van's doors, two plates of carne asada taco and burrito shrapnel came *flying* toward The Astro's back windshield.

"*See* ya!" Raleigh yelled and pulled away quick-like, then slowed down dramatically, as the girls came flapping after us, looking like they were going to start in on the van with their meat juice and salsa-dipped fists.

"Let's hit it," I said.

"Oh, my God!" Jenny said, cracking up despite herself; it was a laugh I'd heard many, many times.

"Nice try, though," I told Rob. "You guys were almost in there, I reckon."

"Thank you," Rob said. "I did give it the old college try, didn't I?"

"He was being sarcastic, Rob," Jenny said.

"The old *junior* college try," I said.

"The old junior college *dropout* try," Raleigh ribbed.

"Hey!" Rob said, mock-hurt but emphatically. "I got my AA I did four years almost at Valley College, okay?!"

"Associate Asshole—that's the degree *you* got," Raleigh smiled. "You are the nicest asshole I know, Rob. One of the funniest, too."

"Why thank you very much," Rob said with a quickened, very Elvis Presley voice. "I do try to amuse myself and entertain my lovely and distinguished band mates whenever possible."

Raleigh said: "You should have used your Morrissey line on her, Rob."

"His what?" Jenny said.

"His Morrissey line. Tell her, Rob."

"You go, 'Do you like Morrissey? 'Cause I'd like more of what *I* see!' Hahaha."

"Nice one," I said. "It's a variation on the 'Are you from Tennessee?' line."

"You got it," Rob said.

"Duh, John," Raleigh said.

"You made that up? Nice one, Robert. Very clever," I said.

"I try to please me, right enough, mate," Rob said in Scouse this time.

Of course we were all delirious by now.

"You guys are *crazy*," Jenny said affectionately. "Out of your tree. I do like a cheesy pickup line, though."

"I am *too?*" I teased.

"I saw the way you were looking at those girls. You're terrible. You're even worse than these two. Like you were trying not to look at them."

"Uh-oh, John—you're in trouble now!" Raleigh trumpeted.

"And totally failing!" Rob said.

"Trying not to look at them is…"

"Somehow worse than actually gawking," Rob said.

"Give me a break. I wasn't even…" I said.

"Oh sure," Jen said.

"They *were* really cute," Ral said in my "defense."

Hardly.

"I *know. Really* cute. The one was…I mean, I would have *loved* to…" Rob said.

"Okay, okay," Jenny, achuckle, said. "That's e*nough*, you guys. *Jeez.* And *you*," she added, turning my way, then turning away.

"How does this sort of thing *happen* to me!" I mock-groaned. "Rob started it! There I am—an innocent bystander, trapped in a van with two mental patients in the front seats…"

"No post-gig sex for *you*, tonight, Johnnyboy—that's for sure," Rob cackled, as Raleigh put on Sonic Youth's *Goo*—the record we almost always rocked out to on our merry way to a gig; either that or *Daydream Nation*. It got us way pumped to be…carrying on to withersoever we carried on to. Playing to twelve people—or a twelve hundred. (Well, maybe seven or eight hundred at Stanford—far and away the biggest gig in Weird Sister history.) And because every band has its ritual, boiling or simmering or whatnot, hither and thither, to and fro.

"How did this become about *me*, the fuck?" I joked, as Kim Gordon sprecht-sang "You are never goin' anywhere, you are never goin' anywhere."

"Jenny's never letting you have any ever again, aren't you, Jen?" Raleigh said.

"Yep," said Jen.

"Run away with me, Jennifer," Rob breathed, making goo-goo eyes at Jen of course. "I was only kidding about old Alicia back there.

She was nothing. What a sea hag. Let's elope and start a *new* band. You know I am in love with you and always have been. Come on, Jenny—what do you say?"

"I love her more than you do, asshole," Ral said. "You know that, right, Jenny? Pick *me!*"

"I can't! I love both you bozos equally not," Jenny laughed.

"I wouldn't even do this in front of you—ever," Rob said and, turning 'round, made like he was going to blast forth a "leglifter."

"Don't!" Jenny said.

"Gross!" Raleigh said.

"Quit it!" I said.

"Kidding!" said Rob and put his left leg back down.

"Can I be in it—you guys's new band?" Raleigh said in a tone that put one in mind of The Beaver in *Leave it to Beaver*.

"Sure," Jenny said.

"I love Jenny more than you do, Rob," Raleigh reiterated. "Plus I was in love with her first."

"Gosh, can *I* be in it, too?" I asked, in a tone that was more Eddie Haskell or Wally.

"No!" all three of them crowed together, and merrily off we sped toward the freeway for a short jaunt on the 5 to get to The Hut.

"No John in band!" Jenny said.

"Yeah, Jenny!" Rob said.

"I love/hate you all," I laughed.

The Doll Hut's one of the weirder bars: the light can only be described as sort of piss-and-tinsel: the stage is right beside the bar area, which is a sort of cage, or as the motif/moniker suggests, a hut. It's mingier than most, this place. And, again as its name suggests, smaller than most—to put you in mind of a doll, I guess. There's room for maybe fifty-five people, seventy tops if the place's packed. Which it wasn't gonna be for *our* gig, as I've intimated earlier. We had a bit of a hard time finding it. It was one of those deals where you got the sense that you were close, but that if you didn't look at the *Thomas Guide* or ask someone, you'd end up in Carlsbad or somewhere. We were lost;

we went down several obviously-wrong sidestreets then doubled back; then Rob clocked a kid on a skateboard with a two-sizes-too-big Belgian army jacket and bright green longish hair porcupining punkishly away from his head—which was, it seemed, two sizes too *small*.

"Hey, *Green Day!*" Rob yelled out the window, over the clackity-clack of the kid's skateboard. "Do you know where The Doll Hut is, please?"

"The what?" he said, and stopped, flipping his board up and into his hands—but only for a bright second before it twirled back to the pavement and he jumped on it and spun around trickily.

"The *Doll* Hut, Rob said. "It's a club. It's supposed to be right around here…"

"Go left at the next light, then right, I think. You'll see an alley on the right. Take that."

"Thank you, Green Day," Raleigh said, at which the skate kid promptly and predictably flipped us off, then propelled himself and his board down a narrow sidestreet.

"Just by looking at you I can tell that your band sucks!" the kid yelled without looking back.

"You don't even have a band, Green Day," Jenny yelped. "Suck my left one!"

"Fuck you, you *bitch!*" the Green Day kid hollered.

"That does it," Raleigh cried and spun the van 'round.

"Knock it off, Ral. Don't fuck around," I said.

"You never let us have any fun," Jenny said, as Raleigh made another U-turn; I caught a quick flash of the kid really jamming now, making his getaway.

"That was a pretty funny line, though," Rob said. "Gotta hand it to him."

"I'd hand him his *ass*," Raleigh said.

"You'd *handle* his ass, Raleigh," Jenny said.

Nice *one, Jenny*, I thought so loud in my head I might've actually said it.

"Are you saying I'm *gay?*" Raleigh said, turned 'round, and touched his chest with the splayed fingers of his right hand, like a gay, pink-and-baby-blue-spotted spider had just alighted on him.

"Watch the road, Ral," Rob said.

""You'll make her a cheeseburger!" Jen quoted.

Everyone cracked up at that one.

"I'd make her the best cheeseburger she's ever had!" Rob cackled. "The one was *really* cute."

"You'd spin her, Rob?" Raleigh said.

"She wasn't a spinner, but I would, I would spin her, for sure," Rob intoned.

"It is very apparent," Jenny said with a sort of philosophical sigh, after the laughter had scattered, died somewhat down, "that The Weird Sisters have been on the road for just a *little* too long."

"It hasn't been that long," Rob said. "Are there any snacks left, by the way?"

"Here," Jenny said and handed him a sack of chocolate-covered Fritos or pork rinds or something.

"Long enough for all four of us to be more disturbing than a chick playing air drums," I said. "'Van fever' has official stricken the Sisters."

"Hey!" Jenny said. "I don't know if I shouldn't object to that. The feminist in me says I probably should."

"But?" I said.

"But the aesthetically-oriented person in me says…"

"It's hideous," I said.

"More disturbing than a drummer singing," Rob interjected and threw Ral a look.

"More disturbing than a bass player reading music charts," Raleigh said, throwing one back.

"More disturbing than watching a bass player try to read *charts*," Jenny laughed. "More disturbing than a singer carrying *gear!*"

"Hey!" I said. "I hope you don't mean me. I carry gear. I carry *your* gear."

"Her purse, maybe, you do," Raleigh said.

"Ooooh!" everyone, including me, oooohed.

"*Burn,*" I said all sarcastic, like the word was twelve syllables.

"Good one, Ral," Rob said.

"Not good one," I laughed. "Good one not! Not even re*motely* funny at all. Average jab. No points. Negative points, in fact, for lack of originality," I said. "You just concentrate on carrying your bag of mega hair products, Raleigh. That's rich—coming from a guy who has an entire bagful of…"

I cut myself off. Or Rob did, rescuing as per usual.

"Yeah, how come you have so many of those?" Rob said. Raleigh gave him this hurt look. "No, really. I mean…" Rob said.

"So many what?" Raleigh said.

"Hair products!" Rob said.

"Band fight!" Jenny said.

"Seriously, Raleigh," I said.

"You guys are *not* nice!" Raleigh said and pulled on his ponytail.

"'Van fever! Van fever!'" Jenny said. "Band fight! Band fight!"

"But I thought you said I was the nicest asshole you knew," Rob said all mock-pouty-like.

"We have been on the road too long," I said. "Several Sisters are clearly losing their already precarious, tiny minds."

"We haven't been out that long," Rob reiterated as the jocularity, as it always needs must, abated. "Ten days is nothing."

"But it's seemed like it—that's for sure! It's been so weird," Jenny said after a little hiatus as Raleigh, changing the music, turned up a cassette of The Carpenters.

The song was "We've Only Just Begun."

"It's always weird," Rob said. "The key thing is whether it's good weird or bad weird."

"And this was…" Jenny said, playing "the straight man."

"Both!" Rob and I jinxed-on-a-Coke.

And of course what else were all four of us, raving away like that, going to do, heading as we were to our last gig of this at once trying and jolly jaunt, excited still, a little, a bit, I imagine, but more jazzed to be going home soon now, but singing along with Karen at the tops of our late and middle twenty-something/nothing lungs.

Bands *are* stupid.

And yet, even though bands are stupid, and I rave on and bitch like mad about all the trappings of the music biz, and rash on Raleigh and chronicle all the silly, nettlesome things about being on the road and the crazy people you have to work with (and look out for), I gotta add here, gotta say this: I love playing rock music more than I can ever tell you.

And you can insert here your very own favorite self-reflexive I-love-rock-and-roll anthem (there are so many to choose from). Go on. Do it now. Get up and play a little air guitar if you want.

No air drums, though, please.

Cheers.

Now: looking 'round The Doll Hut (we found it at last after two or three wrong turns, pulled up and loaded-in for the load-in), I was suddenly put in mind—who knows what triggers these odd, Lockeian Associations of Ideas—of a former friend of mine, a posh girl with five or so names. Katherine St. Margaret Crosley Weatherfield Baranaby-Smith, she was improbably called. How her names concatenated! I wouldn't kid you: she was real. We'd sat, Kath and I, on a vast nougat-colored beach one spring weekday up the blue-green coast in sparkling central California where we both lived. We'd sat and read by the blueberry taffy-colored sea. Me *Tarzan*, by Edgar Rice Burroughs—she Jane, Jane Austen, *Persuasion*. It seemed as though we'd rented it out, that windy beachfront; there was nary a soul for yards and yards. Some idlers bumping a volleyball in the tumbling, miragey distance, some kite-flying kids all crazy-legging down by the murmuring shore. Whitehairs and bluehairs in khaki trousers and tucked-in golf shirts, lapping creamless ice creams by the snack shacks. Busty beach bunny bouncing by on peach beach bike. Flash of white tennies, the slip-on sort, of course, vapid flashing smile. Silhouettes of lonesome joggers padding sand, puffing rhythmically. Sails salaaming on the water. You know the sort of scenario I'm painting here. Promiscuity of palm trees. Sad, dirty bum shuffling by in Neptune-issue, ripped-up, oily loincloth. Beach bums too—but of another demographic/tax bracket entirely. The sky lime and cream at the horizon, Easter Bunny marshmallow-blue up top. Low sun, blah, blah, blah. One swimmer swimming in a silent Technicolor movie shot—far out enough to make no noise. Meretricious gulls wheeling, sandpipers denoting the bubbling spume, etcetera, etcetera, etcetera. A lone, private plane drawing a hazy line in the salt air.

I had unsuccessfully courted Katherine for a couple of intensely dream-slow romantic weeks. Two and a half, maybe. Three at most. The occasional kisses, deep on my part and, yes, probably spuriously so on hers; the laughings-off at my outrageous, run-away-with-me admonitions as we clinked golden white wine glasses *al fresco* at frighteningly expensive restaurants, on the verandah at her place; the incremental crushing of my crush as I realized she was far too down-to-earth/pragmatic to bear the featherweight burden of all of my foolhardy romantic projections—the entire litany of the inconclusive whirlwind "love" affair. Me all thwarted concupiscence (we never slept together, only kissed) passionate-approximate but not full-on heavy duty, her pulling away as I tried to pull her in, her a flurry of restraint and denial, amidst those many, many (for me, at least) breath-arresting kisses. But no disrobing or frisky fondling of any kind beyond a quick pat here, a furtive fondle there.

And she had gamely and bemusedly entertained my really quite preposterous advances for a while. While at the same time being "inexplicably" (of course that's how *I'd* bumptiously describe it) immune to my most chivalric, exaggerated blandishments. Or seemed to. Entertained them like one does relatives of relatives—sincerely enough, but not for long. She let me squire her 'round long enough I guess at least not to make me look too very much a useless fool, and long enough to have her come off as sporting and open. That Katherine. A nice, cool girl, in other words. The kind who gave a guy a *chance*. Or at least the illusion of one. Nevertheless, she was the sort who never *really* takes one seriously. One who *pshaws* your every

earnest, I-really-mean-it-I-think-we're-meant-for-each-other avowal.
One who, to console you, tells you quite decorously: "Look: I make
up my mind about a new man in the first ten minutes. You've heard
about a girl like me—one who does that? Surely you have. Well, here
I am. I told you. I told you at the outset, love. Not literally, of course,
but the signs were there for you to read. You *asked* me—so I'm telling
you, telling it like it is. The last thing I want's to lead you on, John.
Honey, you're sweet and funny and cute and kind, but I've only fooled
around with you (well, you know, made out with you, kissed you, that
is, it's all been quite innocent and, *you* know, *light*, I think) just to see
if my instincts might, this time, have been wrong. You see, however,
they never are. I wonder sometimes. I really do. But there you are. I'm
sorry. I know myself, God knows, too well. I hope we shall always
be very good friends. And I know somehow we *will*. We really will.
Know what? I wish I had 'a type.' That'd make things so much more
thoroughgoingly easier, you see. If I had a type I wouldn't have to go
through all this *je sais pas*, this, *je sais pas* that…you know? No? Okay.
God, who *knows!* But I *don't*, you see—I have to go by instinct. I end
up with the most *cur*ious men. There are so so many better things to
think about in this world, don't you think? No? Okay. Anyway. Hmm.
All right—since you *asked*. Last guy I was serious with—let's see, it
was three years we dated—didn't speak a *word* of English. Greek guy,
so happy all the time. Maddening, actually. Insouciant doesn't even
be*gin* to describe him. I tried to teach him French. Unsuccessfully, of
course. And English was absolutely, impossibly impossible. Somehow
it didn't matter. My boyfriend in college—okay, after all this time, I'll
tell you where I went: it was *Columbia*, okay?; and I went to Miss
Porter's for Prep, en*dur*ed it, that is; I hope you're happy now, 'cause
never tell *anyone* that! Ha! Okay, so anyway he played professional
tennis, this guy I dated. On the tour and everything. Don't flinch!
Don't be jealous! I know you love tennis. We should play sometime.
I'm terrible, or better, only adequate, a 'C' player, 'C-plus', but you
won't mind, huh?! Ha! You're so funny. It's sometimes like you're in
a *play* or something, the things you say, John. Anyway, he was gone

all the time. Never saw him. Radak was his name. Couldn't tell you what he *looked like* to this very day—and it was only, oh, six years ago! Isn't that funny. It was *perfect*...I imagine he had to have been tall. Okay, he was tall. I remember that much. Eastern European-looking. I really couldn't say. Well, most Eastern European guys look, um, *Eastern European!* Duh! Isn't that priceless? Tickles me to death, that does. Anyway, his family emigrated to Greece from Croatia. Now *I* sound like a someone in a play! Sometimes I think I am one. Probably blond, he was. Blond-ish or something. So funny that I can't even really picture him! He kept sending me tickets to meet him in Rio or Barcelona or somewhere and I'd have a midterm or paper or something. Never once went. Might have watched him play a set or two at Newport or whaddayacallit Flushing Meadows for the US Open, but I wouldn't swear to it, I swear. He almost always lost in the first round of any given tournament so what would've been the use of my flying out to watch him, anyway. Try not to be cut up about it, our quote-unquote thing, John; men get over me as easily as they come, um, tumbling. It sounds *égoïste*, I know, but it's true. You'll see. Just you wait and see. In six months you'll go 'Who was that girl I went to the beach with that perfect day?' Seriously. You will."

Katherine said things like that so matter-of-factly that you had to kind of go along with her in a sort of Jamesian, "There you are," way, her kind tone cutting worse than a curse, worse than the hottest hauteur. In the end, she was the sort of wonderful woman who turned out to be too frank and sensible for one to pine after for too long, tarry puppydoggedly around, hoping against hope; one too logical and in some ways too unimaginative to long for for too long, dream of for the long haul. She let one down so easy that it was like one'd never been up. There was something beautiful about it. Beautiful as her smooth brown skin getting goosefleshed, occasionally, almost empurpled, by the too-strong breeze that day.

I went and did the precise thing I knew I shouldn't: I wrote her a horrible poem—whose facetiousness only belied my hopelessly desperate, transparent sincerity. I still have it in my mortified head.

And that's precisely where it's gonna stay: I've already unveiled too much juvenilia this go-'round, you know. There's only so much confrontation with his former pseudo-literary foolishness a foolish romantic fool like me can take, you know?

Take it from me, it, the poem, was *total* doggerel. I don't know where that term comes from, but if it's from dogs howling or cantering over to rip a poop on some parchment an idiot with a quill pen has befouled, then that'd be about right, about accurate.

She must've just laughed and thrown it in the trash. That's what I'd have done. Put it at the *bottom* of the waste basket, sort of plunge it down and stuff like a stubborn stool. How I cringe at the things I've done! You look back on your callow, yearning, gonadal youth sometimes like you were a *Trog* or Australopithecus version of yourself or something. Or like gentlepeople in the sixteenth century must've looked upon the "savages" whom adventuring marauders had brought to Londinium for show-and-tell—the Africans, Australians, Americans, and Carribean people who didn't even *know* they were African, Austrialian, etcetera. They just thought they were just *people*, probably.

Anyway.

What a purblind, goony, romantic dunce! Here's a cautionary tale for you, fellas: unless your name is Ogden Nash or James Fenton or John-John Donne, *don't write a superbabe a poem*—not even of any kind. Not even if you are called P. B. Shelley should you, really; you'll only end up drowning, as it were.

Groan!

Incorrigible punster.

Neither of us had a job at the time I'm telling you about—me because I had just finished grad school after a year off bumming around England (reading books in pubs, having a sort of postgrad gap year by filling in the vast gaps in my readings in the English, French, and Russian classics) and didn't want one, didn't want to do anything but concentrate on my own jolly disillusionment, and she because she was burnt from working too hard "in finance" and had made such a pile that she could skate, as it were, for a while.

Those French majors who go a-conquering the big, bad business world just for a lark, just to see if they can do it—don't they just slay you?

Well, Katherine slayed in many-another way. (In college, and maybe for two or three or seven postgrad years, girls like her strutted into and skipped right out of your life before you could catch your breath or the next bus to Sapville.) Of course she was quite beautiful and intimidatingly tall (if you weren't, that is, at least six-two); her hair in sassy, elongated pixie-cut à la Linda Evangelista and sea-and-sun-streaked blonde. Very East Coast. Which works so well on the West Coast. Exotic, like. Heartbreakingly, uncommonly beautiful model-like, flowerlike face. Of course. Long legs. Of course: 'cause that's what leggy beauties always have. Trim. Fit without working out. Of course. Born to wriggle into a shimmery maillot or little black cocktail dress. Born to buy and live in enormously expensive Italian shoes. Very expensive shoes. A smile that weakened your entire you. The *cutest* little teeth, the type that showcase a bit too much the gums. Had taken, in terms of being hit on, so many hits that she was like Dresden or fucking Jake Whatshisname, the Robert De Niro character in *Raging Bull*. You've maybe met her. Her kind. The sort of preppy person who doesn't say where she was "at school" so that you sort of just fill in the blanks and think "Old Money—*has* to be, a personage of unexceptionable taste and wondrous style." The kind you could picture clacking confidently in plain, classic, full-calf sleek black ultra-sexy boots across the cobblestones of roly-poly Montenegro, tight, short wool skirt, pert breasts ashimmer, free beneath an electric or sapphire blue satin blouse, a sexy yet weirdly pudibund choker of silk and black velvet 'round her super-swan-like neck; or, on a Montana ranch, talking calmly by the snapping fireside, with an easy smile and a fat glass of Cabernet—after a day out riding and shooting, with the western sky smiling down on her.

Where you could *never* picture her is of course where, according to a common friend who gave me a report five years down the line from this, she ended up: pregnant and severely ponytailed, pushing a grim pram down State Street, supposedly living in a flagitious Westside (the wrong side, the bad side, insalubrious) two-bedroom above *a self-serve car wash* (!) with a *much*-shorter-than-her waiter who works, word is, or worked, at our little seaside town's best-loved Mexican restaurant and who also, they say, deals coke.

And it now strikes me that this is the second unrequited sort of über-preppy babe/impossibly-beautiful person I have told you about, which bespeaks two things: shallow me only goes for really pretty, really smart women—they're what I like, okay?—and believe it or not, where I come from in California, there are *lots* of them: it's like you're surrounded; you just come out of a gas station loo 'cause you got a flat and you're waiting for the guy in the shirt with his name on a patch on his dark blue or green shirt to fix it and there one is, asking you for the restroom key; you stepped on a sharp pebble by the beach and you're hopping up and down on one foot and you block one, as it were, and kinda bump into her as she's heading for the outdoor beach shower and you beg her pardon and chat her up and she seems cool and you ask her if you can make it up to her with sushi later that night (she turns you down—let's not feed your appetite for fantasy-encounters five course meals here); or you're at your little brother's Little League game and you turn 'round too fast 'cause he's on deck and hitting .500 and you knock another Betty's snowcone off its paper funnel and she smiles and eye-fucks you so hard and so flirtatiously bites her unreal lip that her six-nine, two-seventy boyfriend right behind her's instantly ready to put to use his two or three jujitsu moves—the ones he acquired on account of he knew this day would come. And come.

It's horrible, horrible, horrible—that little babe-filled, seaside town. Just the *worst!* All these pretty, pretty girls. You just can't get away from them!

That day I'm telling you about, then, Kath and I lay on our respective oversized beach towels (hers terry cloth, monogrammed)—that variably windy day—and sat and gazed at the lassitudinous waves, waves that sounded in the weekday stillness like someone steadily turning over the pages of a crunchy-wonderful book or fresh fish and chips when they used to serve them to you in newspaper. The wind, I remember, gusted up sometimes so that you fairly tasted fresh air, like you were being force-fed your own breathing. I told her I had written more than an album's worth of songs and was thinking of moving to Los Angeles to find a band to play them with. Finishing a dissertation on Samuel Johnson had necessitated me doing something reckless and outré like forming a band. I had to. After spending six months obsessively writing a book about another artist, I'd sworn I would become one myself, or die trying.

It's funny the phrases we use. I wasn't going to die for my art. Starve, slave, suffer, hump gear, lose a bit of my hearing, have days when I was so tired I'd hallucinate, tear my hair out over the most picayune things, subject myself to mild humiliation at the hands of bookers, sound guys, doormen, and barbacks, plus get paid to lose my mind trying to corral middle and junior high schoolers for a substitute living—yeah; sure; that I would do, did do, would or will probably do again. But I wasn't going to expire just for the sake of making music.

And there's nothing like writing a dissertation on someone for kinda-sorta killing off your interest in them: try it sometime, gentle skimmer.

She looked at me, Katherine did, as I declared my not-so-farfetched artistic intentions, like I had just suggested we smear ourselves with tri-tip juice and troll the Santa Barbara Channel at just the time when the water's turning warmer and the spy-hopping great whites migrate south. And her perfect mouth, teeth, lips puckered, protruded, pinked forth in a kissy-faced way and she observed something I shall never forget: "It seems a sort of very hard life, being an artist. Which I'm sure you are."

I cannot convey the dreamy way she said such stuff. She went on: "It wouldn't be for *me*, but if you absolutely *must*, you know... you aren't going to believe this, maybe, but I went out with a very famous musician for a little while...okay, if you must know, it was... oh, I really don't want to say...okay, it was Bruce: I reckon I don't have to tell you his last name, too...I know, I know...but—ha!—there lots of Bruces in music so you'll never know, really. And it might not be the one you're thinking of—'cause a lady never tells, does she? *Any*way, *John*, I never tell anyone about it as it wasn't serious—just a little fling...and anyway I hate it when people drop names or, you know, brag that they've slept with someone famous. And it was only a short time, very short, that we dated. Yep. Well, for a month or so, if you really wanna know. I went on tour with him for a week as well. I know it's a total cliché—don't *say* it!—but, hey, I was young. And he asked me to, so I went. So there."

"Huh," I remember saying, or trying to say. Then repeating: "Huh."

"Yeah. Look: here's the thing: for all the money he makes *now* and of course all the recognition and adulation I wouldn't want to've gone through what he's gone through for all the tea in China. And of course—being famous? No *thank* you! Wouldn't want to be that for *any*thing. I hope it makes you happy, John. And I know that you're going to tell me that you don't want to be famous, are not doing it in order to be famous."

"Precisely," I said.

"Precisely," said she, and continued: "I just *know* from knowing lots of artists from when I worked on Wall Street that of *course* it's something that you *have* to do, but—gosh—it just seems like you're in for having *such* a hard life...such a hard life...such a hard life..."

Her dreamy, old world, hyper-educated voice came imperishably impressively from beneath the flowerlike sun hat she affected without fail whenever she sunbathed, she said. I could swear now, looking back, that her giant eyes had smiled Cassandraishly beneath her fashionable Ray-Bans. Or that there was a certain knowingness in her elegant voice. And I will never forget the gesture with which she shut the brim of the hat—the brim she'd originally companionably lifted so as to make herself clear, make herself heard, as if to say "And that's all that need be said on the matter"—as she lay back down, turning back over, turning her brown satin back to the sea with its thousand tints of blue and green, shifting her fine, round, firm/you-couldn't-help-but-notice-it rump, to read and tan and dream some more.

"Let me ask you something, John," she said dozily, around five minutes later, turning her head with torpid importance. I hadn't known quite what to say, so I shut up for once.

"Sure," I said, all hopeful, genuinely eager to learn. "Go ahead."

"Are these warm little winds what they call Santa Anas?"

"Sorry?!"

"Are these warm little winds…"

"Yes, I think so," I said—kinda stunned on account of it seemed right then that none of the things she'd said had a reality, and that, somehow, some way, I wasn't even really real to her and oh well what the hell.

How strange that it never occurred to me till now, till I bunged in our gear at The Doll Hut, in Orange County, California, on April 5, 1994, with Rob and Raleigh and Jen passing me back and forth with whatever equipment they had to hand, that Katherine St. Margaret Crosley et alia may have had a point. The little reverie I had—who knows what triggers these things?—of the two of us on the near-deserted beach that day had a sort of trancelike effect on me. I remembered later the way she'd, unannounced, stood and braved the rippling windwaves and slit her fine eyes at the bright horizon and the sealine. Then dropped *Persuasion*, flung down that hat, set down those expensive sunglasses, thumbed down her purple-and-white striped, breath-catching bikini bottoms, fingered up her matching, haltered top, and, like some tall bronze Queen of the Nereids, entered the placidly plangent water and effortlessly swum toward an enthusiastically nodding buoy, then disappeared under the salted waves for what seemed the longest time—disappeared like she was indeed going to dive away forever from my specific existence. It was like I was already not even there. In short, she didn't even bother saying "I'm going in."

What was I *do*ing here? The Doll Hut, I mean. On tour. At this hour. With my life. Any working/touring musician intermittently wonders the same thing of a Tuesday night at a rotten, pungently musty club. Of a Thursday night at a decent club, even. Wonder: How many more times can I lug this cumbersome, behemoth amp up a parlous staircase and down a pitch-black hellhole? (With temples throbbing still from last night's post-gig bender, through drumming rain outside?) How many more times can I pinch and thump and jam and wrench my thumb bright blue? Poke myself in the face or finger with a boinging guitar string that draws blood and chafes like a particularly nasty paper cut? How many more times can I let the sound guy yell at me to *turn the fuck down?* Even when my amp's on "two." Just on two, I tell you. Be bedeviled by a bouncer or the late-night pizza-taco that's contradicting everything my stomach's saying this morning? How many more times tolerating a sour bartender (who's "not open till six, man") treating my girlfriend like a total refugee for asking for a little bottle of purified water at 5:58? Can I countenance again having to fairly *will* the piss to spray forth faster as I stop my breath in a too-dark, stinking, retch-inducing loo? Wash my hands soaplessly afterward, almost-blindly raking the soap dispenser for a crust or a crystal of cake or powder, husbanding my ire over innumerable little slights, insults, riotous disappointments, and oversights that all just add up. Vicissitudes, boring hiatuses, delays, questions inane and clownish and germane, unhappy exchanges, unpleasant odors, prodigious discomfiture, cant. Dashed hopes and blasted expectations. Bafflement, foiling. Comedowns, setbacks, fiascos and teasings. Blighted, thwarted, crushed. Things gone, going, horribly, horribly wrong. Crest-or-chapfallen. Fucked on the pavement outside the shut-up venue, with one convex and wilted Chesterfield left and all stores closed. Two in the morning, no place to stay. Short of cash and patience. Long on material for jeremiads like this.

Not that I want to com*plain* or anything.

But really now: How many more people with equally good intentions and innocuously bothersome questions can I talk to before or after the gig when all I want to do is die to the world for three days straight?

Jesus slept.

You guys and rocking girls who've toured? You know just what I'm on about. Ah, but maybe I'm viewing touring through too rose-colored glasses here, painting too pretty a picture. Downplaying the downfalls. Ha!

Some band, as we stacked our gear off in a corner somewhere, were already onstage. Every once in a while, some obscure miracle, some way "out there" outfit, swims into your aesthetic ken, and is on the bill you're on as well. You roll into Omaha, Nebraska or Athens, GA or goddam Boise and up onstage is a group that you've never heard of that just blows you away. These guys/gurls are amazing, you think. I can't believe I don't know them. Such a beauteous ruckus of quintessentially harmonious pandemonium was coming from the stage we gazed up at that we could hardly believe our ears. And eyes. For the band onstage was a Japanese Noise Band that had actual *songs*. Well, they had one, at least—the one they were playing. And if they had one, they maybe had another one. Had to. My old exacting-as-far-as-music-standards-go pal, Sterling would probably disagree ("*Any* band, no matter how basically atrocious, can luck out and write *one* great song!" he often opined), but I was sure that these guys were going to have at least one more "tune" that rocked my world.

Three guys, all facing each other, ignoring the audience (an audience of seven, plus us), rail-thin and wild-haired (great-haired, rather, like perfectly fashioned Napoleonic black shakos had been plunked down on their rocking, bobbing heads). They were cranking out a "number" that had a yip-yip-yip sort of verse (or chorus; it was hard to tell *what* it was), then a groovy, psychedelic passage following that was relaxed and spacey, as the guitar player, this absolute *gawk* of a person, six foot five at least, was coaxing notes out of his axe like he was a one-man television or wire. Like he was playing two guitar parts at once, is what I am trying to tell you. It seemed he was a manic butcher, some fel knight like Macbeth, savaging his strings, owning an electric *Throne of Blood*. Then they went to a catchy chorus that within two bars had you humming along with it.

The drummer was an equal marvel. Keith Moon died when I was very, very young, so I never got to see The Who, the real Who, live. But boy oh boy wasn't this kid, with his shellacked Baby Huey coif dancing like a blackly burning, swaying flame, conjuring Keith Moon's spirit as he flailed away like each drum had to be hit as hard and as many times in ratatat succession as humanly conceivable. We just stood there, Jenny and I and Rob and Raleigh, in a staggered, ragged row, smiling in wonder and joy. It was like they'd beaten into submission a song they'd written. Like they'd whipped rather than composed it, somehow.

You have two ways to go as a performing band and no in-betweens: you can "work" the crowd, acknowledge them to the max, look 'round the room, draw them in, or you can pretend like it doesn't matter for all the world whether there is anyone watching at all. The latter's like giving off the vibe, after a fashion, almost like you hate them, or at least you hate the fact that they're voyeuristically there, witnessing, watching you, waiting for something, waiting for you to give them something, something good, good as can be, live-wise. Either approach, if you do it right, can work. If you do it right, mind. How many times have you yourself, reader, gone to a gig and the band onstage is practically upstaging themselves to get you to like them. The worst is when like a bar or cover band an original band *introduces the band members to the crowd*: that's just awful. Did The Clash ever go: "Hey, guys, now I'd like to introduce you to Mr. Topper Headon on bass guitar! So put your hands together for..."

No they the fuck did not. And if they ever did, they were taking the piss, believe me.

If any of you raucous rockers out there go form a stupid group one day please don't ever let me know that your drummer's called Big Wally or "The Wombat" or that the imbecile bassist is named Steve "but we call him 'Sleeve'"; I and anyone with any taste will instantly hate you *and* your so-called music if I hear that the guitarist is called *Phil*. (Phil's a wanker's moniker, anyway! Fuck *you*, Phil. Fuck off the stage and back to your job at Staples or OfficeMax, stocking and checking mouthbreathingly. Go get me some toner and some No. 2

pencils instead of playing that forty-bar "solo" that pays homage to Mark Knopfler that I and my drinking buddies are starting to take extreme umbrage to here. Okay? Thanks.)

"Sank you!" the bass player said to the mic, to the little crowd, who clapped like mad for them and rightfully, us included, of course.

The bald, be-tatted guy standing next me whooped "Spring Snow!" and kind of clapped at me—as though I wanted encouragement for expressing my enthusiasm for them. I certainly did not. They were great: the first good band we'd played with all tour long. I was thumping my palms raw and wearing out a smile as well.

"Spring Snow!" he yodeled again and the bass player said "Sank you very much!" and the applause died down and the club's stereo came on. (Unfortunately, with a Nirvana song: "Come As You Are").

Two

hink back, if you would be so kind, to my reference re: the bibulous bar bore that ornaments every bar, almost…ready? The Doll Hut had the *king* bore—this "chap" called Barnacle Bob.

"How come they call him Barnacle Bob?" Raleigh asked as Barnacle Bob, ostensibly twigging that we were a band, came bang right up to us.

"I dunno *why* they call me that!" Barnacle Bob said as he thrust his chest right up against Raleigh's shoulder and put his happy, sweaty, winking, smiling face right in Raleigh's; then he let out this massy guffaw like he'd made the joke to end all jokes: "I don't know why at all! *And* don't know why I thought you was a band, you lot! Maybe the musical equipment that's weighing you down presently was something of a subtle clue! Hahaha!"

"Hello, Bob," Franklin, coming up just then, said evenly. "Very funny. Let me introduce you to…"

"Bob's your uncle," Bob said coolly. "These must be The *Weird* Sisters! How d'ye do, The Weird Sisters? You don't half look weird. Ah, I'm only jokin' ya! Look at *you!* [Jenny, of course.] How d'ye *do?* [Ogling her breasts, leering be*yond*.] Hahaha! Only joking you, love. Welcome to the Jungle! I mean The Doll Hut! Hahaha! Don't tell me—you named yourselves after *Macbeff*, right? I knew so. I fought so. Nice one. Very, like, literary and that. Shakespeare, innit. I like you a lot already [to Jenny]—and your sisters [to Jenny's chest again, rearing up on his tiptoes for vulgar, ghastly emphasis]."

"Knock it off, Bob," Franklin said.

"I don't mean nuffin' by it, pretty lady," Barnacle Bob apologized. "Only joking. No offense. You lot are meant to conjure up the witches in *Macbeff*, though, right? I got that right, dint I? I fought so. I was only having a laff…and if I told you [toward Jenny again] you had a beautiful body, would you hold it against…"

"Cut it out, Bob," Franklin said as Bob's goggle-eyes went giant and Bob himself canted too close, I could tell, to Jen.

She backed away as if somehow someone had spat at her.

Dear sweet girl.

"Having some drinks, are we?" Raleigh, turning our way, said.

Stares of great blankness; then Barnacle Bob sort of hoisted his glass in a halfhearted fashion.

"He looks just like Marty Feldman, doesn't he?!" Raleigh said. "You look just like Marty Feldman," Raleigh said to Bob.

"Okay, all right, all right," Barnacle Bob said, twitching his nose with its palpable rivulets of burst-vessel porphyry blue. "I dint mean nuffin'…"

"That's enough, Bob," Franklin intoned, peace-makingly, as Raleigh walked over to one of those mirrors that are also adverts for

Bombay gin or Jim Beam: he never could pass one by without looking to see if he was in it.

"Bob's your uncle, then. S'awrite now. Now: about the whole *Macbeff* thing?"

We said hello and nodded "yeah" to his understanding that we were called after the witches in "The Scottish Play," that we were a brainy kind of band, knew our classical theatrical allusions and blah, blah, blah; and Rob gave Bob a vapid, threatening look and I *almost* declined to shake his hand and Jenny like the good sport she was just laughed and shrugged it all off and Barnacle Bob, who wasn't the publican or the booker or an official impresario or anything— he just acted like he owned the joint—imparted to us the pertinent information that The Jollygoods, the band that was meant to play after us, had cancelled, citing sorrow over Cobain's unbearable demise as the reason why they wouldn't be doing the stupid gig. Hence, Bob said, we could take our time hoisting our stuff onstage and moreover we could play as long a set as we wanted, adding facetiously, "Well, as long as the nuts in the Hut want you to, anyway—the nutters at the Hutter! Haha!"

Oh, like we really wanted to play a long set to something like fourteen people, anyway; and this on the last night of a long (but only metaphorically) tour; at the end of "a long day at the office," as it were.

And by office I mean Pleiadean Waiting Station.

He had on this dusty-black patently "poetic" and "colourful" Mad Hatter-ish top hat, Bob did, with an obligatory regulation hippie feather/roach clip, red and black and white, waving forth from it, and these violet-tinted rectilinear granny glasses that perched atop his very thin, very long beaky or finlike (it was hard to pick *which*) super aquiline and unmistakably English proboscis, i.e. his nose. He got so up in your space that you thought he was going to jump on you like an impertinent house cat. And of course he specialized, as most pub bores do, in boring you silly *and* getting way too close for comfort. Plus the following exciting extracurriculars: advanced name-dropping; repeating himself and echolalically repeating what others were saying; cutting you off when you tried, politely or no, to excuse yourself and go Anywhere, USA but where *he* was; punching you full force in the face with his breath (a potpourri of whiskey, onions?, curry? carrots? a second helping of onions? and double-pepperoni, perhaps); yarning on about how he'd seen some legendary band— Hendrix, Love, Doors, Who, Zeppelin, Sly, Creedence, Airplane—do a *secret show* that him and only around twenty-seven other people were at; collaring or cornering you when you tried to get away (even if it was to *buy him a drink so as to get away from him*; he wasn't having that, oh no, he'd get the next round—though of course he never got around to it, the next round and its getting).

Barnacle Bob, thy type is legion. Many are thee as thou spreadest thyself across the bar-and-clubland, multiplying thyself like a fancy figure in a Fun House Hall of Mirrors.

So as Spring Snow flung their stuff off stage with surprising expediency and admirable urgency, Rob and Raleigh excused themselves to get on with setting our gear up. Jenny, sensing getting trapped or wrapped up in yet another banal-crazy conversation, I imagine, sensibly went with them while I watched, and for a weird second the whole thing—Spring Snow getting off the stage, us readying ourselves to do a completely unnecessary gig—seemed like it was choreographed by Fellini or some mad genius Russian director from the twenties or something. That left Franklin and me with Barnacle Bob. Just grand. And fuck me if old Barn didn't single me out for a regular blather. What else could he do?—I was, after Franklin pissed off to the loo, the only one dumbly standing next to him, i.e. available for interlocutorial harrying.

But before I subject you to his interminable blandiloquent orations (I'm thinking maybe I'll spare you—even though *I* wasn't spared), and describe his toothy, rebarbative smile, a word about the etiquette of multiple-bills and bands and "changeovers" from one act to another. If you are the slightest bit considerate, you start getting your amps and things off stage and down several treacherous, nodose, invisible black steps no less than two or three minutes after you're done playing; right afuckingway. I always made a point myself of wrapping up my and Jenny's guitar leads and hurry-humping her amp and mine and our effects pedals and guitars off any stage we graced like someone being timed, unless of course we were the headliner, the last band of the night; then, good show or bad or just bleh, I threw myself off the stage and negotiated myself down the bletcherous stage steps, then went into hiding as best I could, backstage or out to the van or any available alleyway. If the gig patly sucked, I didn't want even my best friends to tell me otherwise, go patronizingly consoling me down the lane; if the gig was good, I knew that and I preferred to disappear so as not to be subjected to anyone's praise. I have learned, over the years, to take a sincere, thoughtful compliment on the chin— it's only etiquette and you sort of do a good turn by acknowledging as unfussily as possible someone's/almost anyone's good intentions. To deflect a compliment with something like "Oh, you're just saying that!" or "Oh, no I'm not—I'm not all that grand!" is, it now seems to me, graceless and crass. It takes a lot of thought and sometimes therapy to get to the point where you just go "Thank you! Thank you so much!" But in my late twenties what did I know about decorum and how-to-take-a compliment? Fuck-all is what I knew. After a gig I didn't want to have to put such theoretical stuff into practical practice. I just want, and I know Rob did/does to, to get colossally drunk and not talk about the show.

As I watched the guys in Spring Snow lariat their heavy duty, cool snakelike orange-and-black tweed guitar leads and toss their cool Vox amps and Gretsch drums off stage like they were game show participants or like a minor fire was about to go blazing under them, I thought of *course* a band from Ja*pan* are going to be not only efficient to the max, "a well-oiled machine," but also *polite*. So many American and UK bands take their dear sweet, jolly time getting the *fuck* off stage: you so want to chuck their stuff off for them. Some bands, no matter how hard you vibe them, stand there sighing and huffing at 'em arms akimbo. The bass player's got to take twenty minutes scrabbling around in his pockets for his vintage lighter and light a cigarette—plus one for his deputized roadie that takes sixteen flicks and subsequent shuttings of the cap to happen. The singer's no help at all. He's already swanned off backstage and is bobbing for beers in the headliner's dressing room or making for your discontented girlfriend or for his own bright-eyed or totally over-it moll. The drummer takes a *year* to get each wing nut loose on his cymbal stands. He lifts off each stupid "false exciter" (i.e. cymbal) separately instead of porting the whole assemblage off the riser. 'Cause *that*, that would be too easy and logical and just plain considerate. And keyboard players? Don't even get me churning on *them*. One of the reasons why Jenny stopped playing keyboards on maybe a third of our songs a few months ago wasn't just because guitars sound better, look cooler—but because they, those keyboard setups, come off so dopey onstage, and are a total hassle anyway. Even dorky, goonish, super nerdy *keyboard bands* hate it when the dorky, goonish, super nerdy bands they're playing with have keyboard setups big as what's probably in Rick Wakeman's dungeon. I'll bet synthy Depeche Mode, if they ever gigged, early on, with The Human League or Thompson Twins, say, looked askance at all that gear that looks like stacks of chiaroscuro ironing boards and went "Ugh! Get a load of all *that* shite, wouldn't you just!" Unfailingly, the keyboard guy, the guy with the most convoluted mishmash of chords and power sources and goddam antennae or whatnot, is the most lollygagging lollygagger in the entire building when it comes to fucking one's gear the fuck off stage. Get a load of the guy's *hair* too, next time you go to some crummy club gig where a synth band's on. The keyboardist's the one with the poodle-doo or mega-mullet every single time. You don't even have to see him loading his precious synth into its bondage leather bag to tell it's him. You can't miss him: he looks just like Linda McCartney circa *Band on the Run*: and Linda McCartney just after Linda McCartney has gone and put Linda McCartney's finger in a socket.

Keys or no, it's utterly exasperating, is what I'm trying to say, watching some shite band break down after their shite set in what seems like they're moving in slow motion (through shite, slowly).

Anyway, here's barmy bibbling Barnacle Bobby, disciple of Comus, deep in his cups, what he said. I may as well go ahead and inflict it on you, his dubious palaver. You'll have to envision for yourselves how Bob's beetle-brows went up and down with each imparted revelation like so many marionettes or notes on a waterlogged calliope. Perpend: picture him, if you will, with his gnarled, maculate hands clasped donnishly behind his back as he natters on, lecturing-like, his head craned forward like a sort of human crane. He only unknits them, his hands, when he gropes for the gleaming pint or fat glass of rotgut he's got perched on the edge of the bar in the gloaming light of the lurid bar room lamplight. There you have him.

Here's *Bobby*:

"Want me to tell you somefink? [That was how he always, they said, started—by making you his accomplice, like, a *willing* audience.] Well, I will. Don't mind if I do, as the tipsy bishop said to the seductive lamppost. Ha! Now: nine'een sixty noine, it was. Devonshire Downs. Place way *way* out in The Valley. Los Angeles. Ah! The very name. It just—takes you back. Takes one back. Devonshire. Downs. Gotta certain wing to it, wot. Takes me back, the ver' thought of it. Takes me aback, is what it does—to fink all them gigs I been to i' the meantime. Glory! See, I'd come up from Huntington Beach where I hadda squat-type situation wif a coupla pals of the female perwaysion of mine, wink-wink. Wary nice gurls, *they* was. Mindy and Mandy, was their names. But not their real names, if you know what I mean, mate. Unforgettable gurls, them. Nice and *generous*, Barnacle Bob's your uncle; if you know what old Bob's tellin' ya. Right? You wif me? Magical time, the bloody sixties. Never come again and the way we were and all of that. Any road…where waz I? Oh, The Downs. Devonshire. Do you like Jimi, by the way? Jimi *Hen*drix? Fink he's any good a'tall? Rahaha. My, was 'e eva! Comes on, hat off, looks up, winks—tongue out, revs up, one chord, goes on for hours, this one chord, it seems. Maddening. What a tease. And what's he do? Well hell's bells if he doesn't up and starts up wif what *I* thought at the time was a ripping rendition of good old 'Purple 'aze.' But it waddn't. Mindblowing, it was. A simple marvel. He never murdered anyone, but he sure killed that day. The blighter starts likesay making love to 'is axe. Soloing, like. Such an intimate thing you felt a right voyeur. Musical Peepin' Toms, that's what we wuz that 'mortal day. *I* did, anyway, feel like that. Like you'd caught 'im wif his trousers down. Then he goes into this blues thing, Jimi does, bless 'im, and there's Buddy Miles wailing away. The mind boggles like swimmers wifout goggles, it does. They don't make them like that no more, to be sure, don't you know, mate. And you can bet your last fiver on that. Your bottom dollar or Bob's *not* your uncle. Played like they was on fire, that lot. Given Jimi's penchant for pyrotechnics, it's more than possible he *was* on fire, don't you know. Literally and all of that. And yet Jimi himself, by Jove, such a *nice* cove. Just the sweetest bloke. Ever so amiable and humble and modest and such. Genuinely-like. The genuine article, him. Oh, no I never met him, me. Not I. Not personally, you see. It was just, well, someone I knew knew someone who knew someone who knew him. Such a nice chap, Jimi. So they said. I never had the pleasure. Pity about the junk and everything, though—know what I mean? Great shame. You wouldn't have seen him on the telly—too young, you. But on David Frost's talk show, my, was he ever just the most mellow fellow, quite the little gentleman, you know and so unassumin'. All about peace and love and peace and love. As were we all, I daresay. Peace and love's a jolly cliché, innit, but the whole scene really was all about that. Peace and love. Far as the gig goes, the whole thing was unannounced, you see. Or maybe it was organized, arranged. Can't remember. Too many drugs! Those days wuz *filled* wif them—times you'd wake up and wonder not what day but what week it was, my man! What month, wot? R*ather*. Oh I say. You couldn't tie your *shoes*, mate, sometimes. You might think you could Old Mother *Hub*bard in them, but you couldn't fookin' tie the blighters! I been takin' drugs since I was a wee boy and bunking off school ta hie me ta free concerts for longer 'an I can remember! Hahaha! [cough, cough, cough]. Can't get away wif that sort of thing *now*adays, can yer? Puttin' on a surprise show, I mean. I was there when The Beatles played the rooftop, I was—no fuckin' lie, mate. Saville Row. I wouldn't kid you on. But nothing's the same these days. The drugs as well. And, speaking of drugs—let's talk about New Order, a band your press kit says you revere, does it not?… Yeah, I read your lot's press kit. I collect 'em, I do—the bands I fancy, anyway. The booker here passes them along to me; I'm a consultant, like. Musical consultant, that's my game. Sultan of it, me. Sultan of Musical Consulting. Nice one, eh? Anyway, were New Order or somefink to try and do a gig on the low down? Not a chance, mate. Too much red tape. Swat team of lawyers or somefink. Goons an' them in riot gear. Choppers hovering and all of that. But in the old days, the halcyon days, like—the excitement was, like, in the air. Do you know what I mean? Smell that? Smell the air right now, wouldja? Smell it! What do yer smell? Nuffing—that's what. No smell. None. Not a whiff of it. The smell's gone. The smell of excitement. Never see it come a-fucking-gain. Rock's dead now. The record companies just let acts fling any old half-baked LP out there. No quality control, mind. Not *your* band, of course. Haha! Not the *Sistas!* Ha! There's nuffing in it, puff of smoke, nowadays. Nuffing. It's all postures and such. Where's a band like The Move or The Who? Love or The bloody Byrds. Tell me. Yer can't! Might as well try 'n' find in California a porp pie or fish 'n' fuckin' chips like we gets back home. Never 'appen! Might as well ask for a poet laureate like Alfred Lord Bloody Tennyson! And get this: all them hair bands Nirvana was supposed t'have made irrelevant and all of that? They'll rise again. Mark my words, they will. Hair rock *resurgum*, to mint a phrase. Come again, they will (as the actress said to the bishop!) 'Hey, hey, my, my—rock and roll will *ever* die,' if you ask me, mate. I say, you wouldn't have a *drink* ticket to spare old Bob, now, wouldya? Somefink to wet the old whistle? You wouldn't have a…fanks. Fanks a lot. I say, wery kind of you, mate. Wery generous. Not all bands these days so nice to good old Bob. Kids and them. No respect. As ole Arefa Fanklin says t'the faif-ful. R-E-S-P-and all of that. Now. Not so wif the Jap kids up onstage the moment, though: they give me *all* they bloody drink tickets, them did. Don't drink alcohol, they said. Funny, eh? *Sake* they make there, Japan. Gets you *right* pissed. Cracking good band, yeah, ain't they? Set up a bloody racket, all right. But what kinda rock stars they gonna be if they don't learn to have a bit of bevvy, I ask you? No kind of rock star. Rock *star*. Speaking a-which? Would you mind having the barkeep top me off? Fanx. As I was saying—entire band teetotallin', as it might be? Ridiculous. Personally, I don't hold it against them—course I don't! I walked away wif six free drinks. Gave me all their drink tickets! *Wonderful* band. I'm prez of their bleeding fan club now, I am! Hahaha! Now, let's see—where wuz I, then? Oh. Let me tell you somfink, mate. Mind you, them metal bands. Them metal bands'll come again, you mark my words. Unkillable, they are. Unkillable. Now, Nir*vana*, mind you—let me tell you somefink about that band. In honor of Mr. Kur' Cobain's untimely premature unwarranted demise. If I might, an' it please your worships…you see, then, thing wif Nir*vana* was…and a lot of people don't know this. The thing with Nirvana was…"

And blah, blah, blah, blah, blah, blah, blah went on Bob's sort of verbal cadenza. Weirdly, his raffish voice shifted gears or seemed to, at least, from Michael Caine to Michael York to Michael Palin to Peter Cook to Keith Richards to Peter O'Toole to Peter Brook to Richard Burton to Richard Harris to Dudley Moore to *Roger* Moore to Oliver Reed to Lawrence Oliver to Hugh Grant to Richard E. Grant to Tom Courtney to Sean Connery to Michael Caine and back again. He said living in America had majorly messed with his accent. Uh, *ye-ah*. No kiddin'. Practiced aeolist that he was, it was like old Barnacle B. was trying on different parts for the same character in a fringe play. He had that inimitably English thing of sounding both self-deprecating and self-aggrandizing at the same time, like his mouth couldn't make up its mind. Years of being told by their sententious, didactic masters that they knew nothing had turned droves of them, English lads grown old like Bob, into pedants themselves, know-alls.

And some of them into beastly, dipsomaniacal bar bores.

As Johnson says about drunks getting drunk: "He who makes a beast of himself gets rid of the pain of being a man."

And later on, when we were breaking down after an okay-enough set and about to load out our stuff outside to the Astro under a gibbous moon, I spotted him drunkenly address the bright, fresh, red-painted public telephone in the corner. Lecturing to it. I reckon Bob'd run out of faces to melt in that goddam club, right enough, so he'd barnacled onto *a phone booth*. I pictured him even later on in the night having a jowly dispute with a lacquered lamppost, haranguing a varnished garbage pail, upbraiding a gleaming fire hydrant, then punctuating his drunken, disputatious oratory by promptly vomiting on it.

"What an *id*iot," Franklin, coming up to me and witnessing the entire charade, said. I loved him for that; though we hadn't hung out with him all that many times, I'd never ever heard him have a bad word for anybody.

Three

he fanzine world is marked for the most part by quite parochial considerations. Rare is the *worldly* person who thinks it'd be a grand idea to type up his bedsit musings on a bunch of bands from a particular genre, shuffle those jottings lovingly together into a semblance of a journal or review, slap a colored cover with a pen-and-ink drawing or "live shot" imago of the "featured" band on it, and take those "masters" down to the local Kinko's or Copymat and have them collate and staple, say, fifty copies to start so that he or she can then distribute them among the faithful—if he can find them. The editor of any given 'zine is really into, for instance, twee or Malaysian jangle pop, Swedish power pop or hardcore or punk, Japanese girl groups, or revivalist neo-sixties guitar bands who exclusively employ left-handed twelve-string Rickenbackers or something. I used the word "world" by design on account of the fact that the creator of said

'zine really *is* master of his or her domain. He or she can write about—
from any slant he wants—whatever he wishes. He doesn't have to
subject his scribblings, jejune or otherwise, to a censorious editor or
pernickety proofreader or even his mom; he doesn't even have to use
English idioms properly. Her opinions reign supreme. (Gender switch
alert.) She's sort of like the "literary" equivalent of the DIY punk
rocker. Answers to no one. Not even her "following." She's queen. And
she has the "artistic" liberty of making it up as she goes along. She can
be humble and say "Hey, it's only one cub reviewer's opinion," or she
can wax didactic all she wants, shoving her judgments down people's
throats. Going on rants ("Why Are All These New Bands Picking
One-Word Names?" or "Can We Please Not Have Any More Bands
That Use 'Super' As a Prefix, Please?") or geeky, Peter Pan-ish tangents
("The Ten Best Non-Chocolate Candies," "Ten Terrific Cereals I Have
Known") or pasting up silly, superfluous sidebars ("Indie Rockers And
Their Favorie Sports Teams") only *total* dorks would want to read.
It's crazy. It's funny to think of these über-nerdy, modern musical
miscellany scribblers as the descendants of proselytizing gazetteers
and gadfly pamphleteers from the Grub Street circa *The Age of Reason*.

He or she might start by handing out copies, hot off the press,
at gigs like ours, like the one you've just read about. He or she might
not even plan to go beyond Volume Number One. Maybe she's read
How to Start a Fanzine, a "famous" 'zine itself, by some twee pop
chick whose name escapes me right now (she's probably read *How to
Start a Record Label* by same, but reckoned a fanzine is much cheaper,
much more fun, much more "her"). He might deferentially drop off a
hopeful handful at a mom-and-pop record shop, work up the nerve
to chat up the clerk and/or manager—or maybe just bashfully place
(not fling) them in with the flyers and postcards in the nook near
one of the store's windows. Maybe send them to other 'zines who
might write about his 'zine in exchange for a tacit agreement to do a
write-up on them, the other 'zine, up in return in the next "ish" (i.e.
"issue") or so. The cageyer of them might solicit some local businesses
to advertise, even. You can just picture one approaching Mr. Kindlay,

the sweat-covered Canadian guy that runs the dry cleaners on the corner, or prune-faced Mrs. Pinappleous, the sweet old Greek who's got that video store that no one goes to on account of it always smells like someone's St. Bernard took a dogshit in it, explaining incomprehensibly what they're doing in writing about the legacy of Hüsker Dü, the importance of orange juice or The Field Mice, how the issue that Mrs. or Mr.'s considering taking out ad space in might even have an interview from Lawrence (Lawrence!) from Felt or, if not him, then maybe Dan from The Television Personalites.

Television Personalities? Incredible! The entire back page is only twenty-five bucks?! How can up such a deal be passed? Such a nice boy, he—always wearing that worn-out sweater no matter the heat: a little off in the head but such a nice, fat face has he, smiling so, and always with that skin of his like the inside of a candy bar wrapper.

That there is something internecine, dorky, reverential, precious, insular, and idolatrous about the fanboy or -girl is a total given. There is, furthermore, something of the autodidact in every 'zinemaker. There is something sententious too. Sometimes it struck me, in meeting innumerable geeks at innumerable gigs, that they were all trying to out-whisper each other about how they knew about some hot band before the band had even put out a record. That it was one big whisper party, if you will. You wanted to surprise-attack them sometimes with a big, fat hug. Except for the fact that most 'zine girls and guys, curiously, have this weird sort of "please don't get too close to me and *certainly* don't touch me" vibe. How to spot one, a 'zinester: no matter how toasty out it is, he's got a "jumper" on—it's probably mohair; it's doubtless from the fifties; his trousers (they're not *pants*) are perfectly creased, de rigueur vintage, too, probably very slim fitting ('zine people don't have much time to waste eating—there's too much new stuff to check out in order to determine definitively whether it's cool or not). Your basic 'zinette favors dresses that could've been purloined from Wardrobe on a Grace Kelly or Audrey Hepburn flick. She's gotta have some cool, geek-chic glasses, for sure—whether she needs them or not. Jewelry's *déclassé* for sure—unless it's for special occasions like Morrissey's coming to be the speaker at your public school's graduation or it's Paul Weller's or David Bowie's birthday.

Four

lake, the publisher/proprietor of *Pies*, you could've spotted a mile away as a 'zine geek, even if he didn't have the obligatory cardie or even if he wasn't hugging a coupla copies of his latest issue. Here he comes mincing up to me as I wrap up my and Jenny's guitar leads and lasso them into the sticker-pasted, cheap, vintage thrift shop suitcase that the two of us use for all our accessories, pedals, and strings, and capos, and stuff.

"How do you like that Boss Digital Delay pedal?" Flake asked haltingly.

"Hi. You must be Flake," I said. "Nice to meet you."

"You like it?" he breathed, skipping formalities, I reckon. "I find the new ones don't compare to the ones from the mid-eighties."

"Oh," I said. "Do you play music as well? I mean, play in a band as well as have a fan…'zine?"

"Um, no. Not really."

"But you play guitar, though?"

"No."

"Oh."

"So…"

"Never? I like your jumper, by the way!"

"My what?"

"Your sweater. It's cool."

"Oh, this? My sweater? Oh, yeah, 'jumper.' Right! Thanks! Well, I own a sixty-two Fender Jazzmaster—all original, real rare, totally amazing—but I, um, can't really play it. I mess around on it and stuff...I know a few chords but not that many. I do take it out of the case, though. The original case, that is. I wish I could play it; I'm just not any good. I love guitars so much, though; you must, too. Love them, I mean."

"I do, actually," I said.

"The price tag's still on it, in fact. On my guitar, I mean."

"Wow. Well, you should pick it up more often. I love Jazzmasters. I used to have one but I had to sell it."

"Oh, no: that's too bad. Sorry to hear that."

Silence long enough to be kinda nervous-making for both of us.

"So, Flake, I, um..." I started to say. Someone had to say *some*thing here.

"I loved your set, by the way. I think you guys are great. Sort of like The Go-Betweens or The House of Love. But fuzzier. Have you ever heard of a band called Hypnolovewheel?—they're from New Jersey."

"Thank you. Yes. They have a song called 'Bridget Because' that's one of my favorite..."

"You know 'Bridget Because'!? Oh, my *gosh*—I love that song. I love it. No one knows that band, you know. You are only, like, the fourth person I know who knows them. Amazing. Anyway, I only got here, like, twenty minutes ago, so I only caught, like, the last four songs. I'm glad you played some things from the new album. That was killer. I reviewed it, by the way, in the current issue—here it is."

I looked at the page he had the 'zine open to: Four and a half pies.

"Thank you," I said and nodded around twenty times or so. "Four and a half pies."

"Uh-huh."

"That's great, Flake. I'm glad you liked it."

"That's out of five pies," Flake said.

"Oh, that's good," I said. "I'm glad it's not four and a half pies out of ten pies."

"No. Huh-huh," Flake huh'ed *without* laughing.

Yikes: another humming, awkward pause.

"Um, Franklin said we were meant to do an interview?..."

"Is that okay?"

"Of course."

"Do you have time now?"

"Sure. Let me just finish packing up, okay. Won't be six minutes."

"Um, can we have, uh, Jenny do it, too, the interview, do you think?"

"Of course. Hey *Jenny!*" I shouted to her. She was off to the side of the stage; Rob was helping her get her amp off of it—well, not helping, doing it for her. "This is Flake. Come say hello."

Just then Raleigh banged over, having pretty expeditiously put his drums in his cases and stacked them near the loading door: "Is this gonna take real long, you guys? I am hoping not. I would love to be able to get out of here and go home pretty..."

"Raleigh, this is Flake from *Pies*," I said, with meaning.

"You were great," Flake said.

"Why, thank you! *Pies?*..."

"It's a fanzine. About jangly pop bands. I think he did The Posies, last issue. Teenage Fan Club too. Some shoegaze bands he likes, as well. *You* know."

"Oh. Cool. I was just thinking maybe Rob and I could get a ride from Franklin—he said he's going up to LA tonight and I thought if maybe you and Jenny were gonna stay and do this interview that we might..."

"It won't take that long, Ral," I said.

"But I really want to..."

"Just give us fifteen minutes, Ral," I said. "Half an hour, max. You can participate, you know."

"That's cool. Rob and I will just load the van, I guess."

"Seriously. Tell Rob to come over here as well, okay?"

"Okay."

And Raleigh sauntered off.

"Should we sit down?" Flake asked as Jen stepped over to us both.

We went over to an empty table in the back. It wasn't hard to find one; the only people left in the bar were Franklin, Barnacle B. and someone he was ostensibly torturing, the bartender, the doorman, and us; even the sound guy had got the fuck out. Spring Snow—long gone. Flake took a tape recorder out of his satchel (of course he had one of those—it was probably from the Belgian Fire Brigade or something cool like that; very authentic). I'll just give you our responses, if that's okay with you. The questions, banal and otherwise, will be implicit anyway:

"We met through our old drummer Walter," I said. "Rob and Walter were jamming in this practice shed back of Walter's house— halfway between Hancock Park and Koreatown—and looking for a songwriter/singer who was into or looking for something that was equal parts Joy Division and The Beach Boys…yes, that's what their ad said! I thought, 'Hmm, these guys sound…weird! Haha!' I answered it, the ad, and we started practicing seven or eight of my songs. Then we met Jenny 'cause she was renting a room from Walter and his horrible girlfriend, Nastasha. She started off playing keyboards and guitar but she doesn't play keyboards anymore 'cause keyboards, live, are just kinda not-on—*we* think. I dunno, really. Plus she became, in our opinion, a really interesting guitarist on account of she doesn't know *at all* what she's doing."

"I really don't," Jenny said.

"She makes up chords, couldn't even tell you what a basic D or G chord looks like," I said.

"I could tell you what a D chord looks like," Jenny said flatly, correcting me and rolling her eyes.

"Okay," I said. "I know you can. But you know what I mean. She forms cool chords and does instinctually all these things someone who'd been trained on guitar would never think of. We made a record with this British or Irish guy McLeary—he never told us which it was—and after we finished it we finished with Walter 'cause he didn't have the right attitude, should I say, Jen?"

"He didn't have the right girlfriend," Jenny said.

"Hahaha," I said.

Next question.

"No, I had never been in a rock band before," Jenny answered. "I grew up in music, if you like—my mom and dad are both professional musicians and music teachers as well, and I got a college scholarship to be a Music major and everything. But I was just giving private lessons and working in a law firm downtown when I met John. Well, John and Rob 'cause Raleigh came after. I never thought of doing music as a career. And I still don't think of it that way—I'm just having fun, really. Though we're very serious about it, the fun we're having. And the record we made as well—I am very proud of that, for sure. Though I would like a chance to sing a couple of things all over again, you know…but we didn't have that much money. We did it ourselves."

Next question.

"I like The Beatles—just like he does, I guess," Jenny answered again. "I like them too much, I think. And The Carpenters and lots of soul music like Sly and the Family Stone and Stevie Wonder. All kinds of soul music. I like Sonic Youth. I probably like *them* too much, too…both John and I get a record and listen to it obsessively. I mean, dozens and dozens of times. My Bloody Valentine's *Isn't Anything* is probably one we wore out a *few* copies of, to tell you the truth. We love that record. And *Daydream Nation* and *Goo* and…lots of stuff, I guess."

Next.

"If there was one band we would like to open up for?" I repeated. "I don't know…XTC, probably—but they will never play live again. We really like a lot of Creation and 4AD bands. But mostly MBV but we don't *try* to be like that or any of them."

"Cocteau Twins would be amazing!" Jenny said. "We'd love to open for them. But I don't think they do shows anymore, either."

Next.

"Probably The Beatles. If we had to pick one influence. The Beatles. And the influence we have worked so hard to disguise—which is New Order. The *guitar* New Order, I'll just clarify. I'll just come right out and say it. It's probably a lot more quote-unquote mysterious to fib like mad and go 'I never really listened to them.' But we might as well just acknowledge it. *I* love The Beatles and The Velvet Underground and so of course as I write most of the songs we're going to sound something like that plus other things. *We* love New Order. More than Joy Division. All bands have influences they have to try to either hide or get over—I never believe anyone who says otherwise. Do you know the famous story of how Black Francis put an ad in a Boston paper saying he was into Husker Du and The Mamas and The Papas? Pretty funny. Kim Deal was the only one who answered, legend has it, and so there you are. Most bands, most good bands, have two or three wildly different generic-as-in-genre influences that go to make them something original, I think. I won't say we are the most sincere band around, you know. I don't think sincerity in art, if you will, does much good anyway. All those bands from Athens in their earnest way, all their exuberance and stuff. I wasn't into that at all. I think of art as having greatly to do with the first three letters of 'artifice,' you know? Every band is in some way contrived. People came up to us this whole week to tell us that we sounded like their favorite band that they wanted to talk about. It's so funny. You just nod your head. I can't tell you how many people said we sound like The Go-Betweens and we have hardly even heard them—honestly. Fans are so funny. *Bands* are so funny. Even the ones—especially the ones!—who claim that they have no idea what they are doing! We love The Velvet Underground as well. Well, *I* do..."

"I like The Rolling Stones!" Jenny interjected with a sharp yelp, insinuating that I was not a quote-unquote Stones guy.

"Like I don't?" I said. "Anyway, Flake, when we went in to record, one of my preposterously ambitious idea was to try to make a record as good as *The White Album*. I will officially pause here for your devoted readers to laugh appropriately loudly. Now I realize, of course I do, that that is an im*poss*ible task, but *goddammit I tried!*... Yes, we deliberately did a few acoustic songs amidst the faster tracks and shoegazey songs. No one will ever be as good as The Beatles—but you have to try, don't you? And when we make the next album it will be a sort of reaction against the failure of the one we did that just came out.

Know what I mean? 'Cause, to me, all art is failure…but that's another topic and probably too convoluted for this interview! Do you know our friend Jock who has a 'zine called *The Big Makeover*? Of course you do. Everyone does. You are going to have to edit this to death to fit your size and length requirements, most likely, but Jock, bless his little indie rock heart, he just publishes *the entire conversation* with all these bands, coughs, snickers and all…it's amazing. Crazy. Oh, hey, here are Rob and Raleigh…hey, you guys."

"Hi," Raleigh said.

"Hey," Rob said.

Next question.

"We hooked up with Better Records through Stacey, the label manager there—she saw us play in LA and brought a tape of our finished record in to the two guys who run the label," Jenny answered.

"There's only one guy running it now," Raleigh chimed in.

"I don't know if they wanted to announce that yet, or announce it themselves, there, Raleigh," I said in a way that came out, I think, a little too cross.

"The guy who's left believes in space aliens," Raleigh continued; the tone he used was so pat and weirdly factual that he might just as well have been declaring that, sometimes, he liked to put milk on his cornflakes. "Mike Mays. Just today he was telling us about how these people from The Pleiades are coming back soon. To earth."

"What?!" Rob said.

"I don't know if Flake really wants or needs to hear…" I started to say quite loudly.

"I didn't *tell* you that?!" Raleigh said to Rob, utterly ignoring me, as expected. It was, suddenly, as though it was the two of them talking—like Flake and Jenny and I weren't even there. "I thought I told you. Good gig tonight, by the way."

"No way, Beavis," Rob said, meaning to convey his incredulity that the imprint we were on was now being run by a Moonie, not that his bass playing wasn't sound.

"Yes, way," Raleigh said. "I'm totally serious. Ask Jenny. Ask…"

"Do you have some more questions for us—about the band or the record, Flake?" Jenny, coming to the rescue, running interference, queried with a winsome smile.

"Jenny, can I get you a glass of water?" Raleigh asked all sugarily.

"Thank you, but I'm okay," Jen said. "Thanks, anyway, Raleigh."

"Well," I said as Rob and Raleigh, having felt they did their bit and/or had had enough, wandered out (unannounced, unexcused) to the ostensibly now-packed van—Rob for a smoke, most like, Raleigh…who knew?

Flake then asked us if we felt part of a quote-unquote scene in LA and if so, what we thought of it, plus what we thought of Nirvana and if we had any words on Kurt Cobain:

"I don't see us as part of any scene—and I never loved Nirvana, though of course the news today is very sad."

"Terribly sad," Jenny added.

After Flake asked me about my lyrics (and I declined to comment), he got around at last to asking his "infamous" pie question.

"My favorite? Rhubarb, weirdly—though now that I think about it, I never order it!" I said. "I think it's only my favorite in memory 'cause I had it on special occasions as a kid, I think. I normally just get apple. Plain, heated or not, doesn't matter, and not *à la mode*."

"*Dutch* apple," Jenny said, then added adorably: "Peach, though, as well—am I allowed to pick two?! If I pick one over the other, one's going to be upset with me!"

"Thank *you*, Flake." I said. "Franklin has our address so please do send us a copy when it comes out. And thanks for the nice review."

"And for coming to our show. Nice talking to you," Jenny said. "But now you got me thinking we need to stop on the way home and have some 'pie and *quoiffee*,' like Travis Bickle says in *Taxi Driver.* Take care of yourself. See you next time."

"Jenny?" Flake umm'ed as we were walking away. "I was hoping to interview just you for a few minutes, if that's okay? I thought Franklin told you. I wanted to write about you as a child star—or piano prodigy? Isn't that what you were? At least that's what they told me."

"Uh-huh," she said. "I guess you could say that. Sure. Can you guys manage loading the van without me?" she joked.

"We'll try our best," I winked and, leaving Jen behind to finish up with Flake, went out from the blue fug and queasy tangerine-and-pomegranate light of the bar to the yellow curb in front where the van was almost loaded and idling.

Doing fanzine interviews is a bit fun 'cause it makes you feel like your art and opinions matter, like you're legit and everything. Every *artiste* feels a full-on fraud once or twice in a while, so it's nice to take a break from that for half an hour or forty-five minutes or so and talk into some sweet, earnest nebbish's running tape recorder. It also sells records, having interviews in indie rock rags. It sells two or three at *least*. And as Boswell says of the happy times when Johnson lived with his great friends The Thrales, and particularly Mrs. Thrale who was apparently no bluestocking but a very deeply literary lady, "no man" is "insensible" to the pleasures of praise from the charming and knowledgeable in his field.

One

e made it back to our North Hollywood practice space at about three-thirty that night/morning and, with a good dose of that adrenaline that you seem to get going when you are completely exhausted, unloaded all our stuff (not forgetting Raleigh's dumbells) and hoisted and latched the tan back bench back into the rented Astro and headed back to Los Angeles. Raleigh had left his big old faded blue Merc in one of the parking spaces we have back of our domicile so we waited for him to jib away so we could empty the van from there. We'd given Rob a ride to his place in the Valley first, as we were already there, so we said goodbye in a way only close band mates can say. In other words, *I hope I never have to see you again* meets *See you next week for a drink so we can talk about what a wonderfully great and tremendously atrocious tour we had!*.

Are there some things in life where the talking about them afterward, cracking up about them and trading reminiscences, is almost neater than the doing of them? Artic swimming rituals on New Year's Day in Northern Minnesota? Water or snow skiing for the very first time? Losing your virginity to your second cousin twice-removed? Doing your first gig on Halloween in your dumb drummer's living room to a curious (in both senses of the term) crowd, an admixture of a hundred humorless Goths and drunken knuckleheads and a handful of your super-supportive wonder-friends—doing such a gig, *and* you're a jangle pop band with sunny-dark songs about escaping with a good book somewhere beautiful and clean and tearing in your dreaming mind the bright sky into a million wonderful pieces, songs that Goths and knuckleheads are *most* unlikely to like or remain quiet for long enough to get to the first chorus?

Uh-yaw.

Jenny and I didn't even bother bringing in our sleeping bags and personal bags from the Astro; we just trudged upstairs and shed exhausted clothes to the hardwood bedroom floor and dove into bed, sweet bed, cold and clean then warm and soothing, just inexpressibly comforting.

Two

p betimes, relatively speaking, especially after so little sleep, albeit delicious sleep—eight-twenty-five on the dot. To the coffeemaker to get some home-brewed Columbian jet fuel going, which would, I remember telling myself, suit me down to the ground. There's just something about that first cup of coffee, isn't therel: when you get just the perfect amount of milk and sugar swirled into it. None of this black coffee stuff—that's for New Yorkers and people who read Raymond Chandler and Dashiel Hammett. One grapefruit from a bowl of them that must be our roommate Keating's 'cause they weren't there when we set out on tour ten days ago. Jenny already gone by eight; off, poor thing, to work at her job downtown at Johnson & Johnson, the famous law firm. Didn't even hear her get up, shower, and put on one of the frowsty work frocks she effects 'cause she says it saves her dilemma-ing in the morning on what to wear if *every* work dress she has is equally dowdy, uncute. To think the bulk of the seventy-five plus people at her work have never seen her play onstage, never seen how pretty/sexy she can be—except at the Christmas and/or New Years parties I've never escorted her to. Maybe a handful of her secretarial-pool girlfriends and a couple of junior lawyers and that's it—who've seen her onstage, that is. One of whom, I *know*, some guy called *Bran* or something equally egregious, has a major crush on her 'cause at one gig, a Molly Malone's Pub gig, he kept trying to steer her into a corner and was pressing all up close to her, buying her drinks that she nursed, I saw, like anything. Wonder sometimes whether she trusts herself with other men. Yet loyalty's her heart's motif—and I never even consider whether or not she'd "do anything" with someone else. Or rarely I do, at least. I don't know. It's not something we talk about and I'm not sure why; maybe part of me wants her to…unthinkable.

I splash fresh cream and snow raw sugar into the coffee and pad into our vasty-big living room to have a sit down after a too-short lie down. Funny how we get right up to sit right down. Clouds and fog and mist within. Sympathetic, fleeting thoughts of Rob and Ral off to their respective "yobs" as, respectively, telemarketer and office yokel. Reality check for them today, must be, going from a week and a half of fancying yourself a big shot pop star, merrying around a shiny or dull new town each day, laughing with your band mates, doing the requisite college radio interview, haphazard breakfast, maybe lazy lunch if drive day not too taxing, sound check, having the gig go off or not and slaps on the back afterward either way and drinks brought/bought…to, this grim morning, punch the clock and make the java, look sharp, er, what's that? Sorry, sir? Yes. Absolutely. Yes indeed, *sir*. Get on that right away. Yes sir, yes sir, yes sir, yes. When do you want it by? Yesterday? Fine. Ten minutes ago? Dandy. Get right on it. No problem. Coming right up. Office gossip and an hour at best for a crummy lunch out at some dark dump or a bolted repast at one's desk and an endless clockwatching afternoon of looking busy doing nothing. "Playing at having a job," Jenny often calls it. And we, together, made up a little jingle to go with the slogan. *Da*-da-*dum-de-de*-da-*da, ta-ra*. *Play*-ing at *hav*-ing a *job*, ta ra; *play*-ing at *hav*-ing a *job*, hey-hey. She and her fellow college-educated office slaves (more than one of them really pretty, *silly* pretty) each have a corporate lawyer they "take care of." Funny. Thinking this morning of the snacks they keep in there, all part of the so-called "Golden Ceiling," the furtive plan the corporate types have to keep you at work as long as possible, make work like home, guilt trip more productivity out of you, keep pedal properly to metal, your eyes on the prize dangled above you perpetually. The colorfully-wrapped snacks in the break room (I've been to Jen's office several times) would make snack-fiends like Ral and Rob just drool-and-swoon and meltdown sugar-overload-wise.

Then the obligatory traffic-fight home at five or six or seven-fifteen. Jen, I know too well, fakes her way through it beautifully, her day job. She's well-liked there and well-paid too. Rob, as you might expect, hates his but never complains; and Raleigh only shrugs it off as "It's a job" whenever the topic emerges, but you know he'd rather be doing music, music and working out and having cereal and getting "Betties" you thought he'd never have a shot at. Mine—job, that is, for today at least—is as follows: take the van back, ring the temp agency I signed on for a month or so ago as well as the bookstore downtown at which I sometimes work a day or two, stocking and checking.

Or not.

Take the van back, at least.

Just for something to do, a distraction, I snap on the fuzzy telly with this remote that looks like your gran's clicker for her garage at the condo your family had to move her into; and on the box comes *the* news story from Seattle, of course, on the scene near The Space Needle, where a gathering of thousands in reverend remembrance of St. Cobain is expected to take place tomorrow. Hey you plaid-clad grunge kids clomping by in tan or charcoal work boots? Got time for a talk? Reporter holding microphone toward waif girl in tribute-like lumberjack shirt flanked by her two long-haired Seattleite swains, she saying "He was, like, a symbol, you know? With all his beautiful musical talents and everything he did he, like, you know, um, to put Seattle on the map." Pats tawny hair back and puts on self-pleased look, rock boys nod along. "You'll be here tomorrow for the remembrance, the ceremony, that is?" goes Reporter. "For sure, for sure," the three reply. "But," one of the lumberdudes opines, "I'm really kind of, like, angry right now, though, you know?"

"Tell us how you *feel*," Mr. Reporter breathes; "We're all kind of baffled and don't know what to think," another punter offers obsequiously. Reporter in requisite indigo blazer signing off for Channel 7's "Eyewitness News" with a doleful look and a "There you have it. Live from The Space Needle. This is Paul Pickelle. Back to you in the newsroom on this sad day for all Nirvana fans. "

And on comes the follow-up montage footage of Kurt in his cool furry copper-green sweater and great lank hair in unkempt perfection doing "All Apologies" on MTV's *Unplugged* and their "sincere," one-minute eulogy, complete with mosh pit longhairs in obligatory plaid slam-dancing like drunken trolls or Lithuanians. Cue for me to switch off idiot box. I will witness no more Eye Witness News. Pardon pun. Please forgive. Understand.

Things to do: long bathe, luxuriating sudsily in it as feel very dirty, half hour at least; get dressed, clean teeth; sweep out van, bring upstairs sleeping bags and thingumbobs, take break and listen to a bit of Beatles, any bit'll do. Make sure van doesn't smell like bum has used it to cook a squirrel in coffee can or barbeque skunk on makeshift city park grill. (It certainly can pong like that after ten days of four touring artists belching like walruses ; well, three, that is—Jenny doesn't burp; "beefing," which of course Jen never has and never will—*queefs* maybe, but that's *private*, prurient reader; stewing in sweaty, gig-clothes and spilling snack-shrapnel all over the place.)

Have you ever, gentle reader, worn the same clothes for two or three days straight? On account of you're too tired or indifferent to change them? (I'm not talking about underwear—*that* you have to shift daily, for sure.)

More tasks: fill van with cheap gas, the least dear you can find; drive way out of your way to find it. Fill it, your rental, not a drop more than three-fourths full as that's what they, Enterprise Rentals, jotted down when we set out. Drop off van. Sign off as Rep in his immaculate shirtsleeves asks "Do you want to leave it all on the card?" "Yes, please." The card Mike Mays repo'ed yesterday. [Insert prayer here.] Card goes through. Thank you, Jesus. Shake head as Starched White Shirt asks with forced smile once more if we took the Astro in question out of state? "Uh, nooo," I fib, and say to myself, inside my head, *It took us.* Why do they care if you cross the border into Oregon, "The Zone" (i.e. Arizona), or wonderful Nevada, anyhow? Mexico, well *sure*—that's out of the *country.* Kind of. But what's the difference, I always wonder? What's *really* an infraction, more of a crime for sure, is how little money we made on the laborious road. But we did make some. Most bands don't. Limp back home and drink themselves silly, cry themselves to sleep. Pick up where they left off. Go back to their sad jobs as security guards and Guitar Center salespeople, substitute teachers and doormen at bars, nannies and cabbies and valets. Record store clerks and fucking busboys. Trying not to be bitter, trying to find a way to go out on tour next fall, in the spring, in their gran's VW camper van.

Bus ride back and in the little black logbook notebook I tally the rounded-off numbers):

✓ Enterprise Van Rental: -387.00 dollars

✓ Gig Monies: +1989.00 dollars (*approximately*—not too good with math; should just let Jen figure this one out)

✓ Gas Money: Can't find all the receipts but who cares anyway as we used the Gold Card. Have to find more of those in backpacks, jeans pockets, etcetera and send them in to Stacey at the label.

✓ Per diems: -10 dollars each x 10 days= -400 dollars CDs, 7-inches, T-shirts Sold at Gigs: +535.00 dollars

✓ Hotels/Motels: 4 nights at Total of -457.00 dollars (dared not use card for those as Better would flip!)

✓ Miscellaneous Expenses Picked Up By "Band Fund": visit to Space Needle, a matinee movie, guitar strings and drumsticks, toiletries and sundries, snacks, a lunch, etcetera:-76.04 dollars

✓ Total Revenue for spring tour: +1194.00 dollars

Future uncertain. Metaphor for life itself. With Manson leaving, will we still have a label to be on, record for? A label that doesn't promote us properly, hasn't promoted us properly—and one that a thousand and one bands would kill to be not properly promoted by, kill to be on, esp. when one *in* a thousand and one bands gets promoted properly by their record label. Whither The Sisters? What'll we do? Questions abound.

As a band—with or without "Management"—you never really quite know what to do. No move is the right move (and sometimes no move *is* the right move, if you know what I mean). For having served as booking agent I would be entitled to take ten percent of that total for myself for living expenses, especially as I am kinda more than broke right now and need the funds badly.

So, basically, I just had a pretty successful tour—and, basically, I'm fucked.

Three

nice, fun bus ride on an LA city bus sure can make one wax philosophical in all manner of ways. There was I, on the 207, after having dropped off the Astro, bumping along with half your poor, your tired, your lame, your halt, your crazed, your young, your old, Hispanics, mechanics, nurses-in-training (the certified ones are already at the hospital, ready to go, being amazing, saintly), students, the homeless, the hopeless, the fearless, the cheerless, sleeping, chatting, staring straight ahead, laughing like mad to themselves, themselves jostling along—every one of them—the fucked streets of the *real* City of Angels, not candy Bel Air or phoney Beverly Hills or "Above Sunset" aka The Hollywood Hills. Want an inner-city education and quick-like? Break out fifty cents and board one of the darn things, the bus, "The Pooch," and head anywhere.

Midway down Western, just past Santa Monica Boulevard, the bus conductor, a wiry, wizened, can't-really-tell-how-old-he-is black man with jaundice in his eyes and hate in his heart stopped the trolley and started simply be*rating* two little old Asian ladies and one little old Mandarin-ish man, going: "What?! What the fuck you say? What? *What?* I can't under*stand* what you're…learns the motherfucking *Englishes*, man! *Learns* the mother*fucking English!*" Their faces, the immigrating supplicants, the supplicating immigrants, went bright pink, or so it seemed to me, and they just stood there bewildered, impassive, lost, not boarding. You don't want—unless you're feeling particularly philanthropic or contrariwise suicidal—to get in the unbridled middle of something like that. It's a wonder more drivers don't totally *snap* in the course of a literally circumlocuting LA-busing day, boy, Daylight Savings Time or no. I've been carless now for longer than I care to think (I had an old tan Volvo 240 I was in love/hate but mostly love with and I burned it out right after I quit my last "real" job as a substitute teacher—poor thing just up and quit one day: just like I did subbing). Hence, I know of what I speak as I have had to merry along with the rest of the bus-riding loonies and goonies to my various temp jobs and to my bookstore "situation." It can be fun, riding the bus. It can. When it's not unmitigated hell, that is.

The boisterous brakes shriek, then sorrowfully sigh. You feel in your each tooth the sound they make. It hits you, the sound of bus brakes screaming, right in the chops, as though you've just scraped the bottoms of your incisors (slowly) along the entire length of a hot pink brick fresh from a roaring fireplace. Only intermittently can you hear yourself think, what with the incessant shot-like backfirings of the vehicle's exhaust and the engine growling greatly, howling insanely. And that's, maybe, if you are where I am, metaphorically speaking, in life, not a bad thing. I don't *want* to think right now. I'm not used to it. I've been on *tour*, okay? I've been in a sort of nightmare Never-Neverland. There's been no mental prowess/sharpness required. I'm not playing the victim here, you realize; it's just how it is.

You pay your fifty cents, try to sit down before the bus conductor rockets off and you go caroming off one of the handrails on the back of the seats, or boinging off a little old Guatemalan lady's laundry basket; you lurch, are jolted, and you hold on like grim death in anticipation of the rib-jabbing stops every two-or-so blocks. There they are, your strained hands, lobster-red and jellyfish-white, too taut from gripping those selfsame handrails with every unpredictable deceleration. The drivers—they drive *way* too fast. And then the jarring, asthmatic brakes. What are they, these LA bus conductors—retirees from fucking Le Mans or the goddam [fill in the blank here with your favorite race car event]? Next to you, odds are, is *an utterly exhausted person*, most likely Mexican-American, Honduran-American, African-American or Asian-American—'cause that's what Los Angeles does, wears fuckers out. Fags fuckers to the *nth* degree, irrespective of ethnicity. Espeicially if you've gotten on at six in the morning, in the half-dark, with the moon still sailing away in the psychedelic sky, off to work at some hell-center, some sweat-edifice, some horror pit of a jobsite or spirit-crushing nightmare station office space or restaurant whose kitchen resembles a Mercy Seat Hospital loony bin.

Their corpulent or emaciated arms or bulging, crackling shopping bags intrude on your limited airspace, these your fellow budget-conscious cosmopolitan busriders. Their spent heads bob in marionette-ish ways that hurt *your* neck to look at them. Whereupon: in trundles a glaze-eyed, pimple-stippled sixteen-year-old with a hypertrophic baby screaming bloody murder. A spindle-shanked and funny-faced septuagenarian with an immaculate cowboy hat, drunk as fuck. A congeries of horrors—pie-faced, pumpkin-butted school kids and the foul bouquet they bring along with their lemon backpacks and cheap black Walkmans: bacony, salt-smeared, chili-fried, burnt cotton candy, *eau du sweat*. And look at the *faces*, wouldn't you just: here a horse, there a piggy, there a more horsey horse, everywhere a rat-rat. Old McDonald had a farm—and it got on to an LA bus and went a-riding.

And the kids, oh the kiddies, the kids, the kids, the childrens. The kids in this city are soft and crunchy. Human marshmallows, roasted. Bellicose, then Biafra-eyed. Doughy hard. Gooey-tough. Hideously beautiful. Ambulant candy bars. One, getting on just now, cognate-objectively belched a belch that was so bold and voluble and prodigious and gross and jabbering and *lingering* and even-to-*him*-frightening (then funny) that it seemed like he was some sort of trumpetless, modern-day *herald* heralding the arrival of The Burp King and His Merry Extra-Gaseous Courtiers or something—'cause, I swear to God, the next three imp-urchins tried to match his distance and profundity, belch-wise, like they were doing a caroling "round" of crude vulgar offensiveness, competition version. Were a doctor on board, armed with stethoscope, one would be tempted to obstreperously demand she listen to any one of these pigeon-chested children's chests to see if he'd or she'd swallowed an eructating midget or super burping superbaby.

Look! Here comes a stylish, terrifically pretty, thirty-something Latina in a smart, business-blue business outfit who, if you got to know her, might drive you mad in the best way possible. She's smarter than you, better-mannered, happier, friendlier, and *way* more financially stable: the only reason she's on this coach is because her BMW's in the shop. You look around, all incredulity that the conductor's not stopping at the next stop and throwing her off for being too pulchritudinous to ride more than six blocks east. "Back to the west side with *you*, toothsome miss," he might flirtatiously say. "What the heck are you *doing* east of Western, anyway? Don't you know your *place*? You're way out of your element here. Back thataway—out you go, *chica linda*." That you will never know her name, let alone meet her, is a certified serendipity somehow. You will observe her, desire her, but not meet. She gets off two stops later, thank God. Thank God! Goodbye! Had you said hello, and she kind of liked you, and you sort of charmed her by dropping your bohemian front or, better yet, playing it up, and she gave you her number (I mean, she's right to be positively leery of any guy she met on a *bus*), and you went out on a date with her after making loads of effort to "get to yes," and you went out with her miraculously *again*, having blown her away with your wit and charm and quietly confident and really rather astonishing erudition and kindness and debonair sensitivity-for-such-a-jock-and-a-half, and you met her cat, and it didn't bolt when you went to pet it, and you became her perfect gentleman lover on, say, unconventionally, the *thirteenth* date, and you took her home to meet the overjoyed and charmingly skeptical *mamá y papá*, and she fell wildly in love with lucky you, and wanted kids with you, and made you unaccountably deliriously happy and you actually retired from ogling girls like her?—well, get this: *you'd never write another song*. You'd be too busy being ecstatically happy to find time for being that tortured, wallowing, second-guessing thing: an artist. Ha! Of course you'd keep writing if you're the real deal; new joys and heartbreaks'd stoke the fires of your ire and rapture, despite the fact that you've caught the "ultimate" catch. 'Cause there's always a catch when you're talking romantic attachments. Still, a comlier girl you've never "known." Whew! *That* was close! A narrowlier escape you haven't had in a longish time. Good thing she's gone! Big win for the Muses here; way to go, team. (Big loss for you, and cupid, too, however; there went your dream girl; go home and write a song about how you'll never see her again; how she walked onto a bus that took her right into, then out of your "life"; at least there's that; how sad; what a life; bye-bye, dream girl; see you where you'll live now: in dreams alone, in dreams alone.)

Back on board then. Here's a family of *Watchtower*-toting Jehovah's Witnesses, five of them, in descending order of bantam height, weebling their way to the very back. They snap you right out of your tiny, phantasmagoric reveries. As does, *voila,* a crazed crazy in a homemade loincloth, a halter top and Roman-soldier sandals—does he qualify as transgender, or *trance* gender, you wonder?—dancing and laughing his way on, just breezing by the driver, not paying, taking his own sweet time, in his own world, *out* there, corkscrew curls jouncing, mile-wide smile, hearing the Spheres, grooving with them, communing. As the tearaway coach slows at the bench or kiosk just-past the next stoplights you can take in the dolorous smiles and baleful eyes of the so-tired vendors of iced fruits with their endless Ziplocs of delectable pineapple and mango, oranges, honeydew and watermelon powdered with chili powder and a spritz of lemon zest, a rumor of seasoned sea salt. Or see the tire jocks at the *Llantas* shops, all-teeth and cheeks, feigning baseball swings with tire irons, or Western shootouts with their lug nut guns, joking around, goofing around, waiting around, making the best of it, making it through the rarely-easy workaday work day.

Elsewhere, west of Crescent Heights on Sunset, say, the young and the hip and the not-so-young-but-looking-it (they're working out, they're dieting) go dilemma-ing over quintessentially essential things like whether to have the Blue Crab Salad, the Mu Shu Shrimp, the Foie Gras Dumplings or the Dutch-French Cheese Plate. Wanna make a moiety of the Club Sandwich or the Cobb Salad, darling? They're sipping mimosas and Bloody Marias, trashing with giddy panache the reputations of mutual acquaintance while perspiring waiters (who are all beautiful, indefatigably insouciant, aspiring actors, struggling screenwriters, would-be producers, future directors—possible winners of putative Oscars, every one) pop champagne corks over their patrons' laughing-happy heads. Mad traffic sings by; the valets are backed up like nobody's business. During the lunch rush two-tops and anxious three-tops wait and are seated *al fresco*, unshield themselves by way of taking off or looking up over ridiculously expensive sunglasses so they can scan the menu, gossip desultorily, talk shop, talk turkey, huggermugger, shuffle through or shrug off someone's portfolio, talk about the second rewrite, catch up, seal the deal, talk figures, get down to the nitty-gritty and put this thing to bed, start production, *post*-production, preproduction, get our lawyers in on this ASAP, make an offer, turn it down (make them want you; get as much as you can out of it, milk them for all they've got), clink glasses (here's to it!), cut a check, take out an option, decline dessert (think they'll have just one more half decaf, then they gotta run). They hurry into new-leased SUVs or spiffy convertibles with bright blue California vanity plates that read "I AMZE ME" or "PRDCER" or "I MODEL" or "C YA!" or "GOLDN GOD"; "KISS MY A," "ND IRISH," "FK OFF!," "EZ WRTR," "STAR 82," or "YOU WISH!"

Los Angeles. It's weird here.

On their way, they mull over the topics they've covered: Who's left whom? His tell-all said *what*? Didn't you see the thing in this week's *People/Billboard/The Hollywood Reporter* or on the men's room wall at Sushi on Sunset? The trades are "exploding"; the headlines are screaming; hectoring and flashing away, the "paps" want the scoop, the scuttlebutt, the inside story. I don't know what he sees in her! Can you believe it? *I* sure can't. He'll never *brunch* in *this* town *again!* Hey! Why'd I drink so much last night? His kid just got a record deal. I only did a bump or two. The bar at Chateau Marmont was just so packed we almost left. But then just guess who walked right in? Go ahead. You'll never... He sat and had a drink with us, uh-huh, uh-huh, uh-huh...I *know!* I thought I'd died and gone to heaven... What? Who?

I'm sorry it's so hard to hear out here. Waiter! Bring the check, okay? Valet! Bring the Porsche around! Oh, sorry, here's the ticket—it's the black one with the gold…I told you "Keep it close," remember? If you think *she's* crazy wait till I tell you about the second line producer on the sequel! You want weird? You want neurotic? Let me tell you. The chick's a fucking psychopath. The boyfriend's even moreso now. They're out of rehab again but, gosh, you know, I just don't know. *No* one wants to work with her: and he, well, he couldn't get himself arrested if his life defuckingpended on it. There's only so much you can do for…people like that never change. Isn't *that* the total truth? You know she slept with both my exes. I never told you? Seriously? I really thought I told you that. I find that kind of creepy—right?… You ever just can't *sleep* sometimes? Gotta talkta my docta 'bout that, no? This prescription isn't working. I haven't felt like this since law school. Seems I'm always tired these days. The weather's sure been weird of late…nice to see you too, my dear. We'll have to do this soon sometime. Again, I mean. Julie! So nice of you to get in touch. And give my love to Robert, too…you're not together any more? I thought you went to therapy. I thought the couples counseling worked. Oh God, I feel so bad right now. We never even got to talking. That's *ter*rible—are you all right? He didn't leave you for that trollop? That blondie-redhead what's-her-name? He *did?* What an ass that bastard is. What a fucking idiot. I'm *so* sorry, Julie, really. God knows you can do better—jeez! You're prettier by far, you know. I hope you know that *I* think so. *She* can't act to save her life—we all know that. What a horrid little *bitch.* Call my office after Sundance. I'll set you up with someone nice. *Not* an actor—'kay?—this time. Better wait till after Cannes. Okay? Okay. Okay…

They've rolled away, these and other lunchers, in cars that are freshly shining from their bi-weekly carwashings. Heads swivel anytime anyone remotely resembling someone who's "someone" swims into their ken. The umbrellas emblazoned with French and Italian beer or "designer" sparkling water insignia shield them from the outside world, and the *après-midi* sun. The whole shebang, as indeed does the entirety of West Hollywood, smacks of a movie set, with walk-on parts for one and all.

Their kiddies, their brood, the spawn of the well-and-better-to-do, the gentlemen and ladies who *lunch?* Here be the nascent brats in private school uniforms who just got out for a yet another half day: coaxed with Cokes, bribed with gelato, quietened by candy and greasy gourmet pizza slices, loaded and herded into minivans with the promise of unlimited Magic Mountain trips and calzones FedEx-ed straight from New York. Here we are. Here we go. Out and about, it's Mommy and Me—and both screaming. Mommy only inly, her child a howling, mortifying Hyde Jr. or Juniorette till he or she gets designer peppermints and genuine gumdrops from the gumdrop shops on fancy Larchmont, trendy Melrose, Highland and Hollywood, Sixth and La Brea. I want gummybears, mommy! I want "a" entire regiment of gingerbreadmen!

Caitlin, Caleb, Abigail or Absolom don't *want* to, Mommy; I *hate* you, Mommy: I never get to have *any*thing I want.

Later, all around Los Angeles: a kibble-hearted man who's just lost his job and whose wife's going to leave him (she's called her family in the Palisades, crammed two "carry-on" bags and two hanging "wardrobes" into the trunk of her loyal royal blue or plum or cream Miata, just to be sure) will have a major meltdown in a 7-Eleven as the clerk hands him his change in a way that makes him mad (in both senses of the term). To wit: by putting the quarters and nickels and pennies onto the dollar bill in order to hand his, the madman's, change back. Clerks, saving energy, saving time, maybe even thinking that they making the change exchange *easier* for you, the customer, are just starting to *do* that annoying thing circa 1994. That's the last straw and all it takes. He'll "scramble" the money histrionically and make the fucking guy behind the counter fucking pick it fucking up. Then he'll have his Michael-Douglas-in-*Falling Down* moment. Deliver his ineloquent soliloquy, played to an audience of two or maybe three.

On the boardwalks of gurgling Venice, yuppies and off-duty hippies alike will go rollerblading into the tie-dye sunset; 'round the

Silverlake Reservoir, hip execs will jog with their floppy dogs, and stop by the dog park on Silver Lake Boulevard. A symphony of car alarms and almost timeable sirens from cop cars and ambulance vans. Cops and robbers, robbers and cops. Shots. Yes, you can't ignore them. And you have to. All over the Valley, and especially down Ventura Boulevard, the humming bistros fill for happy hour as the sky goes honey-blonde pale ale and a darker, harder blue melting into a sort of more blue—curacao blue. The homeless on Crenshaw, on Wilshire, on Sunset, at the off-ramps of the 101 in East Hollywood— the shuffling mendicants and have-nots with tenantless eyes, them with a hand out for a handout—are heading for anywhere, nowhere at all. The legion of shopping cart-pushers shopping for the detritus of society. Bottles and cans and plastic recycleables. The casteless untouchables, honorary and literal. In garish, remarkable motley, with, say, dirty seersucker jackets and cargo shorts, one poor foot shod, one not, either be-socked or bare and black with dirt. Or no shirt, a black blazer (that didn't start out that way) and a repp tie for a headband. Motorists glance askance at them and accelerate to pass by, tisking their compassion, bunching their mouths in momentary pity, or screwing up their very noses in derision and disgust. Or they express their discomfiture simply by *not seeing them*. Turning the other cheek…away. Like people reputedly do on the dung-painted streets of Kalicut, Mumbai, Delhi, Hyderabad—by *simply not seeing them there*.

Innumerable hopeful people light candles and put on soft music and make out on couches as dusk falls, the dinner one made for another growing cold on plates on countless tables. They go to the movies, to the beach, and to bars and to bed. College kids wait in After Hours Counseling Center lobbies and bitch about their roommates and housemates, their pompous or somnambulistic profs, how hard Spanish Four is or any Upper Division Econ. Flower delivery boys drop off last-of-the-day arrangements by the dozens, their vans veritable Antarcticas on wheels—you have to keep the flowers cold the year round in a climate like this. Friends fall out or reconcile. *Thousands* of joints and bongs are passed back and forth between high school kids or medical technicians, nurses, stockbrokers and construction workers, maids and teachers and people on unemployment; baked; stoned; wasted.

Single mothers laugh at their kids on zillions of gated and not-gated playgrounds; they can't believe how cute they are. Orthodox Jews saunter at sundown off to synagogues in the Mid-Wilshire district, brazenly jaywalk. In the cool glades of Griffith Park, under sweeping trees, people picnic, have lemonades and sandwiches. One hundred thousand million shop girls and stock boys dip into the alleys back of their workplaces for a glamourous smoke break. A teeming multitude go through Customs—they've come from India, from Latvia, from Germany and Israel. From Bangladesh and Mauritania. Canada, Iran, Iraq. A multitude *skip* Customs; they "give it a miss"—in lorries and on foot across the sands of Arizona, the deserts of south San Diego County; they stowaway on just barely seaworthy boats, pay through the teeth to ride on puddle jumpers through margarita-colored evening skies.

And what curious, extraordinary *learning* goes on everywhere! An homogeneous congeries of Korean immigrants, businessmen and entrepreneurial hopefuls, follow their uncredentialed teacher through English greetings and ways to say goodbye; Spanish-speakers erase their accents—or try to. Erase them for a hopeful afternoon. French class, dance class, acting class of course. Metal-work and woodworking for junior college credit. Soldering, pottery, painting, sewing. Poetry circles and night classes setting up Fiction Workshops and Scriptwriters Support Groups. A *Swann's Way* book club munches powdered sugar lemon squares and madelines of course and drinks cups of smoking Chamomile and Earl Grey. Beginning Bartending, Data processing, X-rays, Massage. People study to be clowns and ministers, optometry assistants and industrial draughtswomen, video editors and computer programmers. Night school, junior college, traffic school, gym. People weld car parts or bizarro art projects. Amidst the shit, the blood, the piss, the puke of so many hospitals and hospices, everyday heroes (doctors, nurses, EMTs) go about their heartbreaking/warming business. One thousand million zillionteen cups of paper-cupped coffee get sipped at countless endless AA and NA meetings. Addicts hook up, swap stories (all familiar, all sad), swap spit, swap one addiction for another. Junkies score. Whores whore. Trucks roar. Motorcycles too. The Emergency Wards in Hollywood and Malibu refer to bikers as riders on "two-wheel death traps." Assorted psychologists despair of doing anything for their desperate patients, seek more therapy themselves; the patterns keep repeating, keep repeating, keep repeating; their clients cling, talking *ad nauseam* about the same old muddle, the same old connundrums—with mothers, with fathers, with lovers, with others. The iffy stats are in: more people in "this town" suffer from Borderline Personality Disorder than anywhere else in the world. Do they move here, to be here, to congregate unknowingly? The trees downtown, growing straight out of wonky squares cut into the pounded pavement, are a strange blue and white color, like old people whom life itself has cruelly bruised. Someone jumps (full twist, half-gainer, *Geronimo!*) from the Fourth Street overpass at rush hour while someone else slits his wrists in the warm water of a last bath. Every ten minutes, statistics show: suicide hotline lights right up. Telephone poles get summarily thumbtacked with Xeroxes of pictures of Missing Persons, announcements of yard sales, lost cats, Reward Offered, please call with any information, Have You Seen Tabby, Winston, Pepper, Mister, Blackie, Sherwood, Zorro, Whiskers, Maisie, Bebop, Charlie, Linus, Larry?

A shrewdness of apes flings fresh feces at taunting patrons at the LA Zoo (the poor primates must be *sick* of people mimicking them, making ape-faces, ooh-oohing and aah-aahing up and down and monkeying their arms around); and a harem of ball-balancing seals delights an ark-arking cluster of kiddies with swathes of creamless chocolate ice cream on their chubby-happy faces.

Inspired by Bukowski, Chandler, Fante, Fitzgerald, Faulkner, Ellis, Ellroy, West, Waugh, and Didion, writers in and out of Writing Programs write the first paragraph of their Great American/

Quintessentially Angelean Novels—or put the final period on one. And screenwriters team up, become "writing partners," *viz.* laboring under the illusion that a real writer can have any *compañero* other than the blank page and the poised pen or the suspenseful fingertips at the fearsome typewriter.

Bands have their first practice in diabolically cacophonous rehearsal rooms off Riverside and San Fernando, in Chatsworth and Downey and South San Pedro—or they break up acrimoniously, kick out the singer, the bass player, get the drummer's girlfriend "in" on "second guitar and backing vox." Heshers from Altadena or South El Monte duck out of too-hot practice rooms for a quick smoke and a catty chat about Cobain—how Nirvana *sucked* anyway; and how can you like a band that doesn't have solos? That's not rock! Guns N' *Roses*, man—that was a band. Gimme Warrant, Ratt, Priest and "The" Crüe. Ha! Sounds like an accounting or law firm! Fuck all this grunge stuff; death to it all, man. Metal's where it's at and always *has* been, man.

Cut to:

Two men in their early thirties, say, loping brazenly arm-in-arm down Wilshire near La Brea—quite a distance from "Boys Town," Santa Monica Boulevard, that is, where this sort of thing is more commonly done. They both have "high-and-tight," military-ish haircuts and look like they've just emerged from a vogue gym or a tony westside athletic club. Two sets of fathers and sons, walking past them in opposite directions, take note. Especially as the aforementioned two, a couple, proud and bold, share a quaint, fond, sticky, glistening kiss next to a planterbox plumped with clumps of decidedly *not*-symbolic purple pansies, red poppies, and yellow peonies.

The father and son who are walking upstream, as it were, west on Wilshire, discuss what they've seen. Well, the father does, anyway. The father has noted his son's mouth going all wacky, it's in the shape of a "Z," almost; he can't just pretend the two men they've passed are "just friendly"; he has to say *some*thing, try to explain. He tells his son, who is, let's imagine, nine, that the two men walking together are what is called *gay*. They like each other in the same way (*sort* of) that your mom and I do, the first dad says—and no they aren't married, and maybe they are in love with one another, Tommy, who knows? But there isn't anything *wrong* with what they are doing—they're just made *different* somehow, and that's okay? Okay? Do you understand? You think so? You do? Good. Good, Tommy. Glad we got to talk about it, my boy, I really am.

Now, the *other* father, who is out exercising with his kid (ten-and-a-half or so, let's say), headed downstream, so to speak, east on Wilshire, also realizes that he too must say something, as *his* son's mouth has made more of an "O" figure, a *lasting* "O," one that seems to linger there, Edvard Munchly on his little face. Well, Timmy, the second dad says, what you've just witnessed are two homo*sexuals*— men of the same sex who like the same sex as the sex *they* are. One of them had real big muscles, didn't he, Tim, and very tan skin beneath his tight white tank top too. It looked like he ironed it, his T-shirt, didn't it? Isn't that funny! He must work out a lot to look like that, huh, Timmy. And the one in the sky blue (or maybe it was more of a lavender?) tank top—the shorter of the two—was...well...hmm. Anyway, what they are going to do is, well, when they get back home? *Prob*ably what they are going to do. Well, Timmy, *one* of them or both of them at the same time are probably going to scour each other's prepuces with their lips and tongues when they get home and take a shower together. The prepuce, you see, is the space on your pee pee that is below the *glans*, you know, the head—the part at the tip that looks like the Pope's hat or a bishop's one. Oh, you knew that? You *did*, did you? Got it in your science biology class, huh? The one you have with that nice teacher, that very nice man, Mr. Sell, the one that you like so much? He is a nice, nice man, isn't he. Good. He's got such...a...um...he's got such good things to say about *you*. Anyway, Timmy, a lot of times homosexuals have pee-pees that are like a wolverine squashed by a truck tire. *Or*, a pepperoni log that's fallen on the floor of an unswept barber's shop. There are all kinds of magazines that show these type of men, Tim, in various curious poses and in different, interesting costumes, mostly just hats and helmets and short-shorts (and with *no* shorts) and brand new tan work boots, you know, like what construction workers wear? And you are never, *ever*, ever, to look at them, these magazines; do you understand? Never. That sort of magazine-looking is absolutely positively forever and *always* forbidden to you—understand? You are *not* to look at the homosexual magazines on, for instance, the big giant magazine stand on Hollywood and Ivar or of *course* on Santa Monica Boulevard just west of La Cienega; or if you go to Venice one day—if Mommy lets you, ever; or the giant ones on Ventura in The Valley: all over The Valley, actually. Mostly they are wrapped in tight cellophane, these terribly interesting and forbiggen—I mean, forbidden—magazines. For your protection they are, but sometimes one or two are *not* wrapped and thus they are very, very tempting to curious little eyes like yours perhaps might be. So. *Promise* me you'll never look at such magazines, Timmy. Eschew them, Timmy. (Eschew means "avoid," okay? It's your word for today.) Promise me, son. Make the Boy Scout salute right now and swear.

Ukrainians, Cambodians, Argentines and Filipinos in the streets below the burnt purple and brown hills of The San Gabriel Valley, hills marbled darker brown and deep green and, in places, at twilight, silvered with the last of the slanting springtide sun, brushed or touched with pink, the rocks reddened, with big bulbous pristine white clouds sailing fluffily above them.

A legion or tribe or smallish nation of bums queues for the wonderfully wonderful and singularly labyrinthine, intagliated Central Downtown Library, one of the most astonishing edifices in the city, beautiful and inspiring. They live there for the day, your vagabonds and ragamuffins, among the stacks and desks and reading rooms, the hallways and corridors, display rooms and the sad café.

A scrum of British berks "on holiday" congregates at Ye Olde Kings Head Pub in Santa Monica, two blocks from the beach. Call them "Lager Louts" or "Football Hooligans"—but not to their happy-laughing sunburnt faces, for fuck's sake—what *are* you, mental? These be the mad lads with butch haircuts, butch smiles, skin in need of tons more sanative sun (with sunscreen this time), verb tenses in want of serious rethinking. They hail from Madchester, from Burr-ming'am, from Livapool and Blackpoo: and it's funny how they've come three thousand fucking miles just to end up hanging out with their mates from home. Here be the stupefying, dead-drunk dumbfucks, the pre-Chavs (the term's almost twenty years in the future), the Neandermen, with their glassy eyes and stained jerseys, missing teeth and baying hollow yodels at the match on telly; *regardez-vous* their cacodaemoniacal ghastliness; it's like a minuet, the way they hop and dance around in groups of twos and threes and four, ever shifting, reeling, turning, leaning forward, leaning backward, grasping at each others' shirts and throats, gesticulating at the barkeep for another round of cold Coronas, having a go at each other, taking turns flicking darts and having a slash in the stinky loo. America, la! You wanna drink, mate? Have one on me. Great here, innit? Fuckin' sunshine and birds in wee bikinis all over the shop. Haven't seen a *single* bloody Paki! Not even down the corner shops. Not one wog yet. Rahahaha! This place is paradise. Paradise, innit. Fuckin' *ace*, mate. Cheers, ya? If you were drinking in the selfsame pub with them you'd probably move a-ways away from them, probably be uncomfortable around them, especially when time's called at the end of the night; but you couldn't get away from their lifted, tenor, impervious voices: there'd be no escape from *that*, and from their like-a-face-punch laughter. You'd think: Really? Are you sure you have to be so typical? Can't you breathe through your nose just *once* in a while? Can you not leer, jeer, or cheer when you pop out to the sidewalk for a quick smoke, a little girl drops her lollipop onto the sidewalk or an old dear gran bump-and-grinds by mistake against a fire hydrant, or face-plants off the curb, her wheelchair brodying out onto the street, only to be scrunched by a tanklike streetsweeper?

Chinatown, Koreatown, Little Armenia. Los Angeles. Eternally swirling, imponderable city. Here's my paean—hear it and more. O LA! O City of Angels. O' Devils. And everything in between. The stories, the laughter, the horror, the horror. All those chattering and chuntering people from the edge of the deep blue sea, from merry Malibu to posh Pacific Palisades, from well-to-do Woodland Hills to about-to-be-yuppiefied South Pasadena and down to Carson, Inglewood and Hawaiian Gardens, The City of Industry, Compton, Watts. The births, the deaths, the wonder, the wonder.

And why does the air in Commerce—even as you drive fast on the 5 with your windows fast-rolled up—taste like someone's burning an entire silo's-worth of Goofy Grape Kool-Aid? And why does everyone drive so fast at night (hint: the incomprehensible traffic's too much during the day)? And why does San Pedro, home of the immortal more-than-a-punk-band Minutemen, seem so eldritch? Inglewood so friendly and free? Certain pacific-looking streets throughout The Valley as the most dangerous places on God's green earth?

Tonight the Lakers will win, the Dodgers lose, the Kings (away) give up hope for The Stanley Cup.

On playgrounds, on park grounds, the lure and joy and *agon* of athletic endeavors carries on apace; and through the only lightly smoggy air go sailing volleyballs and tetherballs and softballs and handballs and kickballs and baseballs and tennis balls and footballs and Frisbees and lacrosse balls and racquetball balls and cricket balls (no less, yes—ex-pat Indians/Sri Lankans/Trinidadans cook them up, them clubs) and soccer balls and Wiffle balls and medicine balls and dodgeballs and basketballs.

NB. Contemplating my dear, horrible, wonderful, terrible city thusly, it's like I'm a dog with a cat on its neck, the claws excavating the angry folds in it, the neck, the cat holding on for dear life (holding on like grim death), the dog snarling, somersaulting 'round and 'round to try to shake the damn cat off. It's like a ride a powerful hallucinogenic drug takes you on that you want to stop that won't, it won't. I've got to will it to wind down, put the brakes on, bung a flagpole into the rusty gears of this crazy-go-round; I've *got* to stop thinking, stop churning, stop *writing*. But how can *that* be? Writers write even when they're not writing—they rush back breathlessly to the kitchen table or to the computer just to add just one more thing, subtract an adjective, rip up all they wrote the night before. It's of paramount importance that I quit this mindset and get back to the story.

Oh like *that's* what I'm gonna do.

Just one more paragraph, though, okay? One last semi-panoramic grammatological kaleidoscope or tilt-a-whirl or flight of fancy; one more imaginary interlude or narratal interruption. Like most of the tangentially afflicted/addicted I plead for just one more, just one last one, one more hit or dose or drag.

Hence:

While I ride the bus the gavel comes down on white collar crime, on assorted *desperados* whose three strikes are up—and they're out, off to County then the dreaded Pen, getting measured for an orange jumpsuit. Frat boys boot, hurl, yak, "call for a Buick" and "do the Technicolor yawn," "burp to the ninth power," hork, horf, "revisit their breakfast," or "toss a sidewalk pizza" off blue-and-gold and scarlet-and-gold balconies after much too much daydrinking. Of *course* they also hold meetings to find ways to raise funds to contribute to The United Way and The Red Cross and Amnesty International. Let's not forget their magnanimous Greeky beneficence. Oodles of sorority girls from LMU to Pepperdine to USC to "the other place" go and "salaam to the porcelain john," as well; but it's because they're, duh!, *bulimic*, some of them, and the thought of a weight gain is tremendously tyrannizing. Or because, just like the boys, they're collegiate debauchees. And of course the kids at these well-respected Southern California "party schools" (they're all of them "party schools," especially the handful of jesuitical ones) do fundraisers and charity benefits by the dozens and stuff. Plastic surgeons limn on computers how a patient's new set of tits will (maybe) look. Jejune tennis players chuck their rackets on countless blue or green or gray or red hardcourt So. Cal tennis courts. Chefs and sous-chefs toss shrimp and scallops and shallots into sizzling woks and jumping frying pans: sheer in butter pats, flake in chives, a splash of white wine, make with a rumor of garlic, a splatter of extra virgin olive oil. They beat down the flames 'round a thousand steaks and hissing cheeseburgers; they're having fun yelling at runners or berating waiters all over opulent Westside restaurants or humble mom-and-pops in Montrose or Eagle Rock. In the so-blue, bright white and sparkling harbors, skiffs and sloops and yachts set out (Avons, too); in the hazy white and pale yellow and dull red and perfect purple deserts, off-road motorbikes idle, do "broadies," spill, fly through scorched air. Someone in Burbank flubs a take on a set for a pilot or a sitcom or a pornographic masterpiece—and has to do it all over again, for the thirteenth time that day. Groans, curses, kicked chairs, self-pulled hair. In a recording studio in Hollywood a real live rock star—not one of the Johnny-wannabes I've told you oh-so-much about—takes a break from not getting a guitar solo or a vocal quite right for the thirteenth time that afternoon. His wife and kids have come in to the control room, anyway—a rare day of visiting dad at "the office." The bass has to be replaced on this "side," anyway, the legendary producer from London says kindly, and lights a menthol light 'cause he's trying to cut down, eat right, work out too; there's something about it here, in sparkly LA, that shames one into better shape, that brings out "the fiend within" as well. For for all his goodish good intentions, he's gonna, after the session, end up mowing an avocado-and-maple bacon chompburger at one in the morning before he Porsches out to Redondo to huff coke and swill vodka tonics till sun-up with some birds he met backstage last summer at The Cure. Foils and epees clank and whistle and describe arabesques through/in the air at the really quite poetically-named Los Angeles International Fencing Center. There's a one mile square area in lovely downtown creepy Chatsworth that churns out more than eighty-four percent of the world's porn. Why not? The (arguably) most beautiful and the most (certifiably) sleezy people in the *universe* live right here! Why not put two and two together, so to speak. To be sure, there's one on cable right now somewhere—an LA-made blue movie! You've seen that girl at the Gelsons in The Valley! She used to be a stripper/she worked her way through law school, stripping. At night she adds three x's to her name: Ginnie Sixxx, she calls herself; or Trixxie Foxxx, Anita Kixxx, Amanda Luxxx, Heather Blixxx. Or, uh, maybe it's not her—but someone who looked just fucking like her. There are so many. So many of them. From farish away her face seems beautiful as moonlight on new snow. But up close…. Erm, let's keep the close-ups to a minimum, *hmm? Cut!* Lovers make and break dates, fall out of love and say goodbye with the tritest of phrases, hoping they can still be friends, assuring one another that it's not *you* it's *them*, they've thought about this a long time, and now they know it's for the best, they'll always cherish what "we" had, and sad to say they must move on, move out, make room for someone new. (Why oh why is it always the one who's hurt the other one the most that wants to still be friends? Huh? Why is that? *Guilt*—it must be. 'Course it is.) Lovers fall in love out of pity, admiration, or 'cause one of them's got a smile that's simply irresistible. They hold hands and walk into the future, the future, the future, the future. A future that will, in time, become the past.

And speaking of the past and the future, what, anyway, *is* Time but an imbecile lunatic maniac scaling the gate (the other side of which we quakingly wait?)

There he is, Time the Madman, Time the Unstoppable, Time the Attack-Druid, the Terrible, relentless, horribly in earnest, so fleet, so nimble, so impatient, scrambling to get over it, that gate, to *get* us, there where we *are*, in our insecure gardens, the ones the philosopher told us to cultivate, waiting, waiting, with futile, ready fists or useless shouts of feeble warning before he has us by the throat or the scruff of the neck, or, yes, the balls.

Mean Mr. Time—he means it, man: he's not fucking a*round* here; he doesn't have time to.

He's coming. *He's coming.*

Four

nd so what to do with the rest of the afternoon but make tea, take nap, wake up, more tea (they say Johnson sometimes drank twenty cups a day), debate with self whether or not to pick up the phone and embark on drumming up work and/ or more gigs? Maybe run into our roommate Keating who usually emerges from his room at mid-afternoon, only to drink a wake-up Coke or make dreadful instant coffee (then cereal, which is all he ever seems to eat; the grapefruit are a total mystery, the work of some fruit-elf?), take a shower or wash his hair in the kitchen sink, then motor away to his recording studio, which, like our practice space, is in the Noho Arts District. Keating's amazing: he's up and out of the house in fourteen minutes. You'll get to see him for an afternoon or evening once or twice a month when he's burnt out on recording zillions of bands and needs a few hours off. Sometimes he schedules himself some spare time so that he can go see tribute bands (his ironic passion) and really, really bad bands (his sick obsession). Keating's hilarious: I will tell you all about him: he's a complete kook and ridiculously funny, too.

Nevertheless, and most importantly, I must stave off ineluctable feelings of despair in the wake of post-tour let down. And wait till six or six-thirty or so to make dinner for Jenny so that I can feel useful, or at least not completely useless, feel like a kept man.

Jenny, Jenny my pivotal, irreplaceable band mate, my darling girlfriend whom I love to death and with all my heart and whom I must—I know deep in the heart of my heart of hearts—find a way to leave.

Part Two

One

ell, hello again. *Hi.* Hi, there. Nothing like leaving you hanging like that, eh? Quite the Tantalus move on my part, I dare say. Just when you were thinking how things must be creamy-peachy/hunky-dory between Jenny and me, with our new place put together and everything and the band doing pretty well and all and the two of us living with a cool roommate who's also a fan of the band.

Quite the contrivance, don't you think, leaving off Part One like that? Something straight out of a cliffhanging Penny Dreadful or pulpy, tawdry detective novella. And what's worse, dear reader, is you're gonna have to hang on just a bit longer before I tell you why I am having such a relationshiply-crisis, such a love-related freakout—'cause I have something even more pressing to convey here and that's this: a meticulous account, replete with symbolic *trompe l'oeil* and suspense techniques garnered from various narratal sources and How-To manuals, of *my very first real live nervous breakdown.*

Hurrah!

Two

 didn't go looking for it. It's not like I was going grandstanding and thinking, hmm, what can I do to complete the cliché circle of guy goes on mad tour (that wasn't really all that mad), guy comes home and stares blankly at wall for five days straight, his life ostensibly divested of all meaning, his hopes not just dashed but *creamed* somehow, smithereened, his belief that anything at all's worth doing for any reason or cause is all bollocks, that he's the picture-perfect portrait of total inconsequentiality and despair. You know: like he's trying to reenact, in his own life, one of those songs on side three or four of Pink Floyd's *The Wall* where the singer/frontguy checks out, as it were, and stays in his empty bathtub for a couple of weeks or something. You know the song I'm talking about: "Are all these your guitars?" the flirty cartoon groupie in it asks. You've heard it. "Wanna take a *bath?*"

Anyway, it all started, as so many things that go south quickly do, with a telephone ringing. It was belling just as I walked upstairs and through the door, having walked all the way back from taking the bus back from dropping off the van, from Western down Wilshire to our apartment on Lorraine. I like walking in LA—I often get an idea for a song when I walk around my city. I might get accosted by a crazy person, or a pebble in the eye from an Audi speeding by, but I might get something to "work with," too.

"Hello?" I said to the receiver of the ringing phone.

"Hey!"

"Hi. Who's this?"

"Did you see a review of your record in *SPIN?*"

"What?!" I said. "Who is this, please? Raleigh, is this you? Did you get someone to…"

"I said: 'Did you *see* the re*view* of your *rec*ord in *SPIN?*'"

Pause. Blank. The slowed-down voice had thrown me even further.

"No…" wary I warily said. "Who…"

"Dude! Of *course* you didn't, of *course* not," the hectoring voice continued, "'cause there *was* no review there! And I doubt—good as the LP you guys made *is* and all of that and so on and so forth—that there's *gonna* be."

"Okay," I said.

"That's okay with you? That's all right? Dude! Do you ever care about your so-called career?! Or am I just gonna waste my valuable breath a*gain*, lecturing you on how the music business is…"

"Bob Chalet?—Bob Chalet, is that *you*?" I said. Bob Chalet was this quondam Artist & Repetoire guy who'd come to the gig we'd done months ago at USC and told me he was starting a label on his own: Bob Chalet Records, it was humbly dubbed, or going to be. He was originally gonna call it Playing Records, but he changed his mind and went for the more audacious handle, the more megalomaniacal masthead. He'd stayed in touch with me, us, and had invited me to breakfast at this greasy spoon near Beachwood Canyon he practically lived at; when the bill turned up, he made it seem like it was his big shot treat, his pleasure, picking up the check, even though you'd only had a coffee and occasionally a pancake, or a gooey, blueberry-oozing muffin. Total bill: 11.49 dollars.

Big shot Bob Chalet.

Again aggressively, dogmatically, Bob Chalet said: "How's it *going*, John? Going okay with you and your band? On the path to stardom, are ya?"

"Hi, Bob." I said or more like sighed. "You sound kinda *aggro*…"

"Oh, *do* I? I *do*? So you *didn't* see a review in SPIN—or *Rolling Stone*, for that matter?"

"You just told me I didn't, Bob."

"That I did, that I did."

"Uh, *okay*…what are you up to, anyway—aside from trying to bring me down soon as I get home?"

"Pretty shitty, your tour was, huh? No records in stores. In-stores poorly attended. Shows spotty. Tour support nonexistent as well. Band members fighting almost every day as a result of the rough times on the road? Bad food. Bad backs from fucking sleeping on people's floors? Bad…"

"Pretty much, Bob."

"Am I right or am I right?"

"You're, um…"

"Am I right or am I…"

"What exactly are you *driving* at, here, Bob, may I ask?" I laughed.

"Bob Chalet is calling to tell you that, had you signed with Bob Chalet Records, Bob Chalet personally would've made sure you'd have had at least a three-star review in one or maybe both of those rags. Bob Chalet woulda made that happen, for sure. Bob Chalet would have…"

"Sure, Bob."

"You don't believe me?"

"And besides, Bob," I said, "you didn't *offer* us a goddam record deal—you only talked about it…*ad infinitum*, as I recall."

"And so you signed with those losers at Better."

"Obviously."

"And do you know why Bob Chalet didn't sign you?"

"No, Bob—unless it was because you didn't *have* a label yet," I said. "You were only fucking *talking* about founding one. *Funding* one, more importantly. Haha! You were only at the talking stage. *And* talking and talking and *talking* stage…"

"Shut the fuck up. Listen to me. Are you listening to me?"

"Yes, Bob," I wearily said.

"Now get this: neither does Bob Chalet know why he didn't sign you. It's a mystery to him. It truly is. He's not sure why it didn't happen—and now you guys are locked in to a shit deal on a shit label and in a shit position as far as…"

"We're not locked in, Bob," I said. "In fact…"

"That's not what Bob Chalet heard."

"Oh?"

"Look, shithead, are you going to be a shithead about your shitheaded music career your whole shithead life, or what?"

"Gosh, Bob. I don't *think* so," I said in my most Eddie Haskell sort of voice.

"Yeah, yeah you are," Bob Chalet said. "I pretty much think you *are* going to be a shithead your whole career. The sort of shitheaded shithead who doesn't realize that this is a *bus*iness, okay? The second word of the phrase 'music business' is *business*, okay? Got that? It's a business. You have to ap*proach* it like one, okay? You have a *sort of* hit single, two major station, I heard—gotta buncha great reviews, and your goddam label's just *sitting* there fucking *sitting there*. You know? Why aren't they plastering San Francisco with Weird Sisters posters and promo singles? Where is your *Street* Team? Who are they? Does your stupid label even *have* one? I mean, if Bob Chalet were your..."

"What's a Street Team?" I said.

You know me well enough by now to know that I was just messing with him.

"What?!" he said.

"I said: 'What's a 'Street Team?'"

"Are you serious? Are you messing with me?"

"Yeah, Bob, I think I am just messing with you here," I said. "Uh-huh. Hey! I know what a Street Team is. It's a...hey! By the way, I'm really looking forward to Wimbledon this year, aren't you? I have this ritual going where I get up and make strawberries and cream and sometimes strawberry shortcake and watch as many matches as I..."

"Jesus *Christ*, man!"

Bob, I knew, fancied himself quite the former junior tennis star and fan. I'd gotten him out on the court a couple of times (twice, actually—I gave him another chance in order to see if his first-time court demeanor was only a fluke). You could tell that he used to be okay, or more than okay, but that he'd never get it back, his game. For one thing, he took around four hours, once he got to the courts (way late, of course), getting ready, obviously stalling, or just being controlling—tying on this unsightly banana or blue bandana *just so* and getting his wristbands parallel and setting out his "special drink" and banana and apple and orange wedges and sunscreen and terrycloth towel with his initials on it and having to look a million times into his filthy-dirty, commodious tennis bag for something... you know.

Then he got out and warmed up not by hiting with me, oh no, but by "stretching" or doing some freaky yoga moves that looked like they could only be bought from the guys in the highest ashrams in Rishikesh.

By the time he got 'round to actually "hitting," your hour on court was nearly spent and you had to go to the kiosk and buy another one, hoping to Our Lord and Savior Bob wouldn't neurotically have to start his regimen all the fuck over again if your court was "reserved" and you had to move to a different one, which is a bitch, sometimes.

"Bob?" I innocented.

"*What?*"

"Could you *please* stop referring to yourself as 'Bob Chalet'?! And—hey!—I thought you told me way back when that your label was going to be called Playing Records. Do you even have a label right now, if I may be so bold as to inquire? I mean..."

"What the fuck do you want me to refer to myself as? What the fuck do you want me to call me?" he kind of yelled. Sometimes you got the sense that he was like all three of The Three Stooges at once. He had Moe's voluble irascibility, Larry's hair, and Curly's clueless cluelessness as to how he was or might be perceived. One time I asked him if he had watched a lot of the show as a kid and he just kind of stared at me with this look that conveyed the unimpeachable idea that he was convinced that I'd successfully escaped from a high security mental institution on an uncharted island or somewhere. That's how he was. "That's my *name*, okay?" he continued. "No one tells Bob Chalet what to...hey, Johnny, what are you doing right now? You wanna go get breakfast?"

"Breakfast? It's nearly two-thirty, Bob! It's nearly *dinner* time."

"Bob Chalet wants breaky—that's just the way he is. Sometimes he eats *sushi* for breakfast if he feels like it, Bob Chalet does. If Bob Chalet can't have *pussy*, he wants *sushi*. Don't you love pussy? I *love* pussy. Love it. Did you know that about me? Did you *know* that, dude? *And* sushi. Just that sweet, salty taste of *snatch?* I wish I was face down in a nice, wet, salty-sweet muff right now, I'm telling you. Just going to *town* on that shit. You know? Just sucking on a tasty beaver to end all snatches. I wish I was licking the alphabet on some nice, tasty pussy, right now. Hahaha!"

"I wish you were, too, Bob," I said. "I really do."

"Nothing like it, is there? Nothing. Anyway, besides, Playing Records was a *great* name—is a great name. A *great* name, man. But *Bob Chalet Records* just gave it that personal touch, if you know what I mean. That personal touch."

"That megalomaniacal touch," I said.

"Exactly," Bob Chalet, surely muddled as to the meaning of the "M" word, agreed in his imperious way.

Then I made the big mistake of telling him about what Mike Mays had said about how he'd go out of business if he actually paid his artists the royalties owed us. And that bit of heinous information just drove the indignant Bob Chalet *right out of his crusading mind.* I was glad, when I heard how he reacted, that I'd conveniently left out the bit about The Pleiades People; that would've been the last straw for Bob Chalet. He probably would've rented a great, big, white steed from some movie production company or The Los Angeles Equestrian Center and gone galloping down the 405 and charged in to the Better offices on it or something, waving a stage prop gold-and-silver painted broadsword and demanding grandiloquently to see the SoundScan figures, make the label's accountant slap his double-entry ledgers down on a desktop. Not really for *us*, mind you, but in the name of Good and Fair Executive-Type/On the Side of the Artist Guys in the Record Industry Everywhere, Ltd.—which you could tell he really thought he was *times ten.* Some guys got into "the business," you sensed sometimes, on account of they wanted to be the guy who does ride in on the metaphorical white horse. Maybe because mommy and daddy never gave them enough love or credit, or they were gone all the time to Cancun or Cozumel, or 'cause they themselves got cut from varsity badminton or didn't get a date to the goddam junior prom.

"You have *got* to be kidding me! He said that? He actually *said* that?" Bob said. "So not only are they not gonna promote you—when you guys have what a zillion bands would kill for, what every band would kill for, and every A and R guy, too—but they're not gonna pay you?! Like, *ever*?! And this idiot Mike Mays *told* you this?! Unreal. Whoever the fuck Mike *Mays* is. Who *is* this guy? Who does this shithead think he is—an even more bigger shithead than you?"

"Yeah," I said, adopting Bob's tone, "who *does* he think he is— some Bob Chalet or someone?"

"Ex*actly*...wait. What? You're kidding me, right?"

"Yes, Bob," I sighed.

"Anyway. This is ridiculous. I can't believe this. Why don't you bring Jenny right now over to the joint for some breakfast? We need to talk about this, man. Knock a few ideas around. Bascially, you guys are screwed. John! You guys are getting royally screwed here, okay? We need to talk about this."

"*Royalty* screwed, Bob."

"Don't fucking interrupt me, okay? Don't ever do that. I'm trying to *help* you here, man. And you don't even know it. Or you didn't until just now when I told you. How many times do I have to tell you? Bring Jenny and we'll talk about what you need to do. If you want a chance at continuing to *be* a band, is all. Maybe you don't want to succeed, eh?'

"Not really, Bob," I said. "I don't know. Probably not."

"You're kidding, right?"

"Yeah, Bob. But there's a heathy bit of self-sabotage in *every* ar—"

"Now you listen to me and you listen *good*, buddy. Are you listening?

"Sorry?" I said.

"Shut up. In the music *business*…It's a *bus*iness, okay? Ever considered that? There's two parts to that term. Maybe you have the first part down, okay? Your music. But your business skills suck. Maybe you wanna go throwing it all away like so many idiot bands do. I didn't think, when I first saw you guys at USC, that you were that kind of band, but maybe I was wrong, you know? Maybe I was a fool to think you guys had your shit together. Maybe…I don't know. I really just don't know about you guys. Come on out here. I can tell you guys all about my plans for when Bob Chalet Records gets going. What I'm up to. I can't say much, you know, 'cause it's a bit hush-hush right now and my investors are…Well, never mind. Listen to me! I love Jenny. Jenny's great. Truly. And your songs…Okay, they're *good*, I like them. A lot of them. Mostly. Need more *bridges* in them but what*ever*. But *she's* amazing. You're lucky to have her in your band, you know, man. She's, like, a *ma*jor talent, in my estimation. A *ma*jor talent."

"Abso*lute*ly, Bob Chalet. I concur one *hun*dred per…"

"How is she anyway?"

"Great. Fine. I mean…"

"You have got to leave that lame-o label. Get out of your deal, man."

"She likes her day job, sort of, actually. I mean…" I said, igonoring him, going back to talking about Jen.

"A day job?" Bob Chalet said, like you'd told him something in Old Norse or Polish or Middle English or Farsi; like he'd hardly heard the word. A lot of these guys, these self-appointed/self-professed guys in the "Industry"?—they're rich kids going slumming, mark my words. Trust funders deluxe. A lot of them have big mouths, big allowances, and even bigger dreams, bathing you in the flood of their fulsome orotundity. Fucking big shots, every one of them. All talk. Big balls. *Big* old *cojones* when it came to talking, talking, talking 'bout what they were *gonna* do but of course rarely actually did. Most of the ones you encountered had one of three backgrounds: the first type had uncles and daddies and brothers and cousins in the record biz (Bob Chalet was one of those—but you got the sense that he was *very* the black sheep, *very* the family pariah, and that his uncle, who was one of thirty-three or something Vice Presidents of some hotshot label in important New York, was kinda embarrassed by him, kinda did whatever he could to keep bad, embarrassing Bob on the West Coast, the other coast, way away from him back East); the second type was the self-made high school dropout type, too bored and "smart" and cool to finish quote-unquote lower education, proud of having flunked everything but drama or shop or something (Bob Chalet was that type too); and the third was the kind of guy or girl who, in college, spent all their precious spare time milling around the musty college radio station, shooting the shit, getting their pot-smoking, incessantly socializing undergrad ass sucked by some radio rep at Geffen or A&M or RCA or MCA.

"Yeah, she has a day job," I said ever so matter-of-factly. "She has one. She couldn't *wait* to get home from tour and go back to it. Ha! I have one too—at a bookstore downtown but they don't need me too very often."

"Really?"

"Of course. Whudja think? Jeez, Bob. you're kinda making me sound like someone out of a Salinger novel or something here."

"I love Salinger," Bob Chalet said. "*Great* writer. They had us read him when I went to private school. Did you know I got kicked out of three different private schools by the time I was fifteen?"

"*Great* writer," I agreed. "Love him. Especially his poems."

"Uh-huh."

"Ringo."

"Huh?"

"On being asked about Beethoven. Never mind. And of course you went to private school! I shoulda guessed that. So did..."

"Uh-huh. I got kicked out of two of them, actually. *Any*way..."

"But you just said 'three.'"

"Oh, right. Did I? Seriously: what are you doing right now?"

"Nothing. Recovering. Stalling concerning figuring out my life. Leave it to you to turn a Salinger reference to something concerning your..."

I pulled myself up just in time and changed tack:

"Hey, Bob. Did you know that the term 'negligee' is related to the idea of neglect?"

"What? No. Is it?"

"Yeah. Interesting, isn't it?"

"Makes sense, I guess," Bob said. "*I* speak French. Fluently, man. Well, I used to, at least, when I was…"

"A person, in French, can be sartorially described as 'negligee' and it'll mean he is rather careless of dress. And yet you wouldn't want a woman, one who was into negligees—and who doesn't want one who's not?—to be particularly *careless* about her bedtime attire, would you now? Or maybe you would. Like, en dishabille and stuff, you know. Anyway. I'm not trying to be pedantic or anything—it was just something I was thinking about today as I took the bus back from dropping off the van."

I'd said all this latter bit in my pseudo-Oxonian accent. I was obviously bored and attempting to attenuate said boredom by taking the piss out of Bob Chalet.

"Huh," he said. There was the bright sound of a cheap acoustic guitar being ponderously plinked in the background. I'd seen it, Chalet's guitar, the one time I'd gone over to his house in the hills of Topanga; it was tinged this chocolate box gold and covered with stickers. Real weird. A real no-no as well. "Anyway," Chalet continued. "So, um…How's Jenny *doing*, anyway?"

Another guy all mad for her. There was just no getting away from them.

"Do you think very hard about etymology, Bob Chalet?" I said, then skipped conversationally ahead, quickly, letting the last inquiry remain safely rhetorical. Then sighed once more: "Jenny's fine. Did so well on tour. One of the guys, you know. She's great. Total trooper."

"Etymology?" Bob Chalet said, rewinding the tape. "Is that what you said? *Words*, right? I knew that. Not particularly, Professor," Bob Chalet added ironically, in his own ersatz Britspeak; Bob Chalet, like so many "record people," *loved* those UK types, was una*bashed* about being an Anglophile or Anglomaniac, more like; he knew "tons" of people in London, he said, and went there, to "The Big Smoke," "all the time"/"practically three times a year."

There was a long pause, on account of I had just put down the phone and gone to reheat some coffee from my earlier session with it.

"Hello? Hello?" the speaker in the telephone was going; I could hear it plainly as I padded back from the kitchen.

"Sorry, Bob," I said.

"You just walked away from the phone?"

"Oh no," I lied. "I just had something stuck in my throat. I self-Heimliched and everything's hunky-dory now, thanks."

"Breakfast, then?" Bob said. "Spot of brekky? You know, you talk about books and all a lot, don't you, John? But what you don't know is you're talking to someone who is actually quite well-versed in the Classics."

"Oh?" I said brightly. "Honestly? You don't say."

"I don't. But now you mention it…Oh, yeah, man. *Tom Jones, Anna Karenina, Madame Bovary, Far from the Madding Crowd, Lolita, Vanity Fair*…All those."

"You've read all those?" I said, decorously trying not to sound too very incredulous.

"Seen every one of them—some of them twice, even. Different versions. BBC *and* the feature film."

"Hahaha!"

"Why are you laughing—huh?" He was getting really upset. "You get just as much out of a movie as you do a book—plot, characters, all of that. You get more, in fact. You get the visuals. No one can convince me that seeing the film of something's not just as legit as reading the book of it. *No* one. You get just as much—if not more—from a movie of a book than you do from the actual book of a book. Everyone knows that. Cinematography, *and* story."

"You're incredible," I said.

"Thank you. *Now*: what about breakfast, dude? I need to take a meeting with you to tell you everything you are doing in the music *business*s is wrong. Hold on a sec."

I heard the Bob Chalet Bong go gurgling, then of course the long breathe of potsmoke smoked and expelled. I say "Bob Chalet Bong" on account of Bob was so "wacky" that he'd superglued a colored cutout picture of himself on the façade of his bong in order, I imagine, to "personalize" it and make whoever was smoking with him laugh. Or maybe he did it so that when he was chortling pot while looking in a mirror he could amuse himself no end. And of course the picture of Bob Chalet on Bob Chalet's Bong was a picture of Bob Chalet smoking from the Bob Chalet Bong.

Talk about your stoner *mise en abymes*.

"Are you there, dude? Dude!"

"*What*, Bob?"

"Okay," he continued. "Why isn't your record label paying for you to have a residency in San Francisco right now where you have a song on—what was it I heard?—twice a day on a major station? The big rival—not the major major—alternative radio station?"

"Uh-huh," I said.

I had to move the telephone a bit away from my ear for this next bit: it got real loud, is what I'm saying here; and I will spare you the eyesore all-caps. Just picture lots of advanced or grandmaster sort of yelling, if you would be so kind, counterbalanced by a bit of shrill bark-hollering:

"Why aren't they fucking plastering that town with postcards and posters? Why aren't you guys *moving* to San Fran in order to capitalize on your regional momentum? You should be playing acoustic, you and Jenny, twice a *week* up there—and gigging all *over* the Bay Area. There should be ads on cable TV—those are cheaper than you realize. You should be…Oh my *God!* What the fuck is your label *doing*, anyway? I bet you couldn't find your record hardly anywhere up there, huh."

"Actually…" I hmm'ed, and of course wondered how anyone who was high could yell. Wasn't pot meant to make everyone, regardless of temperament, mellow?

"I *knew* it. I thought so, dude. I knew it, dude. You guys are…"

"Please stop calling me 'dude,' Bob!"

"…totally blowing it. How many shots do you think a band *gets* these days? This is a complete disaster, man. You should be…Oh! I forgot to mention: drag about the Cobain thing, huh? You heard about that, right?"

"Yeah, Bob, we heard it on the…"

"Who's *man*aging you, man?" Bob Chalet abruptly challenged. "*I* should manage you, is what I should do. Except I can't, I might add parenthetically—too busy and your label sucks and is a bunch of pirates and fucking…stoners. Now if you were signed to *my* label…"

"*You* don't *have* a label, Bob," I said.

"Fuck off! Of course I do!" he yelped. "I'm putting it together as we speak. Bob Chalet Records is going to be up and running by Christmas or I don't know what I'm talking about, okay? I'm getting the funding next month. Month after that *tops*. No lie, homie. Middle of next year, BC Recs will be up and running. *Hey!* How about *this*— I'm thinking that my publicist, when I hire one, is going to freak when I tell her that the first band I sign to my label is *myself—as a solo artist.* 'Bob Chalet signs…*Bob Chalet!*' How do you like *that?* What do you make of *that*, huh, John? Brilliant. It'll be the talk of the industry. Take the pop rock world by storm. You hungry? C'mon, man—let's go have some chow. We don't have to go to the regular joint—we could go get sushi…or Mexican…whatever."

Then Bob Chalet strummed a few Spanish sounding, galloping chords, E to F#m, I assumed. The same chords as Love's "Alone Again Or."

"But you know I love the regular joint. Come on, man—what do you say?" Bob said.

"You're hilarious, Chalet," I said. "Oh God, I guess—but you know I don't have a car right now: you'd have to come over to mid-town or Larchmont. I would have to *walk* some distance to meet you,

you realize. Or take Jen's bike. Or you could come and pick me up? But I doubt you wanna do that. Does it, by the way, disturb you when you see a drunk laid out on the pavement in the middle of the day? Particularly outside certain slummy, mid-city *Cervecerias*. You just think, for one thing, about how uncomfortable..."

"What are you *talking* about, man? You're the one who's high here; you're the guy who's baked. Why are you even concerned with that? The encyclopedia-wore-Converse doesn't have a car right now, eh? Forgot about that. Sorry about that—sincerely. Can't be without a car in LA. That's death. Oh well. Next time, maybe, man. Forget it, then," Bob Chalet said.

"All right, then," I said. "Take it easy—thanks for calling…I guess. I don't know why, sometimes, you solicit favoring me with your company."

"Whatever, dude," said Bob. "Later. I'll have to save my lecture for another time. Peace. You guys need a real label *and* a manager."

Big silence.

"Maybe I can ask around and get a showcase for you somewhere. No promises, right? I mean, I got out of being a booking agent years and years ago and never want to visit *that* joke shop ever again. You read me? You know what it's like, right? Didn't you yourself book the little tour your little band just went on?"

"Yeah. Talking to jaded bookers all day long; when, that is, you can get them on the phone. It was worse than having to talk to *you*, Bob."

"Very funny."

"You know I'm only joking you."

"Do I? Anyway, you're squandering opportunities you don't even know about here, John. I'm telling you. Not many bands *have* a *fifth* of what you guys have right now, despite your crap record company. Oh! I forgot. By the *way*: you guys got any *money*? You have something you could invest irrespective of your so-called label? You know you can do that, right? Hire someone outside the label to really promote you. I'll bet that never occurred to you, huh. I bet you didn't think of *that* at all."

"Not really," I said pretty faintly. That had not occurred to me, to us, indeed. We'd never thought we could—wow!—hire someone else, an outside source, to hype us. "No, Bob," I said more boldly now, sighing away as well. "We don't a) have any money to speak of beyond a couple hundred at *best* in our 'band fund,' and b) We never thought about trying to hire some outside agency to supplement what Better is doing."

"Well, then, you are a fool, my friend. A bloody fool."

"I guess," I said, my voice once more trailing way away.

"It's too bad," Bob said, trailing off somewhat.

"I reckon," I said lamely. "Thanks for bringing me down."

"Any time," Bob said. "Take it easy."

"Bye."

"Sorry, dude. It'd just the truth. Don't blow it. Think about it. You guys should hire me, man. You'd be stupid not to. I really like the band. There's no American bands *like* you guys except for maybe—*I* don't know. There's tons of *British* bands and especially New Zealand bands like you, maybe—but your songs are…I don't know. You guys got a definite psychedelic thing going with the super-catchy melody thing. You guys are *good*. You could, with a little help from me, be *great*."

"Why, thanks, Bob," I said, sincerely this time.

"Fuckin' A, I will say that. Anyway. The record's good, man. This McLeary guy's…good, *pretty* good. He's all *right* but…you know I shoulda produced it for you, John. I got the confidence and I got the ears and I got the experience and I got the balls. Know what they call me in the industry? Guess. Guess what they call me."

I had some ideas but you know even *I* wasn't going to voice them here.

"They call me 'The Ears.' 'The Ears'—that's me. Cause I got 'em, man. It's a gift; what can I say? I know music."

"I know you do, Bob."

God knows I would've said anything to get off the horn right then. Not so fast, though; I wasn't getting off that easy.

"You know it and I know it, baby. But think about it, though. Think about this: there's a million fuckin' bands out there just like you that have a good record. And maybe a 'double threat' like you and Jenny together. Mostly Jenny, though. Hahaha! I'm just kidding you, dude. They're *your* songs. I know she writes a little here and there like you told me but… The *difference* is that those bands are out there every *day* doing gigs and in-stores and little kiddies' birthday parties and busting their asses on the *road*. Not really kiddie parties, but you know what I'm saying. Barbeques. Carnivals. Kiosks. Farmer's fucking Markets. Okay—not those. You know I'm over the top here, but you know what I mean. God, I exaggerate a hell of a lot, don't I?"

"Well, you…"

"Don't answer that. Don't answer that, man. Don't say a word. Hahaha! Anyway. Good luck to you guys—I will check in with you pretty soon, okay? You're gonna need it, luck. You have no idea."

"Uh, sure, Bob. Bye," I said.

Any old way, I was glad of one thing: getting out of going to breakfast with Bob Chalet. It was something to eschew. It was also something to do when you wanted to be in the presence of a total industry kook, *and* have your buttermilk pancakes paid for, but it was more of something to eschew. I don't know exactly why having breakfast or coffee with Bob was horrible, exactly, but I shall try and tell you. First of all, at this, to put it oxymoronically, ritzy greasy spoon in The Valley Bob Chalet frequented he knew *everyone*—and was all bumptious about it all breakfast long. Bob breakfasted with the air of someone attending an ambassadorial dinner. He knew the humping busboys (or at least he made it seem like he did) and the grinning cashier (with cute, hip, nerd glasses and tits out to *here*) and the valets in their red velvet vests and the sweaty, sopping dishwashers. (What sort of breakfast spot has *valet parking*, anyway, I always wondered?) Of *course* he knew every waitress like he'd never missed a goddam Thanksgiving at their family homes; and the chef (and by that I mean gourmet *fry cook*) was a guy with long eyes and a smileless expression perpetual whom Bob had to hail and slap on the back and pretend to fence with with a fucking spatula or dinner knife or fluted newspaper or something *every time he went in*. Secondly, you had to wait till Bob had had around twelve-and-a-half cups of decaf before he could impart the platitudinous platitudes re: the record business that he had to impart to you. *Decaf*, I tell you! Like he was getting all *not* revved up on sans-caffeine beverages. With a napkin tucked in to his shirt collar, no less. Who tucks in a napkin after 1842, I ask you, who's not someone in a Scorsese movie? Thirdly, Bob Chalet would sit there with around—I swear to God—three newspapers and two industry tip-sheets (sometimes *Billboard*, sometimes *Hits*, sometimes even the lowly, risibly poorly written and flagrantly pandering and meretricious *Music Connection,* just a *total* piece of shit) and go "Just a second— lemme just finish this, I gotta finish this, lemme just get through this one last article" when you'd been sitting there waiting for him to start in pontificating, on your own twelfth *non-decaf*, exasperated and wired as all get-out, gritting your teeth and feeling your hard, black heart race like a gerbil that's had its kibble spiked with fine cocaine. Jenny had gone with me (I'd pleaded with her, begged) one time and never again. I remember her saying "What a *bozo!*" in the car as we sped expeditiously away in her sensible Japanese car. "No *wonder* I hate the record business!" she concluded. Then, kinda riffing on it, she continued: "The thing is, with these bozos? These sleazy record industry bozos? Those bozos don't know what bozos they truly are, you know? They have no idea. They could look in a mirror and see big red circles for cheeks and a big red nose and a total bozo hairdo and still go: 'Lookin' good, yep! Pretty awesome.' I mean, what a..."

"Bozo?" I'd said brightly.

"Exactly," said she.

Now you're going, "John, John, John. Why, pray, would *you*, an hyper-educated and seemingly quite discriminating and ultra-urbane personage, a personage of pith and moment and possible distinction, hang out with such an obvious superchurl? Must needs ye go and break your fast with such an bombastic bounder and cad as this-a one, as this Bob-oaf, this nimrod, this dunderBob, this *bim?* A bim like him?! Hum! How greatly curious about all *manner* of humanoid personalities ye needs must invariably be! How penetratingly inquisitive-adventurous. How so-very droll. I mean, the imbecile eegit *actually says* that watching a movie's no different from reading a book!"

It must be that there's a masochist streak in me a mile wide. There really must be. Or: that Bob Chalet, who comes from rich oik, is going to have some even *richer* oik with a music biz jones wave a magic wand in screaming Technicolor over Bob's own weird, Larry-from-The-Three-Stooges-haired, oiled-up pate and go: "*Here,* have the presidency of an independent record label. Take it. It's all yours. The most glam-job imaginable. The most ego-boosting, spirit-lifting, psyche-bolting occupation you can fathom. Take it; go on; go ahead; sign some bands; give them good advances and heaps of tour support and loads of advice and tea and sympathy and hoodwinky pep talks and launch them on an unsuspecting pop world. Go for it."

I honestly could picture Bob picturing himself shouting down the telephone; and in some grand manner shoving Bob Chalet Records "down their throats" ("they" being the unsuspecting record-buying, baby-birdy-mouthed masses, the music-lemmings and "promosexuals" at Press and Radio who'd "do what they're told," review and play what Bob and his team would tell them to; and thus receive more knick-knackery, more "freebies," more trips to New York and LA to see more of his bands, more suck-ass kudos, more praise, and, most importantly, more duplicitous promises of a shot at glamorous gainful employment postgraduation in the self-perpetuating, self-congratulating, self-aggrandizing, self-admiring world of big time alternative rock—brought to you of course by Bob Chalet of Bob Chalet Records).

It was weird because, one moment, there Bob'd be—talking knowingly about not just alternative but *all* music, and one's own music in particular. I'd sent him an advance cassette of our record on Better and he'd called me *the very afternoon he'd received it,* he said, to talk about the sequence, and the various keys I'd written the songs in, and the variegated tempos of each song, and how he really liked how we'd laid the "tunes" out like they were going to be two sides of an LP rather than just a CD. Traditional thinking has it that you want to lead off with a great song, but not the best song, not at all; then put another strong one second, then comes "the single." Or maybe it goes forth, if the songs overall on the album proper are good enough. The last two songs on Side One (assuming the album's comprised of the classic ten or eleven "numbers') should be a bit contrasty, espousing the depth of the songwriting, and the fabled "arc" of the record. Side Two (song six) needed to be very up-tempo—as though the listener were starting over again. And then maybe one had to think about closing the record with a very, very, very memorable track, one that left the listener with the feeling he or she'd been somewhere—somewhere he or she would willingly want to return to. You didn't want a record to be too long, outstay its welcome. And that had nothing to do with how long the LP was. It was a matter of sequencing. It was a tricky thing, sequenceing a record, orchestrating it—a job and/or final call often left to the producer. I didn't, or hadn't, rather, left it to McLeary: he was way too mercurial about it, anyway. Every other day he had a completely different sequence to propose to me, fastidiously chicken-scratched onto yellow legal pad paper; so in the end I ended up just pleasing myself. Myself and Jen. Jen who didn't really care one way or another—anything I wanted was fine with her. Rob of course gave the green light to whatever we wanted—and of course Walter had been jettisoned by then. Not that in a million years I would have asked his opinion.

Anyway, there Chalet would be, talking your ear off, melting your face off, acting the fool, and as I said quite impressively recounting and assessing particular particularities re: your music. Very articulate and suave and riveting of course cause his major subject was you, of course, and your work of art. His ostensible subject, I should say. His real theme was, of course, himself. How could it not be? Because then, after he'd butter-basted your ass left and right, he'd come out with something so random, so egotistical and crude, with all the charm, say, of an haunter of billiards rooms, or of a frequenter of bear-gardens or alleys of bowling, that you'd wonder where the fuck the *other* guy, the *other* Bob, the *good* Bob, *went*. But lately the problem had been that the bad Bob was in evidence a lot more than the good

Bob was; I guess that after he'd spewed his obsequious spew about how great your record was, how cool and what wonderful songs you'd written, he had to spend his time telling you everything you'd done wrong by not consulting him, how he coulda told you you shouldn't have put cello on the one song, and that another song was perfect for—I don't know—a fucking French horn or the SC marching band or some eskimo chant group or sampled whalesong or whatnot.

There he was (in my mind), locomoting 'round his fake zinc and scintillant linoleum brand new offices in West Hollywood or Silverlake, making like he had a cape trailing behind him, a flurry of ludicrously attractive interns agitating themselves all 'round him, their collective more-than-fetching décolletages sploshing all over the shop, going "The King is upset! The King is upset!" How one could almost hear the ululating telephones, their shrill trill. See the meetings he'd take with ambitious, anxious managers and booking agents, all salivating to sign to Bob's label the bands they rep'ed. How maleficent Bob would love it as they quailed away, yessing him incessantly, nodding their heads to his every suggestion till they needed a top-of-the-line plastic and soft cotton corduroy neck brace or one of those steel/catcher's mask sort of deals you get when you've had a stage four stroke.

Three

nglish novelist Elizabeth Bowen somewhat-famously said that, in fiction, dialogue is what characters *do* to each other. Speech is action. Isn't that wonderful? Isn't that interesting? And thus, what I am essaying to show you is that I put up with semi-abusive windbags like good old, bad Bob Chalet because...let him do as he would to me, because.... because there was a slim, slivery chance he'd

luck out one day and actually have a label and be able to help us get to "the next level"—the level we felt we deserved to be on, on account of *all* bands feel that the level up from the level they're on is the realm where they deservedly belong.

Tawdry opportunist.

And because all we all of us Weird Sisters ever wanted to do was play *music*, make records and "get out there" and starve and play in front, as you've seen, to anywhere from two to two hundred to two thousand people who might buy what we put out so that we could (*may*be) keep going. You're not reading, gentle reader, about some indie band with junkie or alcohol problems here, the sort of scurrility and scuttlebutt that titillates the masses and makes the gossip mills churn and burn. Raleigh and Jenny rarely or barely even drank—and that left Rob and I who did enjoy a tipple and a toke like anyone of our twenty-something demographic might, but we hardly ever got *wasted*, and *never* before shows. I've never met anyone who could play for shit while they were either drunk or high, anyway. Though I gotta admit I don't count among my acquaintance, any reggae guys or gals! Ha.

Get in a van, book time in a studio, make a record, go promote it, practice, practice, practice.

Me, Jen, Rob, Ral. That's all we ever really wanted to do. And all it was was the hardest thing there ever *was* to do—keep a band alive, alive in a city that eats them, eats them while they sleep, sleep in late or get up early and rally then sally forth to execrable day jobs, day jobs they, as the old adage goes, don't quit…

And yet, with the van returned, and no pressing thing of any real pith or moment to occupy myself with…*now* what? What *now*?

Four

he terrible telephone trilled again around twenty minutes after this, after I'd semi-enjoyably endured bad old Bob Chalet, just as I was thinking about having "a cuppa tea and a lie down" then, without being aware of it right then of course, commencing having my nice new nervous breakdown—but that was, as I mentioned, yet to come. Against my better judgment, I picked up the receiver.

"Hello," I said, with rather, I'm sure, the keenest apathy, the most bored bonhomie.

"Yesss, sir! How are *you* this e-ven-ing, sir? Have I reached a 'Chjohn' who lives on Lorraine Avenue today, sir?" a Punjabi or Bengali-sounding voice brightly said.

Oh no, I thought: *A sales call, a telephoning solicitor soliciting something*. The dreadest of dreadfuls, the worst. This was, mind you, in the days before the things that hold suzerainty over all of our lives: the cellphone and the internet. This was in an era when you had to *think*. Think: do I take this call? Do I really wanna talk to *anyone* right now? That thing called "Caller ID" adumbrated the mobile phone— but not everyone had it in 1994. Nowadays you look at a number, or reckon you'll call them, whoever they are, back next Christmas or Veterans Day; send them an email; text them and stuff. But then, dear readers who are old enough to remember, whose short term mems have not yet been blown out by weed or blow or crystal meth or *life itself*, we had to make snap (moral?) judgments. We had to think on our feet—and maybe put our feet in our mouths. To pick up or not to pick up, to paraphrase The Dane, that *was* the question.

"You must have the wrong…"

"Oh no no no no," the voice on the other end woggled brightly. "Very correct number. To John I am speaking, then? On Lorry Anne Ave-n-ue in Los Angeles, Cali*for*nia?"

"*Raleigh?* Is that you?" I said.

"No, sir. Not Rowel-ly speaking, sir. I am Patramajan: from the A, T and the T *tele*phone corporation, sir—you can call me Patram. Or Pat. Or Mister P.—which is what my friends here call me. So funny. Okay! Let me azzk you a kestion, sir, if you would to be so wary co-operahtive! Vee are *vun*dering if you are still best pleased with our servicings? You are the man of the house, yesss?"

"Look, Raleigh, I know it's you. You must have just seen Peter Sellers in *The Party* or something."

"Ach, there hiss *no* such person here, sir. Azzz I have zed to you, sir! No *Peter*: Patra*ma*jan. That hiss my name, sir. And—as I toldju—I am calling from A, T and the T. A, T and T is the place of busyness of which I am to be calling, sir. Yess. Indeed, sir. Would you care to speaking with my most immediate supervisor? Hold on and I will most assuredly connect you…"

"Oh my God," I said. His voice was like a symphony of one, going up and going down—a symphony being conducted by a tone deaf epileptic or spastic or like when John Lennon used to make "retard" faces and motions onstage with The Beatles.

"One *quest*ion, please, sir—while I am having you on the line: if only you would kindly respond to this one little in*quiry*, sir? Have you been receiving many por-no-*graph*-ic magazines of a ho-mo-*sex*-ual nature in your place of residing?"

"*Raleigh!*" I said. "I know that's you. Not cool. What do you want? I'm busy, okay?"

"I'm most *dreadfully* sorry, sir," the voice went on…Till at last it broke, and couldn't do any more: "Hahahaha!" it guffawed. "What's up, John? How's it going? Hahaha!"

"Jesus, Raleigh. Get a life."

"I can't believe you. I had you going there for so long! *Hey*, John. You *totally* were had, huh."

"Yes, Ral, you got me. Happy?"

"Very. What are you doing? Hahaha! *'Patramajan!'*"

"You kill yourself, don't you?"

"That I do," he lilted, like when the Walter character says "I did not know that" in *The Big Lebowski*—you know, right after Walter wields the gun in the bowling alley and The Dude tells him that Smokey's a pacifist.

"What do you think? Dealing with one of your pranks. Trying to figure out my life and what we're gonna do about this situation at Better…"

"How was your tour?"

"You were *on* it, Ral—you know exactly how it went. Cut it out, okay? Had enough of your fucking ballyragging. I gotta go now."

"I know. Just joking you. What's 'ballyragging'?"

"Hang up, Ral."

"Are we rehearsing any time soon?"

"I hope not, "I said.

"Hey," he said. "Don't get all defensive. I know you don't mean that. You know you love rehearsing. How about tonight?"

"Oh my God! I'm not being defensive," I said. "I *did*. I did love it. Not sure about it anymore. You talk to Rob?"

"Nah, not yet. Pretty soon I will, though."

"Okay, well…"

"Let me know when we are going to practice again, all right?"

"Okay," I just muttered.

"You set up any more shows?"

"I just got *back*, Ral. Give me a fucking break. Why don't *you* set up some shows? I was just talking to Bob Chalet about maybe setting up some…"

"Bob Chalet? Bob Cha*let*?" Raieigh said. "What were you talking to *him* for? That guy. Sheesh. You know he's just blowing smoke up your…."

"Yeah, I know."

"Don't *talk* to that guy! Don't talk to that wink. He's an *id*iot. I don't say that about too many people, but he is one. Totally. Oh my God. No wonder you're all down and stuff. Oh, *hey!* You get any interesting new magazines come in the mail.?"

"No, Ral. Or, I don't know: neither one of us has bothered with the mail yet, I don't think. Why? What'd you do *now?*"

"Nothing."

"Fuck, Raleigh, if you…"

"Just a subscription I thought you might like…Hahahaha!"

"My God."

"You sure you haven't seen any new magazines come?"

"Goddamit, Raleigh…I don't know why I don't hang up on you."

"Seeing as you're such a *hustler* for the band and everything…"

"You didn't!"

"I don't know what I do sometimes. I just like to make people happy. I thought you might like something to read that would make you happy. Maybe Jenny intercepted them and stashed them under your mattress!"

"Maybe Jenny takes them and stashes them under the mattress? You're amazing. Talk to you later, then. You really took out a subscription to *Hustler* and sent it to our house?"

"Uh-huh. Just a little present."

"Jesus fuck, Raleigh. *Hustler's* not even a *gay* magazine. You didn't even get your own joke right. There is definitely something very wrong with…"

"Oh, shit—that's right; it isn't. Damn. It's only a joke, you know. Chill *out*, man."

I could hear him tittering away from the telephone.

"You need intense psychiatric care, you know that, Ral? Like, institutionalized care. Thanks for the 'gay porn.'"

"*Hustler's* not gay? Okay, then. *You're* gay."

"Aren't you at work right now? What must they think of you, taking time off from you precious job to gag-call your band mate ?"

"Oh, like *you* don't," he said, meaning I, too, was a potential mental case in need of greater care.

"Yeah, but I'm a*ware* of it, okay? You, however, are clueless. You can't even wait for one of your stupid practical jokes to be actually *played* before you go telling people what you've ridiculously done to them? You must be so fucking bored that...Your Indian accent is pretty foolproof, however," I laughed suddenly, overhearing myself get all preposterously worked up. "I gotta hand it to you in that respect. Almost as good as the ridiculous German thing."

There was this Nazi voice he did—especially when he was, I imagined, fed up with me ordering him around and getting all miffy sometimes when we worked out the drum parts to songs and what he wanted to do wasn't "right" and Jenny was fresh out of ways to try to help me to get him to see what we were driving at, which was usually something, drum-wise, less busy, more inventive, and different from the other beats we'd agreed upon. Drumming's hard. The drummer has the hardest job in any band. But that didn't mean you refrained from putting your foot down once in a while. "Ja*wohl!*" he'd go, all gungho. "You must to *feel*," he'd say, parodying my futile attempts to play with more finesse, less bam-bam-bam. "You must to play ze zongs with much more sensitivity, ja!"

"You know I am only kidding around," he said, self-exoneratingly, at last.

"I know, Ral. I kid around too much myself. We are an entire generation of people who don't take life seriously enough."

"*Too* seriously. *I* think," he said. "Anyway... *Whatever...* Oh, I forgot! Next weekend I got tickets for all of us to go see Sonic Youth. It'll be like a band outing and stuff. You up for it?"

"Great, Ral," I said, trying to sound pumped. It was hard to get psyched for anything right then—the strain of the tour and the label situation: these were things that were starting to sink in. Plus the fact that I was broke and having problems, as I have indicated, with my girlfriend that I was only beginning to acknowledge, only just starting to put off thinking about. "But I think Jen's going out of town next weekend—visiting her mom or something."

"Okay, then. Hope you to be having yourself a *wary* good day, sir," he signed off in his gag-Babu voice.

And I made another cup of tea and lay down and slept till around five or five thirty, when I knew that, soon, Jenny's unmistakable step would be heard coming up the back stairs.

Part Three

One

here I am, in the creaking, be-winged, grandpapa of a heather-gray reading chair in our bedroom, and I'm looking at the top of Jen's head and stroking her neck and filtering her soft, baby-fine, layered, red-and-ginger brown and almost translucent hair as she takes me into her mouth till I explode and she runs to the loo to spit not swallow, her biggish, wiggly, black-silk-pantied bum bunny-bobbing away from me. She hustles cause she knows I, having a penchant for tall and slim-hipped women, think her ass's too big and roly-poly, and her legs and ankles are "thick" like they used to point out in the thirties and forties when practically all you got to clock of a woman's legs were just to the top of her bobby sox. Jenny almost never fails, when she's just in her undies, to reflexively put her hands palms down back there, as if to fend off my disapproving eyes. She hates that I think that she's not fit. And she thinks that too, which makes it all the more complex. If you met her you'd more than likely think I'm fucking crazy, cracked completely, quite insane. God knows everybody *but* me does fancy her body like mad—her chest particularly. *Many's* the guy of our mutual acquaintance (plus Rob, plus Raleigh, her very own band mates, internicenely speaking) who's commented on what nice big breasts the chick in my band has.

Rob, who basically can say anything to anyone on account of he's so disarmingly charming, went one time when he saw me make a face: "What's your *problem*, John? Jenny has a *great* body. She's just so *soft* and…I mean, what's the *matter* with you?" And then laughed and had the good sense to stop. You do get too familiar with each other sometimes, being in a band together and all.

Back to what's just happened in the bedroom: Jenny is really good at doing that, to be awfully frank. She loves it, loves to.

Why do you like to so much, Jen? I've asked her more than once. How come you *so* get wet when you do that to me? I don't know, she says. I just like how it feels and it really turns me on—I know it does. I get so wet when I know I'm about to do it, and even more wet when I'm doing it. *So* turned on! I like the way you grow in my mouth and when I look up and see your eyes kind of go half-mast and glossy, I suppose. I suppose it's also a feeling of control, control over someone, that I have you in my power; that I can do something to you that make you, you know, *mine* and—not in a bad way, at all—at my mercy. Having almost complete control over you, hearing you moan and give that little snuffling sound or clucking sound and moaning in your throat just pleases me, I guess. *I* don't *know*! It's such a funny question! I just like it, the feeling of your cock in my mouth, the taste of it, of you, and when you come, the taste of *that*, your sperm. (But I don't like the taste of it so much that I want to—you know—swallow it. I know you know that, and that you don't mind, right? Good. I'm glad.) I'm sure it's some sort of oral fixation, that there's *some* sort of fixation *there*, but it's just almost impossible to explain. I don't think any girl can really explain it. Girls I knew in college loved to try, though—try to put it into words; but they always ended up just laughing. A guy sort of seduced me the first time when I was maybe fifteen or something—in the cabin of a pleasure boat. Haha! A pleasure boat! (Sorry.) Fourteen, maybe? That's what I was at the time. Oh my God. I don't know. And after only a little while doing it to him I realized that I liked it and if I'd known I liked it he wouldn't have thought he had to sort of hold my head down, which happens to young girls a lot more than you maybe realize…I just liked it. And I didn't want to lose my virginity to him. You know? Boys just come at you, if you're pretty and friendly. They're terrible. Older boys and they just won't stop. At least I waited till I was sixteen to first have sex. It makes us both feel so good, doesn't it, John? In a way I think it's kind of a jinx—isn't it?—to talk about it! I don't know…I don't *know*! Hahaha! I guess I'm just a bad girl. You above all people know I am. I just love having sex. Who doesn't?

That's what Jenny said. Or approximately. Notwithstanding all she said, and how undeniably sexily she's frankly talked about her sex self, I sort of just have sex with her in order to please her, make her feel loved and wanted, and also because, well, I'm a *guy*, after all; I'm just not—it's that I'm—I'm not into it anymore. I love you so much, Jenny, I tell her; and I'm miles from lying. I do. But not in the way that I know that she wants me to, that every woman who loves one man wants him to. And that's a total drag, I know, and I can hear those of you who've had a little therapy or a lot of it going *"Tell* her, you bastard! Work it out! Get counseling! Go to the library and get some books by Robert A. Johnson or David Viscott or Dr. Ruth! Talk it over—or do the right thing and break the fuck *up* with her so that she, a truly great and bright and pretty girl with so much going for her, can find someone who *does* wanna fucking fuck her sixteen times a day, and who loves her enough to do the tough thing and tell the truth."

Oh yeah, like *that's* what I wanna do, what I'm *way* looking forward to. The thought of letting her go and hence soonly go with some new guy is anathema to me, understandably. Who is *that* magnanimous, anyway? Anyone but this guy, regrettably. Anyone but me. You don't really want her, but you *really* don't want her to be with anybody else. Such monstrous, callow, callous selfishness—I acknowledge it. And I'm working on it, all right? I think I am at least. Isn't that what people in their terrible twenties always say, i.e. rationalize? "I'm working on that!" Working on it by sweeping it, as she doubtless does herself, under the carpet. Hoping the sitch will resolve itself on its own, work out for the best, be resolved somehow. You're working on working out how to put it off and put it off and put it off—whatever it is.

It already stings like mad when I know Jen knows that things aren't all that great between us. But we're such good friends, you know, are so comfortable together, too comfortable, perhaps, okay, probably, but what do you do about that? Start making things *un*comfortable? No one but a drama merchant wants *that*.

When we first met and started dating and playing music together and sort of pumped up each other's happiness, became that *egoisme a deux* thing you read about, when she lived with our old drummer Walter and his horrible girlfriend Nastasha, it seemed that she rarely had her clothes on, Jen. Surprisingly (or not?), you never get tired of it, of *her*. Some girls, boy, they can look (as Jen absolutely does, mind you) all innocent and sweet and be the naughtiest of naughty naughties you can ever imagine. The old sexist saw goes that every strapping chappie likes a lady in the living room and a whore in the bedroom, and it goes like that for a reason: your girlfriend's level of variable horniness is like this big old secret the two of you share. Well, the two of you plus every guy she's been with in the past, of course.

Best not to think about *that*, though, isn't?

Up till now, till what I described at the outset her, we haven't had sex, made love, "done" anything, for more than two weeks now, Jenny and I—what with the tour and the build up to it and now, for me, the let down from it. The horrible come down to come. But, after having gotten off the phone with that *punk* pranky Raleigh and having had my "cuppa tea and a lie down," I'd woken up at around five and ridden Jen's imperial white mountain bike to the grocery store and bought scallops and lettuce and a plump-ripe avocado and a bottle of not-dear white wine and had dinner almost ready when she'd come in the back door. (She wasn't going to drink more than half an eight-ounce water glass of it anyway—we never could keep proper wine glasses around, you see: even "unbreakable" ones got broken so easily when we had a couple of people over or small parties, usually late into the night after successful local club gigs. Only after the good ones, the good gigs, were friends invited over, anyway: if the gig had gone wrong or there weren't that many people in attendance, the last thing we wanted was to be in the midst of even our best chums and "fans" and their rollicking friends.)

Anyway, I had some pretty purple flowers, some white ones too, that I'd plucked from this sleepy churchyard that's two blocks or so away from our apartment; put them in a cereal bowl with some tap water where they started wilting almost immediately, droopy as hell and sad, actually, but it's the thought that counts, you know, and there was no way I could afford to buy her store-bought flowers as I was down to my last penny, almost, with 31.43 dollars in the bank. The experience at the grocery store had been horrible in more ways than just financial, than just a mathematical reminder that I was at this point sort of a "kept man"—one of the worst sort of men one man could be. Very soon, too well I knew, I was going to have to ask Jenny for money. Any self-respecting American male with even a passing interest in Thoreauean or anybody's notion of self-reliance was not gonna relish such an "enterprise" as asking one's girlfriend for a "loan" one knew wasn't never gonna be paid back.

Terrible predicament.

As I was paying the grocery clerk, thinking about what I was facing, the vicissitudes of being me, I made the *ow*-inducing mistake of looking at the "box boy" and asking her for "paper *and* plastic, please" (I was on Jen's bike, was gonna need extra security in terms of portage); when I looked up from getting my precious change I noticed she had just a *screaming* archipelago of *ghastly* pimples on her face, the riveting sort you, unless you looked away instanter, were going to have to stare at for a terrible spell, an amount of time that would seem to you to be light-years, but be in actuality three or four horror show seconds tops. I mean, one of her blemishes, the size of, say, a "florin" that might be used onstage in a big venue production of *Rosencrantz and Guildenstern Are Dead*, actually *shouted at me*, said my name. "Hey!" it screamingly screamed, "Hey, *John!* Yeah, *you.* Look at *me!* Can't take your eyes off me, can you! Riveting, huh. Have a nice day and—oh yeah, almost forgot—*bon appetit!*"

I mean, the poor grocery girl: she looked like someone'd barfed on her face and didn't even have the common courtesy to wipe her down with a handy dishrag. Just appalling, poor thing, and in this day and age when they have superlasers and things for that sort of awful affliction. I'll tell you, I got out of there as fast as I humanly could, and rode home just shuddering, peddling as fast as I could so as to get all winded and thus forget what I'd just seen and concentrate on being prodigiously out-of-shape instead. Sometimes someone's visage makes you wonder if there really is a God or any old creature up in the undefeatable sky. Or if it's not just one big joke to Him in his infinite wisdom and potentiality for ironies of the most vile, grotesque nature. To crown all, leaving, taking my pittance of sundries and stoking them down my backpack, heading for the bike rack outside the supermarket, I clocked a tall bum, Maasai-tall, in fact, a white guy so grimy he looked like a chimneysweep from a remake of *Oliver!* He spotted me too, poor thing, and commenced accosting me for spare change. The way he looked like a giant mutant hare, all teeth and human fur, would be enough for anyone to give him their car or something just to have him go away. Jesus Christ Almighty he was dirty and scary and thin, with a remarkably, disturbingly tiny head.

Now, normally, like the rest of my fellow Angelenos, I have a fair bit of ambivalence about panhandling ne'er-do-wells and inveterate freeloaders shuffling toward you with both hands out looking for a handout when you're just trying to get to your therapy appointment or visit your mistress for a nooner or quickie. Mostly I—like so many—ignore their pathetic pleadings and tall tales of woe at gas stations and (for the less cagey ones) outside dispensaries of myriad potations and libations (i.e, liquor stores). In other palaver, I gives them da money about one-fifth to one-twelfth of the time. Sorry I can't be a bit more precise about it, but if you spend all your time tallying up what perfuckingcentage of the times you are requisitioned for the remaining "Pretty Polly" (cf. *A Clockwork Orange*) that dallies in your pocket, you will either, *I* think, go mad or become something horrible like a sociologist or a Republican.

So I gave this NBA-sized, pea-noggined, lobbying zombie everything I had in my pocket. I dunno: it must have been close to a king's ransom, in bum's currency exchange rate terms: four bucks. Close to the last I had in the whole world.

I don't know why I gave it to him. Something must have possessed me to. Some "fuck-it" impulse or "who-cares" synapse went a-firing; I haven't a clue.

But the bum and my inexplicable philanthropic "fit" didn't bother me nearly as much as the indelible, ineradicable sight of the pock-faced girl did.

When you're on edge or feeling adrift sometimes in life there are things which normally you might shrug or blow off that, now, give you a strange, keen pang instead and upset you, your tenuous equilibrium, your sense of proportion about people and things and all of that. Any merriment or hope you've mustered—right out the goddam window. All I can I say of (as I will soon report to you) the next five days after this is that I had a stunning nervous breakdown: five days I spent staring at the walls, or *a* wall, any wall, and not caring whether I lived or died or whether, for that matter, anyone who meant anything or all the world to me lived or died. Did they, these five dark as I say days—did they have their terrifying provenance in this visitation, so to speak, this odd, chance encounter with the girl with the blasted, spotted cheeks and splendiferously be-pimpled chin? Who's to say, in a Lockean way? I shouldn't at all have been that upset at the sight of her; I mean, come on, I had lived in Los Angeles nearly a year by then and had witnessed many much worse sights.

I threshed the bicycle's pedals through the golden yellow air as fast as I could through the wide gray-blue main streets, then the narrower, more residential and mostly deserted ones, past brown and cream and aubergine buildings, edifices sleeping somehow, lonely in a way only big dwelling places on big city tributary sorts of streets can be, with the odd gardeners tidying up their lawn-work for the day, stoking their tools into ramshackle trucks; and one lone postman puffing away in his bantam blue-white jeep, done with his rounds, perhaps, or with just one last neighborhood to go.

Just be*cause*, just because I'm a madman at times, I unquivered a baguette from my backpack and held it out in from of me, screaming (believably, I thought) "No *prisoners!* No *prisoners!*" like your man Peter O'Toole in Lean's immortal *Lawrence*. I did it on a stretch of street near our apartment, and I don't think anyone saw or heard me; but if they *did*, maybe, especially if they were a film buff or something, maybe they got a kick out of it. *I sure did.* But then again and as you know, I'm out of my tree, my effing mind, totally for the birds. And birds, I think, were my only witnesses for I saw a flock of them like a black shower scatter skyward at my great yalps and yelps and yowls and mad, shouted parpings.

I wonder what the poor people who have actual and not self-induced on account of extreme boredom Tourette's Syndrome go through. Must be fucked. It's fucked enough when it comes on in *my* twist-o, impulsive sensibility and people go a-clearing out the way. All the average averageburghers in America, the art mavens and biography-oriented consumers who croon about how much they love the rock and roll martyrs to sanity—your Syds, your Skip Spences, your Adam Ants, your guys in Badfinger that ended on the end of a last, not-nice rope, your crazy Courtneys, your who-am-I-leaving-outs-there-must-be-someone-else-I'm-missing?—only go glorifying said crackpotmeisters on account of they have never even been close to mental. Otherwise they'd know it ain't no trip to Cleveland. They'd know that being totally mental's kind of a rum deal.

The fruit salad sunset I rode home in (cherry, grape, pineapple, plum, lemon, orange, banana) was the last I'd see of the LA sky for the next five days. I'd forget for a while about looking up—at the sky, at *anything.* As I've intimated, you go out on tour for two days or two weeks or two years—even if you aren't the most sensitive kitten or cat in the litter—, you are frayed as fuck, fucking freaked, whether you have to go back to a dreary job you despise or to having no job at all, or a laughably part-timey one at a bookshop. And now that I think of it, Rob and Raleigh and Jenny had it better than I did 'cause in going back to work they'd have deadlines and responsibilities and projects to "catch up on" and lose themselves in; they wouldn't have time, as I had, to (over)think. They wouldn't just, as I had seemed to, "lose themselves"; they wouldn't have had time to.

On the kitchen table, in preparing for having dinner ready for Jen and at least feeling somewhat useful, I had some special candles going too. Some sort of squat, cheap, overpoweringly vanilla and cinnamon scented ones that were down to having their last spluttering romantic hurrah, burning with their last hour-and-a-half's worth of wavy flames, their melted rims looking like the lips of early Mick Jagger or those wonderful tribal people you seen in documentaries who put pucks of baked clay or cut wood in their lower lips for some reason— to signify their "worth" or something, I don't know, their bride price. You see, I could be a perfectly nice sweet aw-shucks boyfriend when I wanted to be one—almost thoughtful and sensitive, truth be told; a patient listener and genuinely interested in what Jen had to say; affectionate and caring and all of that. The thing was, and those of you who know the first part of *The King of Good Intentions* will corroborate this, she never said all that much, opened up; it was as though she made not-overtalking a sort of mark of distinction. Which is such a great relief when you think about it, those of you who've for the most part had what I would call a pretty common American girlfriend or spouse or partner: those common in every sense of the word types who *share their every thought or notion.*

Not *every* American woman, okay? And yes I know that there are a lot of guys who are a chatty lot, as well.

She'd never show it, Jenny wouldn't, but she had to be bummed to be "back to the grind."

Over dinner I, of course, asked Jen about her day and listened to her report re: how her work-girlfriends wanted to hear all about our tour and how everybody there was glad to have her back. I'd met most of them, her coworkers, the admin-assistants like her, women with college educations from good colleges and universities putting out fires all day long and "taking care of" the big shot, mostly male lawyers at Johnson & Johnson, the firm that employed her and paid her a pretty penny too. The constellation of watercolor-colored flowers I'd arranged on the kitchen table reminded me how, in order to try to win her back after I'd fucked up so bad with the Sarah-Who-Hates-Me chick, I'd sent Jen a nice bouquet of roses, written her long letters of longing, filled with great remorse, called her not-obsessively and just to talk sometimes, tried not to sound like "a broken record" (it was a

term she used quite often), and persistently requested her company—
for coffee, for lunch, for a walk, a cupcake, for "fifteen minutes," for
a drink, for dinner, for whatever. I'd gotten sick off "eating crow"; I'd
taken ample helpings and asked for heaps more; I'd made promises up
the wazoo, grounded for the most part in reassuring her that a) it, that
cheating on her, was something that would "never happen again"—
not "in a million thousand years"; and b) that my promises/love for
her had "nothing to do with my [understandable] fear that she'd leave
the band."

And it'd worked. She'd taken me back. Persistence paid off. Plus
she loved me. Plus *Amor Vincit Omnia*. Plus sometimes you can just,
like, wear a girl down till she just gives up and gives in. And in fact, as
you know, dear reader, she'd taken me in in more ways than one and
we'd gotten a nice big new place together with this record producer
guy, our roommate, Keating, whom we hardly ever saw.

And after dinner that night and even though she was evidently
very tired from a long day we'd gone to bed pretty early after having
fucked and sucked each other like I ever so salaciously told vicarious
you. I had put *The Notorious Byrd Brothers* CD on infinite play on the
tape deck by our bed—do you know the album? It's really ethereal and
not well known, actually. Beautiful trippy effects all over it and many
good, spacey, one-chord songs. You should get it. It's great. Plus it's
got this *awesome* band fight tagged on at the end of it: the band is just
teeing off on the drummer, Michael Clarke, getting all worked up and
pissed-off at him.

And it had given me weird dreams, that record, and I had awoken
after only a couple of hours' sleep and gone out to the living room to
try to read some Somerset Maugham or something.

And in the middle of the night, after, I imagine, I had gotten
back to dreamland for a while, Jenny and I in that remarkably dark
bedroom had one of those pillow-talky conversations that mean at
once so much and somehow so little (so little 'cause you have so many
of them if you are "with someone" for a longish time):

"Jenny?" I said softly. "Are you asleep?"

"No," she said. "I was for a while, I think, but I'm wide awake now."

"Are you all right? What time is it?"

"I'm okay," she sobbed.

"What's the matter? Why are you crying?"

"I don't know. Nothing."

"Tell me."

"I'm not crying."

"Yes, you are. Tell me what's the matter."

"It's nothing. I'm just tired, I guess."

"But you've been sleeping. How can you be tired when you're sleeping?"

She sort of snort-laughed at that.

"I don't know."

Long pause.

"John?"

"Yes, sweetheart?"

"Never mind."

"Please just tell me what's the matter, Jen. I'm sure you are tired. You must be. But you are much more resilient than anyone I know, Jen."

"I just wish…"

"Wish what?"

"It doesn't matter…"

"Jenny…just say it…"

"I wish you…I wish we…I don't think you really love me, John. I wish you did. I so wish that."

"Jenny. Of *course* I do," I said and reached for her and turned her around to face me. Her pretty face was streaming; she'd been sniffling and tearing up quietly, so as not to wake me. But she had. The sheets anent her pillow was a minor lake of teardrops and snot.

"It's okay."

"What makes you say that?" I said. "Of *course* I love you—you're my baby bunny."

"I know but…"

"But what?"

"You're just with me because…because of the band."

"That's not true. You know it's not."

"It is, though. I know it is. You shouldn't lie to me. You shouldn't lie to me ever."

"I'm not. And—no—you don't *know* that—'cause it's not true. Of course what we have is better, amazing, due to the fact that we have a *really* good or at least 'very good enough' band (*I* think) together," I said. "But it's not the reason I'm with you. Not why I love you. I love you so much, Jen. You have no idea."

"You're sure of that?" she sniffed, disconsolate.

"Of course I am."

"You're just saying that, though. I know you are. You're just pretending. Are you just saying that? Tell me. Just tell me."

"That is so…"

"Are you with someone else? Just *tell* me, okay? Are you having an affair? Tell me the truth. Is there someone. Do you still see…what's-her-fuck?"

"Of *course* not!" I stage-whispered. "Jenny, do you think I would have worked—tried—so hard to win you back if I was with someone else, or planning to be? I love you: I don't know what I'd do without you. I…"

"You wish I were skinnier. And taller."

"No, I don't," I lied.

"A 'sexy girl.' I'm not sexy enough for you. You can tell me."

"*Sexy* girl," I said in a mock-flirtatious tone we shared when we used the term we shared—usually when she had on some stage clothes (even if it was a "casual" sort of outfit she was getting into she took hours to get ready—just the longest time) that made the most of her assets. She was always pretty, often stunning, and she could dress very sexily when she wanted to, which was mostly for gigs—but not always for gigs. We weren't by any stretch of the imagination a "grunge band"; we were a fuzzy jangly pop band; but this was the grunge era and lots of girls dressed fashionably down, in T-shirts and ripped jeans and Doc Martens, and Jenny was one of them, but in a stylish rather than slattern way. I always thought she looked better in her "uniform" (tight white V-neck T, faded blue jeans, cute, simple, calf-length black boots) than when she shimmied into, say, a clinging turtleneck black dress or short skirt she had to gasp theatrically in order to get into. She didn't go around in Pendletons or anything, nothing like that; and she always wore a good amount of tastefully applied makeup—the kind that sort of makes it look like the girl's hardly wearing any; but she liked not to have to dress up and be all girly, all "sexy girl" all the time—which made her, as I think she realized, all the more alluring to the average Joe and Jane.

But it was neither Joe nor Jane she was concerned with just then.

"*Sexy* girl," she echoed, and then sort of laugh-sniffled.

I up and got her a yellow tissue from the loo.

"Everyone thinks so," I said, coming back, wiping her nose in the dark.

"So what," she sniffed.

"It's okay. Thank you."

"I know," she joked.

"Of course you are sexy. And so so beautiful."

"Shut up."

"No."

That, for some reason, got her laughing. She hand-dried her eyes.

"Kiss me. Thank you for dinner, John. John-John. You didn't have to do that. We could just as well have gone out. I don't mind trea…"

"Are you kidding?" I interjected. "I'm sick of going out. I don't want to leave the apartment for around six months or so. You know I like to pamper you. I'd make you breakfast in bed every day if you wanted me to."

"I don't really eat breakfast."

"Yes, you do!"

"Okay, start tomorrow morning, then!"

"Except you have to go to work!"

"Thanks for reminding me!" she smiled and sobbed a bit then laughed brightly this involuntary sort of laugh she had when she was feeling depressed or down on herself and I wiped her tear-wet face with my hand and wiped it on my shirt. Then she kind of broke down again a little bit and revealed that she snacked almost all day at work—they had too many tasty snacks, as I think I've mentioned. Rob and Ral'd have been way interested to hear about her work-related "snack-attacks."

"I'm such a pig. You have no idea. I'm as bad as Rob and Raleigh are."

"No, you're not."

"Yeah, I am."

"Are not. No one could be as bad as Raleigh is."

"Well," she snorted a little again, and some junk jetted from her little nose, "that's true."

This time I let her wipe her little nose on my bedshirt.

"I'm sorry we can't just live from playing music. I want that so much for you as much as I do for me, you know. I'm sorry you have to…" I said.

"Ah, it's not so bad. I get into the grind, somehow, actually. And the money of course. I like saving. I am well paid for 'playing at having a job.'"

"And you have a nice car."

"A nice, modest, conservative, boring, unsexy car," she sighed.

"Stop it. You could get a Miata—like Psycho has," I opined absurdly.

Psycho was this crazy, overeducated scientist friend of ours who drove around in a red Miata and was hilariously and quite patly out of his gourd.

"How is Psycho, anyway? I miss him. He's so funny! And Jaz too! Have you talked to Sterling? I miss everyone. A Miata!? I don't think so."

"I know. Haven't talked to them in for*ever*."

Pause encore.

"What are we going to do, John?"

"I don't know. I think things are not good for us at Better with Mike Manson gone now."

"I meant *us*."

"I know you did," I said, and kissed her cheek and her lips and smoothed her big breasts beneath the loose Stewart pajama top she wore no matter how hot or cold the night might be. "That's why I said that. We're *fine*. We are. We're fine. I love you. I'm just…obviously having a hard time right now. That's why I started talking about the band. What we ought to do next. What can we do?"

"I never expected to make a living out of music, anyway, you know. If it wasn't for you, I probably wouldn't even be *playing* music—just giving piano lessons like when I lived at Walter's. I'm glad I am, though."

"Are you?"

"Yeah! The tour was fun. We did well. Mostly good shows and stuff. Raleigh's…"

"An idiot." I said this in a sort of musical way, like it was a lilting motif or something.

"I know. But I like him anyway," Jenny said, sitting up now.

"I know. He *loves* you. They're both in love with you. He prank called me today, by the way."

"Not *Rob?*"

"Of course not. I'll be fifty or something and he'll still be doing it."

"The German…"

"Indian."

"Like, Native Amercian?"

"East."

"Dots not feathers?"

"Right."

"I can't believe that guy."

"He said he sent me a subscription to a *gay porn mag*. Or he thought he did. He thought *Hustler* was gay porn. Our, or should I say my, new subscription should be arriving on our doorstep any day now."

"He did not!" she laughed, shocking herself, I imagine, that she could cheer up so quick. That I could cheer her up so quick.

"He thinks he's fucking hi*lar*ious, that guy. He's starting to reveal his gags before they even get here. Maybe it's for you too."

"He *is*, kinda."

"Is not. He's not at all."

"Well, *I* think he's funny. *I* think he is…"

"*You* don't know. I *taught* you your sense of humor. Or maybe you skipped the lesson where you're supposed to learn that practical jokers are *not* funny."

We had this running riff—a way for me to tease her mercilessly about how hanging around with me, being my girlfriend, had made her a much more witty and funny person.

Naturally, as a highly educated, talented, and accomplished modern person, and one with a pretty healthy ego, she didn't like that one bit.

"Don't you *dare* start in on that again, John! If I hear you say that one more time I'm gonna scream. I hate it when you go around saying I'm only funny and clever as a result of hanging around with *you!*"

"Quiet! You're gonna wake up Keating—even though he's probably not even home yet. *Okay!* Okay," I said and kissed her meaningfully. "I have had no effect whatsoever on your comic abilities! None!"

She smiled and kissed me sweetly, then deeply

"Make love with me again. Make love *to* me."

"You want fuck?" I said, all mock-coy, quietly, in a sort of namby-pamby babyvoice.

"Yes."

"Or make love."

"Both. Uh-huh."

"*Me?*"

"Yes. I want you to come in me."

"*Okay,*" I said and smiled at her and kissed her. "Me want fuck, too. Let's fuck. Me want you, Jenny."

She giggled at my silly Neanderthaling, then wiggled out of her pajamas, top and bottom, and squealed all girlish as I helped her out by tugging the pants off in a trice.

"Just a minute," I said and got up to use the loo first.

Interlude left to your prurient imagination, reader.

And we're back.

After our second bout of amorous exertions, with Jen's hands taking me, my thrusts, my hips, into her with the closest, sweetest abandon, with locked eyes and feelings of mutual (as far as one can ever tell) oneness, that Jungian "oceanic" feeling, we both fell back to what in the morning we testified to each other as turning out to be much more restful sleep, with, for me, intermittent dreams of much weirdness and lingering wonder.

Two

he fact that Jen had brought up the topic of interpersonal relationship-related mendacity, and that, furthermore, ideally and practically it shouldn't be an issue between practically-connubial us, harked back to when we'd negotiated getting back together six months or so prior to this. Negotiated is at once an apt term and a farce: I was in no position to bargain. Not even close. You see, when you're busted, infidelity-wise, and you "come clean," it doesn't just end *there*. Oh no. No way. You know it doesn't. She's gotta know *why* you betrayed her. She's gotta have *reasons*. She's gotta have an answer. Even if you don't know why you did. And sometimes you, the *cheater*, the *fucker*, just don't. You *and* your therapist haven't a clue. It just happens; there's neither rhyme nor reason to it. It's something that's like this calamitous, chthonic inexplicable internal crisis/sexual *chaos* and there's just no accounting for it, there isn't. But to her, the cheat*ee*, that doesn't matter. And moreover, she's gotta have the details in screaming, blood red writing, as it were. All of them. Not in *actual* writing, but you know what I mean. There's something just so lurid and sordid and gruesome and masochistic and ultimately ludicrous and hilarious about it—and it never fails, most times, to come up. She wants to know *everything*. She says that. You might think she

keeps probing just for the sake of rubbing your duplicitous nose in it. And of course, in terms of epistemology, what is "everything," anyway? The truth? What's the *truth*, you might ask. Truth: what is it? And then when you get all philosophical and shit, she just gets more angry and frustrated and upset 'cause she thinks you're trying to pull some semantic jiggery-pokery over on her and she just does not appreciate that shit one bit. No, sir. You can go a-floundering in infinite numbers of ways, trying to figure out what she wants to hear, what will appease her and mollify her and reassure her no end—and you'll still be sitting there baffled (the term means literally "hanged upside-down") as a naughty courtier out of favor with Her Highness The Royal Princess, a laughingstock, in your moth-eaten stocking-feet, with an efflorescence of leaf-and-twig-shaped bruises all over your cavalier-ish precious person.

Her Eminence, Her Ladyship, she doth bee in greate high dudgeon and is most wrothe with ye, fair Sir.

And what if the so-called reason why you slept—even if it was just the one time, just the one indiscretion—with someone else was quote-unquote *just because*, you're even more fucked than the fucked you imagined you were on account of, to her, *that's no explanation*; it's utterly invalid. There has to be more. There has to be something. You wonder sometimes if it isn't the yin or the yang of women's illimitable capabilities to be the nurturer—their Jungian flipside, capacity to endure untold pain, their welcoming of it, sometimes. It *can't* be just "that." It can't just be "because"; it can't be "I don't know why I did it, honey; it sort of just happened"; that's just not good enough; it won't do, and you're not "getting away" with that, not for a million trillion bucks. Forget it. Not happening. People console themselves in matters like this (I use the term loosely, ironically, 'cause it's such cold comfort to "know" anything, in terms of rationalizations when you've been terribly hurt, horribly betrayed) with all sorts of truisms and platitudes and reductive tag lines. We all of us fools—we want to know, to know, to know. We aren't satisfied till we get to the bottom of it! (Unless we're either Fools on the Hill or guru/Bodhisatvas on clouds nine or ten. We're going excavating till the truth comes out! We're gonna find out what happened and why! Ladies and gentlemen readers!) What manner of good does it do us, the "truth," the putative facts? Where does it get us? Anywhere? Anywhere closer to the unknowable stars, to fulfillment, to God and hope and love and happiness? Perhaps it's 'cause it makes us think we matter somehow, the so-called truth does. It makes us think for an adventitious spell that our lives actually count. The good Dr. J. tells us somewhere in his vast scribblings that a man can put up with much, and *more*, and then some; but the one thing he can't fucking countenance for very fucking long *at all* is the thought or notion of his own inconsequentiality. I wish I could find the passage in my well-thumbed *Selected Writings*. Shoot me for a confirmed, inveterate pessimist, but there you go. Some quasi-philosophical days I don't think there *is* such a thing *as* the truth—there are too many mitigating factors, too many variables. And if it has to do with the sexes it's *complicated* as all get-out, *monsieurs et madames*, and that's all I have to say on the matter.

Men are just pigs, many of your girlfriends will tell you, all smug, self-righteous, superior, calmly stirring their smoking, honeyed peppermint tea or knocking back powerful turquoise or apple or lemon cocktails like Prohibition's about to make a comeback, patting a pudibund turtleneck and long, staid plaid wool skirt, or adjusting *down* their already *seriously* plunging *décolleté* while they sashay their way around town in an overstuffed miniskirt. They also say: *They're dogs*, men are, *all of them*—sexual slobs who think through their pants, with their dicks, just disgusting, aren't they, aren't they all? Every last one of them. Don't you *know* that, Shirley, Holly, Valerie Jane? Haven't you figured that out that much yet? Revolting animals. And yet the self-same sex sage will say with her next breath, neither aware nor caring whether or not her utterances are contradictory: "I wish I could just meet a *nice* guy, you know? One who does what he says and says what he does. One who won't ever cheat on me. Where is he? Oh nice guy, oh nice guy—wherefore *art* thou, nice guy, oh nice guy? I *know* there's one out there somewhere. But where? Where *is* that fucking son of a bitch Prince Charming/non-piggy-doggy? God *damn* him."

People: they're so funny. They take it all so personally. Well, they're persons, after all, *some* of them are, that is, so it stands to reason that they *would* do, you know. Everyone's emotionally/psychologically scrounging 'round for a sense of importance, of mattering.

And no man, Dr. J tells us, nor woman neither—and I repeat—can tolerate for very long the idea of his or her own sodding inconsequence. So there you go.

Three

h and in the morning, the morning after Jenny and I had our talk and our lovemaking, wasn't the paint-by-numbers sky just glorious, with a combination of cumulus and nebulous carnation-colored clouds majestically sailing so high and various across the too-blue-and-indigo Los Angeles stratosphere; like tall ships, they were, the clouds—amazing. And the streets stained with the fat raindrops that must have come in the wee hours before dawn. And a strangely sibilant wind coming chillily, whistling through the imprecise or shifted old shuttered windows of our craftsmanlike building, making for a rare, odd frost, bluish and sparkling, on the sills and on the windows of the cold cars parked out in the street. And me, as I heard Jenny's sensible economy car roll away down the narrow back way driveway and spirit her off to work—was I now so low, so low. Contrarily. So unlike those voluptuous and vibrant, cottony clouds on high.

And oh to be among them, floating there, without a care.

It's Thursday now, two days gone from the last day of tour, and I am down, down, down. So down that down isn't the word for it. Can barely get out of bed. Awash in doubtless over-exaggerated agony at the thought of the ineffable *nothing* of my life. How sad! How sorry! How self-pitying and inescapable. Do you think I wanted to feel this bad? I knew too well the type of personality-type who went grandstanding the woe-is-me motif—and it wasn't "me," the woe-is-me-meister role, the put-upon pally. That's not my *MO*, okay? It's not who I am. I know I'm not exactly Mr. Positive Positivity but... Jesus-lord, this is not good, this feeling. I hate sad sacks and fucking pain-paraders! Yet there was I, an I who could hardly-barely levitate from beneath the comfortless comforter—as I've said—and I couldn't, try as I punctiliously might, help it. Why, oh why and wherefore so wan and palely loitering, oh artist/knight-at-arms that seem useless and defenseless? What's the *matter*, poor thing? What's wrong? You can tell me. Feeling meaningless and hope-free too? Burdens burgeoning all around? Nothing's worth a tinker's curse and money's run out with the sense of purpose? Don't know what to do? Oh, you.

What if they gave a nervous breakdown and nobody came?

That's what you feel like, kids. Nobody. Not *a* nobody. Just no one. You feel like looking at a wall for five days straight—and that's precisely what I did. That's what you do. If you were to be asked "Hey, man, what's your occupation? What do you do?" (the query so many people in LA start with...and end with if they don't like your answer), you'd go: "What do I do? Hmm. That's a good question. Um, well, mostly I just sort of despair. That, and I look at this wall all day. That's pretty much what I do. See this wall? That's my job—looking at it. A lot." If they were to inquire as well if it was cool if they blew away your favorite relative or friend in the world, you'd go: "All right. See if I care. Go right ahead. I don't mind *what* you do." It's like you're there, in the middle of the street, just lying there, and you see this tank or artillery truck or giant crane or bloodthirsty hellmonster coming your way and you are all: "Fine. Run me over. See if I mind. See if I care. Really. I don't. I just don't care. Go ahead. Do it."

Describing it now, the near-week I spent in a walking coma, feeling blank, feeling nothing, not even sadness, really, just zilch, zip, nothing? Well, it's indescribable, somehow. And what I and any lyricist worth his Bic-and-college-ruled-notebook might do is *use* it, is write it down, get it down, get it out, come up with some artistic exercise with which to exorcise it, this deep dip into the doldrums.

But *goot Gott in Himmel* the *last* thing I wanted to do was write or even try to. I mean, I only write songs, truth be told, when I am really up or really down, anyway. Writing "on a schedule" or sitting down and *forcing oneself to write some lyrics each day*—that's not for me. I was down, all right. But this was *too down for words*. Literally for words and the playing with them that is songwriting.

Isn't it funny how people go: "Well, *could be worse*." Because it *always* could be, can be. What's even more odd is when they go: "Oh my gosh, *it couldn't have been worse*. [then slowing down for extra emphasis] Just could-n't have been-a *worse!*" Uh, yes it could! It could—whatever "it" is—*always* be worse than the worst worst of it that it already is. Got that? Good, 'cause I'm kind of losing myself here.

Scenario, viz. the topic at hand: Here's *you*. You get kicked out, let's say, given the old heave-ho by your lovely wife of a good six years (she's an accelerated gal, a real go-getter—one year ahead of "the seven-year itch"): she caught you with your nuts barked up against that old chestnut, the secretary's "poonani." The choreography of your life, with its complacent routines and infinitely differentiated predictabilities is interrupted significantly. Things are *not going to be as they were*. Nothing's ever, in fact, going to be the same. *You've* seen to that. Made sure of it with your lack of foresight, insight and sight sight. The homestead hearth's had cracks and then some all this time; and you think, Ah, hell, most marriages and love affairs are decidedly deciduous anyway. Ah, the rebarbative odor of a "broken home"— its first whiffs have wafted over the rooftop, they're mingling with the walls' incipient dry rot. And "working it out," "getting therapy," "working through this," "going on a couples' weekend retreat" or "taking a reparative, exciting, revivifying Tantric sex class together"?

Not options, any of them. Wifey's pissed. Way so. She's in an *ecstasy* of ire and indignation, inconsolable—even if she wanted to be she couldn't be appeased. She's also from a—I'm not going to come right out and say they're *Latino or Russian or Prussian-Yazukan or anything, but they* might *be*—family with a time-tested tradition of vengeance and the Talion law, an eye for an eye, and a limb or a kidney for a tooth or an act of *in flagrante* infidelity. Big surprise: she's taking you for everything you've got. She ain't just playing Killarney here; she's playing for keeps. Hiring a smart brigade of Yalie lawyers.

What could be worse?

Okay—all right—let me have a think here. Lawyers, you say? What could be worse? Well, for one thing, she's banging the lawyers. Take that. All four of them. Sometimes two at a time. When she feels really lost and lonely, too wounded by what cliché-ridden *you* did with "The Chestnut," as she now rather imprecisely yet kinda/sorta-cleverly refers to Charon, the archetypal secretary, she consoles herself a little bit, she says, with a merry threesome, in the full-on champagne-and-cocaine hot tub cliché, so that instead of lost and lonely she can feel strong and slutty, satisfyingly dirty, devilishly pleased. And, well, okay—after two or three weeks of having them, the law men, on rotation she thinks she might be a) in love with and b) pregnant by one of them. Probably, she avers, from one of the times in the one guy's ever-gurgling jacuzzi. He wants her to run away with him to Fiji, to the Faroe Islands, to faraway places, anyway; he sincerely does, the guy whose embryo it probably-maybe-is does. She hasn't made her mind up yet; she's going to inventory and perhaps arraign her feelings and give it a good think. She wouldn't mind living on an island: she's lost quite a bit of weight and spends a goodly amount of time at the gym getting fit as hell, as ever, as she never really truly was when she was with you, 'cause it's hard to get psyched for the gym when you're exhausted emotionally, psychologically, and physically from faking orgasms all the time. *What could be worse?* He, the lawyer-fuck she's fucking fucking the most, more than the others, he, she informs you, is far and away the best fuck of the fucking foursome, of her life, in fact. She's amazed she ever had a problem climaxing. Now she climaxes to the max, she does, and she knows she's looking better than ever in a weensy bikini. He's such a stud, this one legal stud. He oughta be illegal, him. With such a hot cock, adds she, as she tells you about it, about him, over the telephone, making the "c" in "cock" hard as could be—which reminds her: she is going to try and make your *life* hard now, as hard as she can make it. As hard as law-guy's cock is. Big. Sweet. Nice. Cock. She thusly spells it out for you—like a language teacher might to a "slow" ESL class. Nice cocky, she calls to it sometimes—on account of sometimes it looks like an attack dog or attack sea lion, albino version. It's so big, she reports, relishing imagining you squirming like anything; maybe after the third time a-night they "do" it, it hurts when she puts it in her, well, where she never let *you*. It's too big for her mouth, even. But at least it's straight. It's straighter than yours. Yours cants too far to the left. She never told you that, did she? Well, now you know. You have that bit of information. *Rien ne va plus*, she says, delivering a supreme non sequitur. She never told you but now she thinks might be a good time to tell you that *she never came when you had sex.* All fake. Not once. Not ever. Never. Okay, *once*. Drunk. She was drunk the one time. Holiday drunk, which doesn't even count. One time. Big deal. What could be worse? Well, the one time she did come [and here she whispers for extra-dramatic dramatic effect] *she was thinking about fucking your better-looking brother.* And she *was* thinking about fucking your better-looking brother because *that's what she did do*, fuck him, three Christmases ago, at the annual extended-family Christmas holiday cabin, under the pretty, pulsating Christmas tree, with the pretty lights all robin's egg blue and mellow yellow and sperm white and danger red, while you were upstairs passed out on the egg nog and the Scotch, the egg nog and the *cheap* Scotch you always bought because you *are* cheap, you cheap-o cheapskate, cheap as the fucks you had with fucking "The Chestnut," that cheap whore, that cut-rate trollop, that cunt, that *cunt*. How much more cunty can you get than that cunty cunt-whore? None more at all.

What could be worse?! [What a great game show that would be! Take it away, heirs of Goodson and Todman!] What *could* be worse? This could. During the wonderful and lovely telephone conversation you're horribly having with your emotionally frost-bitten wife, the "Call Waiting" beep beeps; just a second, honey, says desperate and despairing you; Hello? Who is it? It's a law firm. The law firm that your wife's been fucking. Yes? you inquire. Yes, *yes*, what *is* it? Yes, what do you goddam pettifogging bastards goddam *want?* What? *You get the registered letter we sent?* the parody gumshoe/tough-guy voice on the other end of the line goes. Our records say you did. So? So what? If you know that already, why call and ask? you respond. So, you obviously didn't open it. Open it. You got and didn't open it? the tough-guy voice goes. No, no—no, I didn't goddam open it, you go. Open it! You have to. It's registered. Therefore. We know you got it, now you're going to *get it!* Get it? Good. Open it. I'll go ahead and hold. Go ahead.

You put the phone down and pick up the letter you've tried to hide from yourself, knowing it can't be good, putting it off by putting it down somewhere near the fireplace, perhaps. At last you open it, expecting poison gas to come a-wafting or a pit viper to come a-lunging. Whew! It' not from the ex-wife! Sweet! But wait. Oh, great: secretary Charon's suing you for sexual harassment. The wanton bitch wants monetary compensation. Knowing her, that wanton, mercenary, prevaricating *bitch*, she'll want *ample* compensation. She'll probably spell it "amble." Well, dear, amble on over. Any time. You wouldn't mind a goodbye/consolation non-conjugal visit.

The letter tells you you won't be hearing from her again; you'll be hearing from the Yalie lawyers, though; they'll be in touch with *you.* Undone! You are undone. And there's an end on't. *What could be worse?!* It *couldn't* be worse than this! It couldn't be more fucked up; you couldn't *be* more fucked. (It's like a foreign language drill in a hefty, only sparsely illustrated textbook that's just *waiting* to give you some nice fresh papercuts.):

Fucked you are.

Are you fucked?

You *are* fucked.

Yes, you are.

Fucked, that is. (You.)

The Fucked.

The Fucked One.

With an unmistakable accent over the *e*.

Translate that into any of the world's languages you care to, kids.

The Call Waiting beep bleeps encore. Yes? *Yes?* Hel*lo*? Who *is* it? What *now*? What do you *want*? It's Charon. What *now*, Charon? I thought I wasn't going to hear from…oh, you change your mind? You're empowered now, huh? Okay. Okay. What do you want? Why can't you leave me…? Harassing *me*, now are we? I already got your lawyers' letter and I can't befuckinglieve you'd…What?! You're *pregnant?* You're pregnant. Right. Sure you are. This has to be some put-on, some sick, elaborate joke. You're not. Not kidding. Stop fucking with me, Charon. I mean, I wish we *were* stilll…What the fuck? What the *fuck*, Charaon? It sounds cliché but…How do you know it's *mine?…* *Huh?* How *dare* I? How *dare* I? How dare *you?* You know I have to ask! I can't just accept it. I can't just blithely go: 'Oh, okay? How much do you want a month? Want the house and the car and the pool I don't have and the stocks and the bonds?' I can't just… You have to give me your word. You have to give me your worthless, good-for-nothing word…Hahahaha! Go ahead, Charon. Tell me the truth. Swear on a stack of bibles. Can you? Huh? Tell me. I'm listening.

And then she hangs up ticked off, but promising she's not about to go chivvying you to death, but that for sure you'll hear from her "friends" again, from her lawyers, that is. Although she does add, with all the unmitigated sincerity of a coy, virginal cheerleader, with all the substance of a *pom-pom*, that she's "rilly sorry things turned out this way"—as though the Fates or Furies have goose-stepped in and prevented her from staying her hand suing you, getting, um, rid of the embryonic problem. As though she has no idea how things got to this stage yet she's just "doing what she has to do."

What could be worse?

Well, okay, this: this could. Just getting warmed up here, see? Proceed to holding weary, afflicted head in hands. Get used to it! It's going to be a too-familiar pose or stance for you. You ought to hie thee down to the olde style department story in the ghostlike part of your town and have your photographic portrait taken like that. It'd be an image they could prop up on a tribute-ish sort of easel at your sparsely-attended funeral so that smattering of mourners could go: "Wow, that picture really captures his down-the-toilet life, shortly before he, well, you know, went tragically *insane...*"

Three days after this, and five days after you last fucked Charon (it was kind of a half-hate fuck, *kind* of, not really, or at least it was a little more rough that what you're used to with her, on account of you were pissed at her for being the cause of why you cheated on your wife; oh and by the by: you don't think of yourself as a "hate fuck" kind of guy, but you could see yourself maybe getting into just a little bit, who knows?: maybe getting into it a *lot* if things keep on getting worse and worse the way they worsely seem to be)—-three days later, as I'm saying here, you go to take a regular old run of the mill/nothing out of the ordinary piss after fortifying yourself with a coupla two, three, four tequila shots for breakfast, and you find your dick's stippled with painful little itchy hillocky blotches; red; firey-looking, with little dips like bantam craters; looking like they're about to be oozing painfully, about to get some attention for themselves; decidedly not ignorable; horrible, in fact. It was probably your of-late o'er-hasty technique with respect to angrily zipping up your zipper that did it, right? *That's* it. Gotta be. You've been under such great stress of late (you idiot, you stupid fucking oafish, dolty *dumbshit*) that you neglect to be ginger with your zipper *and* your pecker, the fiendish, foul, unsightly thing that got you into this, surely. Right? Nuh-uh.

Your trousers aren't to blame, m'boy.

*Hell*o!

Hi, herpes! your doctor, a sort of friend, a regular card, a regular cut-up, says the very next day, his earliest available appointment. *Hey* there. Ooh, that looks nasty, sorry to say. Pretty painful, is it, eh? One

question, all right? Ready? Okay. Shoot? Okay: *Ever heard of condoms?*
Rubbers never occur to you? Johnnies, prophylactics, dick wraps, love
gloves? Trojan makes a good one, my friend. A good, high-sensitivity,
quite possibly sheep or lambskin (also dubbed "natural") *sheath* For
Her Pleasure. You can pick them up even at gas stations these days.
Little League snack shops, Russian Tearooms, Chocolatiers, Sporting
Goods stores, the Narthex of your local Lutheran Episcopalian
Methodist Church—just about everyone sells them, haven't you
heard? Catholic gift shops are around the only places you won't find
them sold. Perhaps you've seen them advertised? They're only on
every other page in every Sports magazine/Men's magazine in the
country. Jeez. Your doc laughs to himself, snaps off his limpid latex
prophylactic gloves, scratches off a prescription for Extra Strength
Valtrex, and has a horrifyingly attractive nurse come in and see you
out after you get dressed. Sorry about that. Shit happens. Life is cruel.
Tough break. Tough *out*break. Ha! Good one. Sorry. Tough stuff, I
mean. Tough shit. It's rough but you'll get used to it: everyone does.
The ones who survive the first six months, that is. Kidding! Not fatal.
Just to your love life. A joke! Sorry! I'll be serious. *Everyone* has it,
nowadays. One in five has it, stats say. Which is, in metropolitan areas
known for a high concentration of randy singles and young or middle-
aged marrieds, tantamount to "everyone, almost." One in four, more
like. Hillary will give you some brochures, some information. You see
the ass on her? Well, you're probably not into ass-seeing just now, but,
hey, come back and look at it sometime: spectacular. Herpes, now.
This is the deal. Are you listening? Okay. High and low, town and
country, its spread can't be stopped, especially among the young and
promiscuous. Though you are neither of those, huh: you're just thirty-
something/pushing forty and philandering. Oh, it was just the one
woman, an affair? Not philandering, then. Wrong word. The word
is foolish, then. Kidding you. It does happen to your demographic
as well. Just not as much. How that helps you I don't know. Doesn't,
does it? Drag. Listen: fling yourself into any bar in any metropolis in
America and swing a dead armadillo and you'll hit three or four who

have it. You are not alone. You *feel* alone right now, though, right? Never sadder. That's normal. Very. It'll pass. This is the worst part. Better tell your wife. Better you do it than the office. Sorry. Better tell this Charon, too, by the by. Make that call. Call today. Make yourself. Put it off you very much should not. You don't want *us* to call her; it'll only make her madder. Tell her to tell her other lovers, if she has them, which she probably does, in spades—they may even be close friends of yours: that happens: that happens *a lot*, a lot more than you think. Not me, though. *I* didn't fuck her. God I *hope* I didn't. Kidding. Haha! She could be with one of them right now, in fact. Some big black guy with a dong like a turkey leg. Or a Jewish guy like me with a dong like a *jumbo* turkey leg. Hahaha! Funny, huh. Sorry. Can't help myself sometimes. Guess you can relate to *that!* One thing we Jews don't get a lotta credit for—having big, prodigious *schlongs*. Just like the poor Irish guys like you have reps for, well, never mind. Anyway, about the pizzles of God's Chosen? Not a lot of people know that—except of course the people we fuck. *They* know. Boy do they ever. They'd fuckin' better. Ha! In terms of anthropology or biology or one of those—it makes sense though. Hear me out. God chooses Jews. Going to need extra Jews because people see you as chosen? by God? Jealous. Want to hurt chosen Jews. Ergo, need more Jews to replace Jews that will be knocked off or evicted on jealousy counts. Right. You with me? If Jews are chosen, by God, to have long fat dicks, women of all sorts of faiths, creeds, and breeding ages will want said large dicks *in* them. More dicks in them, more chance of babies coming out of them. What's that? Oh?! Damn. You're right: without Jewish mothers those kids begot by the big Jew dicks won't really be *real* Jews, as not all having Jewish mothers. Good point. Didn't really think that one through. Well, it was nice while it lasted, my theory. It's just nice to think about sex, isn't it? I spend a lot of my time—let me tell you—thinking about…What's she look like, any old way, this Charon? Any cute? Really? She's pretty? *Quite* pretty? A real looker? Send her over! She need a check-up? I'm *kid*ding. Have a sense of humor, won't you? Have a couple of them. Take two on your way out and call me in the morning. Ha! Funny, huh? Good one. It's gonna come in handy [said very slowly]. A sense of humor is going to come in very, very handy. Read me? Great. *Very* necessary. Inexpendable. Inexpendable? Unexpendable? Inexpungable? God*damn*it, what's the word I'm looking for here? Indisposable. That's it. No: indispensable. Anyway. The Herp! Yikes! *No bueno*. Owie! (I say "Owie!" instead of "Oy vey!—I hate that phrase, so low class, so cliché. As if I'm not enough of a cliché already—a scratch-golfing, medicine-practicing, Jaguar-driving, Princeton-Alumni-ing, Bel Air-residing, devilishly handsome, tall, not-bald, athletic and well-read and happily married Jew. With a big Jew *schlong*. A regular tree trunk between my legs. Ha! Oy *vey!* I mean, owie.) I ever show you my sequoia-like cock? Kidding! I rarely even let the girls I screw get a look at it. Certainly not before I get them in the sack, I don't. No way. I *used* to, in college, but the endless Kathies and Kikis and Kupcakes I fucked would invariably get one look at the thing and go: "Hey, *putz!* You're not putting that thing anywhere *near* me, okay? I gotta Chem final this week and I need to be able to *sit down* for three hours in a row here, okay, Mistah Big Cock? No way are you fucking me with that thing!" Hahaha! Priceless. And if you're fucking thinking that *I'm* fucking thinking I'm Philip Fucking *Roth* with a goddamn MD—well, hey: think what you wanna, huh?! Okay by me. Hahaha. Hilarious. First time my wife saw me without a towel and in the light of day she nearly fainted. Served that frigid cunt right for always wanting the lights out, eh? Joking. About the lights out. Not about the cunt thing. You marry someone in order to have full-time access to her dainty little cunty and then she be*comes* one. A *big* one. Wish I were kidding. Jesus-on-a-corn-cob, man, you can thank Yahweh every goddam day of your life you're not married, my *mein bester freund*. Ain't it the truth. And I'm, as I said, one of the quote lucky ones, one of the happy ones. I love that crazy bitch to death. I love her. I don't wanna *fuck her*, mind you, but I'd walk in front of lunch truck for that twat any day of the week. She's family now. Goddamn if she isn't. Nine years we've been together. Nine! Can you be*lieve* that? Not me. No, siree. Beautiful girl.

She was, that is. I have no problem with her—especially as I have no problem cheating on her. And G-d bless her if she doesn't say jack shit when I come home from quote unquote golfing at one thousand o'clock in the morning sometimes, smelling like a Tampon dipped in amber-colored cheap perfume and "slut-butter." That's a good one, huh. "Slut butter." You like it? Cheer up? Everyone has herpes. Okay. My wife, she looks the other way—like any sensible wifey should. Indeed. *Any*way. Look after yourself. Go easy on yourself. It's the only way. Trust me. And make those calls and fill that prescription.

Don't tell my wife, by the way... *What? Don't tell her what?* That I told you I was happily *married*, of course. She'll find a way to take that shit out on me somehow, believe me. She finds that out, that I'm happy *and* happy I am still *married* to her? *Hell.* Hell, I tell ya. That's what I'll get for it. Hell pure and simple. No kiddin'. She doesn't know I'm happy as hell with her and what she don't know won't hurt her, ya know? How true is that? How true is that saying. Too true—that's what it is. Sleeping dogs lie and all that other cliché stuff. She finds out I'm con*tent* and all, she'll get the upper hand and start using the back of it on my ass day and night, night and day. Day and night I'll get my ass stir-fried by that twat of a wife I love so much. Oy v...Let me tell you something: *every last one of these crazy bitches—even the sane ones—are completely out of their frigging minds and don't you forget it.* But hey: I don't have to tell *you*, do I? Now listen: take care. Be careful. Be a *mensch.* Go have some *fun.* Take up snorkeling or bocce ball. Golf! Try it! Meet some nice girls and don't tell them you have...what you have...until maybe the fourth date. Third date, actually—cause if you ain't banging her by then, fuck her. Know what I mean? Be a pillar of the community for a little while. Take a French class, take a night class, or even Improv—*I* don't know! Do yoga. The hot kind. Something! And most of all: don't worry. You'll be *fine.* A little pain, physical—a lot pain, psychological. But just at first. You'll accept it. People do. *You're* people. You'll do what they do too.

Wait! I got it. Go on a *pleasure* cruise. No kidding. Baja. The Galapagos. Greece. Spain. Ber*mu*da. Anywhere: the Carribean. Hot tamale! The wife and I went to fucking Bogota, Columbia coupla years ago? Holy shit—I gotta tell you the little bitch nearly divorced me on the streets of Caracas, right there on the flagstones or cobblestones or whatchamaycallum. I said 'Caracas' but meant Bogota. We went to Caracas too—but the chicks weren't half so sexy. Anyway. Went into a cathedral, she did, my wife, Marcy did. You want a cup of water? You all right? Anyway. And started scouting around for some priest or cardinal or indigenous janitor to pronounce us unmarried. Never seen her like that. Serious. Crazy with a "K," she is. The dumb cunt thought that's all a Catholic priest had to do—wave a censer or a cross around and—poof!—you're divorced. Boy was she serious. Never seen her so livid, that crazy fucking frigid bitch. I think I will go home early today and give her a pud-pounding that she'll never forget. I wouldn't kid you. What could I do down there in South America, though? I was surrounded. Outnumbered like mad. Everywhere I turned there's some fine hot Latin chick's fine hot Latin *ass* in my face. I'm not rubbernecking on purpose—it's right there, some chick's *great* butt. Jesus, the asses on the girls down there. *And* their *smiles?* Get outta here! Outstanding. Outrageous. It's like some kind of flag they're waving at you. It's patriotism, that's what it is, the way they waddle and sashay and waggle those big behinds around that town for G-d and Country. What great publicity for the Touris Bureaus of South America! Jesus fuck. Jesus Christ. You're just trying to read that rag *USA Today* or the worthless *Herald-Tribune* and have a cup of unbelievably delicious aromatic coffee in some outdoor bistro thing or *plaza* or whatever and choke down half a wedge of coffee cake coated with ungodly amounts of cinnamonsugar and *they're practically lining up to put their unbelievably big beautiful-bitch butts in your fucking face before it's even time for a* refill. Jeez Louise. Columbian girls. I had to have us come back early. I had to get out of there. I couldn't *take* it. I almost didn't make it *out* of there. Let me tell you. Seriously. Practically faked a stomach ailment so that I could just go *home.* You know how they say everyone cries when they leave Hawaii? Well, Columbia— just like that. You're weeping 'cause of the beauty. But different types, see? Me, I was sobbing. And she knew why, Marcy did. She *knew*. For a second there I thought she was actually gonna say she felt sorry for me. And she should. No man should have to take that for too long. *I* couldn't take it there, I'm telling you. Beautiful girls everywhere, just begging for it, my friend. Phenomenal. I had a rod for three days straight. I had to check to see if I'd prescribed for myself and *eaten* an entire bottle of Viagra by mistake. I unpleated every pair of Chinos I'd brought, I know that much. Golf slacks—out of the question. I had to wear a robe *over* my robe in the mornings. God, it was fucking horrible. Marcy g-ddam glowering at me the entire time, asking me why, asking me if I was cold—and there it was, a hundred and twelve in the shade in the morning. She knew what was what. Smart little rat, that Marce. Her beady little pale pink rat eyes got even fucking *smaller*. Smaller by the day. Which lead her, logically of course, to demand a second breast augmentation! Smaller, bigger. Smaller, bigger. I don't think she saw a single painting or native sculpture or craft-piece in a single one of the twenty-seven hundred thousand museums we went to! Watched *me* like a *prison guard* the entire time. Watched me like a hawk. Watched my cock like a hawk—that's for sure. I don't think she saw a single church or steeple or painting or whatsit—Madonna and child—the whole entire time we were there. Had her crazy gaze trained on my codpiece from the time we left the hotel to the time we got back…Never go back there. Torture. Even in the tourist churches and museum bookstores there are girls in these frothy striped skirts that just…By the way, don't you just love *Taking Tiger Mountain By Strategy*. Simply remarkable album. Eno's a genius. Better than Mark Knophler, even. Knophler is very underrated. Better than Springsteen. I can't believe you don't like Springsteen! I've gotten more into music these days. The more I get into music the less I have to think about my wife. It's true. Now she's more jealous of my stereo than my desire to retire in Bogo-fucking-ta. I'm telling you. If I ever get divorced, G-d forbid, G-d for*fend*, I'd be on the next plane, though. *Columbia*— whatta country. And Venezuela, too. Go down there once you get settled with the herpes (which you will—everyone does) and get over the shock of it and the foolish shame. You'll get down and thank me on your blessed knees, my friend. You won't be*lieve* the chicks they got down there. If you like those Latins half as much as I do you'll freak out like nobody's business. I'll pick up the phone one day and it'll be you long distance and all I'll hear is the sound of you weeping with gratitude and unimaginable wonder. Even if you bang three of those va-va-va-voomy g-ddesses a day, you'll still be upset about the ones you *didn't* get to fuck. You'll *never* get to fuck. Everywhere all over the world there are girls you are never going to fuck, my friend. It makes you want to kill yourself sometimes, it really does. All right then. Time's up. I gotta be serious here a sec. Some words of wisdom called for here. Take it very, very, *very* easy on yourself. Be good to you. Maybe no g-ddam *sport-fucking* for a while, though, old sport— sex with people you haven't known for at least ten years. Or at least avoid ones you have only known ten minutes; for two or three drinks, that is. Take a day or ten off, a couple hours at least. Haha! And yet, what's the difference? You already have the biggie here, the one that never goes away, the gift that goes on giving, as they say. Just try not to give it to anyone else. I know you know that. It's just, as your doctor, I gotta say that kind of shit. It's not that bad. People live with it. Often find partners who have it too. You have to laugh—like I said. Better keep your sense of humor handy. That one I just told you to get. You'll need it. Not joshing. Get this scrip filled right away, though. Across the street, the pharmacy. Golf sometime? Or aren't you a member? No? Used to be? I see. Ah, pity then. Some other time. Take it easy. Keep in touch. Goodbye. Take care."

What could be worse?

Your about-to-be-former wife (who used to be excruciatingly beautiful, and still is, though just not to you; she's like one of those one in a hundred million zillion babes like Catherine Deneuve or Susan Sarandon or Diane Sawyer who got *better looking* as they aged)—she won't let you see your kids; you can forget about *them* for a spell, says she. You can forget you even knew them. You certainly weren't remembering their sweet, obedient little angel-faces when you put your demonic dick in Charon. How could you have even hired a secretary who doesn't even know how to spell her own fucking name?! You fucking fuck! You stupid *id*iot. You *fucking* idiot. What a *dumb*shit. I bet she was great at *dic*tation, then, huh? You scum. Was she the only one you fucked? Was there a Tiphany too? A Djulie? A Scathleen or Amenda?

What can you do? What you can do. The only thing you can do: you play Dylan's *Blood on the Tracks* fifteen times a day for two months straight.

Then you really start getting into it, that record.

Nevertheless: you don't shave. You don't bathe. All you seem to do is *age* and look in the mirror each mid-morning out of curiosity to see if you're still there. Yep. There you are. Sure as shit. Sure as shit you sure look like shit. Shit is you. You again. You shit. Oh, great. Just great. That's just fantastic. You live in your Adidas sweats. You haven't worn a pair of shoes for weeks. And moccasins don't count. Why would you need them, shoes? You don't leave, go out, not even to the market or the liquor store. That's what you plug the phone back in for—calling the liquor store to come bring such staples as tequila, anejo tequila, reposado tequila, tequila mixto, blue agave tequila, tequila blanco, two-for-one packs of Marlboro Lights in a box, and a cardboard box brimming with fresh, juicy, horripilated limes.

For the tequila, of course.

What could be worse?

Ta-*da!*

Oh I could—ta-*da!*—kill off one or more of your kids here or have a flaming plane fly into your living room, tragically *not* taking your turbid life but leaving you a tertiary quadriplegic, but don't you think you've suffered enough? I do, too. Don't you think you've been through enough fresh Hell? Well, I do; I do, too.

And so *exeunt* and onward.

Four

ake your greatest fear. Maybe it's cats or horses or Herpes Simplex 09000 or circus clowns popping out of your trunk as you go to put in it the corpse you just made. Maybe it's having to address the assembled Continental Congress in a drunken, tankard-clinking, dizzy dream with all the Founding Fathers grimly-soberly watching you; maybe it's having at last to talk to *your* father or mother about how you feel he or she never really loved your ass—on account of they were self-absorbed, or drunk during the day, or their parents beat them up on a daily basis.

It ain't fucking nothing in comparison to facing a bona fide nervous breakdown.

Know how, in those nine-hundred-page "doorstop" literary biographies that only advanced emeritus-type eggheads can get through, even with the help of a magnifying glass big as your vanity mirror, they go something like: "But then, ominously, with The Great War on the bleak horizon, the great man broke down at long last. Without time even to change out of his favorite best cravat and fashionably rounded, starched white shirt collar, he was ferried off to The Continent with but five tightly banded pumpkin-and-walnut colored *portmanteaux*, four of them symbolically empty. (No one knows why.) There, on The Continent, holding on for dear life to his red-gold-and-black-banded, cream-colored "boater," hands thrust into the pockets of his trademark astrakhan blueberry greatcoat and with his favorite wintergreen tennis shoes on, alas, the wrong feet, he climbed the long climb in the terrifying train from Le Havre to Lausanne; then—unsmiling all the way—up the vertiginous funicular to the sequestered sanitarium in the magic mountains of fairy tale Zunderland, a little-known toy principality north-northwest of

Switzerland proper. Wheeled 'round in an oversized, water nymph-and-dryad-ornamented wooden wheelchair built for two, perpetually wrapped in a "rug" and with one of his own tomes (with uncut pages) on his sad lap (fretting like an old guitar his trusty Cricket bat, which doubled as a cane or "walking stick"), able only to drink tepid Darjeeling (with milk not cream of course and one lump of sugar laced with powerful laudanum) and take a little beef-tea broth on alternating Wednesdays, there at Mont St. Michel-le-Triste-Pour-Les-Pauves-Belleslettristes he [the great man] gradually recuperated in the splendid, summer, Swiss-adjacent sunshine: playing a bit of desultory chess against the knackered pneumatic German nurses; whacking brightly striped croquet balls into the welcoming trees; playing badminton against an imaginary opponent, someone whom he loved like a brother, who got shot at Belleau Wood; chastising chestnuts that he kicked before him at a remarkably balletic trot; writing precisely three pathetic anaphoric sentences per day; failing (we've learned via his doctors' copious session notebooks) to take a normal interest in normal things like masturbation and lawn bowling; drawing poplars upside-down and endless menacing snowscapes and mythopoeic angel-demons in a funereal-black notebook; sampling assorted fortifying strudels (with warm, fresh cream from the local surrounding mountain dairies); sipping hot chocolate swirled with Ceylonese cinnamon sticks and taking incremental little bites from the lambent *pot au feu du jour*—which was mutton most of the time, but occasionally *boeuf.*"

His one witticism, the entire seven months he spent resting, reading, and reveling in butterfly-hunting and *The Varieties of Relgious Experience* by William James, was "*Careful there*, dear fraulein—just *whose* shuttlecock?!" at his farewell banquet (a grim affair, but a sort of nut-based "roast" nonetheless, with just two nurses, both louche and drunk and greatly sexually sated, and a nineteen-year-old visiting psychiatrist intern, the Head Herr Doktor having flu, plus suffering from undiagnosed tertiary dementia and a morbid obsession with lollipops and gumdrops).

The first weeks had been rough: he'd had words with the hospital post box in the pristine entryway, imagining it a secret fascist agent. He'd challenged a visiting, soon-to-be-expatriated fellow poet-friend from Kandy to a cribbage match, the loser of which would have to run 'round the grounds three times naked, backward, while pretending to shave off his beard with a trowel. On a night of the brightest moonlight the Head Nurse had caught him in bed with a younger nurse she'd [the Head Nurse] been "experimenting Sapphically with, for more reasons than just Case Notes." Mayhem, utter. Angered shadows dancing and flailing and pots and pans flying in cartoon silhouette through pristine, insupportable air. Sometime at the end of the first fortnight he'd beaten up a closetful of broomsticks, adopted a Conquistador's helmet meant only for show (the sight of him in it, walking 'round in his authentic English flannel nightshirt, upset the archetypal twelve other patients), and spoken fluent Iroquois— to his own great hallucinogenic surprise, never having studied it, nor even heard it, that wonderful, guttural dead tongue. He'd sallied forth across the gumdrop meadows, *literally* running away with his own imagination, skipping, dashing, jogging backward, laughing raucously at the too-close sky. Here we can envision him recording on canvas the watercolor-purple and burnt orange sunsets, standing at an easel with paintbrush in one hand and a metallic tumbler of fortifying wine or Schnapps or a jam tart in the other, striking mock-duelist postures from his days as a champion amateur fencing fanatic, much to the chortling nurses' great amusement. Picking the wild mountain flowers, the golden strawberries, some thyme. Then, after great hope of earlyish recovery, must needs come the desperate and supine time, the seemingly endless weeks of being greatly, profoundly *down*. The singular Collective Unconscious. Or the *too* conscious—couldn't sleep, couldn't eat, couldn't move, couldn't care less. The knocked-down-and-out black spell that lasted a full, petrifying month. His head an anvil, shining from the pounding; his heart a dormant forge, cold, ashen, mortifyingly dark. The denying of visitors. Strictly *verbotten*, company was, but the great man's great friend, a famously prolific and unpublished poet, one Charles McNickle O'Grady, persevered and pounded the tall, dark, and handsome desk at reception and was eventually granted a short and fruitless audience at his, the great man's, clammy, restive bedside. No light of recognition shone in his too-blue eyes. No faint smile of friendly warmth or sentiment traversed his pale and trembling and spittle-spackled lips. No gesture of acknowledgement...?"

Or something like that.

Well, me/I/I for one never really (really) understood before what the fuck they, those ponderous biographers with their big, bright, gray or russet beards and serious smiles, meant by stuff like that. And now I do.

Try to describe it? What it's like? Good suggestion. Thank you; I think I will, cheers. Here goes: I can't. Can't. I will say, however, that time's never seemed so *present*—and not in a good way. Get this: I'd look at the clock and after what seemed like an hour—I swear to you—only a minute and half'd passed. It's a black cloud of unknowing beyond or behind or what-you-will, the cloud of unknowing that we all of us know. And the fact that you've no idea when or *if* it'll pass only adds to the anxiousness. You just don't care. It goes so far beyond *ennui*, so outstrips the mere childsplay that is *accidie*, that you can't even imagine.

If we are all of us Administrations-of-One, in terms of the governance of our lives (husbanding our strengths, marshaling our forces, emotionally getting and spending, thinking incessantly about the Commonwealth that's inescapably *us* while simultaneously—one hopes—trying not to be too much of an arsehole about it), then a nervous breakdown's a regime change with no one there, a *coup d'etat* with no new pretenders to re- and displace the old one or ones, an ousting without a new boss to meet the old. It's a real mess.

Fantastical, grotesque, it's everything that you can't say it is; unreachable; untouchable; indefinable; unthinkable; immeasurable; appalling.

A sneaky hyena taking a man's hand when he's not looking, snapping the bone in one crunch and the blood fountaining, splashing out like a gargantuan Roman candle.

A staring into the gloaming, seeing something that's at once there and isn't, something looming, something dreadful.

The dull, dead, dreary-beyond-dreary feeling of palpable, unbearable emptiness, hopelessness, wretchedness, despair.

The dolorous doldrums mingling miserably with the howling fantods.

Kites sampling the intestines of your inner Prometheus.

Your pores ponging like a bad brisket sandwich left out in the Texas sun.

Sharp glass shards slowly-gently pressed into your tender toenails just as you come out of a long hot bath.

Hideous, nightmare-ish—like trying to swim to safety in a pool of coldest syrup.

Just a blankness falling freely falling through you, morbidly gloomy and beyond melancholic.

A bitterly grievous shocking shriek on a whitely foggy night.

"Prufrock" divested of the funny bits.

The Waste Land stripped of…nothing.

What one kneeling before being decapitated must feel.

It's an awakening in a cold and misty wood, and knowing you're lost in it, and the terrifying feeling just after you've called out in your loudest, most desperate and hollow and give-away voice that your cries might just as easily summon a vicious circle of wolves in a wolfpack or a buccaneering, unbreakfasted bear as it might bring any help at all—a blind Boy Scout on crutches with no topo map and a severely low IQ or summon in another lost loser like you who's maybe a closet cannibal?

Ha!

And the horror right there—a bat flying at your face again and again: it's *not* giving up on getting one of your eyes, maybe both, till it gets one at least. There: a puff adder that's got into your tent, then your sleeping bag. There it is; it's on your leg; it's got you; it's *got* you. Nice puff adder. Nice boy. Please don't bite me, please. Please don't.

And then you scream.

It's a deadly, banal, boring person droning at you at a party that never ends, never seems to be about to, and even when it does, he follows you home, this boring bore, matching your steps along the cold rain-wet dully-sparkling cobblestones, or down the pink crunchy cinder path by the public park where you try unsuccessfully to dodge him; he gets his foot in your front door (you essay to get *yours* in his *ass*, but he artfully dodges your every ridiculous kick; he laughs and bares his unspeakable teeth; jigs 'round your dining table top; dances a hornpipe on your sofa; clicking his heels he demands to know what's for afternoon tea *for the next six days at least*—and then when you don't respond he folds his arms most petulantly and retreats to a corner for a major sulk; then when you least expect it he spins 'round and trots over to your fridge and helps himself to a slice of iced lemon cake, skimming up some extra icing, scalping another part of it, the cake).

You can't think where you know him from. He seems oddly/vaguely familiar but for the life of you you can't place him. He doesn't seem to be *leaving*. Not anytime soon.

Now he's got your *carving knife*, the sharpest, most formidable one in the rhombus-y woodblock; he posts it into the smack-middle of your kitchen table, said knife, then plucks it out again; smirks.

What do you think you're going to do with that? you ask. You bastard, you add.

Where's your cat? he says.

I haven't got a cat.

I heard it, you liar.

I don't know what you heard—but you didn't hear a cat.

I heard its craven meow. I heard it fucking scratching in your cat box. No one has a stinking cat box if they haven't got a stinking cat to go stinking with it.

I do.

Don't give me that. You lie. Fetch it. Fetch the feline fucker for me! Fetch that fucking feline fucker. Now!

[What the hell. What's the difference? You hate that cat anyway. It eats, sleeps, shits, hunts, eats, shits, prowls, sleeps, eats, hunts, sleeps, shits, eats, prowls, hunts. *It's like a fucking aristocrat from the Eighteenth Cent!* Fuck it. Fuck that cat. He can have it.]

Here. Take it. Take it and bore it to death, why don't you? Like you did me, you stonily say.

I'm going to scalp this cat while you watch in horror. See how boring you find *that*.

Go ahead, you say... Where the devil do I know you from, anyway? How do I know you? I know you from somewhere—I just can't place you. [quietly] You devil.

Really?! It's okay if I scalp it? he says.

Sure.

You're sure?

I just said so.

Quite positive?

Why not?

[Narrowly, incredulous, almost offended,] Sanctioning me lopping of the top of Pussy's purring head, are you now?

I don't mind. Help yourself. See if *I* care. Be my guest. Go right ahead. Have at it. There's a whetstone if the knife's not sharp enough for your liking.

Honestly?

Fine. You didn't answer my question. Who the fuck are you—and what the fuck do you want, anyway?

Quite sure?

I just said so: what are you waiting for, bore? Scalp him. Scalp him good. Scalp him well, I mean.

[Up he holds Kitty. By the scruff, what else. You shrug one shoulder slightly, narrow glazed eyes, blink your ineffable indifference, place your arms akimbo, tilt your tired head.]

Not gonna stop me? says your intruding interlocutor. Stay my hand? Wrestle me to the ground and turn the blade to my bared neck? Threaten to end me?

Fuck off, twat. You wouldn't be worth it, whoever you are.

No: fuck *you*, you fuck.

Go fuck yourself, you stupid boring fucking cuntface. Look at your *face*! Just look at it! It's a cunt, all right. It *is!*

Make me, fucker. Make me fuck myself, why don't you?

I'm not gonna help you. You *are* fucked, so *eat my fuck*, you cunt bitch.

Suck my fuck, fucker.

Eat me.

Blow me.

Bite me.

Bite your*self* with those nasty green teeth you've got, you boring bore, you say.

Are you getting bored of calling me boring? Who's boring whom now, huh? And *don't* talk about my teeth, fucker!

Ha! Everyone else does! You come boring into a room, and it's all anyone can do not to laugh and point and go: "La, look at them diabolical choppers on that poor beast! Just you *look* at those creepy, viscous, crapulous green things—disgusting! He's not stopping at just making the whole room yawn; he's got to gross everyone out with those…"

They don't. They do not. They never.

They do. Every time. Always.

Never.

Always. Everyone stops and gawks. Everyone.

Liar! They wouldn't *dare!*

Kid yourself—go ahead. You're like the *bad Tooth* Fairy. A monster. You fucking Stonehenge-face. You…you… Do you know what you look like?

No: tell me.

You really want me to?

Be my guest.

Sure you can take it?

Give it all you got. See if you can hurt me! Go ahead. Try.

It's going to be a bit anticlimactic now, though.

I don't mind.

Sure?

This is boring!

Oh, *now* he gets it! That's rich.

Just say it. Unless you're too scared to. I mean...

[long pause; very uncomfortable.]

You look like a pumpkin carved by drunken retards! Or a walking set of Jerry Lewis-ish joke dentures.

That all you got? [pause] I do not. Take that back.

Put down the imaginary cat.

The cat's not imaginary! I have it here!

You *did*, but it got away and now you're just a crashing bore with a pretend knife in your hand.

Am not. The knife's real too.

Ha!

Meanie!

Ha!

That's it. I'm never leaving! I'm stopping with you for*ever!*

Fine. Take the spare room—except there isn't any.

Not gonna leave.

Okay. Make yourself right at home. Take one of the bedrooms. Take my wife...

Please.

Funny.

Sure?

About what?

No objections?

I've just told you, you squeal. [in a most threatening tone—the fake breeziness has been summarily jettisoned] Make yourself at home—move...right...in. See if I care. Let me get you a marigold pillow *and* a comforting comforter. Like a nice pale blue goose down one? There's a blue and a lovely fluffy black with a just-washed slipcover. I could bring you in an egg nog or a nice hot cup of tea. There's cocoa—I have some of that. I could warm some up for you right now and plop a nicens bit of strawberry marshmallow into it, if you like. They have designer marshmallows now, if you didn't know. Nothing like a nice hot cup of nice hot strawberry marshmallow cocoa to cozy you up real cinnamon good. Make you feel right welcome and the rest of it. Go on, sit down. Take a load off.

Think I will, thanks. You're quite sure?

Positively. You must be exhausted going 'round that party exasperating everyone and bringing them down. Making them panic like that seeing you heading over, assailing them with some topic they couldn't give a fuck about. Looking 'round for an escape hatch, someone to nod to in order to excuse themselves. You've been hard at work tonight. You're regular royalty at it, making people want to kill themselves to get away from your utter uninterestingness. You're like a baronet of it! A baronet of boringness. Ladies and gentlemen, the Baronet of Boreshire, the Earl of Yawns! What do I call you, anyway?

Finished?

Uh-huh.

Said all you wanted to?

Maybe.

And you really don't mind if I stay here a while?

Oh not at all. Not at *all*.

[darkly] You wouldn't be funning me, now? Having me on?

Not a bit of it.

Mean what you say?

See what I mean?

Pardon?

Sorry?

What?

[Intensely penetrating.] *Why?*

Huh?

What do you think you're doing here, anyway? Who do you think you *are?* Get the hell out of my house. Now! This isn't some play. This isn't some fucking stage or something. Sir Harold's not directing this. There's no Frobsher Peabody waiting in the wings, tapping the wainscoting, wanting to give us notes on our perf…Listen, you: you can't just come barging in here posing as some boring character in a boring setting in a boring play!

Oh no?

No?

Can't I?

Leave! [now eyes narrow as they can get, as can be got.] *Who do you think you are?!*

Huh?

I said: Who do you think you are?

Who do *you* think I am?

Sorry?

[Methodically, slowly, rhythmically.] I said "Who do *you* think I am?" Tell me.

I just told you: you're some fucking boring bore who's a nuisance to the world, basically. You ruined a perfectly nice party, then you barnacled yourself to me the rest of the night, at my elbows and heels like a flipping corgi, like one of those horrible ankle-biters; then you came crashing crashingly in here, boring me left and right, going on and on endlessly about essentially *nothing*; and now when you've been asked to leave—quite politely, I might add—you make even more of an annoyance of yourself and…What do you think you're doing, anyway? Get the fuck out. Get the fuck out of here.

What? You just asked me to stay! You *like* me. You *want* me around.

The fuck I do. I was being sarcastic. Go on, you. Out! Now. Scram! Are you so fucking thick that you can't even tell when someone's being…

No.

No?

No, thank you.

That's better. Very good.

What is?

Nothing.

This is ridiculous, he says. I'm not finished yet. What's the matter—don't you like me?

I don't b*elieve* you. I can't b*elieve* this! You're done here, chum. Piss off now. Time for you to be on your way. Let me get you a helmet.

A what?

A helmet.

What might I need a helmet for?

You're always *crashing*, you crashing bore. That's what crashing bores by definition do. They go crashing around crashing into things…and people. Hence…

Who—*me?*

Yes. Bye. See you. Find someone else to harass and annoy.

Me?

Who else?

Me?

What kind of fucking idiot are you, anyway? Yes, me—I mean you. Goddammit! Leave, please. Please?! Avaunt and quit my sight!

Well. All right, then. I'm tired of having you in a metaphorical headlock, anyway. I know when I'm not wanted.

[He gets up from the couch perhaps where, having left the kitchen, he's been parked, sighs and pads toward the front door. He's nearly there, it's looking good in terms of him exiting, but then—unable to help yourself, knowing better but going ahead anyway—*you* say…]

No, you don't.

What?

You don't. Know when you're not wanted. Or you'd have left hours ago.

You invited me, though. And if you really wanted me to beat it, you wouldn't keep interjecting things.

[beat] *I* did? I invited you. You, an in*sufferable* bore.

Naturally.

You must be joking.

Oh, no. Not in the least.

Of course you are.

Not a chance.

Go on.

I'm *you*, don't you see? I'm you! *I* am *you*. You can't get rid of me. I'm yourself. You can't get rid of your*self*. How in the world do you imagine you could do that? Impossible! Short of suicide, of course. When someone's you, yourself then you're stuck with them. You're who you are and that's that. Surely you must see *that*. I'm you. Your very own self. *And* your own personal paltry little stupid doltish insignificant dumb lame deaf blind drunk fucked ludicrous utterly nonsensical big, fat horribly unbudgeable dull gray stabbingly boring hellaciously silly little completely absurd unbelievably grinding relentlessly yawning caustic banally atrocious nice friendly little captious crapulous dingy dumb fucking preposterously ponderous endless nervous breakdown. You have to confront you: you're having a nervous breakdown. It's what they're *about*.

Uh, all right.

Uh-huh. Like, hel*lo*. About time. And you in effect invited me in. Of course I got my foot in the door. Of course. But who opened the door I got my foot in, huh? Who did? You did. You, that's who.

Really.

Absolutely. Why are you resisting this?

Why stop there, then? That all you got?

Ahem! Let's see: vicious, noxious, nettlesome, niggling, noisome, nullifying, no-good nervous breakdown. Hounding, harrowing lingering, stupidly-dopily, menacing, dungeon-dark, and dripping with stink, with foulness and pestilence, oozing odors, an ecstacy of ugliness and self-blight.

Okay, then. Have a seat, won't you? Get comfy. Sit back down. Get comfy.

All right.

Fine. Charming. Wonderful.

Don't mind if I do. Plus *you like me.*

You're serious!

You do.

You're kidding!

You want me here. Admit it. You like this. You're into it. All the flippant facetiousness in the world's not going to mask that. You're wallowing. It's an active passive thing, when you think about it.

Oh? Oxymoronic and all of that.

Yes. [beat] I'm not so boring now, am I? Not quite the rude boor you thought I was.

Yes, you are, actually.

[Small-ly] I know. It's just the way it is. In the grand scheme of things. One person's sorry little meltdown is just…

You do? Rubbish! You *know* you're a total bore? 'Cause most bores don't even…

Uh-huh. No avoiding it. I'm *terribly* boring—not just boring boring. And there's just nothing either you or I (or I should say "we or I") can do about it.

Nothing?

Nope.

Thought not.

There you are, then.

Flat-out fucked. It's too bad, really.

Indeed.

Completely.

Agreed.

How long are you going to stay, anyway? Your voice, by the way, is incredibly grating. It's like an unfledged owl that's been stepped on by a junior high school bully.

That's up to you, how long I stay. Or should I say I/you it's up to. Up to us. But just you, really. You alone are in this together with me, who's you, if you get what I've been telling you so uninterestingly for the past half hour or so.

You don't have to get personal. So…defensive and sensitive and tetchy. You're looking at me like I just shot a baby penguin in the face.

348   John Andrew Fredrick

How can it be avoided? Of course we are.

And there's no helping it?

Not now.

Later, though? Maybe?

We'll see. Wait and see.

So it's like a psychodrama of one.

Fair enough.

And there's going to be nothing to...

Ameliorate it? No. Not at all. Good word, though. Nice diction. And think about it: in a way, you've already made friends with it, with me, with your breakdown.

Friends? Regular old buddies?

Definitely. Want me to bake you a batch of pity-biscuits?

Very funny. Wait. So it's an...an...allegorical...

Tête à tête with yourself. That's right.

Tête à tête with myself. But a harrowing one, of course.

Of course. Much worse than what you've encountered dealing with me. Wait till I leave and you're on your own...with you.

I see. All right. One more question, though? Why, if you are me and I am you, do you have such fucked *teeth*, then? Sorry to bring it up so blatantly. But I mean, mine are...

Perfect, almost?

Well, yes.

Straight and white and upper middle class?

Yeah. Of course. What else? You're not going to go taking umbrage now or anything...

Why should I? No. Think about the "alter" in alterego. Something's got to be opposite, hasn't it?

Oh. Right.

[Smiling "toothily"] Uh-huh. Exactly. The darkside's gotta have a *dark side*, if you know what I mean.

I get it.

Precisely. Now: let's get started. Get going getting going... nowhere. Ha! Let's get to work sending you reeling and swirling for the next, oh, how about a nice archetypal three days in a row—just for starters? How's that sound? There'll probably be a couple more—that's par for the course for the condition we're in here—but an archetypal three days at the start sounds just about right. Let's get you *so* depressed, feeling so *o*ppressed, that you stare at one or two of these nice walls, basically, for three *as I said* days, and see how you do initially, hmm? Excellent. Sound good? I'll come back on—let's see—Sunday or Saturday, perhaps, to check on you and see how poorly (or in reverse terms *well*) you're doing at this. I won't say "with" as that's a prepositional ambiguity I don't think I have to explain here. Then we'll take it from there. See what wants doing. All righty? That okay with you? You might as well say yes 'cause it has to be; you've no alternative, you realize. You're stuck with you.

Okay. I suppose. Thank you.

Oh, don't *mention* it. My pleasure. Can't say it's *yours*, of course—but you know what I mean. Goodbye now. I'm taking just about everything about you—your sense of self, identity, sense of humor for sure—with me. Your sense of humor: you'll be needing it, but you won't have it; there's the rub. I can't help you, you know. Only you can do that. And probably not even you can help you. It depends on what happens. It completely depends on you—and it doesn't at all, you understand. You're stuck. And you have no idea what's in store for you. Words I could use like "You're going to feel as exquisite and yet as dull and blank as silver paper" would, will, can have no effect on you. Impress you not in the slightest, you see. Because your feeling is going to be the absence of all…Well, I won't spoil it! Ha! *You* will. Hahaha. I will say that you're going to wonder, once we get started, if it will never end, if you will ever come out of it, what you're about to go into. Understand? No? Of course you don't. I could tell you that, when you're done, if one is ever done breaking down (there's a bit of eschatatolgy for you!), that you're not going to be able to describe what's happened to you any more than I can tell you right now what it's going to be like. In other words, we'll both be wasting our breaths. People go and talk about "indescribable" things. Isn't that funny? They have to try. Fools! They talk—or try to—about things they say are indescribable. How ridiculous. How perfectly contradictory and, well, frankly, *human* (i.e. stupid). I *could* tell you that it's a living limbo or a purgatory-in-life, a hell you can and can't feel, and you'd still have no reckoning of what I'm talking about. None. There's *really* nothing more to say. So you may as well begin.

I know.

No, you don't.

Well, then. Be seeing you.

Goodbye, then. Good luck. Though that's of course. You'll be lucky if you…

Good*bye!*

Part Fou

One

ell, then, how d'ye do again, reader? How are yas faring with mine little storybookling? Fairly fatigued with all this tall talk of depression and ennui? Well, I shall spare your lord-and-ladyships any further excavation of the doldrums, any more exfoliation of the aforesaid blank, tiny-big terrors and get on with the tale, get on with life, as life itself and all of us must inexorably do.

So, Jenny came back from work that night to find me like a human cloudburst, acid rain variety, sitting slumpen in the reading chair, unshowered, unshaved, unshriven. I had not answered the phone (not that it rang off the hook anyway—one of the worst things when you are coming down from the at once frenzied and frozen activity of a whirly indie rock band tour is how nothing regular-issue good old everyday existence is) or "done" anything but sit there in the gray reading chair in our room and memorize this wall, that one. At that stage, early on as it was, I couldn't have defended myself against a cream puff or a milquetoast; nor bested even an individually-wrapped packet of tea. Yeah I was down, all right. I did hoist myself up effortfully all of once to turn on the telly long enough to in turn my stomach as this was the day of the vigil for poor Cobain.

The "News" was of course all over it. Tori Telegenic and Michele Microphony and Carl or Cathy Cathoderay were shoving their mics in the faces of any plaid-garbed-fuck they could find malingering miserably 'round the general vicinity of The Space Needle. The grunge crowd with their sad, long mugs in symmetry-synch with their mopey, long locks—I could take all of five minutes of it, the mock-empathetic reporters acting seriously sorrowful and the great unwashed/inarticulate getting the op to be on the box and parade a few spare feelings.

I had better, sadder things to do. I switched the television off and got back to business, the business of breaking down.

And it was work, you know: it takes persevering at; you've got to be committed, committed to putting your "all" into feeling wretched; it's nigh on impossible, in fact, to *have* a nervous breakdown without keeping it going...breaking...farther down. You can't just *sit* there. Hahaha! I laugh cause that's exactly what you do do! (There won't be much more of this, don't fret; we're nearly at the end of it. Supposed self-dubbed regal guy, king of good *etcetera* that I am, I'm not going to Richard The Second you to death here and drag this out so that I may as well ask you to "sit upon the ground and tell sad stories of the death of kings" and have you feel like reaching right into this novel and throttling me, "choking me out," doing me harm.)

Jenny was, of course, alarmed and "had never seen me like this." Fucking A—*I* had never seen me like this, either, my dear. She knelt there, before me, oh so differently from the sexy genuflections I was telling you about earlier. And of course you can imagine now, if you would be so kind, her asking me repeatedly what was wrong? (Of course *I* didn't know; plus, the answer could only be *Everything. Everything's wrong.*) If there was something she could do? (Nothing.) If there wasn't anything she could do? (No, I'm sorry you have to see me like this, Jen. So sorry. Really.) If I wouldn't she would rather put off her long-scheduled trip to see her music mastering martinet father up north in Northern California? (No, not for the world? Please don't worry—I'll snap out of this.) If I was quite sure it was something I was gonna "snap out of"? (Probably not, I said with bitter humor.) If I knew how much she loved me and hoped I would be better sooner than later? (I did. I would. I thought. Who knew?) If I knew how smart and talented and accomplished and driven and unique I was? (And dashing, and devastatingly handsome, and Bondlike, and Mozartian?) And dashing and devastatingly handsome and charming? (And charming? Some charm, Jen, real endearing...I'm really fucked up here.) She said she knew; she asked if I didn't need maybe to "see" someone, talk to "someone," get help? (No, I don't think so. Thank you, Jenny—really. Go on your trip to visit your dad. Thank you; I love you too, I said as though I was trying to convince myself.)

And off she went that night to south of San Francisco, a sleepy super-suburban place called San Carlos, to see her bad dad whom I'll tell you about when I get around to it. But not before she left me forty bucks that I left for as long as I could where she set them, the two mortifyingly ignominious twenties—on the dresser. And not before she asked me again and again and again and again and again if I really, really, really, really, really wouldn't rather she stayed and looked after me.

No. I would be fine, I lied.

Keating was not in evidence for the next three days, all weekend and the Friday—or maybe he just came home at four hundred in the morning—so I had the whole entire vast frosty apartment to myself and my anhedonic self. Maybe I didn't hear him come in or something but, seeing as I was up for three days, unable to sleep, I reckon I would have heard him come in, even though he's quiet as a lamb. It must be, the way he causes no disruption ever whatsoever, because he's got his head in some wanker's turned-to-eleven Marshall stack all day at his studio; or some horn player with a chip on his shoulder the size of Ontario's blaring away at him from all of two feet six inches. Keating's funny. I keep on threatening to introduce you to him, but he's just not around, and—last mention—one must remember that neither am I. I'm gone.

After three days of the modulating mulligrubs, of memorizing the walls, as I said, of doing a swell job of not washing, not cleaning the teeth, not napping, not caring, I had a sort of a singular revelation. I thought to myself: *Thus far, you've been the sort of person who, in careful consideration of his problem, his predicament, his plight, the sort of person, I say, who says "I am gonna take this lying down!" That's been* you. *Now: Let's try a new you; let's essay a fresh angle, shall we. I know,* I said to myself. *I've got it! What if I try and drink my way out of this?!* Maybe in the not-so-distant past you've tried to think your way out of things; now try the aforementioned. That's it, thunk I. I'm gonna try and drink my way out of this! You reach a point with a cold or flu, dontchu, when you *Eureka!* and pop down to the old walk-in liquor closet and go: "Right, you sniffling, sniveling, craven fucker. Right you sorry, sordid *affliction*. I've got just the antidote to *you*. I'm going to drown you, you bastard, with the help of my old friends Jack or Jim or Scotch or Mark as in "Makers." You've fucking had it now, illness; your hours are numbered. We've all done that. Feed a fever, get a cold or flu fucked up. Granny's old adage, innit. Your Irish Gran, at least. That was her all over. All over the floor, that is. Laid out like a late carpet. Gurgling Celtic and making out with a pin cushion, her great battleax bustier nearly up over her hoary head like a fencing or a surgical mask "at ease," her great, billowy knickers in more of a tornado than just the obligatory twist.

So what'd I do, you shouldn't wonder, about my realization and subsequent decision to get my old pal Al Cohol involved in my situation? Well of course now I plucked up the plucky funds from the likesay bureau top where Jenny'd plunked them down and hied me to The Glug Store for some budget tequila and margarita mix. Johnson told Boswell, apparently, that a man in my state, a man with "constitutional melancholy," must needs "divert distressing thoughts, and not combat with them." Fuckin' A. I knew a diversion tactic that you could buy at any market you stumbled in to. I had a plan. A plan at fucking last. I hadn't eaten, hadn't slept, hadn't bathed. Other than that, I'd taken real good care of myself. I needed a plan. A plan for Johnsonian diversion. I must've missed the road so much these past few days that I was trying to simulate still being on it while simultaneously remaining stationed, save a few feeble bathroom or inconclusive kitchen trips, at my chair.

The closest liquor store from where we lived on Lorraine wasn't within rambling distance so I psyched myself up for yet another bike ride on Jenny's white bicycle—put a cardigan on (inside out but what matterethed that, forsooth, when I meself was inside out indeed), shod myself with just-washed Converse All-Stars from under-the-bed, and sallied forth storeward.

Mistake.

For when the clerk rang up my purchase (a sixer of Becks, one bottle cut-rate tequila, two limes, one liter Margarita Mix, one little airline bottle Grand Marnier) the bill came to 45.41 dollars. Now you know I only had forty bucks to work with, the amt. Jen had left me. Something had to be sacrificed. We all know we have to make sacrifices sometimes in life, right? So of course I sacrificed the Grand Mariner cause if you have to make cutbacks well you'd better just reconcile breaking-down self to having regular margaritas rather than Cadillac ones.

"Got a Band-Aid to go with that?" I asked in too-stentorian a voice as the clerk made adjustments to the bill.

"Vhat?" said he.

"Can I have a *Band-Aid* with that, please?"

"We don't zell Band-Aids here, zir. Why you need Band-Aid?"

"Why? 'Cause you just *gouged the hell out of me* and I am *bleeding* all over your *shop*," says me.

Blank look returned.

"You guys sell sleeping pills, by any chance?"

"No, zir."

"You ought to. You must take them yourselves! How else would you ever sleep at night?"

"Goodbye, zir. Have good day."

"Yeah yeah yeah."

"Dat's vhat Beatles zed."

"Real funny."

Let's get back to the story here: permit me to try one more time to tell you what it's like, breaking down: you itch, you do, like a hopeless scoreless junkie. Your skin isn't yours somehow, that thing you live in—*gone*. You live the adage "He's not comfortable in his own skin." Now you know what those pundits, mystics, bodhisattvas who coined that shit were fucking talking about. No matter how quiet it is, where you are and all, it's loud as hell. Pandemonium-in-the-head holds sway and you can't make it stop. People get depressed, just regular-old quotidian down, they usually go to sleep for as long as they can, retreat into the dreamlife and hope not to wake up one day. You have a real breakdown, it's the opposite: you remain awake for days and days, not being able to turn you off. At least that was my experience. It might be different for others—whoever they are. You see: they, those others, don't matter when *you're* going through it, having it out with life itself. Sad/true. You don't wanna ever be the kinda guy who fucks-a-give about nobody but himself; but nervous breakdowners just can't do that, just can't care. There's no one but you, the you whom you don't even wanna be anymore. Does this make sense to you? God, I hope not.

You keep on tearing at your sweatshirt, sweater, favorite T-shirt, turning it into a V-neck. You can't bear to have even your trusty gold and blue St. Christopher touching your neck, dandled over your figuratively crushed chest. You can't bear to take it off. What if it's a talisman? What if it's a lucky charm? You aren't taking any chances, spiritually speaking. You'll pray to any god or totem or fetish object or farfetched Nobodaddy in *The Encyclopedia Britannica* or the history of religion. Your crotch, when you catch an unlucky whiff of it, is a Romanian weightlifter's backup gym bag, the one that's languished unlaundered in the corner of his basement these thirteen weeks; imagine a dreamscape by a young and especially foul-tempered Ingmar Bergman after a bad night, sleepless and querulous, in wintertide Sweden; it's the unbrushed breath of a four-time kimchee-eating contest winner; the armpit of any spotty putrid teenage boy off any red-blooded American-football-playing street; it's the milk you mindlessly left out on the counter before you went away for a week; it's a smelly devil, yeah: it's alive. Lot's wife well could have told you "Don't look!" But you never met her, did you? It's been forever and a day since you've read *The Bible*. That's a-gonna change. You're starting soon as you can find it amidst your pretty Penguins in jumpsuit orange and thick jet black and shiny Plumber's Plastic gray.

Two

ow, when Jenny had left she'd checked, really checked, with me to see if I had rather she didn't go; and like a good and selfless boyfriend I had told her please, not to even think of it, I'm perfectly fine, don't worry about me (but do—go ahead—I'm a mess and I know it—this is fucked—what a drag). It was one of those very much unspoken things between two people who know each other so intimately well that many key discussions are about things that don't really need to be discussed because both parties know what should go down in the dim midst between them that they indeed see themselves and each other through. She knew that my already-guilt for letting myself get so uselessly low would accelerate if over-concern for me was the cause of her missing seeing her father; and we both knew that I was in no shape to be seen going through what it was obvious that I had to go through. I said goodbye to her like you say bye-bye to someone going off to summer camp. With the wishfullest wishes and all godspeed you fare thee well.

There are two kinds of people in this very troubled world: people you like, and people you don't. Jung, co-father of course of all things psychological, said there were two categories too: extraverts and introverts. Nice one, Carl. Quite right. But there are also these: people who want, when they're sick, to be left the fuck alone to ail and suffer and sniffle and sob *solus*; and people who want attention and solicitous nursemaids of any sort and cups of herbal lemon nutmeg tea made with love and shit and all organic of course and brought to them on oyster-colored gold-rimmed salvers interlarded with Medieval mosaics of Persian or Prussian blue and purest verdigris.

My tone ought well inform you of which mind I incontrovertibly am.

Sorry for the convoluted syntax but I am just trying to amuse myself in a boring world. Aren't you?

Do what you will, kind and gentle reader, but *I* want to go into a hole and verily die when I have the flu or leprosy or something—and the same goes when I am head (as in psyche-spirit-mind) or heart sick. Same deal. Quarantined dreams are what I want to dream.

Three

hus, in the wake of my voluptuous sadness/aloneness and borderline catalepsy it was weird when Jen came back from her trip on the Tuesday night of the week after we'd come back from tour. It was strange 'cause I could tell that she felt like something of an intruder in her own home, a home she paid my rent on. She was being timid and awkward, like she was fencing around something or other—probably me, the idea of asking, really asking, how I was doing. A lot of times, someone you care about/love, you may not wanna *know* the extent to which they're fucked up. That's understandable. Like you're protecting both of you. Scream and stomp all you very want, ladies and sensitive gents, about the "i" word, but there's got to be such a thing as being too in-the-know about your SO. You've taken them on, love-wise, relationshiply-speaking, now you gotta take their intimate shit on. To some extent for sure you do. It's not always or even often pleasant. That's why the vogue term for it is "Significant Other," as referenced beforehand/above. Stuff's significant now; it *means* shit—it affects you and you can sweep it under the carpet, as they say, but it's there, like the dust and the lint and the shed skin and the hair you've lodged under the emotional Persian rug with your love-

broom. You've gotta sweep *some*thing. You can't just stand there with the love-broom in your mitt. Couples who tell you, all crowy-like, that they "deal with stuff with each other as soon as it comes up"—bullshit. Bullshit, horseshit, dogshit, just shit. *We* talk it out and work it out immediately, right away," they chirrup smugly and look at each other all coupley, full-on dew-eyed. Nonsense. Nobody can do that. You dealt with everything, right away, that comes up between two people who live together and fuck occasionally and dream together and scheme together and "discuss" who hasn't done the washing up and the fucking hoovering and the paying the gas bill and the fellatio and the cunnilingus, you'd do nothing *but* talk about "what's really going on between you." You'd have no fun or time for yourself whatsoever. Everybody sweeps stuff under the rug. Agreed: the *less* you sweep the better. Do it too much and you have a fucking attack armadillo or resentment badger of *relationshit* stuff under your rug and he's grown, like, sabre-tooth tiger teeth and a Francis Bacon-horrorhead and he's hungry and unpredictable and, most importantly, quick and *vicious*.

Jenny and I had this inside joke when things got pretty bad in the old we're starting to wear on each other's nerves department: did you ever see *Repo Man*? The cult classic, quintessential quirkfest eighties flick? Otto, this callous fucker, just takes the fuck off on his girlfriend, splits; and as he's leaving, she goes, "But *Otto*—what about our re*lat*ionship?!" All exaggeratedly whingey and stuff. And Otto, classically, screws up his fucked face and goes: "Fuck *that*." So anyway, when things got baddish one of us, to relieve the tension, would go "But *Otto*…"

Ah, philosophy.

I sometimes wondered whether we made a jest of it, of "us," because we both of us were fundamentally pessimistic about "relationships" to begin with.

The good things re: Jenny and me—well, not *really* good, but kinda/sorta good—were a) that I was snapping out of it, pretty much burned out on being down; and b) she had the usual massive migraine that visiting her dad usually brought on. Of course I am being facetious here: I have never had a migraine but from the looks of it it looks absolutely appalling, like something you wouldn't wish on your worst enemy or any of the odious Boston Celtics, those biters and whiners—not even horrible Kevin McHale or the dreaded Ainge or the even worse Dennis Johnson, that freckle-faced fuck.

"I left you messages," Jen said. "A couple, I think. You know how my dad runs me ragged when I go home. Did you get them?"

"I didn't check the answering machine once, I don't think. I must've heard the phone ring, but…"

"Oh, honey."

She must've been aware that I, in a normal state, would've been anxious/concerned about any news from our label, and, when healthy and somewhat happy, would dive on any ringing phone like a G.I. trying to save his buddy from "getting it" from a Nazi hand-grenade.

"I'm not so bad now. It was just dark, you know. You have a headache?"

"Mmm. Terrible."

"Go lie down—make you some herbal tea? You must be completely knackered. Put on your pajamas and get into bed."

"Thank you. I think I'll change the sheets first," Jenny said.

"Probably a good idea," I said.

Jenny had some very soft classical going on the bedside boom box we had next to our vast California King, king-size Slumberking, and I brought the tea in and set it down in the room she had to have dark as dark could be when she got a migraine.

"Here you go."

"Thanks, John."

She only really uses my first name when things are really good or really bad. And we both knew the tea was just a gesture, most times; she just wanted kindness. The tea, in her super-sensitive state, would make her wretch and choke, most like.

"You had an awful time?"

"You know. I've told you. My dad just shows me off to this just endless stream of guests when I go back to visit him. It's worse somehow than when I gave recitals as a little kid. 'Play the Chopin!' he demands while he's has having these little old ladies serve him coffee and just pounds of pound and coffee cake. I never get a break just to relax up there."

"I'm sorry," I said. "That sucks."

"And of course he rags on me about playing rock music."

"And on me?"

"Of course. Always."

"What a *snarge*," I said.

"Totally. People never change. They just don't," she added lugubriously.

"Try and sleep now. I'll come in later and rub your feet and go down on you."

"Okay."

She didn't even laugh. Probably would've hurt too much to. Poor Jen. Sucks.

"Just kidding about the foot rub," I joked.

"Okay," she said with a pained, wan smile. Poor Jen, I remember thinking. Must be bad. Worse than usual.

We had this thing where sometimes I would lick her nice and slow when she got migrainey—sometimes an orgasm-flash would "help" or at least attenuate the otherwise indomitable pain. Plus I liked taking care of her in that way, licking her till she writhed and breathed faster and faster and came. I know I've told you that I didn't really love our sex life but oddly, symbiotically, I was just as much of a pleaser as she was; and I loved Jen, I really did, and do. Going down on her didn't always help her. Maybe twenty-five percent of the time. But I was happy to do it: what guy's not gonna be? Plus, sometimes, when we were having sex and she was on top of me she made these faces that were disturbing—like she was another person. Of course we all know that that face, since it was categorized in the immortal film *Office Space* as "The 'O' Face," can be just as funny as it can be a fright. But Jenny made really distressing ones that no way in the world would a polite or even marginally sane person allude to: her pride would receive a sort of mortal wound, I knew, if I ever even hinted that—again, sometimes, not all the time—she freaked me out when she orgasmed. It was all the more "coupley" and a singularly strange thing between two people in the wake of the fact that, in intermittent moments of tenderness and letting her guard down, she would tell me sometimes that she loved how I looked when I came inside her, that I looked so peaceful and happy and, yes, grateful and even "beautiful."

How odd we all are, each of us, every one; all and sundry a cloud of unknowing.

Her dad, though?—what a fucking *fucker*, speaking of odd, speaking of unsightly. I had only met him once, and that was enough, thank you very much. The kind of guy—well, *ogre*, which was our nickname for the sad sod, "The Ogre"—the kind of guy, I say, whose goddam periwinkle or tangerine *ascot* gets in the way of him giving *anyone* (and especially a guitarist/singer-songwriter who's dating his daughter, living with her) a chance or a break. Fat, gammy, rheumy, whiny; dissatisfied, moochy, know-all, crabby; sad, tragic, woebegone, wheezing; snobby, superior, rude, bumptious; hectoring, greedy, irresponsible, improvident; captious, caustic, acrimonious, fractious; capricious, pampered, put-upon, scheming; over-busy but ultimately indolent; baleful, *strange* (weird voice, ghastly mirth-free laugh), toadying, obsequious; sycophantic, calculating, quixotic, querulous; choleric, arrogant, cantankerous, belligerent; contemptuous, sneering, domineering, haughty; miffy, rancorous, paranoid, fraudulent; virulent, tetchy, dumpish, greedy; fretful, catty, splenetic, nettlesome; meddlesome, derisive, censorious, closed-minded; quisling, priggish, woulda-coulda-shoulda-ish; churlish, oafish (kind of a churl-oaf), prematurely emeritus; whingeing, monomaniacal, sanctimonious, toffee-nosed; dabbling, *amateurish*, grasping, sentimental; name-dropping, proud, loud, vain; dandyish, meretricious, sententious, brazen; overbearing, pontificating, fussy, cynical; invidious, perfidious, ridiculous, censorious; defeated, effete in a kind of *macho* way, garrulous in a taciturn kind of way, didactic, dolorous, explosive, diva-like; humbugging, pretentious, maudlin, self-centered, narcissistic, megalomaniacal, mouth-breathing, woebegone, curmudgeonly, and just plain *lame*, Jenny's dad, *Ted* (a snarge's name if there ever was, the *snarge*), just wasn't really all that cool of a guy.

"Plus phoney," I could imagine hearing Jenny's sad-heavy voice going: "Don't forget that. I can't prove it, but I think he's Romanian or or or Bulgarian or something and he shaved off the 'escu' or 'ovich' from our last name in order to Anglicize it. I just know he did. Transylvanian, probably, like a…va…I don't even want to say it. An emotional…what's that term you used the other day? Emotional phlebotomist. I don't hate him. I don't. Well, okay, I do. But…I just…I don't, *really*. Anyway…the name change thing: he won't admit it, but it's true. He's totally ashamed of his heritage; totally; I guess it must come from growing up in the thirties or something when people were openly prejudiced against Eastern Europeans or something. He must've thought he wouldn't get jobs playing in big bands in the Big Band Era and on albums in the witch hunt fifties like he did if he went by the 'escu' or whatever. Ignorant Americans thinking he was a communist or something. A 'Red.' But still, how sad. My dad's only 'politics' consists of 'making contacts' for his next two-bit home grown down home job playing weddings and bar mitzvahs, that's the extent of them, you know. Or sub-contracting them out. Unbelievable. That plus scheming about how he can get me to quit playing rock music and go back to practicing piano for nine hours a day and hating him *and* my life. No *thank* you, dad. Go live your own life now. Have another waffle. Have one with strawberries and extra imitation whip cream—and find someone else to think about and meddle with incessantly, okay?… Meddle in? Whose life to meddle in incessantly. That's right. That's what I meant. *Thank* you, dad, thanks a lot…I love my dad, I do. He and my mom made so many sacrifices to make me a serious musician. I do owe him everything. Or so much, at least. He's the best. And the worst. So he's *everything*. Ha! Oh my God. But sometimes he just… Know what? This is kind of funny. Sort of. You know how all little girls in the sixties thought that when they grew up they were going to marry Paul McCartney? Well, I thought that too—even though I wasn't around very much in the sixties.

Kiss me. I know: that was funny, huh? So I had this picture of Paul from before he got all hairy? I put it up above my bed. And of course kissed it good night, sleep tight every night. Well, my dad saw it and made me take it down. So I put it up in my closet. Which became a kind of shrine. Ha! He was so outraged when The Beatles came along and got all popular. 'This,' he would scream and shout, 'this is *the death of music!* These no-talent bums and their long hair have ruined everything!' And there my mom and I and some kids from the neighborhood he of course gave lessons to would be shouting right back at him: 'Be quiet, dad! Leave those Beatles alone!' My mom and I still have a good laugh at that. They just made him *livid.* There's no other word for it. [prodigious sigh.] I just do better when I don't see him for a longish…But I *have* to, though. The guilt just kills. It's kind of…God knows what he'd have done had our name ended in 'berg,' 'stein,' or 'man'! He tells people we're 'Prussian' and *Irish*—ha! Do you believe that? Like Prussian's better. (Irish! Do I look Irish to you, an 'Irish' guy, 'Scottish' guy? No. Of course not!) There isn't even *a* Prussia anymore, is there?! Is there? The big scary dark family secret is he ran up some completely insane amount of debt and skipped out on it, went, like, underground. First to Oregon—where every total freak and complete loser and renegade goes to give up on life—right? Oregon! (Oregon's really pretty but it totally creeps me out!) It's all these self-righteous humorless *freaks* making their own beer and joining ultra-conservative groups while smoking *pot* and wearing *tie*-dyes. Gun-toting transsexuals and *millions* of people just like my dad—people who have run away and are trying to hide from all their problems in *other* states which they have run away from. Be sure to book us a show there again, okay, John? Oh my God—it's wild up there. Beautiful though. And Portland's cool. Then he moves to where he is now in Northern California where it—being 'on the lam from Uncle Sam'—is sort of celebrated, actually. Certain parts of it, I guess. My mom and I don't really know what happened there but ironically now it seems he had to move away from the place where people who have to move away from something *move to.* Also, he has these *freaky* music nerds up there who practically *idolize* him for doing it. He's so weird, John. They think he's some kind of folk hero-slash-music martyr-slash-icon or something. Ridiculous. Especially the way he talks like some ultra-conservative or whatever. Sickening. He does live to keep music alive, I guess, though. He's like this crusader for music education. That's good. He's not all bad. Just such a *dreamer*. He thinks some university's going to give him some endowment or neck-medal—though, because he's 'underground' he goes on and on about how he could never emerge and claim it. You don't know what it's like to have a 'sad' parent—and I have *two*. You'll meet my mom one day. Completely different, though. My dad tries to get me to invest my money in these pyramid scams every time I go home—or make me give him money for some rare instrument that needs work so that he can sell and triple 'our' investment. Unbelievable."

No wonder Jenny was, contrapuntally, conservative to his wildness, frugal to his spendthriftiness, practical to his pipe dreamy, uncomplaining to his whingeing, etcetera, etcetera:

The Ogre'd had a series of failed curiosity shops specializing in musical knick-knackery and, sometimes, day old baked goods. Currant buns, honey buns, cinnamon buns, hot cross buns, pound cake. You know the shop. Every small and big American town has one. The kind of cluttered little store that sells lute strings; instruction books (greatly yellowed and somewhat petrified) on Beginning Yodelling; books with titles like *Know Your Oboe* or *The Compleat Historie of thee Harpsichord, Vol. I*; sitars with two or three pegs intact and a couple of rusty, boinging or fugitive strings; lavender or rose-colored recorders and gimcrack pennywhistles; cymbals that'd crashed like trash can lids in a twister; pseudo-Medieval stringed things of dubious or downright hokey authenticity; piano bench seat covers with tapestries of capering revelers and horned mythopoeic beasts; plus other junk.

Jenny said sometimes she'd come home from boarding school and The Ogre'd have set up a glass case next to the glass case at the front and there'd be exploded cream puffs and burst tarts, almost fruitless, overblown cinnamon twists and jelly donuts with all the jelly oozed out of them. "And of course what would happen would be they'd all just get eaten—mostly by him—but by my mom and me, as well: to the point where you could hardly get through the halls of our house. I got so fat coming home some weekends. Like I was dying to get back to school where you couldn't eat *anything*, anything at all, the food was so bad. Slopped down on your plate on a tray. Boarding school food—ugh! You know my dad's a hoarder, right? Just awful. Even now he has these giant stacks of endless music in zillions of manila folders, all tied together with twine so that his hallways to this day look like a paper drive. It was such a higgledy-piggledy life we led. My dad—he has never thrown away *anything* in his entire life! Not once. Not a used tissue. Well, his relationship with my *mom*, he threw out that, but that's another story. What kind of message does that send to a kid? That nothing is trash, for sure. But that nothing isn't, either. That everything's the same! You'd go to the kitchen and be taking out the trash—I or my mom would—and he'd go 'Hey! Where are you going with that? What's in there, might I ask? Are you sure that's just trash? There isn't a diamond or a Fort Knox gold brick in there and you're about to throw it out?!' So that putting the garbage out became an act of secrecy. You're standing there with something just gross—a bag full of cans with mold hair in them or something; a dead mouse and some spaghetti scraped from the dinner plates—and he wants to look at what you've got there. Crazy. You didn't want him to spy you going out to the bins for fear you'd have to stop and show him what was getting jettisoned. Gross! Sad dad. You can imagine how few of my friends ever came over—let alone *boy*friends when I was old enough to have them. Which was never, if you ask my dad. Of course, he wanted to prevent me from ever even *speaking* to a boy till I was, like, twenty-three or something; but he was thwarted on that one cause the music school I boarded at was coed. *Very* coed, actually. It made me go kind of boy-crazy, the way that repression and controlling behavior always seems to, doesn't it? Plus there was this Lacrosse Academy just up the road, right on the lake, just like us. But you probably don't want to hear that, do you, John? Even though you always say that people's sexual pasts don't ever matter? To me they do. I wouldn't want to hear about *you* and all those college girls—I really wouldn't. I don't know why. It's totally silly to be jealous. But I am."

I'd only met him, Mr. Jenny's Dad, at this past Merry Christmas-Christmas: that time of year where people are either at their jolly best or their neurotic worst, it seems, or a disturbing, synchronous combo of the two—and his first move was to tell me in no uncertain terms that I was *not good enough for his precious brilliant beautiful prodigal daughter.*

Now a *truly* self-deprecating if not genuinely humble guy like good old Rob might get away with deflecting/diffusing such an affront/situation by concurring, going: "Oh, I *know* I'm not, *sir*. Not at all! It's amazing that such a perfect angel-of-perfect-perfection even deigns to *speak* to such a one as me." But I (knowing *me*) would probably come out with something like: "Oh, I know I'm not, sir. I can't believe she lives with me, let alone nightly takes my throbbing johnson into her willing, supple, lascivious-looking strawberry mouth. And while she does it? She likes me to pull her cherry-hued hair. Not too severely, though. But like I'm her master, basically. She likes that. For sure she does. For sure. It's great to meet you at last, by the way. How are *you*, sir?"

Like some quasi-valorous character out of the goddam *The Fairie Queene*, I see Dad-Ogre, I go up against said Dad-Ogre. That's Redcrosse Knight-like *me*, boy. That's just who I am. Not shy of breaking a lance with ye, shoulde ye be non-gentle and most uncool indeed à la Mr. Jenny's Dad. Decidedly not shy of breaking a lance, O ogreous one. Just not how you'd think.

It's not that I'm defending Jenny's goddam honor or even mine; it's just that such affectedness and snobbery chafes to the max, and scarcely can one with even a shred of dignity let such behavior pass. I can't let snarges like that get away with it, whatever it seems they're getting away with. Just being generally snargey, I guess. It's not right. It just isn't, don't you think? The ineffable effrontery of the guy! Like, *wow.* You're not serious, you want to say. You can't be. Come on. You can't really *mean* that, can you? And then you realize that the bellicose fuck opposite you *is* serious. Dead serious.

"What my daughter is doing with someone like *you* is anybody's guess," he hissed or lisped or huffed or puffed, and this after "knowing" me around a full effing fifteen minutes, cocking his splendiferously wavy-haired head like a gun, his jowls owling into a ruffle of sneers, melding with the folds of his butterscotch ascot above his blood-red sport jacket. "You're some sort of gui*tar*ist, are you? Jenny's told me some things about *you!*" he remarked, distending his dandyish moustache, the kind where you shave the top bit maybe a quarter inch, straight across, à la Clark Gable or someone equally fey and supposedly dashing. He'd made a face like someone had just held up a hank of burnt hair to his unsuspecting nose.

I swear to God. He'd said that. "Someone like *you.*" Right to my face. Right in my face, more like. The mind boggled. The eyes goggled. The mouth wobbled. It must have done. The thoughts toggled—between getting up and leaving or just laughing in his face. Did I have a quippy comeback at the ready? I did not. Counter this crude, inhospitable volley with a witty sally? No. Get up and slap his fat, flushed face with a white glove from his own collection, lodged in some dresser drawer marked "Drum Major Accessories"? Nay. Did I flare up, rage out, storm out, or get into a great pet or giant wax or furiously call him out for a treble-chinned blackguard, cad, and bounder? Nuh-uh. Did I, I ask you, with the air of a personage taking calmly a piece of choice snuff, demand satisfaction, stating that it was immaterial to me whether it was to be swords or pistols at twenty paces, at dawn of course, on a nearby heath or moor, if said preferably misty and cold heath or moor might be booked and available and convenient for the purposes of two belligerents (as we doubtless now were) dueling? *Non, chers madames et monsieurs.* Did I, contrariwise, with the demeanor of a personage turning his back on a duke or earl, get up and gain access to egress, without even indicating that it was my intention to return post haste to Jen's and my hotel in order to get a good night's sleep in order to repair as soon as possible, come morning, to *Southern* California, where such insults as I had suffered, and in fact the entire unpleasant *rencontre*, were almost unheard of, at least among gentlepersons of good *breeding* and refined *taste*? Absolutely not. No, no, no, and no. There wasn't even a sort of *esprit d'escalier* sort of motif. Not even. Not at all.

I find that the best thing to do in situations such as these (even though I've never *had* a situation like this) is something almost formulaic. And here 'tis: 1. Give appropriate look of prodigious disbelief, accompanied by slight, well-timed lifting of incredulous eyebrows. 2. Make slight but unmistakable snort of huffy derision, indicative of how such a uncouth observation (i.e. not being good enough for someone's daughter) is beneath one's dignity to notice verbally. 3. Lift leg for "leglifter": proceed, if one is gaseous, to beefing in offender's fucked face while shouting "Merry Fucking Christmas"; if one is not gassy or it is not Christmas one may resort to Bronx cheering/"raspberry"-sounding sound, preferably jabbering, baboon-ish, and prolonged. 4. (As alternative to 3, if too squeamish to execute or consider beefing or mock-beefing the hilt of bad manners, as one should): Quote the immortal Jeff Spiccoli when speaking to Mr. Hand in that timeless teenage classic, *Fast Times at Ridgemont High*: "YOU DICK!" Then 5. Take offending fucker by the ascot and dunk said fucker's offending head *and* neckwear face first into whatever drink he's drinking while he's busy snubbing you. (It's great when it's a tea cup or like I said a thimble-cup that he's drinking from, on account of you can have fun trying to fit his head into it, the drinking-thing, jam it right in there and repeatedly.)

Of course, I'm having you on. What I *really* do, and I hope you do it too, is be *overnice* to someone overbearing like The Ogre. I get this blank, vague, vaguely bored, fake-*kind* look on my face and go with it, wear it proud, wear it well. There is no way I ever let on that I am discombobulated by the barbaric behavior of barbarians behaving barbarically. Straight up. This is one instance where an anti-phoney like me is in favor of phoney. Where it's necessary. Where it's right.

That drippy, miserable Christmas (just the interminable afternoon and early evening, actually, and thank the Baby Jesus Jen and I got a hotel instead of staying with him in his dusty old, crusty old Old Curiosity Shop of a ramshackle, wood-troll's house where he lived with two older female "assistants" opening and shutting the queasy avocado-colored curtains and porting endless trembling cups of horrible weak tea) old Ted had offered me *The World's Smallest Drink*. Well, *he* didn't; he had one of the flibbertigibbet women who solicitously ninnied 'round him all day do it, pour it out and hand it to me. It was—I couldn't make this up if I tried—a *thimble* of rose wine. Tell a lie: a thimble*ful* of rose. Wow, I couldn't help but say, *thank you*, thanks so *much—cheers!* Thank you *and* your ostentatiously Muskateer-ish Van Dyke. I wanted to ask right then and there if they had a *Guinness Book* lying around somewhere I could puff the dust off so that I could check if I was holding like a couple of errant hairs you've just brushed from your tux, *the world's most mean libation*. There are—I think we can all of us, sane and insane alike, agree—fuck yous and fuck yous. This was a real fuck you. You couldn't even fling such a drink in some snarge's unsuspecting face! You couldn't even fill some offending fucker's well-deserving *ear canal*; it was just like drinking wine-flavored *air*. Or it would've been, had I condescended to drink of it. (I remember looking around for somewhere inconspicuous to set it down and, strangely, it was too small to dispose of without drawing undesirable attention not only to it, but to and especially oneself.)

Drink the thing, look like an idiot; refuse, look a *double*-idiot. An utter ass. 'Twas *the* picture-perfect illustration of the old adage about how you "can't win for losing." (A dumb phrase, by the by, that everybody understands and that nobody can explain.)

Hence, Ogre two, Me zero.

I mean, I'm not a guy who comes to your house expecting trussed Cornish Game Hens in truffled raspberry sauce with Hollandaise dripped over sautéed baby vegetables; a brandy snifter rimmed with ancient Inca gold; slippers and a smoking jacket and a plush white terry cloth bathrobe in the dew-spangled morn.

I mean, that'd be *nice* but…

I don't need an aperitif before dinner or cloudberry sorbet or to gargle homemade custard and bread pudding for "afters." I don't need my throwpillow fluffed or my feet bathed in milk *or* dark chocolate fondue. I don't require a glass of Chateauneuf du Pape *any* year. You don't have to make a low bow to me when you open the door or give me a gift basket wrapped with transparent rhubarb or marzipan-colored wrapping paper or get me high on Hong Kong's finest or point Havana's best my way and spark it with the lighter Humphrey Bogart used in *Casablanca* (if old Bogie indeed even used a lighter; I can't remember—it might've been matches). You don't. For my part, and in return, if you are a good host, I will be a nice guest: gracious, appreciative, amenable. I'll probably be a good guest anyway, *sans* the "if." I promise not to yell "*Cat* box!" right when I come in the door to your malodorous abode; furthermore, I won't make faces at the brussels sprouts or try to feed them to your dying dog (of course I won't fucking *eat* them, nor will I place cooked cauliflower into my open gob—I mean, I'm not in*sane*—but I'll rather daintiliy knife them to the far side of my plate, and push them around so that it looked like I politely tried to down a few of the vile things). I won't kick your dog, dying or otherwise—even if it mistakes my pantaloons for a mobile fire hydrant,—or look derisively at your coffee-tabled *Koran* or the menorah on your mantle. I'm a good guest. I'm a better host, for sure. But I can play the game. I know how to behave. And for a super softie I'm kind of a hard guy.

Well not *really* but, hey, I didn't as a child walk several blocks each week the tough, hardscrabble, dreamlike, and sunkissed sidewalks of Montecito to my fencing lessons just to back down from a mere dad-ogre. No, *sir*. Courageous and redoubtable and plucky were my middle names. By the age of nine I had trespassed through the treacherous orchards of many-a friendly avocado or citrus fruit farmer, and braved the darkest parts of Disneyland with just one parent holding my tremulous, greathearted hand. And speaking of that tender organ, I had had my tender young Jean-Jacques-like aorta broken by no less than four girls at my prep school whom I had valiantly failed to speak to for four years straight; and I had exchanged misfired fists with several boys almost half my height and weight. Riskily, at puberty, I had brazenly stuffed both hands down my bellbottomed "cords" while watching *The Avengers* in our rumpus room while my mother was busy baking pies and making tea in the deceptively comforting fug of the open, whistling kitchen. (Mrs. Peel—you'll never know what chances I and my vaulting hormones willingly took for your sacred sake! To this very day I think I might have made you a good husband, especially as your phantom TV husband never materialized, nor was, to the best of my recollection, ever even alluded to?)

Inspired by The Beatles' legendary magical mystery holiday at Camp Rishikesh, I had sported a child-sized Nehru jacket, itchily crisp and quite bright mauve, to sixth grade basketball practice, and come home with this treasure *and* myself in utter tatters, ostracized, ridiculed, seething, weeping and indignant on behalf of John, Paul, George, et alia—but particularly George, about whom *Teen Beat*'d reported that he had just loved it there and felt he'd found his spiritual home, until of course that bad, naughty man Maharishi had been exposed as the sort of randy dwarf who, well, exposed himself and his holy nakedness seemingly to any woman-novice who was blonde, or who'd had even a walk-on part in a feature film in limited release. And again: inspirited by the aforesaid John Winston Lennon, MBE, and his indelible quip re: "Not knowing whether there was such a thing as genius or not, but if there was he was one" [many *sics*], I had penned no fewer than twenty-two half-finished folk/pop Beatles-ish songs, all in the tricky keys of G and C (plus occasional Em) by the time I'd turned twelve and a half. A double-edged sword for certain, having written one's first double album so young! What musical Mt. Everest's might be left? Any? Doubtless an early-on crisis, perhaps adumbrating the one I've just dragged you through, keelhauling you on land, reader, via the back of my metaphoric Corvair or VW Van. (Want to hear something really trippy? One of said songs had been called "Barnacle Bill"—a pretty ditty about a man who wouldn't let go of the submarine he'd been cast away from for not being a serious-enough submariner or "bubblehead." Pretty strange, eh?—given the fact that some almost-twenty years later I'd meet the Barnacle *Bob* you've heard a bit about/from.)

As a merry, madcap, dipsomaniacal collegian (to my mind, collegiate alcoholism doesn't really "count") I had adventuresomely stolen a Christmas tree from a lonesome lot (with the mischievous assistance of my Catholic chum who worked there); and I had faced the music and some men in too-tight madras trousers after having been busted for drunk-driving a golf cart into a tree right next to the clubhouse as three of my frat friends (of course iconoclast *moi* was "GDI" all the way) had pusillanimously scrambled to the parkinglot, and their convertibles, and safety. Ah, freshman year. My only American-university *annus mirabulus*, the next three being (mis) spent in the south of England, at an institute of "higher" learning (hashish is what I am alluding to here) that shall for the sake of the innocent and the guilty go nameless.

O ogreous one, O bad Jen-dad!—my pretty, little, Irish nanny handn't taken me to the dangerous, pristine beaches of Central California for supervised surfing and delicious picnics just to puss out in front of the nancyboy likes of *you*. (Dangerous on account of all the putative boners my pubescent self might have got in front of said nanny as a result of all the gorgeous girls splayed 'round on soft-blue-and-yellow-striped beach towels, shifting positions as they toasted themselves even more tortuously golden-smooth in the quivering midday sun.)

Thank Krishna comely Celtic Nanny (name: Nancy: yes, Nancy: Nancy the Nanny) told me once in her sweet, kind, lovely, lilting, little Irish way: "Johnnyboy, you're an almost-teen now, aren'tcha, a fortnoight away from da big tirteen? If you're startin' ta feel a certain—how should one go put this?—tingle *groin*ally, in the groiny *area* then, down *there*, ya know, you can always *excuse yourself* like the proper little well-bred little gentleman you most certainly *are* and dive headfirst into those salt waves of tender green and delicious blue—the cold salt water should take care of the problem, the, er, let's call it an "elation," and straight up. It's what your own dear da's done forever now, the dear sweet priapic man—or at least every time *I've* been to the beach with him." (And wouldn't you know it, it was just my fucked luck to find, just as I was developing "feelings" for Nanny Nancy, that she was about to be extradited back to "the old country," though I never was told why or about the circumstances of "the authorities" having gotten wise to her been an illegial alien.

How odd life is! How strange. How very. And how strangely betrayed I felt when the truth came as it sometimes does to light and I did learn that "the old country" turned out to be neighborly *Canada*, and Nancy not Irish at *all* but just kind of playfully weird and bored and actressy and enamored with affecting accents of all kinds. Thank you, Nancy, whithersoever you have roamed, wherever you have gone nannying on to, perhaps impersonating an English-speaking Czech or Serb and Argentine, a Latvian, or a girl from New Guinea. What's the craic, Nancy? Cheers and how you goin'? You who helped me whittle my sapling powers of concentration as you played countless hours of "competitive" chess with me—your impossible breasts, full, deep, too-ample-for-your-five-two-frame, smacking of eau du lavender and saltwater. How unwittingly wily you were, potentially deflecting my each move with every quiver of your riveting bosom, making me forget from time to time what "castling" was, or which piece was The Queen, causing little me to Freudian slip as I tugged your just-in-reach pleated blue or gray or white tennis skirt and asked you to play "chest" with me, thusly eliciting your most musical and Irish-ish laugh. And me, lonely, maybe-brilliant me, so many times left parentless, on the humming tarmac at Montecito International, Nanny fingering daintily away one galloping teardrop from my too-tanned freckle-face, chucking me under the chin so sweetly, tousling my Regular Boys Cut towhead, holding my one hand, the other of course pocketed in order to hide yet another ambiguous "elation" in my short pants as mummy and daddy waved one last time before the plane's greedy portal swallowed them once more, once more on

their merry way to check on our beachfront properties in Cozumel or
Saudiland, Tasmania, The Yucatan.

Anyhow, it wasn't as though Jenny hadn't warned me about him,
L'Ogre. About his strange pride, weird ways, and distinct lack of
noblesse oblige. About the muted abuse and the credit he took for her
every talent and commendable attribute. You know the kind of stage-
dad I'm talking about? Some old biddy would be there, that Xmas Eve,
and trilling on about how she'd known Jen from a little girl, yeah-high,
so cute, such cheeks and big eyes, vast talent, what a prodigy, barely
able to find the foot pedals on the baby grand, and how she, the old
bag, had been there at Jen's first recital, at six or whatnot. And The
Og would portentously go: "That must've been the year I finished my
nine-hundred-page dissertation on Mozart's…What *was* it, Jenny?
Blast it all!—can't even begin to recollect it now; it's been oh-so many
years of toil and struggle and *some would say* underappreciation?
[smarmy smirk here] Oh *Jenny*—what *was* my thesis about *any*way?
It wasn't about World Music, I'll tell you that much! Aha-ha-haha-
ha!" And there he'd go making her tell a cluttered roomful of clucking,
music-playing super dweebs all about *his* academic glory days, or
some obscure bigshot piccolo flute player he'd had a "jam session"
with on trombone and accordion and a stand-up bass and bass
ukelele. Impercipiently nattering on as though *he* of *course* considered
such chatter chattel, not worth the candle, the provence of airheads
and minutiae-meisters, but that the entire room could kick it around
discussion-wise for the next six hours if they *really* felt they truly *must.*

Sickening.

Yeah: I knew the whole sorry story. Well, her side of it, at least. The
only side I need boyfriendily know. The side I would automatically
boyfriendily take. Hers. Of course. What do you *think,* for heaven's
sake? Of course her side. Of course.

Some while later, when Jenny and I had become *super* codependent,
then hopeless and defeated and hollowed-out/estranged, with her
leaving me heartbroken and then the band (and me carrying on with
it without her), not having spoken to one another for *years*, a fan of

The Weird Sisters, this guy Tyrone, white (I specify "white" 'cause the fuck kind of *white guy* is named Tyrone?), a mutual acquaintance of Jenny's and mine, had told me that her father, around a decade after this, had tried to kill himself with a fork. And not a fork fork—a tuning fork.

[Now I realize that you are suddenly agog that I have just "blown" the plot of the novel here and told you that—*quelle surprise*—Jenny and I are no more. To me, plots are for graveyards. And all couples split up eventually. Even if they are together till one of them or both of them dies. Hello, death.]

It was understood, and I was infinitely grateful for it, that Jenny wouldn't ask me to boyfriendly-like go with her to take off some of the bitter edge of having to deal with him, her dad, this trip. The once was enough. Game, set, match. There was no way I could take it. I mean, these fussy, fastidious prima donna types, aren't they invariably the ones who, while they're whinging about some super minor thing, have some egg yolk plastered like a heraldic mark of medieval venerie right there on their smoking jackets or something. We'd been invited, Jenny and I, for a follow up/depressing "brunch" at the Ogre's that morning after the little soiree. So up we schlepped from the budget motel and motored over only to be subjected to Jen's dad's constant matitudinal moanings: "Jenny, the girls [his house slaves/mates, aged fifty-eight or seventy-four or something] have served me a plate where *the bacon is touching the eggs*—touching the *eggs*, I tell you! This won't *do!*"

And all the while he's got a snot-ribbon unfurling down his sleeve, or some jam like a sort of man rouge on his jellyfish jowls, or a be-crisped bacon bit saluting you from between his aquamarine teeth.

Having to endure that again—'twould have been horrible for all concerned anyway on account of The Ogre was of course the sort who made his mind up about you and goddam if you would ever prove his first impression wrong. That much was certain. You know, I've never met any woman before or since who was more genuinely cool in terms of leaving me alone when I didn't wanna talk ad infinitum about my problems.

Hey world, hey universe, isn't there *too much sharing* going on already? Can't we all just shut up for a little while.

Well, you can anyway. I have another story for ya: Had this art history prof in college during my first year. (This was before I fucked off to study in England.) Great guy. Nice guy. Knew his stuff. Brilliant, in fact. The monotone kind of brilliant, sadly, but brilliant nonetheless. Great writer. Writer of books. Books and beautiful articles. Unimaginably knowledgeable. No less than seven undergrad degrees and a PhD of course. Not cute in the way some academics can be but squat, kinda—squat and plumpish and bald. Totally bald, ideally so, bespectacled. One of those poor bastards who at twenty-nine or so doesn't look a day over seventy. Had these big, black, round, yellow-tinted, Truman Capote-style glasses. Always dressed in a seedy sorta crumpled-looking almost jet black shiny suit, white shirt, black tie. Boring beyond. Droned on and on. An avatar of tedium. A baron of banality. A marquis of monotones. A duke of dullness. A king of uninteres*ting*. And so on. Humdrum voice like an ungrounded Marshall stack on "ten," going: "Zzzzzzzzzzzzzzzzzzzz. And then, in late fifteen twenty-four, he zzzzzzzzzzzz'd and went on to zzzzzzzzzzzzzzzzz. In zzzzzzzz, in fact, he zzzzzzzz'd and there was much zzzzzzzzzzzzzzzzzzzzing and zzzzzzzzzzzzzzzing." Lecture Hall, Art History 101. Survey type of thing, 400 frosh. So much information to regurge that you ended up retaining *nada*. The text thicker than a freshman's head on a Sunday morning. Indo-European pottery and cave paintings to that guy who put a shark in formaldehyde and mounted it at The Tate. Kind of prof who could bring you to tears in five minutes. Near-tears of crushing drudgery, having to listen to him. Prof up there, at the lectern, all in hall under hot lights till the slides start, banal facts, banal dates, anecdotes of great banality, boring allusions to History-history, students asleep and deeply, splayed all over those lecture hall seats with the retractable desks for note-taking, kids bashing themselves mechanically in the face *with* said retractable desks in order to try to stay awake, back of hall looking like the Gettysberg fields a couple of days after the great conflict, kids with mouths open horribly, heads lolling, drool on shining chins, in pools at feet, saliva everywhere, kids doing The Impromptu Charleston from slipping on the drool as they leave class crazy-leggedly, sleepwalking out, gross snores, startled snorkles, grown girls crying from tortuous boredom, big boys too, sighs, legs and arms thrown over seats two rows away—you get the picture. And if not asleep, making a run for it after the TAs took roll, walking tiptoe so as not to wake their deeply slumbering classmates, out the communicating doors of shiny maple—to the entryway and freedom.

And guess what the cruel collegians—at least a dozen or so, many of them frattish—called the guy?

That's right: *The Fly*.

"You going to The Fly's class today?" one of one's classmates might inquire. "Can you show me your notes later, please—if you can stay awake, that is. I gotta do…*anything* other than go to that guy's unreally boring class, man. I'd rather study sta*tis*tics or watch the paint dry on the new Athletic Center! Help me out, okay? The Fly's a walking narcotic!" Or this: "Oh my God, you guys! A guy in the front row of The Fly's class *actually answered a question while he was asleep!* Man! I was right be*hind* him—I swear to God! He was snoring like a tablesaw and fuckin' *in his sleep* he goes: 'Gainsborough, I think, Professor!' And The Fly just kept on lecturing. It was completely *classic*. I'm telling you. He took off his glasses and wiped them; and there's just these *huge* black eyes, like, staring up at you from down there in the auditorium? Totally out there, man. *Fully* surreal. Amazing. The full-on weirdness. Like when you're paddling out an there's this humongous wave coming and you can't even believe it cause it wasn't, like, *there* before—and now it is. Rad."

Everything about the guy spelled Fly, Fly, Fly. Utterly uncanny—anyone might perceive it. As he'd turn sideways at the lectern, for instance, clicking to and looking up in apparent rapture at the next colored slide, the professor's badly cut jacket (so very American) would invariably flap open to sprout black wings, semi-diaphonous in the white light of the streaming projector. His sort of squiggle-mouth, the avatar of an upended "Z," sat square in the middle of the circle of his perfectly round, Pickwickian head, a button-nose (almost a no-nose) punctuating the caesura of his at once convivial and impassive countenance, myopic obsidian eyes twinkling behind those great black-and-yellow-tinted "eyes-of-a-fly" sort of glasses. Then, for overkill's sake, there was the fact that thick black curly hairs from The Fly's *backhair* tentacled up from his shirt collar; you could see them if you were conscious enough to stick around after class and catch him up close and personal before he buzzed away and out one of the lime-colored sidedoors on either side of the great podium.

Oh the humanity.

That was The Fly.

That's the backstory. The *story* story's that there I was, feeling all sorry and genuinely sympathetic to this kindly, caring man who was guilty of nothing save being *mosca*-like in appearance and voice and demeanor and dress, and me hating that everyone I knew had given the guy this unkind epithet and shit. So there I was in class one day and staying awake as per usual (yes: a hefty dose of NoDoz over-the-counter amphetamine *was* involved, but still) and taking copious, furious notes, sitting in the back with my best friend BJ with whom I took so many classes freshman year—and this *actual* fly, real big, quite a big, fat fucker, actually, flies into the long, blonde, thickly luxurious hair of the blonde babe sitting in front of us. And as The Fly (I will call him this just this once, for dramatic purposes only) is up there lecturing, droning on like his life depended on it, filling us, surf churls and sparkle bunnies, wonks and party jocks and junior scholars, the thirteen-or-so-out-of-four-hundred who are awake, in on the importance of *Les fauves* or something, this as I said *actual* fly goes weaving its insecty way down the hair on the back of this chick in front of us. And she's earnestly taking diligent notes and stuff, leaning forward like a madwoman, probably herself trying like crazy not to fall asleep. And suddenly she sits up like she's just had this total rev*elation* about French painting from the late nineteenth, and she fucking perks up, like I said, and then *abruptly leans back*, her hair with the actual fly nested in it to all intents and purposes *barked against the back of her chair*, trapped there, probably smushed.

And much to my and BJ's great chagrin we both *totally lose it* and start giggling like *any*thing (like you do sometimes in church or at a funeral, or when a toddler does a full bellyflop into a Koi pond—just after one of his parents has bellowed how the kid's gonna be a future Federer, Jordan, Mays, Gretzky, Sonny Sixkiller or Tebow), then laughing like crazy people when all of a sudden the chick leans forward again and the actual fly flies, all woozy and stunned and stuff, wearily away, in dream-slow sort of motion, like it was drunk or something on her leave-in conditioner or straightening mousse or whatever. And The Fly, who's been I swear to God impervious all semester to the sound of mega-snoring and people groaning in pain from being so bored, *stops the lecture and glares right at us, me especially.*

Me, well-intentioned *me*, who's been sympathizing with the poor, somnolent bore the whole term and kind of clucking and smacking his lips in disapprobation, making a smirk of remonstrance, whenever anyone calls The Fly "The Fly." Taking his side, so to speak. Standing up for the poor fuck.

And The Fly throws BJ and me out of his class. The droning stops. Students who've been in hibernation mode all semester perk up and sit up and sleepily rubberneck. The Fly's greatest sympathizer—moi—is an apparent turncoat/Benedict Arnold. The tsk-tsks ping-pong in Sensurround round the lecture hall. Suddenly everyone's a super-sanctimonius saint of Fly-devotion, appalled that such a ones as rude we two would treat him so. Mortification is mine and BJ's name.

Helas! Helas! O honte, scandale, horreur, et stupidite! Helas! Helas! Quel dommage!

Can't win for losing—Dear Phrase: I know the meaning of you now.

I remember readying myself to rue the day I was born lest the students get so comfy with the cruel label that they'd use it to the professor's face. Imagining scenarios like this, say: an unfeeling/waggish kid in the front row for instance just blithely raising his hand to say:

"Professor The Fly, sir?"

"Yes, Dumpkin?"

"I was wondering if there's any truth to the rumor that Van Gogh, sensing that his 'lady friend' had gone back to turning tricks, nearly lopped off *another* ear and intended to send it to a *different* whore entirely?"

"No, Dumpkin. Next question, class. Any questionszzzzzzzzzzzzz? Any at all? [pause; squints strenuously; spots innocently fresh-faced coed midway up the hall]. Yes, Jane?"

"Dr. Fly, I'm an Entomology major, and I'm wondering why weren't insects of any sort—wasps, flies, roaches, bees or termites— depicted by any of the painters of the High Flemish Renaissance? Surely a fly or June bug is as fit a subject for the human condition as The Crucifixion or The Infant Jesus, if not more so? Common house flies, for instance, must have abounded in Biblical times—as a result of poor sewage systems and such, outdoor eating practices and whatnot. Why aren't there any flies on the food in the depictions, for example, of The Last Supper? I mean, it's almost all fruit. Do you have a theory you might share?"

"That's a phenomenal question, Jane. Let's see. Well for one thing, zzzzzzzzzzzzzzzzzzzzzzzzzzz was occasioned by the zzzzzzzzzzzzzzz- zzzzzzzzzz; and if we consider zzzzzzzzzzzzzzzzzzzzzzzzzzzzzz, then zz zzzzzzzzzzzzzzzzzzzzzzzzzzzzzzzzzzzzzzzzzzzzzzzzzzzzzzzzzzzzzzzzzzzz zzzzzzzzzzzzzzzzzzzzzzzzz. Do you see?"

"Yes, um, I think so, professor. I think I was asleep for part of that."

"Very good, Jane. Anyone else?"

[long pause.]

"Yes, you in the back? Go ahead. You in the red shirt that also looks black, orange, green, and yellow."

"Professor?"

"Yes, yes. I said go ahead. You have a question, do you?"

"This is a two-part question."

"All right."

"First of all, is all that buzzing down there that you're doing going to be on the midterm? And, secondly, have you ever seen that movie with Jeff Goldblum?"

So I guess that's why I don't like epithets and think they're pretty uncool and pretty inhumane and everything. And, of course, BJ and I went the next day to the prof's office in order to say sorry and eat crow and ask for seconds and put our tails between our legs and other platitudes of contrition and remorse.

Epithets, boy.

But there are exceptions to every rule, right? And I'd had to make one for The Ogre. I mean, I hadn't been given a *choice* when it came to *him*. There wasn't an alternative. I mean, he was an ogre. He *was*. It wasn't a metaphor. It wasn't.

Anyway, Jenny was such a great girl like that, in that "great girl" category, had shewn herself to be such time and time again, when it came to knowing when to back off. She was just so nice and understanding like that, at not nagging, not prying, not pushing, not insisting, getting it. Maybe because she wasn't all that hot herself on blurting out her every woe and tiny tribulation and major objection to and dissatisfaction with our relationship, Otto.

Fuck *that*.

I didn't end up going down on her that night, prurient reader: our master bedroom was so dark and still and suffused with the cumbersome atmosphere of physical and psychological suffering (Jen's new, my recent, troubles) that sexy oral sex was the last thing on my conscious or Jenny's dreaming mind, I imagine. I think she slept twelve hours that night. Must have, poor thing.

Four

n the morning I got up and made Jen honey-toast and tea for what must have been again a shock re: having to get up early and get ready and bolt right back to work downtown. Winkling the last of the orange clover from the little flatulent honeybear, I set a little butter-colored plate before her at the kitchen table. She asked me if there were any messages for her while she was gone and I told her that I had let the phone ring and the machine get it for nigh on five days now and that I would listen to them and ring her later at work if there was anything interesting.

She told me again how sorry she was, so sorry I had had "such a hard time" and that she had been thinking about me the whole time she was driving to No. Cal; I returned that I was looking forward to spending some time with her when she got home that night from work.

"And we ought to rehearse, you know," she added, knowing it would make me happy to think she was thinking about the band as well. "You know, I actually kinda miss Rob and Raleigh, believe it or not."

I laughed and said, "I know. Me too! It's funny how right after you unload gear for the last time and stuff you go 'I never wanna see any of these so-called band mates of mine again! (Present company excepted, of course.) And the next week, there you are, missing them, having drinks at Boardners or El Coyote like the tour was the time of your life."

"Like none of the bad things or bad gigs ever even happened," Jenny said.

"Exactly."

"Huh."

I looked up from my cooling coffee. "When I was in college, my roommate BJ got really stoned and wrote down *It's not the conquer— it's the quest* on a piece of scratch paper; and for a while there thought we had found the key to life. We affixed it to the fridge with a plastic magnet replica of Warhol's iconic VU banana. Reductive, yeah, but true for all that, nevertheless: you have these grand dreams of doing something, making records and doing gigs, and you go and do them and it brings you this high for only a little while—then you go right back down, especially when it's all over and there's nothing more to look forward to except finding something more to look forward to. And no matter what you get, it's never enough. There's never enough good reviews. Or *bad* reviews. I *like* bad reviews. Bad reviews are funny, I think. And every time we sell some CDs at a gig I wish we'd sold just two more. Or get a check from ASCAP for radio play and wish it was twenty-seven ninety-five instead of twenty-seven ninety-four. [Our first check from college radio had come just before we started the tour I told you about.] It's funny. It's just…it's just ridiculously hard. I can't even believe it sometimes."

"I know," Jenny said—but not with words: with her big cinnamon eyes, the ones that seemed to me to be so inconsolable sometimes, somehow. Remember? Like nothing you could say could make it all significantly better. Maybe you do. Jenny was/is so smart you can't put much by her. She can't be snowed. At least, I don't think so. You never know with girls. You think you do, but you don't. It's what they have in reserve. It's what they have on you. It's their not-so-secret weapon.

"In a way," I continued, "it's kind of like making love—having a band. You can't sort of store it up. You have to do it again. And again and again."

"*Speaking* of which…" Jenny smiled in what for a sec looked like a pained way that she flinched back from in an instant and evinced sweetness and light right away again.

"That's what they say, I guess," I said. I was distracted by my own solipsistic thoughts and wasn't really all that paying attention. To Jenny, that is.

Then I perked right up.

"Do you have time? What? I mean. Really? You want to? Is your head suddenly better?"

"Not really, unfortunately. Neither. We'll talk some more tonight, okay?"

"Okay."

"Take it easy today, okay? Don't be so hard on yourself."

"Okay. But I really need to…never mind. I'll sort it out. Don't worry. Love you."

"Love you, too."

Then I kissed her meaningfully and off she went again downtown to her yob and her same-old workaday world while I went back to not knowing what to do with me or anything, for that matter. Talking of authors and their solicitude about fame and fretting about how to maintain it, Johnson told Boswell something that revealed that an artist's career was something happenstance, that all of us needed that big, unpredictable thing: a lucky *break*.

"Uncommon parts require uncommon opportunities for their exertion," he said. Thinking on my indigence, coupled with my awareness that so many bands with less talent, less charisma, less chops, and inferior songs, were way more popular than *we* were, I remembered also the doctor's observation that "slow rises worth, by poverty oppressed."

With these cold-comfort truisms I consoled myself for a philosophical spell.

Part Five

One

eep. "Hey, John and Jenny. I am in the studio for a week or so so my hours will be really screwy. Just thought I would call you guys in case you're checking the machine. Called to say I hope your tour went well and catch up soon. Okay, bye. See you sometime. At the apartment or come by the studio if you feel like it. Hope you still like music. Hope you still like *each other*, actually! The band, I mean. Not you two. Okay. Bye." *Beep.*

Beep. "This is Rajamaharata Singh from the Consulate of Myanmar?. Vee ver hoping to, ah, uh, in-ter-est you in our In-ter-na-tion-al Amnesty for Sex Offenders Program. Please to call back at your earwee-est conwenience!" *Beep.*

Beep. "This is a message for Mr. John [static noise in background]. Mr. [static noise in background], this is Ron Johnson of the Waverly-Waterman Mutual Investigative Collections Assurance Group of Ohio, taking over your case from the previous collections compan*ies* in California. We are calling on account of your past due Student Loan account of…" [*Fast-forward.*]

Beep. "Hi, John, hi, Jenny. It's Stacey. Give me a ring at the label when you get this. It's Monday sometime after four, I think. Talk to you soon." *Beep.*

Beep. "Juan! Sterling. What's the *story*, brother? Tell it to me. Never heard from you guys all tour so I assume it went well. Or horribly! Hahaha. Call me back or die. Hi, Jenny!" *Beep.*

Beep. "Hi, John. It's Alicia. Do you want to work at the bookstore this week? A couple of days, maybe? Hope your tour was great. Are you guys back yet? Call me. Let me know." *Beep.*

Beep. "John. Are you there? It's me. Pick up, okay? Just checking in on you. I hope you're better. I'm, um, really having quite a time here, if you know what I mean. Miss you. Love you. Bye." *Beep.*

Beep. "Hi, John. It's me again. You can't call me, I don't think, but I wanted to call you to say I hope you are okay, okay?… Really. It's Jenny, by the way. Hahaha! Bye. See you soon." *Beep.*

Beep. "Dude! (Hey, Jenny.) Call me. Chalet here." *Beep.*

Beep. "This is a message for Jenny from The Weird Sisters. Hi, Jenny, my name is Tim Simmons. I'm the manager of an artist on Warner Brothers you may have heard of. Well, I hope so! Ha! I'll tell you who it is when you ring me back. Please call me at your earliest convenience at two-one-two-six-four-eight-oh-two-five-two. Thank you. We—our management company—saw you play with your band at some club sometime a month or so ago, I think, and were very impressed by you. Call us as soon as you can." *Beep.*

TWO

ast-forward with me here, if you don't mind—let's use the metaphor of a double-album on cassette 'cause cassettes are *au courant* circa the time of our story and kinda/sorta like love and indie bands: not really meant to last. They warp, the tape goes all stretchy-tight, then crinkly-slack; you leave them in your car in the hot parking lot outside your summer job and you come back and they're like your brain on strong psychedelics, if that's your thing. They oxidize and wobble and you sort of reflexively speed through the not-so-great songs and the tape makes that shriek/squiggly sound like when you step on the tail of a dozing house cat. You find one under the seat of your car—you

thought you lost it—and it's all sticky with splashes of root beer or melted peppermint and, yeah, there's some hair gummed/bunged in there and you clean it off and have to stick a book of matches in the player to get it to play straight and it's *The Best of Bread* or Siouxsie and the Banshees' *Once Upon a Time.*

Three

o anyway: first things first: The first call I returned was to—big surprise—Stacey at Better Records on account of there was something ominous in her unmistakable voice and of course neither one of us, reader, can get that talk with Mike Mays out of our minds. The one where it became ringingly apparent that the head of the label was out of his mind and then some.

Stace told me that Mays had left for Santa Fe then Roswell, New Mexico, taking one of the two big white record company cargo vans with him. Mark that. I mean, we didn't get to use one of the vans when we were out promoting…ah, nevermind. What matterth it? It was funny to think maybe Mays was off to help the people of The Pleiades move somewhere like Huntington or Garden Grove. Stacey and the rest "weren't sure when" he was coming back. The "or if," I thought, was something tacit. Uh oh. Big surprise *numero dos*: where the hell else would he beam off to?! A Hopi reservation maybe? The latest National Weather Service reported locus of a streaking UFO? Newly popped up crop circles in Nebraska or ancient stone circles in Oxfordshire or Wiltshire. Zimbabwe or Zanzibar? Who knew what internal clock of chop logic these alien-theorists set their wicky-wacky watches to? I know I'm mixing up the metaphors here like an apothecary/pastry chef, but jeez-in-a-manger, no wonder reactionary types in the so-called "flyover states" look at Californians north and south and break out the old chestnut that we're just a mixed bag of *fruits and nuts*. Those good old boys and girls are onto something. You wanna meet some kooks—come out west. Take a few home with you, do.

Stace'd added that since the other Mike, the Mike who had been on our side, Mike Manson, the nice, normal, blue-button down-wearing, quiet, cool, pop not "rawk" guy, was out of the picture, not to expect much in the way of support from the label anymore. Not that we'd gotten all that much in the first place. In fact, she revealed, Mike Mays had drawn up a new contract or "deal memo" for The Weird Sisters that stipulated that, were Better Records to choose to "pick up the option" on the band's next album, Mike Mays himself would not only select the songs we'd record, but also produce, arrange, and sequence them. ["Why not throw in that he'd do backing vocals and hand-letter the goddam album credits, already, why didn't he?" I suggested acidly. To which Stacey responded with a knowing *pfff* of a knowing laugh.] She went to to say that we, the Sisters of Weird, would have to agree to do at least 200 tour gigs (not counting LA shows) in support of the album, and expect the same sitch as with our debut: no tour support from the record label. All the truant Mays and Company were asking for was, in essence, *total and complete artistic control.* Plus a sort of indentured artistic slavery in the wake of the fact that we would all have, without help from a booking agent (unless one came along), to mortgage our lives and jeopardize our jobs in order to shill for a record that we'd had marginal artistic participation in.

Wow.

Stacey said all this in a tone that suggested that she was trying hard not to flinch or wince, that she was sorry to have to be the bearer of bad news, and that it wasn't going to do either of us any good for her to editorialize or interject a load of sympathy into what she was only obligated to tell me—beyond, that is, a few sighs and a few *tsks* or syllables that suggested "*I know, I know*—I didn't draft this shit up, okay? What can I *say?*"

Plus clichés like don't shoot the messenger, mind you. Pretty please don't.

Stacey said she could fax a copy of the deal memo to this copy shop I used on Western, and that, as she was rooting for us and considered us old friends, we should and could take our time thinking over Mays's proposal. There was no rush, and, as she'd mentioned, no one knew when he was coming back to work anyway. She joked that maybe he'd end up living in a teepee somewhere near Area 51. Then she said we'd talk soon and to take care and maybe get some good LA shows in the meantime? And good luck on account of "how tough it was out there—with so so so many bands vying for the little spotlight available."

"Hold on a minute, okay? Franklin wants to talk to you. I'll transfer you now, all right? Okay, John. Talk to you soon, okay? Bye!"

"Hey, John."

"Hi, Franklin."

"Don't get down, okay? You guys are a great band. A *great* band. Unlike with most bands, there is an actual purpose for you to be one. To be a band. You're going to be fine. Though of course if everyone 'got' you, you'd be a lot more popular than you are right now. Not everyone's going to get you, right? You do know that? I thought so. You don't have giant illusions, do you? I didn't think so. That's cool. That's good. If you want my opinion Mays is an idiot to offer you such a ridiculous contract—I mean, we aren't even done working the record you have out now. And we're not going to stop doing that—I want you to know that."

"Thanks, Franklin."

"Seriously. Don't sign that thing. Use the momentum you have going right now to try to find a new record deal. Use the reviews and the airplay and all of that. You're free to go, you know. You don't owe us anything, and you guys deserve to find a home that's right for you, a place where The Sisters are a priority, not the afterthought of a guy who, well, smokes dope and dreams of aliens rather than thinking about how to make you as popular as you deserve to be. Seriously."

"I know. Thank you, Franklin."

"You'll be all right. Say hi to Jenny for me, okay?"

"Okay."

"The two of you are really, really good together—a great co-front team. The more Jenny sings the better for you guys. I don't mean that, like, for you not to sing, right? Don't take that the wrong way. It's just that it's very powerful when the two of you are singing together, so keep that going! Plus, you know, Rob and Raleigh are getting better and better together. The tour really helped—I can tell, honest, just from The Doll Hut gig. Even if it was only a short tour like that one was. Furthermore, I'm totally sure you will come up with even more great, catchy pop songs and make an even better record than this one was."

"Thank you, Franklin. You're very kind. Cheers."

"Don't mention it, John. Hang in there, John. Don't let it get you down. Book some shows and I will invite some friends at other labels to come see you, all right?"

"Sure. I appreciate it. Thanks, Franklin."

"Hey, guess what?!"

"Huh?"

"*The* weirdest thing. Before he left for New Mexico or wherever, Mays gave Barnacle Bob a job in the warehouse!"

"No way!"

"Seriously! Somebody quit the other day and we needed someone to get in there right away. Now, every time you go out there, out to the warehouse, you gotta watch out for some English drunk operating a forklift, muttering to himself about the good old days of rock and roll or some band he saw in nineteen seventy-four or something. Wild— let me tell you. It's crazier than *ever* here. You're better off..."

"That's hilarious, Franklin. Watch out! Take care, okay? I'd better go. Have a lot of calls to return."

"I will. You as well. I'll be sure and send you Flake's interview with you guys when it comes out."

"Cool."

"And do let me know next time you are playing, okay? I'll try to get some people down. I come up to LA a lot, you know."

"Cheers."

"Goodbye, then."

"Goodbye."

And I got to thinking as I'd hung up the phone that so many of the evils and sorrows of this vast vale of tears we call the big, bad world came from one of two things: thinking either too much or too little of oneself. In terms of over or underestimating oneself. That's what I mean. Not thinking about oneself, though that could be a down as well. And by extention, in my case, troubles came from over or underestimating one's tiny little indie rock band. People were always, whether at a gig or in a newspaper or fanzine or major mag, at the grocery store if they ran into you the afternoon after a big show, on the telephone or the US Mail—people were always, I say, telling you what they thought of what you were doing. Unsolicited, like. They'd tell you "Great gig!" even if it sucked, cause they sometimes, just like you, had good intentions and wanted to relieve your angst, if they could, if only for a moment. They'd tell you sarcastically "Nice *job!*" if they were envious of you and bitter and struggling to have a crummy little band themselves, or if, deep down, they didn't really like you as a person and were only pretending to be friendlylike. They'd tell you all about whom you reminded them of (just so they could convey to you the idea that they were hip, and up on all things modern musical). You'd get the most odd compliments. You'd be told you sounded like/ reminded someone of some band you never even heard of, or some band you couldn't stand, or someone's uncle's garage band from the potshops of greater, outer Amsterdam. Anything. Everything. Keating always told Jenny and me that when, in his professional capacity as producer-guy, he had to go see a band in order to see if they were worth his time working with, recording—when he found that they were unlistenable, had no songs or couldn't play, couldn't in a million years be withstood, he'd always opine: "Wow. You guys were really *loud* tonight! *Really* loud."

And, Keating said, nine out of ten bands would take that as major compliment. Ha! Like that was some kinda coup. Something to be proud of. And what does that say? What? It says, basically, that like I always say: Bands are Stupid.

So then, this: in an artist, in a person, any person, hubris or relentless self-deprecation?—both very bad. Both very perilous. Erring too much one side or the other could result in one's eventually going positively *bonkers*, ending up the parkie who lives in a sleeping bag or tube tent and seldom washes but rather drools on himself, parked amidst perpetual pigeons, muttering to himself or rhapsodizing in the unblinking morning sun, consulting the clouds, cradling a forty of malt liquor or an exploded, orphaned teddy bear. The whole Aristolelean maxim "Know Thyself" seemed geared toward staving off such a state. People who knew themselves, faced themselves, didn't kid themselves (kidding others *about* themselves seemed okay, kept thing from getting too heavy), didn't set themselves up for the big, bad fall. Old Aristotle, he was just looking out for us. Looking out for other people. Which was the avenue to happiness. And yet how could you not be solicitous/worried overmuch about yourself? How could you be disinterested with respect to *you* your*self, you?* Trying to be something, do something, get somewhere, go—how could you *not* do that? Trying too hard for anything—a girl, the making of a work of art, a prize, a pony—anyone could tell you only (often) lead to you *not getting it.*

And yet you had to try. You had to give it the old college try. You had to. You're fuckin' stuck, mate. Ha-ha! [mock-bitter tone here.] Living in England for a year, all those years ago, those halcyon "varsity" days, seeing all those Brit kids look down at anyone who even *seemed* to be trying, who even appeared to be effortfully going for something, anything at all, even a sandwich or a second cup of earl grey, and me for a spell trying to *be* like that, all devil-may-care, all "I don't know how I got this—I just turned up, on a whimsical whim, and, look!, they just kinda awarded me first prize!"; England made me realize that that was just not my style.

What to do, what to do?

I'd already tried having a nervous episode. A lot of good that did. I'd tried drinking my way out of it. Ditto that. What to do?

Four

eep on returning calls. That I could do. Call the rest of the band and organize a rehearsal, then a meeting to fill everyone in on the latest Better Records travesty. Call Sterling, for instance, my brilliant old fellow songwriter friend and *phantom* "rival" on account of he didn't play music anymore on account of he quit trying. Call Bob Chalet and let him gloat like mad over the latest ridiculous news from Better. Call the bookstore I part-timed at and get some work. Call Keating and say hello and hope you are doing well, roommate whom we never see. *Not* call the collection agency re: my student loan on account of what was I going to tell them—that I'd wire them in good faith ten of the fifteen bucks I had left? Promise them I'd sign over a royalty check soon as it turned up in our mailbox (i.e. never)?

Sterling's line was ringing when the "call waiting" beep beeped and I switched calls. *Please don't be Raleigh*, I thought. *Anyone but him.* Even though I did need to talk to him, see when he could work out some new songs.

"Hello?"

"John?"

"Rob! Hi. Hey, listen…"

"Hey. Sorry to interrupt. I am a work, so..."

"What's up, Rob?"

"Quickly: Do you want a three-day job—working on a music video shoot? Dan V. from The Pubic Palace days rang me and asked if I knew anyone who needed a production assistant gig for a few days. Do you know what a PA is? I can't do it, or I'd do it, you know? It's a good gig. Hard work. Very. But...Anyway...Interested? You'd have to get going, like, twenty minutes ago..."

Rob was talking faster than I had ever heard him talk before.

"Rob! I am. Definitely. I know what a PA is. I *think* I do...Um... Un-huh," I said, not at all very certain, but I did know it was an acroynm. "Production assistant."

"Right. The pay, he said, my friend Dan said, is really good, but you have to get out to the desert *now*. I mean, leave *right now*. The crew and the whole shoot are already out there, shooting. I wish *I* could do it, actually, John. The pay's great. But I can't take off any more time from work to, um, work."

Rob always slayed himself. He was like me in that respect: just trying to amuse himself as much as possible in a sometimes most *appalling*ly boring universe.

"Yes, of course," I said. "And thank you for this, Rob. I owe you one—big time. But I don't have a car right now, you know."

"That's okay, actually."

"How's that?"

"Listen: can you drive a lorry truck?"

"A what?" I laughed at the pleonasm. Rob was always good for one of those. I think I told you he told a radio interviewer that we got "A per diem per day" and that we were "Really happy to be on the road also too as well." It was as though he was, linguistically, covering all the bases. Running over them and tacking back again, actually. When he realized he'd Yogi Berra'd again, he'd sometimes try to top his own spoonerism. Say something like: "It's just great being on tour on the road and everything!"

"A big old truck," Rob said. "You know. I mean a lorry. That's it. Sorry. There's a lot of physical labor involved here too, Danny said—I should tell you that. Lifting things, working non-stop. I think he said it was a box truck or something. A commercial kind of thing. Big, like, *really* big."

"Sure. I guess. I mean, I can drive a *van*."

"I think this is a lot lot bigger. Like, huge."

"Gulp," I said, sounding it out.

"I know, I know. But it pays three-hundred-bucks-a-day. With a bonus, maybe, Danny said."

"I can drive a *space* ship for *that*."

"I thought so," Rob laughed. He gave me the number of the production office and told me to ask for Sheila. I thanked Rob profusely of course again and rang the number he gave me and at first they had no idea what I was talking about (those of you who've worked the blue collar-ish jobs in Hollywood will know what I mean when I say that production company offices during shoot times are total cacophonic *madhouses*—and that's putting it mildly), but then, after I kept saying "Dan V., Dan V., his old roommate told me to call. Dan *V…*" the Sheila person finally got it ["Oh, you mean *Danny* V.! Of course! Okay. I know who you mean!"] and instructed me to get there *ASAP* on account of the lorry was waiting for me to drive it out to Joshua Tree to where the shoot for [and she named some band that I thought started with a "W" but I wasn't sure because she seemed to be carrying on five conversations simultaneously with people in her office] was. She'd work out the details of my W-2 form and Social Security number and all that stuff when I got back in three days. I said cool and hung up and got dressed in jeans and my Doc Martens and remembered to bring a sweater and a parka (the desert at night in spring is super cold). I called a cab and called Jen to tell her what was up and I was out the door when the phone trilled and on a whim I rushed back and picked it up and it was Sterling, my dearest friend and favorite Angeleno *raconteur* and *bon vivant* and record clerk, whom those of you who've read *The King of Good Intentions* know and maybe even love already.

"Juan! You just rang me and hung *up?!*"

"Sterling! I am out the door. I have to go to the desert to work on some hair band's video shoot! I can't talk...I..."

"Unbelievable. What band? You haven't even told me about your tour!"

"I think they said Warrant or Whitesnake or something...I couldn't make out..."

"How ugh! That's hysterical!"

"I know, but it's money. Really good money. Listen, Sterling, I need to split here."

And here the horn of the cab went *beep* in the street outside so I told Sterling bye and that I would ring him when I returned and I scurried downstairs and away we went lickety-split to an office in West Hollywood on Santa Monica Boulevard where a new and certainly different rock and roll-related adventure—and one that was going to change my life in the most unexpected yet profound, extraordinary way—awaited me.

One

hat are you *thinking, mate?!*" a longhaired, redbearded giant in a tan *faux* flak jacket and brown, ballooning cargo shorts, and brand new eight-eyelet workboots—it must have been the director himself—barked into a megaphone or whaddayacallit bullhorn or something, at *me*, from maybe seven or eight feet away. He had a beard like a Norse God or just a regular old Danish guy on a ferocious berserker. Here's what he added, from on high, as it were: "Who told you to *walk back here?* Hey, PA—no one told you to?! Who told you to *do* that?! Did *I?*" [and here he pointed theatrically to himself as though he were one of the über-persecuted, an honorary Kurd or Armenian or freckle-faced, redheaded stepchild...well, he *was* a "ginger," actually, so...never mind].

"Did *she?* he continued, beetling even more his already beetling brows. [and here he pointed to *the prettiest girl I had ever seen* who was standing next to him and, *I* thought, smiling my way with her incredible blueberry eyes].

"Jesus Christ Almighty—who hired this guy?" he added and looked around with a look of fucked appeal to the four or five other "staff" who stood fairly close 'round him—the camera man, the really pretty girl (remarkably tall, black hair and too-blue or better yet *sea-blue* eyes, short-shorts of olive drab, boots, wearing a preposterous, floppy camo hat on her pretty head), a couple of ruddy, burly fuckers with gargantuan biceps, grips maybe? best boys?, one of whom might have actually been a woman (like a drag queen-looking type personage you might encounter at a drag queen drag race, if you've ever been to one, which I have not, and never will, not even if I am kidnapped and dragged there myself, for I should find a way to commit *harakiri*, even with a screwdriver or a cheap pen, before they, whoever they are or were or would be, got me there, I assure you), and a slim, tall, slick-haired businessy-seeming/kinda smiley guy in a really nice suit-and-tie and holding a plastic, see-through clipboard whose pages kept fluttering like a shuffled deck of playing cards. There were some other people too, off in the distance near a truck with a carrier bed the yellow Camaro [that was the car in the scene at "the shoot"] had been ported in on; they weren't part of the shot, seemingly, the people, so they just concentrated on a) hurrying up and waiting, as the classic "industry" phrase goes; and b) gobbling whole chickens plumped on plastic plates and slabs of ribs and racks of roast lamb in woodblock-sized chunks with mint sauce and school-supply binder-sized wedges of chocolate cake parfait with raspberry sauce that sparkled like fake blood in the hot sun.

"I'm so sorry!" I pleaded sincerely, faltering big time. "I thought... sorry about that. I didn't..."

"You're not being paid to *think*, mate!" the director yelped, throwing one hand up in the air like he was trying to get rid of it, employing the biting politeness that's part of the atrocious legacy English people left for Australians like I *think* the director was. "Is that what you think you're being paid to do out here—*think?* You are not to even *think* that to think is what you are being paid to *do.* [And here, with the last seven or so words he slowed down as though to sententiously emphasize what an idiot I was, and what a patient kind nice Boddhisatva and all-'round hallowed-one *he* was for pointing out with such careful clarity my imbecility to me and to anyone else in hearing distance.] Is your walkie-talkie even *on, you fucking...?* Oh my *God!* Get back in the goddam Camaro, PA! *Driver,* drive him back to the checkpoint, okay, driver? Who the fuck *are* these people?! I mean, where do they find you people—Greyhound Bus Stations? Bowling alleys? The Gutter? *Har*vard or something?"

He said this (mercifully, not into the bullhorn this time, but just as loudly, it seemed) just so that everyone standing there plus the stunt driver driving the hot rod could now proceed to the bit where they got to look down on me piteously/contemptuously/and with great relief that the director/tyrant guy/carrothead wasn't screaming-barking-fuming at *them* for once. It was like one of those giant searchlights they break out at opening galas or Christmas pageants or nighttime wartime had gone strafing across my fucked and mortified face. Deer-in-the-headlights woulda been grossly understating it, what with how fucked the fucked look on that fucked face of mine musta fucking been just then. Egads, I was blushing and making my mouth do that unsightly thing where you appear to be trying to swallow your own lips. "God*dam*mit!" he concluded, like a reverse benediction. "Let's do this bloody shot again! Let's actually *get* it, this time. Please? *Okay?* Please? Pretty please with clotted cream and raw organic unsweetened sugar on top? Here—put this back in the jeep! [and here he handed one of the "grips" a fat satchel] *Cameras!*" the director guy said as I slunk back into the passenger seat of the fire orange red Camaro and shut the door just in the nick of time before the driver spun it 'round on the stretch of desert highway and we peeled out and hurtled back up the road around three hundred yards or so this time so that he could get in position again.

"See that button in the middle of that thing you're holding in your *hand?*" the driver nodded and Belushied one eyebrow, his right one, the one that was pointing accusingly, in other words, directly *my* way.

"Uh-huh," I winced.

Where else would I be holding *it,* I thought, however. But of course I didn't say that.

"You push that to the 'ON' position, Swifty," he said.

"Oh. Right. Duh," I said.

"Duh," he said. "Here we are."

"Cheers," I said and got out and went over to the side of the road and stood there squinting back toward the crew as the driver, more kindly this time, sort of shouted "Don't mention it" and swung the rumbling hot rod back around, kicking up plumes of green-gray dust and of course in the process frosting me aggressively with sand and gravel shrapnel and exhaust fumes and cactus needles and iguana guano, probably, jackrabbit carrion.

"Two-forty-two, two-forty-two! Do you read me? Over," my walkie-talkie—one that had '242' stenciled in white on it—clarioned.

"Affirmative," I talk-coughed into it. All authoritive and shit. Then added tentatively: "Over?"

"When I give the signal, tell the driver 'Go!'" the voice crackled. I thought it might have been the beautiful girl's, but of course I couldn't be sure.

"Roger," I said.

"Who?" the voice said.

"Roger. As in 'got it,'" I said thickly.

"There's no 'Roger' here," the woman's voice said.

"'I'm sorry?"

Beat.

"I'm just messing with you," the voice said. "I'm totally kidding."

"Oh."

"I'm Katie, by the way. And 'go' is setspeak for 'take off as fast as you can.' Do you think you can remember that?"

"It *is?*" I said in a you-know-what-kinda-tone. And if you don't, I'll help you out: I said it mildly sarcastically.

"Unh-huh," the Katie chick said. She gave a sort of puffed, plosive CV laugh, but it wasn't mean or anything. "What's your name?"

I told her, then added. "You're the assistant director or something? The one with the absurd hat, black hair and sort-of-pretty fa..."

"Hi, John. Nice to meet you."

"You, too."

"I like this hat. Now: do you think you can do this without screwing it up this time?" she lilted.

"Yeah, of course," I said.

"Good. 'Cause that's about the last thing Colin needs right now. Colin The *Great* needs right about now. The Great Colin. Isn't that right, Colin?" she added in a louder manner, her sunny-bright and rather mocking voice glancing off the walkie, a lifted aside, more pronounced of course now that she wasn't playfully disparaging this Colin character, presumably with Colin Someone himself standing right there. "He didn't hear me. He's busy yelling at someone else now. Someone not you, I mean. Hahaha!"

"Okay," I said, uncomfortable as all get-out, but trying perhaps too palpably to inject a bit of confidence into my tone. I didn't know who Colin was for sure but it must've been the bullysome big shot redbeardo; furthermore, I was thinking in general that *I* was the last thing *anyone* on this job needed—I had absolutely positively virtually no idea what I was doing. I had no idea what I was doing the entire time. From the time I got the keys to the truck at the production office to the time I turned them in in the morning three or so days later, I had no idea.

As for Katie: there was something about the way she said "about" that made me think she was East Coast, possibly full-on Canadian. Plus, earlier, I had heard her say "doring" for "during." What was that all about, I wondered, "doring" the short time she was talking. And by the by: when I said she was the prettiest girl I had ever seen what I mean is *she was the prettiest girl I had ever seen.* Like someone could walk up to her any hour of any day of the week and go: "You know what you should be? No, not a mere moll of a movie star. Nothing that typical. Nothing that banal or prosaic. You know what *you* should be? You should be Snow White at Disneyland, like, every day of your life. Times Wonder Woman times Grace Kelly crossed with Ingrid Bergman and Ava Gardner mingled with Natalie Wood when she was alive. Times a real live human person, thespians being kind of the walking dead no matter how pretty or whatnot. That's what *you* should be. You look like you were drawn by some masterly Bottichellian idealist or something. Are you *for real?* 'Cause I don't think you can be." And I don't mean she actually looked like some obligatory paradigm of beauteousness, some cookie-cutter/too-beautiful-to-be-real ideal. You know how someone can be just so too perfect? Too good-looking? Frightfully so? So pretty you're kind of scared of them? Like nothing's even remotely the matter with them? Great teeth, great hair, nice body, sweet smile, super cheekbones, big eyes, great ass, all of that and a bag of overflavored crisps—and not be fetching in the least? Banally beautiful? Lacking that all-important *je ne sais quoi?* That certain something/way about them?

This wasn't that.

Not at all.

I mean, sometimes you go to the movies or the theatre, to some dazzling matinee perf of a sparkling Shakespeare comedy at the original Globe in high summer or to some dumb yet utterly, stupidly wonderful Bond film in its first exciting week—and someone comes on the stage or screen and you go: "Oh my *God*: that is *the* stunningest

face I have *ever* seen!" And her name's Thomasina or Genevieve or
Gemma or Tamsin or something? Bridget or Bailey, Katherine or Kat;
Anne, Amory, Aubrey, or Amelia? You know the nomenclature: the
type of handle girls *you*, Mr. guy *not* called James Bond, could *never*
handle have, yeah.

And she's got that flaw, that perfect little teeny, weeny, eenie,
meenie flaw that makes her even more unbefuckinglievable. Maybe
it's one tooth that juts out to, likesay, tomorrow, or one of her irises
is hooded just a slight bit too sultriliy, or there's a mole somewhere
that looks like it's about to give a speech, or one earlobe is mariginally
wonky and pendulous, or her nice square posture-perfect shoulders
have a port wine mark that looks like a miniature map of French-
occupied Algeria—*I* don't know.

The something *wrong* that makes the person's pulchritude
just *right*.

Well, hell: that was Katie.

"You didn't screw it up!" she laughed. "That kind of stuff happens
all the time. Just not to him, you know. Haha. Don't mind Colin. He's
just an asshole, okay? Not really. I don't really mean that. He's…I don't
know. He's a…*director*. I mean…never mind. He's fine. I mean, people
go trembling in front of him and he's actually just…never mind. Sorry,
I…They're *all* like th…Anyway…"

"*Right*," I said. "Um…"

"Why am I telling you this?!" the Katie chick laughed, heading
me off at the pass, as'twere. "Sorry about that! I mean, honestly!" Then
she sort of snorted and laughed again, at herself. "Sorry! I can't believe
I just did that."

I was of course about to obsequiously say "He *is* an asshole—
absolutely! You've never been more right in your life," but I caught
myself in time and refrained; he might have been her full-on fiancé for
all I knew. I could have easily added that truly ridiculously beautiful
girls like her, it seemed to me, were always putting their pretty fingers
to their plump, siren-ish lips to say "I can't believe I just did that or
said that."

Boop-boop-dee-doop.

How many times have you, reader, heard an über-beauty observe stuff like the following: "I'm *so* terribly sorry—I can't be*lieve* I just backed over your foot or toddler with my shiny, new-car-smelling convertible with that new car smell"; "I'm *so* terribly sorry—I can't be*lieve* I ate your special birthday cupcake/the placenta from your firstborn that was in the freezer/the wedding cake you had wrapped in ten layers of tin foil at the back of your freezer"; or: "I'm *so* horribly insensitive—I can't be*lieve* I just said that your just-home-from-hospitial infant was positively hideous"; "I'm *so* whimsically guilty—I can't be*lieve* I stole your husband the pastor without even *try*ing!"

That's what mega-pretty girls *liked*, what they seemed to enjoy greatly: having ample occasion to say such stuff, a plethora of suchlike coyish blunders, occasions, that is. They *liked* to. They Marilyned down the lane and left a singular huggermugger behind, then oopsed on their merry way away and, skipping maybe, swinging their various nicely-designed and tastefully *au courant*ly upkept purses or a compact copy of the O.E.D., let you deal with the consequences while they went off to meet a professional hockey or polo player or oil tycoon (just to see if he was as cliché as his métier suggested he might be) for an expensive and complex and probably mesmerizingly scintillant ice blue or diaphanous green melony drink before they went to the airport in order to catch the late flight to Aruba or Antigua. It happened all over the world like that. They could like nuclear physics and the mid-period plays of John Webster or Christopher Marlowe; they could adore making apple martinis or strawberry crepes with hand-whipped whipped cream; they could relish playing golf or water polo or doing elaborate sociological surveys of and papers about people who'd spent most of their lives living in doss houses or igloos; they could give half their money and three-fifths of their free time to volunteer causes and Rotary Clubs. They could do all this *as well*— sure. But what they liked *best* was wreaking havoc with your world— if you were a guy, that is. That, to them, was *fun*.

Guys never *mind*, mind you, if their worlds are havocked and wreaked with. Guys never particularly *care*—*if* the girl who has done some dastardly thing to them is one of the Snow Whites, the chosen, like this perfectly imperfect Katie incontrovertibly was. We welcome it. *I don't mind at all at all that, tearing drunk down the street in a heavy, high-end Volvo or powerful BMW, you just tipsily bashed into my just-bought yacht right after your car insurance lapsed, we tell them. Back up over it as well, if you want, lovely little lady. Go ahead. Be my guest. Knock the rudder off if you want. Get it good. Let me direct you: I can help here if you wanna blow off some steam and take out the engine on the thing as you fishtail away. I don't mind. Go for it. Do it, cutie. What do I care? I just want you to be happy, have a nice time, wreck as much as you've a mind to, get it out of your system.*

Just then the Colin guy's Aussie voice cranked over the walkie-talkie asking Katie who the hell she was talking to and could we please just get this shot and get the fuck out of here and move on to the next one?!

"Okay," Katie said. "Who *did* hire you, by the way? I am merely asking for information. 'I merely ask for information, Lane.' (Ha-ha! That's from Oscar Wilde.) Anyway, I've never seen you before. Is this your first time working on a shoot? It must be."

"It is, actually," I said. "And probably my last."

"Ha!" the Katie girl said, but without laughing initially, but then she sort of burst out chuckling. "Probab*ly*, probab*ly*," she added.

"A friend of a friend," I said, continuing, focusing on the intial question. "This guy Danny."

"Danny? Really? Danny did?"

"Yeah."

"Which Danny?" she said. It was as though I could feel her crinkling her eyes intensely in order to commemorate the inquiry. "Tall? Skinny? Dishwater blonde hair? Kinda sour? Kinda *crabby?* But terribly handsome? Like a good-looking, conceited crab. Conceited and arrogant both?"

"I *think* so. I think that's him. I only really met him yesterday. He's a friend of a fr…"

"Looks like he's cross all the time? Pissed-off? Narrowing his beady little cold blue *eyes* at people? Even though everyone just a*dores* him and thinks he's totally hi*lar*ious?"

And here I could hear the director yelling something, but I couldn't make out what it was; and besides, I was thinking just then, as a sort of delayed reaction, that, hey, my great friend Sterling and I quoted *The Importance of Being Earnest* at each other all the time! Katie and I had so much in common, it seemed!

"I guess so. I don't really…I didn't pay that close attention to…" I said, trying to remember Danny better so as to impress her with my acute observational skills, my magnanimous, self-effacing, genuinely genuine and unalloyed and sincere interest in people other than me. Even *guy* people. The vaginaless of this earth.

"That's my little brother!" Katie interjected. "How funny! How is he? I never see him when we're working. Not even during breaks. I don't really see him when were not, either. How's he doing? Is he okay and everything?"

"He doesn't look anything *like* you, though! That's really your brother?" I sidebarred.

"He's adopted."

The way she said that was very ironically matter-of-fact *and* like she was scolding *me* somehow, for something. It was the weirdest thing. Maybe she was putting a two-and-two together that we're meant to jibe in the sense of she had said he was terribly handsome and I had said she looked nothing like him and therefore, by The Transitive Property,…

"Oh?"

"Not really. That's just what we tell him all the time. Family joke."

"Nice. You say 'doring' for 'during,' you realize."

"I know, I know. Everyone here says that."

"Right," I said. "Got it."

"He looks like me more than you think," she said, getting back on track, as it were. "My hair's not really black, you see. You can still see my natural color in it. They had me dye it in case one of these metal chicks on set—excuse me, one of the *Talent*—who were cast in this preposterous...in this *wonderful* video...in case one of the models... Oh, forget it. Nevermind. Sorry? [she said to not-me] Okay. Gotta go!"

"Go?" I said. "Did you say go as in 'Tell the driver to go?'"

"What?!" she said in a panicky way. "No. Not at all. Not yet! Wait, okay?"

"Okay. Sorry. That was close. So you're an understudy for one of the video vixens as well...Is that what you're saying?! Hahaha! What a Renaissance woman!"

"Very funny. Better not kid around like that, though. I'm serious. You're going to get us *both* in trouble, *John*. The driver might misinterpret you and..."

"Waste gas? Drive an extra hundred yards?"

"I'm really not kidding," she said so calmly and authoritatively that it was a bit...scary.

Big pause.

"Who *are* you, anyway?" she continued, lightly though, easing up on me—or so it seemed to quixotic *moi*. "*I* haven't seen you work any movie jobs. Or music videos, for that matter. You kind of look like you're in a *band*. *Please* don't be in a band...A guy in a band."

Her mocky voice went all mock-macho on that last bit.

"Me? A *band*? No. I'm a spy," I said. "It's my métier."

"Oh?" she fluted. "*Really?!* 'Métier, eh?'"

"I *was* an Oxford don but I got 'sent down,'" I said.

"Dons can't be 'sent down,'" she said. "Only undergraduates."

"*I* know that. It was a joke," I fluted right back. "What—did you *go* there or something? You seem like the sort of girl who might've gone to..."

"Yes, actually."

"*Really?*"

"Surprised?"

"No…Why would I be? I just…"

"I don't look like 'Oxford material'—is that what you were going to say?" she said, taking umbrage it seemed—or mock umbrage, maybe—and hung fire.

I dodged her question with one of my own: "What were you, then? A Rhodes Scholar or something? So you're not just stunningly, impossibly okay-looking and funny, but also athletic and brainy?"

There was a discernible pause and my heart jumped up to my suddenly parched and throbbing throat and I thought I might have gone too far, flirting-wise. Maybe she hadn't heard me say that last bit. I sure did hope so. But before this Katie girl could say something (or not say anything) some more squiggly-sounding orders got squakwed and she urged "Get ready! Ready? Go! Tell the driver to *go!*" to me and I said "Go!" to the driver and he revved the engine like it was going to fly apart like a child's toy "funny car" or a Deluxe "Hot Wheels" from the sixties and the Camaro roared away down the road in the queasily wavering heat haze and the juddering tires made big black smokey skidmarks as the thing, fishtailing, shook madly away from where I stood and then jetted straight and fast as thrilling, smelly hell down the glittering-with-tiny-silver-glass-bits/blue-hued road. I looked away to the surrounding brownly purplish mountains and crazy huggermugger of great red rock formations/Acropolis-like boulders and at the Joshua trees in glorious, imperial bloom all around me (that each seemed—without getting *too* trippy here—to have a personality of their own) and the stiller-than-still cacti of various scary-looking types and the untumbling tumbleweeds and vast patches of yellow sand and dirt-white sand and random, castaway tree limbs and the painted blue-and-cotton skies and lonesome telephone poles clotheslined hither and thither and the backroads and azure shadows on the ground from the clouds above.

"Okay, *cut!*" the director ordered.

"Walk back, two-four-two," my walkie-talkie told me. "That's it for this shot."

"Roger," I said.

"Roger?"

"Roger *Fry*, I meant," I sillily jested.

"Huh?!"

"But he was a *Cambridge* guy," I sort of mumbled. "You know, cause we were talking about Ox..."

"Oh, right," Katie's voiced said. "Bloomsbury Group. Hahaha! I almost said 'Froup!'"

"It was a dumb pun," I said. "On my part," I added.

"I *know!* You're weird," she said, with another, stranger laugh to go with it. "And we say 'copy' in *this* profession, by the way. Not 'roger.' Okay?"

"*I* know."

"No, you didn't!"

"Thanks for the information, then," I said, then added in my most deep, manlyish voice. "Over. I mean, *copy*."

"You don't know *what* you mean, *John...*"

"O-kay," I countered.

"Hey, John! John, listen: 'When you get to a fork in the road, take it.'"

"I'm sorry?" I said, and thought *Wow, this pretty chick has said my name around three hundred times now.* What a cool girl. Unless she's having me on. In that case, whatta bitch. People love to hear their names. The groovy English Goth/pop band Love and Rockets told us so on their splendid, acoustic-y *Earth, Sun, Moon* LP back in 1987.

"Yogi Berra."

"Sorry?"

"It's a Yogism. Yogi Berra?"

"Oh, right," I said. "Dodgers. I'm kidding," I said. "Giants, right?"

"You're teasing me."

"No!"

"Yogi Berra," she went on in what again seemed a not-unself-consciously haughty manner, rather mutely playful, "quite famously said: 'When you get to a fork in the road...'" Katie's voice, slowing down singsongily for each word, went. "That just cracks me up every time," she added.

But then her walkie or mine made a sound like a fat, completely dehydrated log bursting in a crackling fire and I lost her; I sort of speedwalked back to where the orange car was smoking and the little "second unit" crew were standing (smoking as well, gagging on their fags like they just lived through a hurricane, everyone but Katie, that is—she didn't smoke); and as I walked up, I saw the Colin guy deftly flick his still-lit ciggie into some very flammable-looking bushes and I heard the Colin guy say to her "Come away, my dear—on to the next thrilling scenario" in an oleaginous if not downright florid way that sent a shot of utterly irrational, spite-filled jealousy-of-the-Colin-guy right down my sore spine, all the way down to my even more sore-from-hoisting-things thighs, and they (she and the Colin) hopped into one of the jeeps with Colin driving and they, the two of them together, pealed away brodying down a dirt road toward the shoot's "base camp," with the sky above them an as-you-might-expect cerulean blue and the puff of dust from the tires of the jeep appropriately dusty and puffy.

Two

he preceding scene took place on burning, pounding desert sun, mid-afternoon Day Two of my terribly wonderful and terribly terrible and mercifully brief stint as a production assistant on a candy-ass, heavy metal music video. I found out it wasn't Whitesnake or Warrant but some newly signed to a major label band of headbangers called Warrior.

Jesus Lord and Holy Spirit, help us stop our ears, we pray.

Day One, I did two hours of teeth-gritting, finger-clenching hours driving the enormous white lorry in whipping winds, with even bigger trucks whizzing by and daytrippers in fancy Japanese and German autos honking at me as I peered tensely at the tinselly mirrors and white-knuckled all the way to the site of the shoot. The site of the shoot was somewhere in Joshua Tree National Park, California. I had received a veritable Magna Carta of orders from a parliament of movie set people types as soon as I parked the truck and hopped crampedly down from the tall cabin. There was a scaffold going up, tall as hell, with wrenchmonkeys and lighting guys, perfervid fellows, Tarzaning all over the chiasmus of aluminium bars and wood boards, drilling and hammering and shouting and breathing. Tents, trailers, mobile homes, generators galore (like big white bugs), ant-like people humping things and running around and shouting and gesticulating, enormous camera rigs, rows of trucks and jeeps and cars and motorcycles on a motorcycle transporter.

And me.

I remember stretching, and yawning, and looking around in naïve wonderment and advanced awkwardness in the vein of "what in the *fuck* am I doing here; I have no business being here." Like in the movies and such: like how a guy deplanes and—wow!—there's Vietnam, the hot air of it, it really exists, it isn't a dream or a brochure or instructional movie in gritty black-and-white; there they are: the sights he's never seen before, the veritably indescribable, here it is, right in front of him, teamingly real. He really *has* been shipped overseas to fight the war good old boy LBJ said Vietboys exclusively were meant to fight.

Golly gee!

Shortly forthwith (I should say "shortly forth*width*" in homage to a guy on set I—I swear to God—overheard who actually used that "expression" as he was telling a story from another video shoot), the orders began: the commands commanded, the shouted shouts, the screams screamed, the yells yelled, the demands demanded. It seemed like the *waterboys* (and girls: serious Title IX was going on here: girls equaled boys) even were queuing up to boss me around. I mean, *gleefully* queuing up. Like sport or something, it was for them.

NB. Ha! There's no such thing as a "waterboy or girl" on a movie set, reader: I made that up. Though it wouldn't be to hard to imagine sets having them. And calling them *Hydration Associates* or *Canteen Specialists* or something and treating them like, um, waterboys in real life maybe get treated?

Quasi-anaphorically speaking, here goes:

I had been ordered to empty onto the rock-hot, rock-strewn, deserty ground the entire contents of the truck I had driven in in; I had been told to put some tarps down and make piles of like things.

I had been ordered, once all the junk inside was on the ground, to bung it summarily back into said truck and drive the truck an hundred feet down the side road it was parked on and empty it out all over again.

I had been ordered, by Danny V. who came up as I had reloaded (he said he recognized me from one of our gigs; Rob had invited him, he said), to reveal "Who the hell told you [me] to do that?" And I had learned that some wag of a desert-billy local crew member had, "making" me for a total greenhorn, played me a dastardly trick in an idle, impish moment. I had emptied out the truck without, I discovered under Danny's tutelage, the benfit of the nice long treacherous at first but later extremely valuable steel ramp that tongued from under the back doors. And I'd told Dan I had no idea "who had told me to do that" on account of everyone I had seen looked exactly alike, in plain white T-shirts or plaid flannel long-sleeved shirts rolled up or waist-tied or blue button-downs, with cargo shorts in brown or tan, workboots and beards or five o'clock shadows and floppy hats or silly-looking trucker-caps, the ones with the white front with something on it like "Desi's Tavern" or "Lonestar Beer" or "I Like Bosoms" or just a picture in silhouette of an upturned dinosaur being fucked by a genie or a bunny or a clown.

Danny V. just said "*Jesus*, some people—*id*iots!" and walked away fuming, talking on his crackling walkie-talkie. But not before he gave me the scoop on the shoot, which was: a day of humping stuff all over the sandy desert; a day of shooting the hair metal band doing cool tough-guy deserty things like having a "hot" bim of a metal chick model who kinda looked like them make out with them, having hot rods peal out and huff plumes of blue-black smoke and tan-pink dust all over the joint; and, on the last day's night of filming, having a concert with the band rocking atop one of the mountains of red stone while fireworks shot all around and the bims danced sex-kitten dances (in slutty bikinis and fuck-me pumps, natch) all around and then everyone in the video seeming to be consumed in a *fire* that symbolically symbolized their *desire* to *rock* till they *dropped* or they'd be a *liar* if they told you anything *other* than that they wanted to *rock* and never fucking *stop* till they were dead or bald or had to go jobs at Costco in the Lumber or Patio & Garden or something, after having gotten haircuts so that they could get said jobs at Costco, or WalMart, or Thrifty's, or one of the myriad Chuck E. Cheeses that were springing up in suburban areas where white people were White Flighting to.

Blecch.

At least that's how the video "script" was "written." There might be some other shit shot if the director and the art director and the set designer and the record label people and the band's manager and the band's manager's assistant manager and the band could all see eye-to-eye about it, Danny said, filling me in.

"Cool," I said. As if it mattered what I thought, or that I knew what in hell was going on.

In the truck was the following mostly heavy, quite unwieldy material: several…oh who cares; it was a lot of heavy, hard to carry metallic stuff and a mess of unwieldy folding chairs and "apple boxes" and big black road cases filled with plutonium or something equally burdensome and cumbersome.

I had been ordered to join a quartet of PAs who were attempting to carry twenty feet in deep sand a dolly that weighed one million pounds—when, seeing me as a weak, albeit tall, weakling who stood nary a chance of even getting a purchase on such a machine, let alone hoisting it, a chick with a flat top haircut kept in place with a red bandana pushed me vigorously and (*I* thought) a touch too ostentatiously out of the way and away they scuttled, like a human centipede (with legs, obviously, missing).

I had been ordered for a short spell to "fan" (as in keep cool with hand-held little electric propeller fans) the four bimmy models who were meant to "go with" the four members of the band. Each of whom was stripper-pretty and makeup caked. A big-haired, golden-skinnned, nice-butted foxy brunette bim matched up with the dark-haired, wolf-faced guitarist; a big-haired, poodle-ish, boy-faced redhead bim paired off with the flame-domed, Doberman-miened drummer; a big-haired, big-eyed, vixenish blondie bimby went with the tow-haired, kitten-nosed singer; and the poor Bassett-mugged bass player got kind of a canine-looking chick with humongous breasts (meant, ostensibly, by either a merciful God or herself or her personal, on-call plastic surgeon, to distract one from looking at her dogface) whose hair wouldn't stay all that big so the makeup people had to keep scurrying over to her to embiggen it with long-ass plastic wide-pronged combs and fireplace pokers and trowels and wizard wands and can after can of ultraflammable hairspray.

Now: another asidely aside:

Feminists of the Great Wide Wonderous World Unite if you want, all you want, against me. Go on, then. Form protest clubs and cabals and bluestocking-ish, indignant societies of suffrage and outrage. March, picket, protest and write your congresswoman. Cry Caricature! Misogyny! But I, *moi*, me, *yo*, I for one did *not* instruct or encourage these women to:

    a)   wear dresses that looked like they'd been aerosol'd on.

    b)   wear lipstick-red fuck-me pumps eight-to-ten inches high.

    c)   stop going to school in the sixth or seventh or eighth grade.

    d)   hang out at The Rainbow or The Roxy instead of The Downtown Library Learning Center or the various The Berlitz Institutes sprinkled all 'round our fair burg.

e)   get as much spray-tanning and "augmenting" as they or their boyfriends or benefactors could afford.

To crown all, I had been ordered virtually to "stand by"—stand right by, that is, the director himself, The Great Colin—to see if I needs must "run" for something. Another PA had apparently been instructed to bring him a Coke with lime. But when the drink came, there was a lemon in it.

'Zounds! Goats and *mon*keys!

"I said a *lime*—not a lemon!" the Colin-guy director screamed. "What *are* you—color blind? A fruit bat? Can I please just get—just the once, mind—something done *right* around here? *Once? One time?* Or do I, as per fucking usual, have to do everything my*self* and grow a bloody orchard by my*self*?! Katie! *Katie!* Where the fresh *hell* is *Katie!* Is this what I went to *art school* for? (It is *not.*) Is this what I went to *film* school for? (*Neg*ative.) Is this why I starved in bloody *Camden* for more than six months, writing, writing, writing—studying the masterpieces of Fassbinder, Herzog, and Henry Jaglom?! (I *ask* you!) It is *not* why I went to art school, to film school, to the St. Martins College caff and ate soda crackers with Worchestershire for almost a week! I want a lime *Coke* and I want it *yesterday!* God *damn* you people! How can I *work* like this?! Hmmm? I have, I say, precious *little* patience *left!*"

You (if you were me) wanted to say: "Hey, *Beard*by! Hey, *Red*ford! Yeah you with the ego to match your stentorian bullhorn-that-you-don't-even-*need*, blowhard. Hey, *you!* Hitchcock! Hoity-toity, bro! Gimme a fucking break. You are an unreal cliché-on-wheels, you are. Unreally so. Can you *hear* you? Wow."

I mean, I don't like it when people treat redheads all shabby, treat them like, um, redheaded stepchildren, as the saying goes. But still. A cunt is a cunt is a cunt, to quote your gran. Isn't that so? And when I am crowned king king, and not just the king of good intentions king, shabmeister guys like Colin The Great? Straight down to the dungeon with them. Or better yet, straight into the stocks. Buckets o'moatwater cascading o'er their hey-wait-how-did-this-happen-to-me heads.

Sponge-throwing contest organized—all welcome! Free dishwater for all subjects to dip their porous projectiles in. Hear ye, hear ye! Come on down! Step right up!

'Round lunchtime I had been ordered to *eat* (the ever-smiling Crafts Service people dished out chow that was *incredible*), and I had been ordered immediately to *stop eating* and immediately get back to work humping things in the immediate vicinity of and according to the whims of those capricious ones who needed the stuff humped "yesterday at the earliest." Humping, humping humping—sometimes with Danny V., sometimes with a bunch of irony-free people who seemed to be *happy* carrying unwieldy bags of sand across the sand.

I had discovered muscles I never knew I had.

Humping, humping, humping—I have used this term so many times I oughta just stop right here and go write for the movies: the *pornographic* movies and make a gajillion of the big bucks and stuff and get my *own* matching bimbos and bright white, blue, orange, red fireworks.

It is good, I might add, to discover money, charms, buried treasure in your backyard, rich and kind relatives, athletic and academic skills you never knew you had. Good it is for all of the above. Indeedly-do.

Yet do note that I did not include the word "muscles" in the aforesaid concatenation of goodnesses.

I had *not* been ordered, after dinner, around eight that evening, to find my truck and hide in it all night long so that no one could find me and harry me into humping more things, faster, faster. But that's exactly what I did—hide in "my" truck. I ordered myself to get the hell away from anyone with a walkie-talkie or a voice or eyes to spy me and have me lift an elephant over a pole-jumper's bar or whatnot. That's the craven, blessed truth, reader: I hid and eventually slept in the lorry so that no one could boss me around and destroy as much of my tender muscle tissue and rather even more tender human dignity. And in the morning, the day I was telling you about, I got up at around six o' clock, sore as all get-out and sand-dusted like hell (you can bet I looked around carefully to see if anyone was gonna clock me emerging from a berthless, sleeping-wise, lorry truck and maybe send sneaky me home, without pay, without said truck, having to walk all the way back to LA); I hopped down, brushed myself off, brushed my teeth with no water chaser of any kind, and waltzed in the most ungainly, Devils-Island-guy-dragging-a-chain-into-the-middle-of-a-swamp fashion over to the Crafts Service area for delicious, aromatic coffee and homemade-tasting and plenteously iced cinnamon rolls and fresh squeezed orange juice and stuffed French toast and English and Canadian bacon and farm fresh eggs and hot Swiss chocolate with imported marshmallows and caviar and champagne with truffles, fois gras, and toad-in-the-hole. Kidding about the last few of course— but it seemed like, if you asked nicely and smiled widely, you might actually get something like that. I don't think the very richest Romans in olden timey Roman days ever ate like that. You know: how they were supposed to have stuffed a baby crocodile with skylark livers and lamb dumplings and mother's milk and roasted it inside an almond-and-fig encrusted wild baby boar.

Something like that.

Apropos of dinner the night before: there had been two eating areas: one with simple tables and some random umbrellas and one with a tarp of royal purple with golden tassles dangling from it, obviously off-limits to all but the director, the record execs, the DP, the assistant director and their assistants—but not the assistants' assistantsn: no way—and the quote-unquote Talent. I had passed by there on my way to the area for the crew (peasant green in color, the tablecloths were), and the elite on the set had, as I trundled by as quickly as I could, looked up from their plates with looks on their faces like bears in the wild who, having salmon with lemon or something, hear something and get ready to growl or claw lest that something try to wrest away their respective feasts. I didn't look *too* hard (of course I, the entire time, and for all the reasons I've been presenting here, tried to be as inconspicuous as possible), but I thought I saw two or three guys with "butter beards." They must've been having Crab and Lobster Delight or something. Scallops and jumbo shrimp medley in *le soupe beure*, maybe.

And of course, this being LA still (in effect—all of Southern California, from The High Desert to desolate Catalina, is Los Angeles), I got accosted, almost as soon as I plopped myself and my plate down, by another PA who was a working musician.

"Hey, man," he said, doing that head-and-chin flick thing that "cool" guys do. "Hey, man. Don't I know you? Aren't you in Weird Sisters? Jangle pop fuzzy psychedelic band—you're the singer, right?"

"Yeah, hi," I said and shook hands. "John. *The* Weird Sisters. And I'm not the only sing…"

"Alexi," he said. "What's going on, man? So you're working this shoot too, yeah?"

"Um, hm," I said.

Then the inevitable.

"You guys are the ones with that really cute chick playing lead guitar and singing too, huh."

"Yeah," I said, forking some garlic mashed potatoes with sugared plantains swimming in hot black pepper *negra* sauce into my ravenous mouth. "My girlfriend."

"Oh, yeah? She is, huh? Cool."

Then the other inevitable.

"I've been meaning to see you guys, man. I've heard of you, but I haven't, like, heard you, you know? I don't think I have. Have I? Anyway. Maybe I read about you guys somewhere or someone told me or something."

This all I took in with the appropriate obligatory blankish look. I'm not so hot on analogies but it was like the awkward moment you get when you're stuck in an elevator with someone you maybe work with and whom you'd just heard some gossip about. Or like when you tell someone you never liked their friend and they tell you said friend just found out he had lupus or just lost his house or had to join the Navy on account of he got someone's young wife pregnant and the husband-someone was gonna kill him if he ever saw him on shore again.

Then the super inevitable: "You oughta check out *my* band, man."

He flicked his bowl cut hair cut, super straight and dyed Peter Murphy black, back into his eyes and kind of nodded his head like he was listening to a tape of himself right just then.

"We're called The John Bonham and Cheese Sandwich. We got a review for our fourth CD right now that's in *NME*."

I did my blank look thing I save for actors and quote-unquote fellow musicians.

"I'm sure you've heard of us," he said, his heavy-hooded eyes going even more half-mast.

"I *think* so," I tentatived.

"We're changing the face of music, actually—with what we're doing. We've made *four* albums in *two* years. One of them we recorded in one single day, only. An afternoon and night. One of our albums, we did."

"I *think* so," I tentatived again.

"Think what—heard of us, or what?" he said, his chewed food on unmissable show as he provocatively waited for my reply.

"Yeah, uh-huh," I said.

I mean, even *I'm* not *that* unflappable, impassive, pokerfaced and impervious. And besides I *had* heard of his band, *and* heard them. This Alexi "cat" was notorious for burning through band members up and down the west coast, from Vancouver to San Diego where he hailed from. San Diego where, in the fourth grade, reportedly, he'd announced that, as an auto-confirmed genius, he had nothing more to gain from traditional "alternative" schooling. On tour, he was legendarily known for kicking his band mates in the face as a "good morning" while they slept on the tatty couch in some rabid fan's basement/marijuana "grow room" in Nebraska or New Mexico, and for fistfights onstage and in general and for general, all-purpose dementia, megalomania, and delusions of grandiloquent grandeur. He had kicked a fan in the chest for heckling him and telling him to get clean and stop smoking laudanum and pharmaceutical opium. He had kicked a fan in the *face* for saying "We love you, Alexi! You're a genius!" He had punted a punter for yawning from the third row of one of his gigs; he'd leaped off stage and butterfly-stroked over the first two rows to get at the poor obsequious chap and kick his shins in. Alexi, asked about it, the punching, in an interview, said he'd punted him, the punter, because he could punt him, and because no one in the bobbing throng would dare to intercede in the mad, violent doings of a zany "genius." He berated people for liking him, liking him, that is, without being about to quote from his songs and/ or recite them backward. He brooked no fancy sycophancy, Alexi didn't. No one was safe from him and this appalling, cross-eyed, crazy "brilliance." He took riffs from The Who, melodies from The Zombies, feedback screes from The Velvet Underground, snippets from lyrics by Dylan, his vocal tone from any British guy sauntering drunkenly down Denmark Street circa 1968, and more lyrics from poetry for high schoolers like Lawrence Ferlinghetti and Kahil Gibran and Robert Fucking Frost—and, lo, he went and called it Art. People lapped it up. People thought him avant garde, cutting edge, an agent provocateur, the rock messiah, the Second Coming of John Winston Ono Lennon-McCartney. People with IQs in the two-digit range did, that is. People turned up at his gigs just to see whom he would fight with (the choices were: the guys in his band, the guys in the audience, the guys on the road or stage crew, or a girl he was dating or who was merely rumored to be preggo with his lovechild); or just to see whom he might call a "sell-out" for liking the Rolling Stones or kittens or homemade ice cream. On his first, celebrated trip to NYC to play CBGB's, a bedraggled film crew of UCLA students in ragged tow, Alexi had dragged a fire extinguisher into the street from its glass case and punched it out, berating it for forsaking "the true cause of rock." A chapbook of his fawning letters to rock luminaries such as Paul McCartney, Peter Gabriel, Morrissey, and that wizard from Boston (the band, that is) had come out from a subsidiary of The University of Oregon Press, a limited edition, printed on matte, wrapped in vellum, and signed with a quill pen dipped in Alexi's own spittle and flem. The police turned up at most of his gigs. The *Police* (the band, that is)—on almost-speaking terms again for just one night—were spotted backstage when The John Bonham & Cheese, etcetera had first gone to England to play some Woodsprite or or Lawn Gnome or Fairy Festival or Splendour on the Grass/Day Out type thing. Sting (Sting!) had given him a hug and a sweater or "jumper" he, Sting, had knitted himself that was made out of a weave of certified virgin Welsh wool and his (Sting's) famous philanthropic wife Trudy's golden brown bobbed hair. Stewart Coupland had looked on and scowled (mostly at Sting) and Andy Summers had looked on and felt like the luckiest guitarist in the world, "just glad to be there, here, or anywhere, really." Some wag writing for *Melody Maker* had reported the whole thing in neo-Pickwickian prose, run and interview rife with malaprops and spoonerisms, and of course all manner of twaddle and cack on the part of Alexi. In the pages of that stalwart, super fickle, trendoid rag, Alexi had crowed that Charles Manson was one of the greatest neglected American songwriters. Old Charlie and himself, of course. And that Aleister Crowley was the greatest undiscovered American writer. He'd added that one day he'd hoped to make a record, in prison, no less, with Manson himself.

"That sounds cool," the idiot reporter had cravenly riposted.

There was a pic of Alexi tipping a bota bag back, streaming Spanish wine into the eye of someone sitting behind him on a plane flying over Greenland as he and his unmerry band made their inargural sally to Blighty.

Yeah, I'd heard of him. Of all the braggy cunts in Rockland, Alexi of The John Bonham, etcetera, was the braggiest of all. Like everyone in the underground scene in Los Angeles, Jenny and I had heard "the buzz" on his band before there even was a buzz on his band; and like every other in-the-loop musician we'd gone to see him play a tiny club in Silver Lake—some secret show or invite-only industry showcase.

You know.

Yes we'd seen him play—for one and a half "songs," that is. And that was it: out-of-there!

He'd opened with a bang—by banging, that is, a tambourine that was missing most of its metal jingles against his guitar strings for fully fifteen minutes, berating the audience, calling us "quiblings"

[sic], telling everyone "shut the fuck up" (over and over), and daring us not to declare him the coming messiah of indie. His cowed band stumblingly lurch-crept up onstage and droned along with him on "A" (playing Vox Teardrops and Hagstrom 12-strings, all of them epically out-of-tune) while Alexi sang in a markedly studied and impressively unwavering Welsh accent, making sure to add a few hundred *Y* and *CW* sounds to his superlispy, whispered vocals.

The effect was oddly mesmerizing—like if you saw a Gandhi or Sri Sri Anyguy yelling prolongedly at a parking lot attendant or a small child building a sandcastle, the Gandhi or Sri Sri guy with, say, a popsicle or Fudgsicle or something in his hand, or like if you saw a monkey playing an accordion virtuosoishly while a drunken midget danced while "conducting" using his record-breaking mustache.

"I've never hit anyone but my little brother in my life," Jenny had observed, shouting into my ear, shouting over the din the Cheese were making, as we watched in awful awe as Alexi snatched the triangle from "his" triangle-player's hands and did a solo on it with a profoundly smug look on his face; "and that was probably with just a pillow during a pillow fight," Jenny continued; "but I want to punch that guy in the face *so bad* right now, I can't tell you. I think I might be able to 'take' him, too. What do you think, John-John?" she'd said. "Should I *bop* him one? Should I? I really *want* to."

There was a shady booker (what a redundancy!) at that gig, I recall, who was notorious for stiffing bands and sifting the "the door" (i.e. the money that people pay to see a band) and moving your set time around and putting four extra acts on the bill at the last moment. Jenny and I knew this guy on account of he had, months earlier, given us a midnight-on-a-Tuesday slot (a shit slot, that is) at his paltry, dirty club. Of course we couldn't get more than ten people down to the show for a slot like that; and the guy had given us nothing but hell for it; and any time he saw us at a friend's band's gig or something he gave out this smirk like I don't know what—like he was all smirky and stuff. He was positively not our favorite, this booker, whose name was Grott Golding; not in our good books. I remember him weaseling over during the set, all smiley and whatnot, socking you in the face with stage-three bourbon-breath, going "Aren't they great?! Aren't they *amazing*?" And me going, sarcastically, without Golding catching on, "Oh, yeah, in*cred*ible."

"The guys in Nirvana were at a show of ours a year ago," Alexi continued, uninvited, unprovoked, of course, accosting me encore, before I could think of somewhere I had to be. I was kind of wishing one of the assistant assistant directors would come 'round right then and order me to move a pyramid or a jet plane over one of the really red rocky formations that towered in the nearish distance. That'd have been preferable.

"Oh?" I parried, yawning grandiloquently, making no attempt to stifle it, doing it on purpose, in fact. I mean, you aren't going to *stop* people like him from going on and on. You're just not. Just as you're not going to stop me doing everything I can to try and stop guys like *him*. Plus, of course, I was beyond exhausted. Plus, as I always or often say: "Sometimes a yawn is a brilliant retort."

"Individually—and this is no bullshit—," Alexi continued, "*each one of them* came up to me and started kissing my ass. Separately, they did. No kidding. Kurt Cobain, Dave Grohl, the other guy. Novalis somebody. Yeah, that's him. Telling me I'm a genius, basically. Two guys in this *big* British band (I can't tell you who, of course) actually wanted to suck my dick when we played this festival with them in Lichtenstein. Literally suck it, in fact. I don't think they're even *fags*, man. They just, like, totally got off on what we did just as much as *we* get off on us. And a reliable source told me the Buzzcocks were maybe going to reform just to do a gig with us."

"Umm," I managed, choking on a delicious piece of super tender barbequed chicken breast.

"Kurdt Cobain said I was the future of rock, in fact," he superciliously continued. "Before he died he said that. Swear to God. The most influential music *lawyer* in The United States, Hyron McFarsom, Esq., told me he wanted to become a homosexual just to become part-time lover of me. Do you know him? He is a total friend of this guy totally cool booker called Grott Golding who, like, brought us along in LA. He has told thousands of people about my talent. At North by Northwest, New Music Seminar, South by Southwest…hell, he's thinking of starting his own international music conference jst so we can headline it. How rad is that? He told me himself he was the most important lawman in America. And who am I to nonbelieve him? Have you ever met him—big guy, four chins, loud, baying voice, knows everything about music? Crazy guy? Always starting fights with people. Always threating to sue them or punch them out? Hilarious. *Great* guy. We're totally his favorite band of all time. I mean…"

"I don't think I do," I managed.

"He told me so, man—and I believed him. End of story. Hahaha! He punches more people than I do! Well, he threatens to. He threatens to punch you if you don't agree with him about The John Bonham and Cheese Sandwich, that's for sure, man. He saw the Stones before they were even called the Stones, man. That's what he told me. Do you believe that? Most people consider him a bloated oaf but he's really loud in his support of The Sandwich, man. The Sandwich is changing the entire music industries, man. We're doing it and the revolutions— plural—we are starting are beginning, like, well—what am I saying?— they *are* happening, like, *now*, dig? That's right—you heard right: revolutions. We aren't just starting *one*, okay? We have several going right now, my band and my fans. Pay attention. Get ready. The times a-changeling and all of that, man. A film crew filmed me for three years, man. Before I even had a band. They filmed me in my sleep! (Parenthesisly, I play over two hundred instruments. You probably didn't know that. I didn't even know that till I just, like, picked up a few new ones that I had no idea I had the abilities to, like, play.)"

With greasy fingers *and his fork*, Alexi parted his lank hair theatrically down the middle just then, like Moses doing the Dead or Red Sea or whatever, and gave me *that* look that brazen, lying liars almost *always* prevaricatingly give you—the look that simply begs you in a way to contradict them. The look that accompanies invariably the little verbal tics like "in fact" (as though saying it substantiates it) and "no lie" or "swear to God" and "and this is no bullshit" (as though such a phrase magically just *guarantees* a mendacity-free anecdote or accolade). Some are subtle about it, some obvious. Damn near all betray themselves. Maybe not every time they lie, but those surefire "tells" are *there* more often than not. You just have to be aware of them, look out for them. If you care. If you want to, that is. Plus this: liar-guys like that often get all bumptiously up in your air or face space when they're fabricating away. They get up close, I imagine, in order to add the *insult* of their drunk-on-themselves presence to the *injury* to the quote-unquote truth that they're inflicting. It's like they are swingeing at the truth, punishing it.

Rock's gotta lotta liars and braggarts, boy. Don't think otherwise.

And of course I didn't, didn't contradict him. I *should* have advised him to try the *jerk* chicken, that's what I shoulda done. Ha! And I was incredulous at myself for having endured so much of this idiot's balderdash. I couldn't eat fast enough to try to get away. It was like I was unceremoniously entered in an eating contest of some sort. I thought I was going to choke on my chicken.

"I couldn't *name* twenty instruments," I jested instead, adding "Sorry, *man*—forgot I gotta go make a phone call. See you" before he could pick up his rodomontade where he'd left off. He was like a one-man orgy of rodomontadery.

It wasn't a lie, me having to make a call. I thought (my worn body thwarted my addled brain) I had told Jenny I would try and call her. I couldn't remember if I did or not—tell her that, that is. I was quite confused and super knackered. I got up and Fribee'd my half-finished plate into a rubbish bin and went to a trailer Danny'd told me about that had a phone for we prole-plebes' use and dialed home but I got the machine so I just told Jen hi and that I was okay but worked to death after one day and not to worry and that I loved her more than peaches.

I love you more than peaches: another inside joke.

I forgot to tell her who I'd just run into; I must have been attempting precipitately to block out the just-made memory.

Some things, some people, you just can't unsee, unhear.

Three

nd the relentless, blaring, hair metal soundtrack for all this—Days One *and* Two (speaking of things you can't unhear)?

The "song" by Warrior that was being turned into a video consisted of the following: a tarted-up and overplayed/almost more-than-parody of Led Zeppelin's "Rock and Roll," *drum-wise*; an exceedingly unpleasant, squealing, chainsaw-sounding speed-metal-riff stolen from Van Halen's "Panama," *lead guitar-wise*; a dull, thudding, repetitious, rumbling bassline that couldn't have been purloined from anyone save a (drunken) beginner player devoid of rhythm, *bass-wise* ; a chugga-chugga set of cliché chords ripped off from Ratt's "Round and Round," *rhythm guitar-wise*; and, to crown all, a higher-than-high-pitched, atonally shrieking vocal that, *idea-wise,* must have been nicked from a demonstration record of sound effects that they used to make in the sixties (e.g. "Lonesome Train Whistle," "Calliope at a Country Fair," "Speakers Cacophonying at Speakers Corner of a Sunday Afternoon," "Infant with Croup Crying," "Siege of Cranes Flying Overhead," "Child Being Brutally Spanked," "Child Being Savagely Whipped," "Big Ben Sounding Twelve o' the Clock," "Gush of Water Cascading Through Some Unsuspecting Personage's Window near the Flooding Ganges," etcetera, etcetera), *singing-wise.*

In fact, the Warrior singer guy's voice sounded like an arthritic banshee who's just had its big toe stepped on by a mastodon or Land Rover *mixed with* a eunuchy Vienna Choir Boy being singed repeatedly with a gleefully sadistic blacksmith's redhot forging iron *crossed with* a cat being torn apart by a band of baying coyotes *mated with* a bobcat rogering a house cat *merged with* a baby seal being casually clubbed by a one-eyed, cretinous, salty seafarer *times* Maria

Sharapova hitting a forehand with all her horrible, obnoxious, grunty-shrieky might. I'll go you one more and say it was like when parts of your teeth scrape across something nasty/slippery as you dubiously bite into a something-burger from a mystery joint (like they, your choppers, misfire kinda) and you simultaneously hit your funny bone hard on a sharp edge while landing on a broken sprinkler head with your coccyx or "tailbone." If that sounds nigh-on impossible—pulling off a tremendously bumbling trifecta like that—well, maybe. But it can be imagined. What can*not* be imagined, humanly conceived, is how atrocious the "tune" by Warrior was; *that*, mere words cannot convey. I reckon I could liken it to biting repeatedly the inside of your mouth. You know how, chomping a caramel apple or a nice slice of filet mignon, sometimes you do that, then almost immediately *do it again?* Well this *was* doing it again and again and again. It was that ouchy.

Pitch-wise, the voice itself was higher than Cheech *and* Chong having a two-on-one "bong off" with Snoop Doggy Dog.

It was just shy, *range-wise,* of what that iconic RCA Victor poochy, Nipper, with his adorable floppy ears, could hear.

It was horrible, just horrible. But somehow the guy's voice was horribly befitting of the unbelievable horribleness of the horrible "song." The song whose title I never learned the name of—and thankfully. 'Twould make it, I reckoned, much easier to get out of my head if I never learned what it was called. I would have to get other songs, good songs, into my head, I was sure, in order to get this song out of it (my head); but the thing was that it was the kind of song that, when it wasn't busy making you want to kill yourself, *makes you never want to hear a note of music again, never in the rest of your life*. It was abominable. *I* abominated it. Everyone did. Except of course the four preening, prancing, poofy posers in Warrior. They jumped up and down, it seemed, every single time it came over the gargantuan stack of megaspeakers the soundman and best boys had rigged up.

The to say the least ostentatious chains 'round the band's collective necks jangled and jounced. They tore with delight at their frilly, tux-ish shirtfronts. Apelike, they clapped their leather, stud, braceleted wrists together and shook their hair out and played air guitar (if they were the guitarist) or air drums (if they were the drummer) or just stood there mouthbreathing (if they were the singer and bassist) and "rocking." In their veritable periwigs, they looked like so many bobbing or bopping Daniel Defoes or William Congreves. They shook their skinny-ass butts in their leather pants like they were dancing girls or Laker Girls. Even if it was on for a mere three seconds (the sound guys futzed relentlessly with the sound equipment—you'd just be standing there, taking a break or biting into one of the ubiquitous energy bars that got passed out like Halloween candy to keep you sugared, working, going, humping—and the Warrior track would punch you in the face like the speakers were right next to your ear, it was that loud), the foursome would start headbanging to their own "tune."

I did give the song a name, myself, however. The name I gave it was "The Most Horrible Song Anwhere, USA." I thought that that kinda summed it up rather tidily.

So anyway, the night of Day Two was basically all of us "on crew" standing 'round watching Warrior mime their song as they stood atop a really paradigmatic and admittedly beautifully-lit ochre mini-mountain of rocks while orange-red-lemon-and-blue fireworks shot incessantly from behind them, rippled through the air around them, and the counterpart bims danced corybantically in front of them (waving firey torches of firey fire like pyromaniacal cheerleaders) and wag-strutted all "sexy" and stuff beside them. The director, that Colin guy, at one point had to yelp "Cut!" on account of the bassman had rocked so hard that his wig (not a metaphor—he was bald as hell) had flown off and landed at the feet of the shortest vixen, who'd tripped on it in her thigh-high boots and gone a-pratfalling, nearly skidding off the big rock. It was like she was performing some sort of gag race at a church picnic where you had to hunch over *and* lose your footing for as long as you could, making your arms windmill madly, while shrieking dunderheadedly.

I couldn't make this stuff up if I tried, believe me.

The director had *not* stopped filming, however, when the singer's actual hair—doubtless doused with excess mousse and extra hairspray—had caught fire: it was the last take of the night anyway, and one might reckon that the Colin fellow and the editor would have a good laugh at the footage of the flailing frontman attempting unsuccessfully to slap out the flames firing from his on-fire head until one of the fire safety people on hand (one of whom was a midget, I shit you not) had scrambled in seeming filmic slow-motion up the face of the rock/plinth/acropolis/palladium and hosed the poor singer down with the extinguisher he'd effortfully lugged up with his person. Only then, when this last farce was ostensibly on film, had Colin The Great shouted "Cut! Cut! Cut! That's a wrap for tonight! In fact, that's *it*, everyone! Brilliant! Brilliant job, all!" Then all and sundry burst into applause of ambiguous purport. All except of course the singer guy, who, instead, burst into tears at having burst into flames, his cardinal hair (hence: identity) once a trademark, now in plaguy-gooey messy shambles. For a second there, I thought that the scathing way the singer looked at the wig-wearing bass player betokened a scrap, wherein the former would try to appropriate the latter's hair-piece, but I was wrong: instead, a roadie or grip or somebody lumbered over with a magnum of Jack and they all, I saw, took a swig out of it while the bass player whipped out his dick and, for a lark or maybe just because they were in a band together, pissed on the drummer's drum kit. It probably wasn't even the drummer's real drum kit—just some prop thing—so what the hell would he care? He himself probably whipped out his own cock and shellacked the damn thing, for all I knew. But of course I didn't stick around to see.

Four

o what do you think?" Katie, sidling up to me, had said after the first hour of night-filming. And she'd skipped away before I could answer. I watched her playfully put her knee into the condyles of the femur, popliteal region, of a tall guy standing next to her surly brother.

Saucy hussy.

And why had that parochial little act bugged me so much?

She smiled this mile-wide smile and he turned around after buckling, kinda, and frowned in a very aggro way—until he saw, presumably, who'd "done" him the little trick; Katie was standing out of the way, looking at the set, trying to act all innocent till she couldn't contain herself, presumably, any longer and looked the tall guy's way and cracked up completely. He gave her a wave "get outta here, you," and the intimacy of it, probably utterly innocent, made my already errant, erring heart go boom. And she bolted away again toward where the director and the camera guys were.

Around two in the morning, the set having shut down, the shoot completed, wrapped, put to bed, Danny had me hump and hump *mucho* more stuff back into my truck, and some other trucks (there was no humping myself hidingly into a truck this time).

"Your sister's amazing!" I'd ventured; goonily, I realized, between deep breaths, the huffs and the puffs: "She's hilarious. So funny and, um, she's really articulate."

"Yeah, right," he'd scowled. "Gimme a break. I mean, she's okay. You don't know her. You wouldn't say that if you knew her."

"Of course," I'd said before I could stop myself.

Base betraying cavalier-of-falseness.

Danny screwed up his mouth: "You talking smack about my sister, man?" he said.

"No! Not at all. I mean…"

"Ah, I'm only messing with you," he said, but he wasn't smiling. Then he said: "Good working with you, though, man. Nice job. Not so bad despite the, er, entertainment."

"Yeah, right," I said. "Seriously."

"If you ever do another of these shoots you'll find you don't even hear the awful music, after a while. And I *like* metal. Hey: don't leave without getting paid, okay? It's cash-on-the-line, this job. Find me first thing in the morning and I'll take care of it—I'll find you one of the production managers."

"Thanks, Danny," I said.

Then around an hour later a guy (red bandana, bushy sideburns, chummily gap-toothed and smiling widely—thought it could've just been the way his mouth was shaped) I hadn't met or seen before kind of shouted: "Hey, man—you gotten any sleep this whole shoot? You look exhausted" and I said "No, I don't think so; I don't think I have, actually," and he shook his sympathetic, disbelieving head and said something into his walkie-talkie and told me to follow him and we went off to a giant silver trailer where he gave me a fat, soft, warm blanket and a pillow and a berth across from an empty berth and I must have fallen dead asleep in my dusty T-shirt and sweatshirt and Bermuda shorts, just barely getting my dust-covered Docs off before I drifted off to dreamland.

Coda

"ood morning," Katie said as I opened my eyes. "How'd you sleep?"

"What time is it?" I managed; there was a little faint red light on in the front part of the cabin where we'd bunked across from one another. "Where am I?"

"Joshua Tree. Hi, John. You snore...a little."

"*You* snore," I yawned and rubbed sleep and furtively tugged at my groin, adjusting the blanket as a decoy, mmm-ing as I did so. "Who are you again?" I said through blanket, having pulled it up and over my head.

"I so do not," Katie said and, reaching over, straining to do so, wrested the wooly thing back down again.

"You so do so. Be quiet, please. People are still sleeping."

"You were totally asleep the whole night. You couldn't know that. And I *don't* snore!" Katie said.

"Well, okay," I whistled; "If you say so. Yes, miss. What are you doing here, anyway?"

"Sleeping, obviously. Without snoring."

"It's this cute little *girly* sort of snore, actually. A sort of adorable little diminutive somnambulist murmuring."

Then I did a quiet, quite ludic, grotesque, and pathetic imitation of a woman snoring quietly, embarrassedly, stertorously—effetely, making what must have been just a hideous face.

[This was all said in the quietest of voices, by the way—at least the part of it after I'd said "I so do not."]

"You break out the sesquipedalian ostentation this early, before coffee? Before you're even *up*?"

"Not so *loud*," I shushed her back.

She laughed.

It was still dark out; something like five, five-thirty-in-the-morning, just before sun-up—who knew? It could've been a year from then, I was so disoriented.

Yet, wishing I could make out her plump pretty scarlet lips in the anonymous darkness, I was conscious enough to be able to tell Katie was just waxing censorious because she liked me, kinda, *may*be, and she was nervous about it. Or seemed so. Or I was just wishfully-thinking/projecting it. She didn't want to, like me, that is. I was right there with her: I don't really want to like me, either, but I sort of have to, on account of I do, I have to admit to me, say such enormously preposterously entertaining things. I mean, you have to give me that. Plus as I might have mentioned around a zillion thousand times she was, even then, first thing in the a.m., goddam beautiful, even with her hair aswirl, a mess, and with her nice mouth slack and the endearing cuneiform lines from a cheap pillow on her nice left cheekbone and faintly freckled neck.

"Oh my God. Were you watching me *sleep?*" I said, archly.

"Ha! You look like a little boy. With your little fist beneath your head. No, though. I wasn't 'watching you sleep.' Whatever do you mean?"

I gave her a stern look. Playful, but only I could have known that it was, unless she was good at interpreting affectionate smiles and sundry affable shakings of the head.

"Maybe a little, I was," Katie said more than coyly. "Okay. I admit it. Okay. I was."

She gave out then a stifled titter and tossed off the sleeping bag that was covering her and rolled her long, lovely, sitting-up self out of the bunk and stood up and, with just a no-frills, practical white bra and shorts on, started scrabbling at the bedding in order to try and find, presumably, her top. She was just standing back up from leaning over to find it and about to put it on when I got up and stood up next to her, balancing my right hand on the ledge above me, and put my left arm very, very gently around her waist and kissed her on the back between her shoulder blade and her spine, nearish her neck. Not at all wet, not at all long—sweet, keen, fond, friendly, liberty-taking, yes, of course, but not too much so (or so I hoped).

But of course *way* too intimate, brazen, surreal, familiar, startling enough to elicit a fat smack in the face and a princess-ish "Well, I declare" from even the most ribald and game "damosel."

"What are you doing?!" she laughed but of course sort of indignantly, in a loud whisper. Then more quietly-serious: "What do you think you're *doing?* You can't just…"

"Nothing," I said in a sort of automatic of course way, not decanting my feelings but rather pouring them right out on the floor.

"You can't just…I ought to…I mean. Really?"

"I'm not going to apologize," I said in a supercilious way that impressed even me. "And I have to say, I'm kind of impressed by you, Katie."

"Oh, so that's what you do when you just feel like doing something and you're so very hard to impress—is that it?"

And of course I couldn't tell if she was angry or pleased. Quite possibly she was both.

"I'm sorry?"

"Huh!" she said. "I mean…*really!* You just…You…"

"Well, sort of," I said, bailing her out, as it were. "*I* don't know. I *guess*. Listen: can I call you sometime when we get back to civilization? May I, I mean? I would like to see you, is what I'm, um, saying. Can I see you? Katie."

"I don't think so."

"Take you to Paris or Buenos Aires or to see the Dodgers play the Expos? Will you give me your number? May I have it, please?"

She looked down and shook her head in a way that of course I assumed mean "no" but then she lifted her powerfully bright blue eyes to me and said: "Why?" with a sincere scoff in her pleasant, unfamiliarly accented voice. "Let's go outside, okay. I don't want to wake…"

"Because I would like to know you—that's all. And I don't usually…"

"Do stuff like kiss girls' backs when they're not looking?! Something tells me you do do that…And you have a…"

She paused, then shifted gears, it seemed.

"You can't just *do* that!" she said, then, poignantly, added my name. "You know? *John.* You can't just…"

"Are you cross? Oh, come on. It wasn't anything. I just felt like it. Are you upset with me? *Katie.* Honestly? You wouldn't *be* so upset if you didn't…"

"No. Not really. I mean, *maybe. Dam*mit!" she said and gave out a little laugh and it seemed she was laughing at herself now, and neither of us was really moving toward the mobile home/trailer thingy's door and I almost put my hand on her cocked hip—I mean, she was right there, in the half dark, and her warm breath was right on me. "I don't know. I don't see how you can just…I mean…God, I've said that phrase around a hundred times already, huh?"

She looked at me meaningfully, self-consciously, and buttoned the last button of the soft, plaid, longsleeve shirt she'd put on over a tight blue nicely shimmery tank top.

"I don't know. Thanks anyway, though. I'm quite flattered but…I can't."

"Why not, though? Why not? Obviously we…"

I was going to say something dreadfully cliché like "have a connection" or "have something" or something lame like that; thank God Katie interrupted me just then. Thank God she did.

"Tell me why you want my number, again? You don't even know me."

"That's a malady I'm trying to remedy," I said in my best mock Oscar Wilde voice. "Will you have lunch with me this week, Katie? Say you will. Say it."

She laughed again, noiselessly but kindly somehow—incredulous, but kind: "You know what? Guess what? I've *seen* your *band.* Danny brought me to one of your shows. I know Rob quite well, actually. Well, kinda. From when he was roommates with my brother. He's great. I like Rob a lot."

"You're so coy and clever! 'Please don't be in a band.' Marvellous! How do you get away with saying such stuff? How can you…"

"I don't know. I like people? I'm a friendly person? I like to make them feel good about themselves? I like banter and fun conversations that aren't too heavy? Or people who go *pressuring* me into..."

"Okay, okay, okay," I said with an "and so?" sort of tone. "And I am not pressuring you, okay? Just maybe nudging you in a very respectful and forceful sort of way—admonishing you that there's an—how can I put this—that there's just this thing that's going on between you and me and there's no sense pretending otherwise."

"Oh?" she said. "And what makes you so sure about that?"

"I'm bluffing, actually."

"Oh, you are, are you?" she tisked.

"What else? Tell me something else about you."

"What a horrid demand! You're kind of pushy, you know."

"Not pushy," I said. "Just curious. And very, very attracted. Anyone would be—attracted to you, that is. Come on. It's not to be helped, okay? It's not something I chose or anything. These things just happen sometimes. And...I don't know..."

Now *I* was laughing at me and big time.

"Oh, they do, do they?"

"You know they do, Katie. What else do you do besides boss people around on video shoots and get hit on by directors and astronauts and billionaire playboys and whoever?"

"Oh, I don't know.... I'm a writer. I write. I have a dog...I like sushi...I grew up playing sports...I was a tomboy. I lived in London for a couple of years after I graduated college..."

"You write? That's great."

"I don't know—is it?"

"Sure. And you're pretty good, are you, as well?"

"I don't know. You're so weird! How should *I* know? *Some*times I think so. Sometimes I think I am—think I might be. Not often. I don't know yet. I've only written two or three things I really like."

"Of course you are—a writer, I mean. With that wit? What 'things,' though? Screenplays? Please don't say *screenplays*."

The look on Katie's face suggested I had captured her, a simulation of the timbre of her voice at least. A look came into her intermittently glittering eyes that passed just as quickly as it had appeared.

"What's the matter with scween…I mean *screen*…Haha! What's the matter with *screen*writing, anyway? I'm so tired right now!"

"Nothing. Uh, it's just…"

"You think it's a *jejune* thing to do, I'll bet. Just a typical…"

"Well, um…I never said…I love that word, though. Nice one."

"Well I like it. Screenwiring. Screenwriting. So there. (God, I just can't *talk* right now! I haven't had more than three hours-worth of sleep in row in around two weeks!)"

"That's terrible."

"It's money. It's work. I really like my job. Obviously. Anyway, what I *mean* is, I want to create something—write a movie—that I'm really-really proud of, you know? Isn't that what anybody…"

"Uh-huh. And have you?"

"I *think* so. No, probably not. I don't know, though," she said, giving out a strange little curious laugh.

Then I looked up and right into her eyes, holding her gaze abnormally longly, it seemed. She didn't flinch: "And you *like* writing, then?"

Right then I thought she would be punctilious/sensitive enough to grasp the idea I was trying to get across: that I and, in *my* opinion, anybody worth anything intellect-wise was suspicious as hell of anyone who said they liked or especially if they claimed they "loved" writing. That the writers who were, it had always seemed to me, "the real deal" hated it just as much as they loved it. I mean, I've never ever ever met anyone who was any good at all who said writing was anything less than water torture or having to go with your in-laws to a Streisand/Celine Dion double-bill or to the opera, no matter what flavor opera.

"You *like* it?" I said in order to make my terribly overt, skeptical point.

"No. Of course not. And yes, of course I do. That's what you want me to say, isn't it?" she said, then changed tack with a wry smile like the whitest moon when it looks like a slice of incandescent lemon, sitting pretty and inspiring in the midnight western sky. "Yes, actually. I do. *Fuck* that: I really do. Not always. But sometimes, yeah, I think I am writing something worthwhile and maybe even original."

I couldn't tell if what she said was said with the utmost confidence or if the whole thing was a total front or sham.

"That just means you're probably *good*," I said patly, with a smile of my own. Then I gave her my aforementioned theory.

"But you probably look down on it, huh, *John*—screenwriting. *John*. Like someone's not a 'real' writer unless they're writing a nine-hundred-page novel that rivals *War and Peace* or Thomas Mann or something...I know *your* type."

"I never said any such...You've read Thomas *Mann?*"

"Of course. Have *you?* Well, let me tell you something," Katie continued, narrowing playfully her very blue, scary blue, at once terrifying and enchanting eyes: "I enjoy it. I do. So *there*. I love film. I've done my homework and have watched enough Buñuel and Bergman and Leni Riefenstahl to...Hey—how come you didn't ask me if I liked your *band*, anyway? You didn't ask me what I thought."

I just shrugged.

"Oh *I* know: you're gonna go ahead and tell me *you don't care* if people like your stuff, your 'art'! Plus you're some Shakespeare freak as well—is that it? The whole band is or something? I do like the name. It's pretty cool."

"'Cause it doesn't matter if you do or not," I declared with respect to the question re: how I hadn't asked her in particular if she liked us.

"Oh?" she said, without the slightest hint of discomfiture.

There was an obvious pause. Tremendous, in fact.

"*Did* you?" I self-deprecatingly said in a mock-desperate, Woody Allen-ish way.

"Yeah, actually," she generously said, and more magnanimously chuckled. "It was good, the show I saw. You guys were really good. I don't see that many LA bands who have..."

"Were you going to say 'actually'—I hate it when people say 'Actually, you guys were pretty good. It's a total 'damned with faint praise' sort of motif. As though they're all surprised that anyone they know could be..."

"That's funny. I get it. Anyway, I will say I don't think you guys should have the girl—Jenny's her name, right? Isn't it Jenny?—sing as much as you do, though."

"Oh?"

"You have a much better singing voice than she does. That's just my opinion..."

"Thank you kindly."

"You're quite welcome!"

"No, I'm not. Well, I am but..."

"Are you being sarcastic? I can't tell when you're kidding and when you're..."

"Everyone says that. You don't know me well enough, I don't think. Of course you don't. And blah, blah, blah," I smiled. "I don't like talking about me. I'd *much* rather..."

"What?"

"Never mind. Seriously, though: you're not just saying that, are you? Like I said, it doesn't matter to me if you..."

"No. I wouldn't just say that—actually, I wouldn't at all. Hahaha! You're welcome. It reminded me a bit of The Jesus and Mary Chain. Not a lot, but a bit. Less fuzzy. Like the melodies of them, though. They're my favorite band, actually. Maybe the Go-Betweens too? You guys are great. I would go see you again. You *know* that, anyway, so why even..."

"Thank you," I said. "I mean it. That's very high praise. Wait...you know the *Go*-Betweens?"

"I said 'reminded' not 'rivalled' or...Yeah, I know the Go-Betweens. They're not that obscure. They were on Capital in the States, if I recall correctly. I was a DJ at my college radio station."

"*Ox*ford had college radio?"

"Junior year abroad. No, at college back east. It's a bit of cliché, I realize, but…"

"You total prevaricator!"

"I said I *went* there—I didn't say I'd *gone* there."

"Where did you go, then?"

"Cornell. The last picked of the Ivies. Well, us and Penn. 'I would found an institution where any person can find instruction in any study.' That's our motto. It just means we are the least exclusive Ivy. Least selective, I mean. And I grew up in Canada: Montreal."

And it suddenly struck me that Katie was like so many people who'd come west from Ivys who didn't want to tell you they were Ivy League on account of a whole discussion ensued, normally, and they were sick of it, the discussion, or at least so over it, let's if you please talk about anything anything anything else: boating or badminton or the beach or Bali and how we'd always wanted to go there for, say, two weeks and get lost and go the full Bohemian motif, live on the vanilla sand in a hut by the mist of a nearby waterfall that's part of a placid, see-through lagoon.

"You're being serious now?" I teased. "I knew it! Ha! I *thought* you were Canadian."

"Well, I am."

"That's pretty impressive, though, eh?'"

"What—being Canadian? There are quite a few of us, you know. And you had better stop right now with the 'eh's.' okay?"

"It was just the one," I said, all coy and stuff. "But okay. No, Katie: Cornell."

"Well, one can but try," she said in a mock-posh accent. "Listen: you should get dressed and get breakfast or coffee at least and paid and get out of here. Oh, you already are dressed. You know what I mean. Put on your boots and scoot. It's over for you guys. The crew, that is. *I* still have a whole day to do, however. Probably well into tonight as well."

I came a little swaying, moony step closer to her then. There was so little room. The floor was spongey. She was so close to me anyway, there in the sparse space of the trailer. Her head was bowed. I put my hands on her hips. Both hands this time. She put her incredibly beautiful black-haired bedhead on my shoulder.

"Don't…" she said and sort of half-stepped away. But I wasn't having any of that. She came back over with not a lot of physical coaxing and rested her head on my shoulder redux. "I don't want to like anyone right now. I'm not dating right now. I'm sorry. I mean, I just…I just got out of something."

Of course you're not going to be surprised when I tell you that, to my mind, the "note" in her voice suggested that she was trying to convince herself as much as she was trying to convince me.

Percipient participant.

"That Colin guy? 'The Great Colin?'" I said.

"*God*, no!" she said and looked up, then broke away from me. "He keeps asking me out, though. So obnoxious. How'd you like working on a ridiculous video, by the way? Not to change the subject or anything…"

"I'd say I was little inclined to try to shine—as a PA, that is—as one could possibly be."

That made Kate laugh.

"At one point, in fact, I hid in a…never mind."

"You what?"

"Nothing."

"What? Tell me! What did you do?"

"I hid in a truck. Just for a few hours. Are you going to dock my pay?"

"That's hilarious. And I don't have anything at all to do with your pay, by the way. But that's brilliant. And not the first time I've heard of someone doing that. That sounds like something Rob would do, actually."

"It does, doesn't it?"

"Pretty hard work, huh?"

"You have no—I mean some—idea."

"I do," she laughed. "I've PA'ed before. It's brutal. I never hid in a truck, though."

Now it was my turn to give out a knowing little chuckle. "For Jesus' sake, Katie, people—and often *fe*male people—with arms more broad than my *thighs* were constantly *finding* me and stuff and barking at me to pick up a golf cart or a monolith or a box full of uranium or something and move it across the softest sand. *Quick*sand, sometimes. All day. I just couldn't…I mean, I was sore in ways…I think an actual pirate ordered me around at one point. Did you guys go back in time and hire pirates for this thing? I thought he (or it: I wasn't sure what sex it was) was gonna cuff me at one point or make me drink 'sack' from a bota bag…"

"Oh my God. Stop," Katie laughed.

"Shhhh," I whispered. "*Quiet*, Katie."

Then she gave out a that kind of stifled involuntary laugh that signaled that she knew she was going to have to get herself under control.

I looked at her: she looked right back. And gave that smile you smile when you don't want someone to know you're smiling at them and fondly.

Or so I rather assumed. And I drew her, wriggling but coming, acquiescing a little in her manner, in her body language, to me once more.

"Do something with me this week, please," I pleaded, holding her just a shade tighter now. "Anything, Katie. I don't care what it is. Coffee or…"

She moved away a touch and put her hands flat on my chest.

"I *told* you, *John*: I don't want to *like* any…Know something? Want to know just the one thing? You already use my name like we already *know* each other. It's really quite distract…Do you even know that you do that? Are you aware of what…"

I pulled her toward me a little tightlier; knowing what was coming, she turned her head and laid her cheek over the top of my left shoulder.

I shook my head in a tsk-tsky way: "Too late! We already like each other. It's totally obvious. You know it. I don't mean to put it all Cary Grant in *To Catch a Thief*, like Cary Grant in *To Catch a Thief*," I needlessly and obviously nervously repeated, "and stuff but it's obviously obvious to both of us. It's obvious, Katie. It'd be obvious to anyone who even *looked* at us. Give me your number, please…When?"

"When, what?"

"When did you 'just get out of something'? You're five eleven, aren't you?"

"Oh, right. Um…I don't know. A year ago? I'm closer to five-foot ten." Danny and his ridiculous little hockey club friends really teased me when we were…"

"A *year* ago?! That was your last re*lation*ship? A girl like you? Girls who look like you normally have about a ten minute coffee break between guys. We need to dis*cuss* this!"

"I know—right?" she chuckled. "There' something *really* wrong with me. I'd better get back in therapy to deal with all the time I've already spent in therapy! But I am, I'll have you know, not the kind you described."

"The kind that…"

"Jumps right into a new relationship ten minutes…"

"Yeah, I was just kidding."

"Yeah, right. But you're right: there is something really wrong with me."

"There's something wrong with *everyone*, Katie."

"I know but…"

"I just spent four days staring at a wall, *I* did."

"Are you serious? Really?"

I kissed her lightly, gently on top of her head just then.

"Uh-huh. I kind of melted down after this tour we just did. Everything kind of just…"

"I'm sorry," she said. As she looked up her eyes went all kind and even bigger somehow after she sort of blinked as a way, I thought, of evincing sympathy.

And I kissed her twice, thrice on the cheek just then.

"I'm fine now, but thank you very much. And that's *great* that you're obviously not the sort of person who jumps from one guy to the…Do you realize how *rare* that is? Especially in *Holly*wood. You know?"

"Yeah, well…" Katie said, and sort of extricated herself from my arms. "There's really only one thing wrong with you that *I* can think of." As we moved together toward the mobile home's door, she looked at me in a way that seemed quizzical, deliberate, deliberating. "That I am not giving you my number, you mean."

"*Very* good, Katie…" I said, kinda fatuously-flirtatiously.

"*Stop* that! You have got to cut that out, *John*…"

I just stood there for a sec. It was one of my very best instances of doing absolutely zilch. All my counter-intuitive instincts screamed *act, do* something, and, miraculously, I just did zip. I, without knowing it, without wiling it, had played it cool.

Amazing!

If my eyes twinkle—if they do twinkle: I can't be certain, naturally—they must have done just then.

"Do you have a pen?" she, turning 'round, vouchsafed at last by way of answer.

"I don't need one," I said in a way, you must understand, that was simply declarative and not melodramatic.

We stepped outside, with me on the landing, the first steps down from the trailer, Katie in the doorway. There must be some ancient Greek expression for "woman-standing-elegantly-in-the-doorway."

We both looked up, as people do in doorways at the end of novels and who have hopes of some sort. We both looked up and saw the last of the sparkling stars, then the just-appearing clouds etching themselves across the endless desert sky, touched bright orange-pink and sun-up gold, heliotrope and bold red with slashes and swaths of brilliant purple, with strands of turquoise appearing incrementally in the dawning dawn, like a painting that comes cinematically into focus, rich by richer color, till it, the sky, that is, at last went all-blue, with the cirrus clouds looking like they were at once streaking across and standing still in the still firmament, like filmic shrapnel, diffusive, beautiful; and the cumulus just hovering, lovely and puffy and low on the milky blue-white horizon.

Do you know what I mean?

It was really picturesque and you-had-to-have-been-there dramatic, is what I'm trying to tell you.

Then Katie said "Oh, okay: you can remember it, then?"; and then she slowly recited the seven numbers, pausing after the first three. And as I repeated them she—a bit both saucily and not, it seemed— asked *over* me if I was going to remember that and of course I said yes of course I will yes of course I will. Yes.

Reprise

s I thresh and thresh through the unignorable, imperious past and sift it and make a plaything of it (for it needs must haunt me somehow, however benignly) and conjure up these essentially dreamlike scenes and mix metaphors here like a literary apothecary and make my single, humble, and unhumble, and, dare I say, singular observations on them, those scenes, and think up the proximate words that people spoke (and arrange them in my head and then syntactically on the page, as artistically and realistically and, when I want to make you laugh, preposterously as I can); when I think as well of the words that possibly went *un*spoken or the further words that were part of the *sub*text of the words used, I think, hey, wow, *These things really happened, more or less, you know? This is what went down.* When I think they, these things I'm both chronicling and making up, really happened to me (and didn't) and to the people I was fortunate or just-so-happened to know (or imagine)—well, then, God only knows what conclusions, what deductions, if any, we might draw from them after I have limned them here and, beforehand, in my mind, and pushed them as it were 'round the page to make them sing or moan or laugh or, one Aristotleanly hopes, "instruct and delight." For nothing, espistemologically speaking, means what we think it does during the time it's happening; it's only later, in reflection, as it's gone, at once queerly evaporated and still present in the immemorial memory, part of the great internal so-called *came-before* that we all harbor, and to varying degrees treasure, and try to measure, and falter when we try to remember exactly what was said (knowing that memory is never exact, never complete, always something we embellish or sketch or etch, filling in or up the gaps we meet up with, anyway)—it's only then that a semblance of meaning emerges, after

the shuffling's accomplished and "the hurlyburly's done," when the battle with memories and words is lost and won. Only, and unreliably, then. Only in our ever so selective and duplicitous, we-can-count-on-it-to-be-unreliable, oxmoronic memory: what in part we use intermittently to provide us with hope, something promulgated, and with past pleasures, the silhouettes and simulacra that stir or slumber deep within, what we've stored or shored up, kept like ephemeral keepsakes, preserved, maintained; and use, yes, to pain ourselves with as well, involuntarily or no, as reminders of what went wrong and how what we did and said will pang us in a sudden trenchant flash we thought we might have curtained or blocked off, and make us flinch within when we see in a lightning way what went (and how *we* went) so maybe mortifyingly, humanly awry.

Little boats, little boats all of us, dolorous and delightful, one and all of us all, fighting and breasting and riding out the variegated tides and swells and lulls of time that carry us inexorably on, inexorably along, merrily or unmerrily, gently or otherwise down the stream(s) of consciousness.

And I also think: here's where, with Katie fatefully giving me her number, as it was just something that happened, for whatever random or pointed reason, for whatever "why" or "why the hell not"—here's where we might stop for now, an appropriate place, a very good enough place to stop and have a think and take a break and take a deep, deep breath and wash or brush our hands as if to say *That's that, then—nice while it lasted, on to the next thing.* So that's all for now, then. The third and last installment of this humble little megasaga will come your way, if you care to peer into it, care to continue, sometime soon, one hopes, in the perpetually uncertain, *l'avenir*, the to-come, yeah, the sometime soon, soon as I sort it out, get it down and sorted out.

And, to be sure, having come thus far, dear reader-reader, having seen what you've seen here, heard what you've heard, skipped a bit, perhaps, or read some parts all over again 'cause you thought you might have missed something in this once-upon-a-time—you must (like anyone might be) be sitting or lying there wondering what's going to happen with The Weird Sisters and their label problems, their internecine problems, esp. the Raleigh problem, and the walking, talking, barking conundrum that is the odd, obnoxious, insolent, officious, importunate, arrogating Bob Chalet? The fall tour that's four-or-so few months from starting. How's that looking? How's that going to happen; or if it does, how will it go? The possible recording of another record, keeping momentum, and keeping together and not having any more unendurable nervous break downs and things.

And Jenny. And Jenny. And Jenny. And Jen.

I've gone and hyped you up meeting Keating the roommate/ producer and you didn't even get to, really: all you got was a phone message and some vague allusions, quick vignettes, and scattershot promises. And what about the Scather, the Psychster, the David, Jaz and all our friends from *The King of Good Intentions*? Will we ever meet up with them again?

And the menagerie of LA types who swim willy-nilly and daily, it seems, into one's ever-shifting and positively unbelievable ken? What of *them*?

And Jenny again, brilliant, pretty, adorable, boundlessly talented *her*: what's gonna happen with me and her? What's in the unthinkable stars for *her*, she, herself—in love and life and rock and roll? Saddled as she is with what she's saddled with. One worries for her, about her, dear Jenny, Jenny-dear, one does—she whom we know at once so much and so very little about, whose *hamartia* ostensibly *is* that she won't let us, let us in, let her guard down, reveal the real her.

And John and Jenny, Jenny and John. What of *that*? Them/us. Especially now that this charming, exceedingly beautiful, eloquent, equal parts (seemingly) *femme fatale* and über-up front Katie chick's come into the picture? What about seemingly insouciant *her*? You're not going to be*lieve* what goes down *there*—in a possibly recidivist way. Or, come to think of it, maybe you will.

It's just—it's just that—it's just that, well, it's just that I'll just have to tell you another time.

The End

JOHN ANDREW FREDRICK

was born in Richmond, VA, and grew up in Santa Barbara, CA. After receiving his PhD from the University of California at Santa Barbara, he formed an indie rock band called The Black Watch that has released seventeen records to considerable acclaim. He lives in Los Angeles.

CPSIA information can be obtained at www.ICGtesting.com
Printed in the USA
LVOW06s0301290715

447925LV00002B/6/P